RECOLLECTIONS

OF A

NEW ENGLAND BRIDE

AND OF A

SOUTHERN MATRON.

BY CAROLINE GILMAN.

NEW EDITION, REVISED.

NEW YORK:
G. P. PUTNAM & CO., 10 PARK PLACE.

1852.

RECOLLECTIONS

OF

A SOUTHERN MATRON.

"Me thinketh it accordant to reson
To tellen you alle the condition
Of eche of hem, so as it seemed to me;
And whiche they weren; and of what degre;
And eke in what avail that they were inne:
And at a knight, then wol I firste beginne."

CHAUCER.

NEW YORK:
G. P. PUTNAM & CO., 10 PARK PLACE.

1852.

PREFACE.

THE "SOUTHERN MATRON" was penned in the same spirit, and with the same object, as the "New-England Housekeeper"—to present as exact a picture as possible of local habits and manners. Every part, except the "love-passages," is founded in events of actual occurrence. Should it be thought that the views of human life in the two works, as has been suggested in private, have too much sunshine about them, I can only reply, that, to have made different descriptions, I must have resorted to imagination instead of fact, as far as my personal observation is concerned.

Perhaps, had I examined the details of the police-courts for my Northern sketch, or the registry of the magistrate-freeholders for my Southern, I might have found gloomier scenes; but they would not have been such as Clarissa Packard and Cornelia Wilton would recognize in their daily experience.

Some apology may be necessary, as a matter of taste, for the frequent introduction of the negro dialect; but the careful reader will perceive that it has only been done when essential to the development of individual character.

I am indebted to one Northern and two Southern friends for the original materials of the story of *Betsey, the servant-maid*, the *Deer Hunt*, and *My brother Ben's education*, all of which I have modified to my narrative.

C. G.

Charleston, S. C., 1837.

RECOLLECTIONS OF A SOUTHERN MATRON.

CHAPTER I.

OLD JACQUE.

"Onward,
O'ershadowed more by the green underwood,
Some slight-raised mounds showed where the dead were laid.
Few gravestones told who slept beneath the turf.
(Perchance the heart that deeply mourns needs not
Such poor remembrancer.) The forest flowers
Themselves had fondly clustered there—and white
Azalias with sweet breath stood round about,
Like fair young maidens mourning o'er their dead.
In some sweet solitude like this I would
That I might sleep my last long dreamless sleep."

ANNA MARIA WELLS.

"He sought him through the bands of fight,
Mid many a pile of slaughtered dead,
Beneath the pale moon's misty light,
With form that shuddered at each tread:
For every step in blood was taken."

W. G. SIMMS.

I WRITE in my paternal mansion. The Ashley, with a graceful sweep, glitters like a lake before me, reflecting the sky and the bending foliage. Occasionally a flat, with its sluggish motion, or a boat, with its urging sail, passes along, and the woods echo to the song or the horn of the negro, waking up life in the solitude. The avenue of noble oaks, under which I sported in childhood, still spread their strong arms, and rustle in the passing breeze. My children are frolicking on the lawn where my first footsteps were watched by tender parents, and one of those parents rests beneath yonder circling cedars. Change! Sameness! What a perpetual chime those words ring on the ear of memory! My children love to lead me to the spot where they may spell the inscription on one princely monument to my grandfather, and hear the tale I have to tell of the fair, the good, and the brave who sleep in that enclosure, sacred to the domestic dead. There is but one inscription there, for we were as one.

I sometimes feel a joy that all are here—my grand-parents; the mother who gave me being; the baby-sister, who looked like a sunbeam on the world and passed away; my first-born, he who was twined to my heart's pulses by ties as strong as those which call up its *natural* vibration; my noble brothers, and my poor cousin Anna, who planted herself the rose that blossoms on her grave! The sun gilds the cedars with his brightest morning hue; *they* shelter the sleepers from his noon-day beams; and when the moon rises over the cleared fields, showing an amphitheatre of distant woods, the cedar-mound stands out in full relief, and those dark sentinels seem to guard the dead. I thank thee, Heaven, that all I love are here!—that stranger-dust mingles not with mine! The tumult of the city rolls not across this sanctuary; careless curiosity treads not on these secluded graves; nor does the idler cull the blossoms that affection has planted, or that time, with unsparing hand, has hung in graceful wreaths or clustered beauty around. No rude sound disturbs the silence. The whippoorwill softens, by her melancholy lay, the mockbird's tale of love and joy. The hare steals lightly over the hillocks, and the serpent twines his silken folds among the herbage; yet do they not mar, like man, the sacred relics of memory, nor with jest and profanity disturb the gloom.

My grandfather fell early in our national struggle for liberty, and his bones might have whitened on the battle-field, had not a locket, containing the fair hair of my grandmother, suspended from his neck, revealed him to a faithful servant. Good old Jacque! How often have I climbed his knees to hear his stories of the past! I even love to recall the peculiar accent with which he beguiled our evenings, when appointed by our parents to superintend the younger servants in their absence. I can fancy I see him now, in winter, throwing the oak logs or lightwood knots on the wide hearth, standing (for he never would sit in the house, even in the presence of the children, unless when holding us on his knees) with a perpetual habit of conscientious trust; or, in summer, seeking some sunny spot, and, with his blue handkerchief tied round his head, employing his feeble hands in net or basket-making. Rarely could he resist our Southern entreaty of, *Do, if you please*, daddy Jacque, tell us about grandpapa's locket, and how he died.

Jacque had been intrusted with the entire control of his young master's household during the term of his education in Europe; and while the confidence placed in him had somewhat increased his self-conceit, it never induced him to take a liberty beyond those which his peculiar situation authorized. Roseland, from the beauty of its location and its valuable paintings, was frequently visited by strangers in the absence of its orphan proprietor, and it is a singular fact that Jacque was never known to ascend the hall stairs on such occasions. He pointed out the way with a bow and flourish of profound respect, and met the guests by a private stairway after they had ascended.

His master returned, married a lovely and highly-educated Southern girl, and the following year Roseland was made doubly beautiful by the birth of a noble boy, the pride of the house and plantation. This happiness was not of long duration, for the times approached which tried American souls, and the young father was called from the peaceful sunshine of his home, from the caresses of his wife and the prattle of his child, to the wild and stormy hardships of war. The night before his departure his wife led him to his likeness by Copley, which still hangs in the hall, and perused his lineaments long and earnestly. She gazed on the manly form beside her, then on the graceful but inanimate representative, took in the loving glance of the living eye, and compared it with its calmer image; then, with a bitter sigh, sank into his arms. The young soldier comforted her with a husband's love, and drew her to the bedside of their sleeping boy. Little Henry started from his repose as they bent over him with whispered words, clung to his father's neck a moment, and then, closing his eyes like the bell of a twilight flower, sank upon his pillow.

With his beautiful wife still resting on his arm, the father took from his desk a locket containing her hair, threw the black ribbon from which it was suspended about his neck, and kissed it fondly. The night passed heavily away, and darkness heavier than night hung over Roseland, when, on the following morning, he departed, attended by Jacque.

In an engagement with the British, Jacque lost sight of his master; the enemy were victorious, and the Americans retreated, leaving their dead unprotected. When the pursuers were exhausted, Jacque searched with anxiety among the living, and, finding no trace of him, returned with sad, cautious, but resolute steps to the field of death. Among the disfigured remains he vainly endeavored for a long time to distinguish him; he who had so lately reposed in the arms of happy love, had found a cold and bloody bed with the promiscuous slain, among whom not even faithful friendship could detect his semblance. At length Jacque found on a mutilated form a locket, with its braid of auburn hair. He shook his head with an expression of satisfied grief, and wiped the bloody jewel with his coat sleeve. Then bearing the body to a stream, cleansed it reverently, dug a grave, and laid it in its place of rest. Touched and kindled by affectionate remembrance, he knelt on the pliant mould, and offered up an untutored prayer.

It was a dark and stormy evening when he returned, and my grandmother had kept her young son awake, with gentle artifice, for companionship. A footstep was heard in the piazza, and Dash gave a growl between warning and recognition, while Henry, clapping his hands, exclaimed, "Papa! papa!" His mother started as Jacque entered, and exclaimed, "Where is your master?"

Jacque was silent, and stood wiping from his cheeks the streaming tears.

"Tell me, Jacque, for the love of God," cried she, clasping the negro's arm, "where is your master?"

"Jacque got no maussâ now," said he, sobbing, "but little Maus Henry."

A long and piercing shriek broke forth from the widow's stricken heart, and she fell senseless on the floor beside her frightened son.

The intelligence spread rapidly through the plantation. Shrieks and lamentations were heard from hut to hut—wild gesticulations were seen by the kindled torchlights among the young, as they cried, "My maussa dead, poor me!"—while the old, rocking on their seats and lifting their hands, responded, "The Lord's will be done. *He* knows."

The following day all was calm but the widow's heart; there the bitter strife of a *new* sorrow raged like a tempest. Even Henry's presence was intolerable. Poor boy! his very step was harsh to her, as, with a paper cap and wooden sword, he marched about her apartment, threatening to revenge his father's death.

Jacque was for several days revolving a measure of importance in his own mind; and at length, determining to give it utterance, went to claim a few moments' attention from his mistress.

She could only shade her eyes, as if to shut out too painful an object, and with one hand pressed closely on her heart, as though to hush its tumult.

"Jacque don't mean no disrespec," said the negro, bowing, as if his errand had something in it of dignity; "my missis know dat as my missis is poorly, and Maussa Henry an't got of no size, Jacque has to turn over what is best to be done for de family; and one grêat trouble it is on my mind, dat my maussa, what provide like one lord even for niggers, let alone white folks, should lay out mong de wolf and varmin, when we could gie 'em such good commodation here, and keep our eye on him, to say nothing of Christian buryin."

My grandmother was instantly roused; and, starting up, with an animated voice she said, "My dear, good Jacque, can he be brought to me? God bless you for the thought!"

A motive for action was now given her, and her heart seemed lightened of a part of its burden. It was a consolation to her to take Henry by the hand, and go forth in search of an appropriate spot for her husband's grave. It seemed to her excited imagination like preparing an apartment for an absent friend.

"Here, mamma," said her prattling boy, "is a pretty place. Papa used to stand under this tree and throw chips into the pond for Dash to bring to me."

"No, my son," said his mother, musingly; "it is too far. I must see the spot from my window. Look, Henry, at the cluster of cedars on that slightly-rising ground. See how the sun shines on the tree-tops, while all beneath is gloom! Like my hopes," she continued, mentally, "so lately seeming bright when all was darkness. That shall be the spot, Henry," she continued, "and you must see that I am laid there too."

The boy looked wistfully at her, and said, "And where shall I go, mamma?"

He had unconsciously touched the right string; and, as she stooped to kiss his forehead, she patiently resolved to wait God's will, and live for him.

While these scenes of tenderness were beguiling the feelings of the widow, Jacque, with a band of fellow-servants, went on his melancholy errand. Even to the imagination, which only partially illuminated the uneducated mind of the negro, the contrast was strong between the aspect of that now silent field, and the recent period when contending forces, with weapons flashing in the sun, and faces tinged with expectation, and footsteps timed to the march of war, had passed before him. It was a moonlight night, one of those nights which seem to exaggerate brightness and stillness, when Jacque led the way to his master's rude grave.

"'Tis a pretty sight, my young maussas and missis," he used to say, when relating this story, while we stood with inward tremor, almost expecting the pictures of our grandparents to start from their frames; "'tis a pretty thing for see one corpse lay out handsome on he natural bed, wid he head to de east, and he limb straight, and he eye shut, and he white shroud, and de watchers sing psalm; but 'twas altogedder onnatural to see my poor maussa wid de ragiments on, and de varmin busy bout him, and de moonlight shine down, and de owl hoot. Dem niggers (natural fools) get scare when we get to maussa self; den says I, 'My men, how you been let folks say dat we have Christian grave, while our maussa, what fed us and kivered us, was laying mong wolf? It's an ugly job, but to it, my men; and as it is a disrespec to sing 'heave ho,' one of you strike up a hymn to help us on.'"

There was no ear to listen to those sounds as they rose up on the midnight air, no eye to appreciate that intrepidity which could conquer the dread of superstitious ignorance. I am wrong. He who formed *hearts* in one mould did not disregard them.

They placed the remains of the soldier in the coffin brought for them, and closed it reverently.

The widow, nerved for the obsequies of her husband, reclined in silence, with Henry by her side. Friends from the city and neighboring plantations sat or stood in whispering circles, shrouded by scarfs, and hoods, and weepers, each holding a sprig of rosemary twined with white paper; the glasses and pictures were turned to the wall, and every article of taste covered with a white cloth. Labor was suspended, the household servants stood in the piazza clothed in mourning, and the field-slaves, with such little testimonials of external respect as they could beg or borrow, arranged themselves below. The coffin was brought to the piazza, its costly ornaments riveted, and little Henry held up to see the inscription. In the city, after a recent decease, the widow would have remained secluded in the formality of grief; but in this case there seemed to be a call for a representative mourner; and, taking Henry's hand, she followed the six negro female *waiters* dressed in white, with napkins pinned over their shoulders, who were preceded by the coffin, which was borne by his people, attended by the pall-bearers, friends of the deceased. The procession passed on, followed by the servants, to Cedar Mound. The coffin was lowered, "dust to dust" was pronounced over it, and the earth fell upon its glittering decorations. Henry clung to his mother, crying, " Papa, come back," while the lamentations and shrieking howl of the negroes filled the air. The widow looked on with zealous scrutiny until the last spadeful of earth was deposited on the swelling mound; then taking her son home, retired to her apartment, where her heart only knew its own bitterness.

The boy soon forgot, in childish blessedness, the funeral of his father, and his notes of happiness rang through the mansion; but how achingly did his mother's thoughts for lingering years dwell in sad revery on her husband's grave. And it is on that spot that my eye now turns. She trained the various vines over its white paling, and planned the monument sacred to her first beloved. There little Henry loved to play with the falling leaves, or gather spring flowers; there his mother laid her head, crowned with reverend honors; there my mother lies; and there may my limbs be borne when God shall call my spirit. But no gloom rests upon it. It has always been a favorite scene for the children of our household. It is not enough that grief should go there and lay down its earthly treasure, or that old age should moralize beneath its shades; happy voices, like Henry's, may still be heard in its enclosure, and the crisp and fresh winter rose that my own Lewis has thrown in my lap he gathered from poor cousin Anna's grave.

CHAPTER II.

COLLEGE FRIENDSHIP AND COLLEGE LOVE.

"Look, when I vow I weep; and vows so born,
In their nativity all truth appears."

Midsummer Night's Dream.

"Too soon, oh all too soon—will come
In later years the spell,
Touching with changing hues the path
Where once but sunlight fell."

FRANCES S. OSGOOD.

FROM the day of his father's death, Henry was monarch of all he surveyed; his mother gazed on him with eyes of untiring love; the elder servants fostered him with protecting pity; and a troop of young ones followed his steps, to serve and sport with him.

The softness inspired by constant indulgence was counteracted by the scenes of danger to which this very indulgence permitted him to resort. He managed a horse incredibly soon, and, long before a city boy had poised a gun, was in the fields winning his own dinner. Though startled by his daring, his mother soon felt pride in the deer's horns and fox's skins that he suspended from the hall, and the fish caught by him tasted fresher than from any other hands. Henry was one of the busiest beings on the wide earth. His horse, his hounds, his rabbits, his terrapins, his birds, &c., gave him incessant occupation between his hours of study. He was a lad of wild and warm affections, and no one knew whether he threw his arms around his horse's or his mother's neck with the most ardor. With great quickness of capacity he contrived to glean an education from his private tutor, and was fitted for college. Long were the discussions on his future destination; at length it was decided that he should enter Harvard College, and his mother, with a sweet magnanimity, consented to give up her boy for those long, long four years.

It was Henry's sixteenth birthday, on a spring morning, when his travelling apparatus was deposited in the piazza, and he stood with his mother to see Jacque turn the last key. The field-hands who could form any excuse had gathered to bid him farewell. They were all very sad, and one (his nurse) was weeping bitterly. The negro children stood on the lawn with a thoughtful air, watching the preparations for his departure. Henry was determined to bear the separation like a man, but Jacque was unusually irritable. He kicked the dogs, called the little boy who held the travelling-bag a "black-faced nigger," and hit the leading horse such a blow on the side of the head, that his mistress called him to order.

"Eberyting go wrong to-day, missis," said Jacque in an apologetic tone.

Grandmamma and Henry dared not trust a long embrace. Why should they, when her arms had encircled him sixteen years, and when she had stolen to his room the night before and slept on his very pillow, while his cheek unabashed nestled close to hers? He shook hands with all the people, and "God bless my young maussa!" was heard from one to the other as they courtesied or bowed low at his farewell. "Don't cry, Nanny," said he to his nurse, as her audible sobs struggled through the apron she had thrown over her face.

"Old Nanny an't gawing for see Maus Henry no more in dis

worl!" said she. "Nanny live long enough now, if Maus Henry no stay wid dem dat raise him."

Jacque had stood somewhat aloof, as if he did not consider himself as belonging to the general group; and it was not until after Henry was seated in the carriage with his tutor, that, with an evident struggle and a preparatory hem! he said,

"Good-by, Maus Henry. Take care you no dishonor de family. Keep straight, my young maussa, walk close.* Jacque can manage missis bery well, and notting an't gawing for trouble she; but who gawing for take care of Maus Henry but God Almighty?"

Henry was admitted pretty fairly at Harvard, and his collegiate life flowed on happily. No one rode such spirited horses as he; his coat was cut with the latest touch of fashion; the tie of his cravat was a study, his flute inimitable; the graceful solemnity of his bow supplied the want of deeper knowledge; and a happy facility of expression carried him over his recitations; many a poor student blessed his liberality, and many a dull one his quickness; the cheerfulness of his manners won him golden opinions; and he who had been attended by slaves from infancy was seen carrying his own bowl of milk† or chocolate across the college-yard, with a bow and jest for all; his classmates caressed him, the fair smiled upon him, and Henry Wilton, the southerner, was pronounced a noble fellow.

He graduated with a secondary college honor, but it was sufficient to hang a splendid dinner upon. Happy they to whom his invitations came before any other sealed up the avenue of acceptance!

The young graduate was the star of commencement-day.

* These expressions are very common among the negroes, and signify, be correct: be pious.

† A custom for which the meals in the commons hall is now a substitute.

His sparkling countenance, graceful manner, fine oratory, and a few appropriate compliments to the ladies, bore off peals of applause, while more elaborate essays were unheeded by the audience. He had secured for his entertainment the splendid line of Boston belles, who, in floating veils and flower-wreathed curls, with "lips apart," leaned from the crowded galleries to listen to —*him!*

A richly-prepared table was laid under a decorated awning on a green in an enclosure, about a quarter of a mile from the colleges. Thither his guests resorted after the exercises were concluded; and Henry, flushed with success, floating on the very clouds of youthful excitement, led the way, with the *mother* of Lucy Sullivan on his arm. And Lucy followed with his friend Winthrop. Was it an August sun that kindled up her cheek in such a glow of rosiness, or was it that Henry, as he guided the mother, looked back on the beautiful girl, and catching a fold of her veil, retained it gently in his hand?

It required no little circumspection to thread the mazes of the Cambridge common on commencement-day. At one moment they justled against a square-capped professor; at another came in contact with a crowd around a merry-andrew; now a gowned orator, with his colored ribbon or medal, the badge of a society, swept by; and now they were impeded by flocks of children hurrying to the booths for confectionery; here was a mob of rioters simply kept from violence by constables, and there pressed a bevy of laughing girls in the airy dress of a ballroom, escorted by young collegians.

The excitement was increased by the ordinarily quiet habits of the Cambridge residents. Over that wide, open common, then diversified only by a few graceful elms, usually brooded the deepest silence and monotony, scarcely interrupted by the thoughtful student conning to the air his appointed task, or the laggard hurrying to his recitation. And the airy-decorated figures of the city ladies were equally opposed to the simple costume of the Cambridge girls. Indeed, until within a few years, one might almost know a Cambridge lady by the plainness of her attire and the absence of external accomplishments, contrasted with the cultivation of her mind.

Henry soon saw his guests seated at his rich banquet, and attended them with cheerful grace, while the little pleasantries of untasked intellect flew around. What was wanting to his happiness? On one side was Lucy Sullivan, with a mingled look of trust and bashfulness varying on her young cheek, and on the other his classmate Winthrop, pledged a friend for weal or woe.

But, as the festivity rose, Lucy's brow began to sadden. "You are silent, Miss Sullivan," whispered Henry. "I go the day after to-morrow, and this day should be sacred to smiles."

He stopped, for he saw a tremulous motion on her lips; and, before she could control herself, a tear stole down her burning cheek. He withdrew his eyes from hers; and, selecting a piece of myrtle from a bouquet near him, carried it, unobserved but by her, to his lips, and laid it on her ungloved hand.

A few honeyed words were spoken as at the close of the dinner he committed her to the care of a Cambridge friend, and Winthrop and himself sallied to the college hall to join the commencement dinner-party, to which they were entitled as graduates. The company had dined, and were just rising to unite in the hymn which, from an early period, has thrown a sacred charm over this literary festival. The venerable president, clergymen collected from every quarter, statesmen, lawyers, graduates, and invited guests, all stood reverently, and responded with the tune of St. Martin's, as two lines at a time were read by one of the professors.*

There was no coldness in the solemn strain that uprose from that assembly, but busy associations were in every breast, as they thus linked their *alma mater* with religious responsibilities.

This feeling was a happy preparation to Henry and Winthrop when, retiring from the hall linked arm in arm, they resolved, to visit Sweet Auburn,† to view the glories of a dying sunset together, and pledge again their vows of friendship. They were

* PSALM.

Sung statedly at the Commencement-dinner in Harvard College, to the tune of St. Martin's; the company standing.

"GIVE ear, ye children; to my law
Devout attention lend;
Let the instructions of my mouth
Deep in your hearts descend.

My tongue, by inspiration taught,
Shall parables unfold;
Dark oracles, but understood,
And own'd for truths of old:

Which we from sacred registers
Of ancient times have known;
And our forefathers' pious care
To us has handed down.

Let children learn the mighty deeds
Which God perform'd of old;
Which, in our younger years, we saw,
And which our fathers told.

Our lips shall tell them to our sons,
And they again to theirs;
That generations yet unborn
May teach them to their heirs."

† Now Mount Auburn Cemetery.

full of sweet communing, and poured out those feelings which youth only knows. They carved their names in a circle on a tree, and exchanged books, those precious ties for intellectual friendship. Henry had traced on a Horace the trite but expressive couplet—

> "Where'er I go, whatever realms I see,
> My heart untravelled fondly turns to thee"—

and Winthrop wrote on a rich edition of Gray's poems the following extract:—

> "Ah, te meæ si partem animæ rapit
> Maturior vis, quid moror altera,
> Nec carus æque, nec superstes
> Integer?"* HORACE.

They lingered in this heart intercourse until the rising moon lighted up the distant spires of the city, and tinged the Charles with its quiet beauty. How often had they on that very spot looked to this moment as a bright and verdant point in their existence! It had come; the ties of four years spent in growing manhood were to be severed. Were they happy? If they were, happiness has sighs and tears. With hands clasped in hand they looked far down in each other's hearts, more busy with memory than hope. They could not tear themselves away. Again they gazed on the Giant's Grave—they lingered on Moss Hill; they plighted solemn vows in the Dell, and a tenderness, shaded like the parting twilight, stole over their souls.

It was a sultry night; and the moon's rays, usually so clear and cool, were like the noon sun to Lucy Sullivan, as they came through her curtained window and shone on her restless slum-

> "Alas, if thou untimely haste away,
> Half of my soul! oh why should I delay?
> Why keep the other half, its value gone,
> Bereft of thee to languish here alone!"

ber. A sound awoke her, a single flute—the tune, a familiar air of tender farewell. With a delicious tremor she started, threw off the cap that bound her braided hair, and looked from behind the folded curtain. The music ceased; a well-known figure stood leaning against a tree, gazing upward. Not a word was spoken. Why speak when every pulsation of the heart tells a tale of tenderness? Lucy held her very breath, and not until the serenader moved, waved his hat, bowed with a low obeisance towards the window, and disappeared, did she seem to respire; then, with a sigh that appeared to bear away her very being, she sank on her bed and burst into tears.

In a few days Henry Wilton departed for the south. A vision of one with a depth of tenderness in her blue eyes, which would have made them grave but for the buoyancy of her step, often came across his memory as he stood on the deck of the vessel, and gazed on the *northern* stars.

Three years elapsed, and he married an Edisto belle, with "whole *acres* of charms;" and when memory asked, "Where is Lucy Sullivan?" echo answered, "Where?"

At a still later period he visited New-England. Colonel Wilton—for papa had acquired honors—was *introduced* to Mr. Winthrop, senator from —— county. They shook hands, spoke of the politics of the day, and parted.

And Lucy Sullivan, where was she? For a brief space the myrtle was cherished, partly in tenderness, partly in hope, and laid within the leaves of a book near a sentimental rhyme. Time passed away; and one day, when William Russell, after urging his suit, had placed unchecked a golden circlet on her forefinger, and was leaning over a book watching her eyes to know when he should turn the leaves, a withered myrtle sprig dropped from the page, which with her handkerchief Lucy quietly brushed away. It fell at her feet, and was crushed by an unconscious movement. The house-maid sweeping the next morning wondered how Miss Lucy could drop so much *litter* on the carpet.

And thus ended college love and college friendship.

CHAPTER III.

THE COUNTRY FUNERAL.

"Why should old age escape unnoticed here,
That sacred era to reflection dear?
That peaceful shore where passion dies away,
Like the last wave that ripples o'er the bay?
Oh, if old age were cancell'd from our lot,
Full soon would man deplore the unhallow'd blot!
Life's busy day would want its tranquil even,
And earth would lose her stepping-stone to heaven."

S. GILMAN.

"Years have past—
Yet still,
When by-gone days do visit me,
Some secret spell
Enchains me to that spot, and once again
I meet the soften'd and religious glance
Of that fair matron's eye; and though my ear
Hath listen'd to rare music—
The full deep cadence of some queen-like one
Trying her harp's fine pulses, and been stirr'd,
E'en as an instrument with cunning sounds
Of ravishing vibration, yet not one
Seems now so grateful to my thirsting ear
As that fond son's '*my mother!*'"

MARY E. LEE.

MAMMA possessed more than "whole *acres* of charms," for though not brilliant, she was good-tempered and sensible. A demure look and reserved manner concealed a close habit of observation. She would sit in company for hours, making scarcely a remark, and recollect afterwards every fact that had been stated, to the color of a riband or the stripe of a waistcoat. Home was her true sphere; there everything was managed with promptitude and decision, and papa, who was a politician, a candidate for military honors, a commissioner of roads, a churchwarden, a "mighty hunter," and withal an active planter, was glad to find his domestic arrangements quiet and orderly. No one ever managed an establishment better; but there was no appeal from her opinions, and I have known her ever eloquent in defending a recipe. She was well entitled to her opinions; for though papa often returned from the city or the chase with unexpected strangers, I never saw her laboring under embarrassment. Her sausages were pronounced to be the best flavored in the neighborhood; her hog's cheese (the English brawn) was delicacy itself; her curds, made in a heart-mould, covered with nutmeg and cream, won the hearts of many a guest; her clabber was turned at that precise moment when a slight acidity tempers the insipidity of milk; her wafers bore the prettiest devices, or were rolled in the thinnest possible consistency; her shrimps, pickled or fresh, were most carefully prepared; her preserved water-melons were carved with the taste of a sculptor; her hommony looked like plates of gathered snow; corn and rice lent all their nice varieties to her breakfast; and her boiled rice answered to Shakspeare's description, for "each particular *grain* did stand on end," or, to use a more expressive term, *crawled.* And all these delicacies were laid on your plate so silently, with a look that seemed to say, "No one will observe you if you do eat this little bit more." An orange leaf, which when crushed in the hand sent out a pleasant odor, was laid on every finger-bowl. A cheerful fire blazed on the bedroom hearths in winter, and flowers ornamented them in spring, while I was early taught to lay fresh roses on the pillows of strangers.

I recollect mamma most distinctly at the breakfast-table. She entered the room almost invariably followed by her maid Chloe, bearing her small basket of keys. She wore a neat morning-dress, with plaited frills, a tasteful cap, her hands decorated with rings, holding a handkerchief of exquisite fineness, and her gold watch suspended from her belt, with its face outward. Chloe, with a turban of superior height (for there is great ambition in the fold of a negro's turban), stood behind her chair with the basket of keys. Her usual office was to dress and undress her mistress every morning and evening, and perform all offices of personal attendance. To her taste mamma often referred in the choice of a dress for the day, for Chloe's taste was unquestionable.

We sat while papa asked a blessing in a low tone. This is a patriarchal and beautiful custom, connecting, as it does, earthly blessings with "the Giver of every good and perfect gift;" but it should either be performed in the Quaker style, in silence, or with distinct and earnest emphasis. My brother John was a bright, observing boy, and yet, at the age of ten years, he said to mamma in a whisper one day, as if fearing he was asking something wrong, "What does papa mean by *tol lol* at the end of the blessing?"

"John," exclaimed she, "is it possible that you do not know that he says 'our Lord?'"

"I always thought it was *tol lol*," said John, blushing to the very eyes.

I mention this fact, for it actually occurred, as a passing hint to those whose duty it is to lead the religious thoughts of the young. One clear idea is too precious a treasure to lose.

It was through similar carelessness that, while kneeling beside mamma at night, or standing to recite my catechism to her every Sabbath, I learned the Lord's Prayer, that simple yet sublime gift to man, as "Our Father *chart* in heaven;" nor was I disabused of this impression until my own mind wrought it out for me by after-reflection.

My best religious impressions were derived from my grandmamma. Her suffering heart had felt their need, her strong mind had tried their value, and she possessed the golden faculty of turning earth's fleeting sands into the scale of heaven.

If ever the cradle of declining age was gently rocked, it was by those who circled around the venerable form of my grandparent at Roseland. A certain tenderness gathered over papa's manner whenever he addressed her; there was even a softened gallantry in his air, as he led her to the coolest seat in the piazza, or the warmest by the hearth. A lofty beauty still sat upon her brow, the same which dwells on the features of her portrait, by Copley, in Roseland Hall. Her hair, bleached like snow, was as fine in its texture, and was singularly contrasted by the sunny curls of her youth. The influence of her manners was evident on the plantation, producing an air of courtesy even among the slaves. It was beautiful to witness the profound respect with which they regarded her. Nanny, Jacque's sister, was her waiting-maid, and herself a fine specimen of that quiet, graceful respect often discerned among our elder servants. Nanny still lives, and is my especial care. On sunny days she is brought up to the piazza in an arm-chair, where she revives from a gentle stupor at the sight of familiar objects. Her children's children play on the lawn, but I sometimes think my Eleanor awakens stronger interest even than they, from her resemblance to her mistress. A few ideas only linger on the old woman's mind; the strongest of which is breathed in the form of a prayer that she may "walk in dis worl so to see missis in heaven."

One autumn evening, in my childhood, when the sunset began to look cold, and the first whirling leaves were brought to our feet, we arrived from our summer residence on our annual visit to Roseland. Premonitions of hastening decay had been seen in grandmamma, and she had evinced a gentle impatience to be once more an inmate of her favorite home. She could no longer walk without assistance, and papa proposed that she should pass on directly through the hall to her bed-room.

"I will rest here, if you please, my son," said she, quietly; and as her still speaking eye dwelt on the likeness of her husband, we understood her.

"If the people wish to see me, let them come now," said she to Nanny. Her will was a law to us, and the negroes were summoned, while we arranged pillows for her to recline on the sofa. She received them kindly; to one giving a word of advice, to another of comfort; she inquired into their wants, and expressed her sympathy in their joys and sorrows.

"See that mammy Sue has extra blankets this winter, my son. Daddy Charles tells me he is too feeble to mend his own roof—set some hands to work upon it before the cold weather."

Jacque had stood behind her chair with Nanny during this interview.

"Jacque," said his mistress.

"My missis," said Jacque.

"You remember your master, Jacque?"

"My lor, missis! me an't got no membrance, if me an't member maussa, just like a yesterday."

"You know where I am to be laid?" said grandmamma.

"Yes, missis, Jacque know berry well;" and he wiped away an unaffected tear.

"I must tell you all how d'ye and good-bye together," said she, "for I am going very fast;" then extending her hand to each in turn, she said a few more words of comfort and blessing. "God bless my old missis!" "Many tanks, my old missis," was heard amid stifled sobs, as, with their aprons or handkerchiefs to their eyes, they withdrew.

Grandmamma rested a few moments, and we stood in silence "Cornelia, dear," said she to me, "you are the eldest, and most resemble your grandfather, and I will give you *the locket*;" and she suspended it with a beautiful chain from my neck. I could not speak, and my brothers, with a sudden understanding of the scene, stood with looks of sorrowful earnestness.

I glanced at the locket through my tears, and they flowed faster as I traced a gray lock entwined with its bright ringlet.

"Henry, my son, I will go to my bedroom," said she. On reaching the door, she turned round deliberately and gazed on the portrait of her early love. We saw her lips move, but her voice was not heard. Then, recollecting herself, she said, "Excuse me," with that graceful and lofty air so peculiarly hers.

She never left her apartment again. A rapid but gentle decay came on; so gentle, that when my brothers and myself were told that she was dead, and saw first the bustle and then the careful tread of mourners, we could scarcely comprehend it. But we did realize something appalling when we were carried by papa to take a last look of his beloved parent. I never saw him so much moved. He kissed again and again her pale forehead; and then, with a long, long gaze, dwelt on her features, so still and unanswering. I can comprehend now that gaze. I know how the mind rushes back, in such moments, to infancy, when those stiffened hands were wrapped around us in twining love; when that bosom was the pillow of our first sorrows; when those ears, now insensible and soundless, heard our whispered confidence; when those eyes, now curtained by unlifted lids, watched our every motion. I know the pang that runs through the heart, and I can fancy the shrieking voice within which says, "Thou mightst have done more for thy mother's happiness, for her who loved thee so!"

Then, however, I experienced not this. A fearful awe overpowered me, the feeling of the supernatural. I fancied that the eyes were opening—I saw the shroud heave on the cold breast —the white sheet waved—I reeled, and should have fallen, but for papa's arms. Oh, dark, dark moment, when the fear of death is roused without its hopes, and we see the gloom of the grave untinged by the dawn of salvation.

I was carried from the room, and aroused by the strange contrast without. True, every face was serious, but there was the bustle of preparation—a cool criticism on propriety. Jacque and Nanny were reverentially covering the portraits of their beloved master and mistress with a white cloth, preparatory to the funeral. I saw that though their eyes were full of tears, yet not a fold was left on its smooth surface; and mamma, who had been a most dutiful and affectionate child, warned the men who were bringing the coffin not to graze the mahogany table. I felt a shock upon my youthful mind when I perceived these seeming incongruities; but I have since found that there are two currents running through every heart, one rising from our high immortal nature, and the other springing from sensations immediately about us. All we can do with the latter is to bear with them, and turn them, if possible, to good.

It was on that mournful occasion that I felt the first struggle of conscience in the vanity of a new suit of mourning. I tried to be, perhaps I *was* sorry in assuming it, but glanced at the mirror to observe if it was becoming. I remember my brothers' looks of importance as they dressed for the funeral, and my correcting their pride in order to screen my own. John and I walked together after our parents to Cedar Mound. He irresistibly stepped into a march. I twitched his arm. Still he stepped forward with great manliness. "John," said I, in unaffected indignation, "are you not ashamed to march at a funeral?"

Thus, even at that early age, we betrayed that love of observances which, though necessary to our earthly condition, may check so fatally our spiritual growth.

Neither John nor I realized that our venerable friend was gone until we reached Cedar Mound. Then the recollection of her last resting-place burst on our young hearts. How often had we strayed there with her, and heard her gentle voice in love and tenderness! How sacredly had she tended those flowers, and told us that we, like them, would die and bloom again! The coffin was lowered; we should see her no more on earth; and, as the birds sent forth their songs, and her tame fawn came forward and gave a wistful look on the grave, our youthful voices rent the air, and we felt the mournful truth that we had indeed lost a friend.

Venerable, even beautiful old age, beautiful when the glow of kindness lingers on the wrinkled brow and animates the lips! Let youth catch thy parting rays, which illuminate it as the dying sunshine illuminates the sapling and flower.

Virtuous old age! we will listen to the lengthened story of thy large experience. Even Heaven scorns not to add up thy gathered store of goodness, and thou shalt see it in glittering numbers on the "book of life."

Dying old age! Let us dwell on the link connecting thy form with eternity, and then gaze on the soul's chariot, as, disencumbered of clay, it rises heavenward among the parting clouds!

Grave of the aged! Let us all pause often at thy sanctuary, where the waves of this world roll off, and leave us alone with God!

CHAPTER IV.

MR. JOSEPH BATES, THE YANKEE LAD.

"A shallow brain behind a serious mask,
An oracle within an empty cask,
He says but little, and, that little said,
Owes all its weight, like loaded dice, to lead."
Cowper's Conversation.

My education, and that of my brothers had been generally superintended, except when the boys were at city schools, by a succession of governesses. I beg pardon; this honorable name is not popular in America. I think we speak of them as young ladies who *stay* with us to teach our children. Our winters were passed at Roseland, with an occasional visit to Charleston; our summers at a Pine-land settlement; and this arrangement rendered it necessary that our teachers should reside under our roof.

John, and Richard, and I had fairly grown beyond petticoat government. When called upon to recite, we laughed behind our books, and turned our lessons into fun. When reading in history of the *irruption* of the Gauls, we spread several plasters, and handed them to our teacher, with the direction, "To Miss Susan Wheeler, to cure the disease of the Gauls." One day, when she entered our room, she observed our heads bent over our books, when lo, on our raising them, she found that we had covered them with colored wafers, which gave us a fearful but grotesque expression. When we recited an account of the origin of writing by hieroglyphics, we let a paper drop from our book, describing Miss Susan in the Egyptian mode. This primitive style was more than Miss Wheeler could bear, particularly as we unkindly adverted to some personal defects. Ridicule is the hardest draught in the world to swallow, and she told papa she must decline teaching us in future. Mamma never interfered with our education, and her passive virtues as a mother remind me of a tribute of praise I once heard given to a clergyman by one of his congregation. "We have an excellent minister; he never meddles with religion, nor politics, nor none of these things." She was scrupulously attentive, however, to our dress and general manners, and her care put to shame the mother who, on being asked by one of her children to comb his hair, answered, that she was busy sewing for the children in Burmah!

In consequence of Miss Wheeler's resignation, papa sent the following advertisement to the Charleston papers.

"A gentleman of cultivated mind and polished manners, with proper credentials, will hear of an eligible situation as private teacher for a family of children in the country. Inquire at this office."

"You rogue," said papa, tapping me on the shoulder with his riding-whip, "and you little rascals," shaking it smilingly at the boys, "don't think to play any more of your pranks! I will put you under a man's care; so look out; you have made Miss Wheeler as thin as a fishing-rod."

We really loved our teacher for her amiable temper, and, turning to her, half choked her with caresses, exclaiming,

"*Do, if you please, don't* give up teaching us! We will *behave.* We will *behave good.*"

Her determination was not, however, to be shaken by our entreaties, and she soon departed to another family to "incline" more docile "twigs."

I remember the *debût* of our new tutor as if it were yesterday. Having had no tasks for several weeks, we were revelling in all the glory of country freedom. One day, when our parents were out, we proposed an excursion in the woods. John rode on his beautiful mare Jenny. He had amused himself the night before by manufacturing what he called a Robinson Crusoe dress, that is, trimming an old hunting cap and jacket with racoon skins. Not satisfied with their regular position, he wore them now with their back parts in front. Equally intoxicated with fun, Richard and I mounted a mule together. He exchanged my bonnet for his hat, while I put his hat over my tangled curls. Jim, our favorite attendant, a reckless black boy of sixteen, rode a horse which we were not allowed to use, and triumphed not a little in the *caracole* of his steed, while our mule paced quietly along. We were attended by an immense retinue of little negroes, some with infants on their backs, and others pulling along those who could run alone, determined to keep up with us as long as possible, and all making characteristic remarks.

"Bro'* Jim ride more better dan Maus John, for true," said one.

"Ha !" said another, striding a gum-tree branch, "gie *me* one horse, and I show you how for ride !"

If I have described our appearance correctly, language is inadequate to represent the clamor that was issuing from the group when, turning a point on entering the avenue, we came

* Brother. The terms daddy, maumer, uncle, aunty, broder and titter (brother and sister), are not confined to connections among the blacks, they seem rather to spring from age.

in immediate contact with a gentleman in a buggie. We thought directly who it *might* be. I confess I felt prodigiously ashamed, and quick as thought exchanged head-gear with Richard. The stranger was evidently startled by this singular assemblage; but collecting himself, said,

"I reckon you can tell me if this is Colonel Wilton's *farm?*"

"Yes, sir," said John, bowing politely, for he had a good deal of his papa about him: "this is Colonel Wilton's *plantation.* Boys, run ahead, and open the gate for the gentleman."

A scampering commenced, and tumbling head over heels, with an evident desire to display their agility, the most active reached the gate leading to the lawn, where they stood respectfully, until the stranger, who sat particularly straight, passed through.

We held a consultation, and at last concluded that our parents would be angry if we did not go and entertain the visitor.

After a necessary smoothing of hair and washing of faces, we sallied down to the apartment where he sat, as erect as an arrow, with the palms of his hand joined, and the fingers crossed, except the two forefingers, which stood out straight.

We lingered outside the door before seeing him, to compose ourselves properly; with now and then a suppressed *giggle*, and now an urgent whisper to each other to go first, or an occasional application of my brothers' heels to each other's backs. At last, in a general scuffle, we were all precipitated forward together into the presence of the stranger.

We scrambled up, and, after a few stifled *snorts* (the only word that can express the act), contrived to compose ourselves; speaking was out of the question; a word would have upset our gravity. Richard stole away, while John and I sat kicking our heels against our chairs, until a note on papa's silver whistle announced his welcome return.

The gentleman arose, and, after a preliminary remark, presented papa with a paper from his large flat pocket-book. I peeped over papa's arm, and read with him—

"This is to certify, that Mr. Joseph Bates, the bearer, is in good standing with the church and congregation at ——, Connecticut. EZEKIEL DUNCAN, *Pastor*."

I did not then interpret papa's smile; but I have thought since how ludicrous it must have seemed to him to receive a certificate of good standing in a church, when he had advertised for testimonials to a teacher with cultivated mind and polished manners.

While papa is receiving the solemn introduction of our new candidate, let me recall his history.*

Mr. Joseph Bates was the son of a Connecticut farmer, that race of men who, by their high moral qualities, contribute so much to the stability and honor of our country. Joseph, when a boy, was employed in tying fagots, driving the cows, husking corn, hoeing potatoes, &c., &c. He attended the district school, which is open in New-England the three winter months, when work is *slack*. There he was taught reading, writing, spelling, and Daboll's Arithmetic. It was observed that he was never so happy as when he had washed his hands after work, and sitten down by the kitchen fire with an almanac in his hand. Perhaps sufficient praise has not been awarded to these little vehicles of knowledge, these national annuals, which, gliding noiselessly into the retreats of ignorance, throw abroad rays of science, and warm up the germs of heart and mind.

* In illustration of this description, I beg leave to state, that a Connecticut gentleman at the South told me recently, that he asked a *pedler* who had come from his neighborhood if the increased tax had not injured the members of his craft. "Oh, I don't know," said he, "I guess not, as they have pretty much turned schoolmasters."

Joseph sat for hours with his eyes fixed on the crabs and scales in the zodiac, with a kind of mysterious delight. He looked to the weather department with the faith of a child, read the wise sayings with the voice of an oracle, and was even known, as a shrill blast came whistling through the door, shaking the very settle on which he sat, to exclaim,

"See, winter comes to rule the varied year."

The only joke he was ever heard to utter was from the same fruitful source.

Joseph availed himself of his privilege of a quarter every year at the district school up to the lawful age of twenty-one. He could cast up accounts, and wrote a tolerable hand, but was no nearer to the mysteries of the zodiac. It is customary for young men, in his quarter of the country, to associate themselves in a class for the winter months, under the teaching of the parish clergyman, who is willing to advance the cause of learning, and aid his scanty resources, by a trifling pecuniary compensation from an evening school. At the age of twenty-one, Joseph became a member of the Rev. Ezekiel Duncan's class, to which, after a hard day's work, he resorted, with hair duly sleeked over his forehead, and well-brushed Sunday suit. Access to Mr. Duncan's instruction and library for three months made a wonderful move in Joseph's mind. Familiar with many things, which made his good old parents, aunt Patty, and sister Nancy stare, he began to think himself competent to any intellectual effort.

At this period the captain of a Charleston trading schooner came to —— to visit his relations, and renewed a boyish intimacy with Joseph. This intercourse produced a restless desire of change in our incipient tutor.

"I calculate, captain," said he, after a long stroll through the town, where the sailor had gone to indulge those associations which come up like young verdure over the most hardened souls, "I calculate it's pretty difficult to git edication down at Charleston."

"Dreadful difficult," said the captain; "I reckon they an't much better than niggers."

"An't you agreeable, captain," said his friend, "to my going down to Charleston, and trying what I can do to help them a trifle at schooling?"

The captain thought it would be a praiseworthy thing, and matters were laid in train to effect the object as soon as possible. Mr. Duncan was the only person opposed to the project; but his advice, though delivered almost in a tone of warning, sounded feebly on Mr. Bates's excited tympanum.

His sister Nancy laid out a pocket piece, which had been kept for show, in buying him a third Sunday shirt; his mother sat up day and night to knit him six pairs of worsted hose; two were of blue yarn, two of gray, and two mixed, for variety; and his aunt Patty, whose pet he had been from childhood, borrowed the suit of a New Haven apprentice, who had *run up* to see his friends, to cut out Joseph's in the last fashion.

For some days he was seen in frequent conference with a pedler—they approached, retreated, parleyed; once or twice there were signs of actual warfare; but at length Joseph came off, we know not at what loss, with a large silver watch, which he boasted kept excellent time. Joseph humored it, as we ought to humor our nervous friends or capricious servants; and when he found that it actually lost one quarter of an hour in every twenty-four, he said, philosophically, "he guessed that was better than hurrying him to death by going too fast."

How fortune favors enterprise! The second day after his bargain he called at one of his neighbors to bid them farewell.

There was a great commotion among the daughters, and a scramble to get something from one of their parboiled hands.

I must stop a moment to say how sweet and healthy farmers' families have appeared to me in my northern excursions, just dressed from their Monday washtubs, sitting down to their afternoon sewing, with smiling faces and sanded floors. The scrambling among the young ladies continued, until one said, "You might as well let him see it as he's got to."

"It's nothing to be ashamed of, Prudence," said another. "'Tan't no present to cut love."

Prudence's cheeks grew a deeper crimson, until the suggestion that "to-morrow was ironing day, and she wouldn't have no time to finish it," induced her to draw out a braided watch-ribbon of various colors. It was observed that Prudence's hand trembled with unaffected trepidation as she pursued her work. Joseph rose to examine it, and by degrees the family (as families will instinctively do) disappeared, and Mr. Bates gained resolution to offer a faithful and affectionate heart to the blushing girl.

True love! Whether thou broodest with white plumage over the souls of the gentle and refined, or spreadest thy heavier flight near coarser hearts, thou art sacred still! Go on thy blessed errand, scatter thy gifts in palace and cottage, and let the young listen in joy, as they hear the rustling of thy wings!

Prudence's blushes were not diminished when her sisters observed, on their return, that the watch-guard had advanced but one knot, and that was done wrong, and their jests came full and free on the embarrassed lover. Happy had it been for him had he wedded his Prudence, and remained a "hewer of wood and drawer of water!" Appreciating affection would have smoothed his path, and labor sweetened his repose.

Such was the man whom my papa was obliged to welcome as

the teacher of his children, for he had not the heart to turn him back after his long journey. I wish there was a register of looks, that mamma's might have been entered when she first saw him, and took in his whole figure, from his greased hair to his worsted hose. He was all angles. You would have judged him to be a mathematician by his elbows, sooner, perhaps, than by his phrenology; for his hair, being cut in an exact line over his brows, left but little display of his organical developments. A perpetual embarrassment in the company of his superiors made him stand like a drake, first on one foot, then on the other; and while with one hand he fiddled at Prudence's watch-chain, he smoothed down the hair closer on his forehead with the other.

I could divine, by Chloe's increased demureness at dinner, what her notions were of our new inmate; but her expressed opinion was reserved for her mistress's ear when she undressed her at night. Jim's looks were less equivocal. As he wielded the fly-brush, he peeped out of one corner of his eye at the stranger's proceedings, scarcely controlled by papa's warning expression; and when Mr. Bates, picking out the orange-leaf, took up a finger-bowl and drank down the water at a draught, he was obliged to make a precipitate retreat to save his character as a good servant, which is one who sees everything without seeming to see.

Alas! how many young men have plodded, and pushed, and been coaxed and hustled through a kind of education in the eastern states, and then presented themselves as teachers to the children of southern gentlemen!

CHAPTER V.

MR. JOSEPH BATES, THE TUTOR.

"Wandering through the southern countries,
Teaching the A B C from Webster's spelling-book."
Halleck's Connecticut.

'*Strepsiades.* So, you like overlooking the gods from a basket?
Come, Socrates, dearest, get down from your rafter,
And tell a poor fellow the thing he's come after."
Clouds of Aristophanes.

From the unrestrained freedom described in the last chapter, we were called on the following morning to take our first lessons. John was not forthcoming.

"Where may your brother be?" said Mr. Bates to Richard.

"He has *marsh'd* his *harnd* on the *dray*," answered little Dick, feeling in his pocket for fish-hooks.

"Wha-r-t?" said Mr. Bates, with a tremendous drawl.*

Richard repeated his first reply.

"I don't conceive," said our teacher.

"Sir," said Richard and I.

"Write it down, if you are agreeable to it," said Mr. Bates.

Little Richard was as backward in chirography and orthography as he was in pronunciation, and Mr. Bates was more puzzled than ever. He turned to me for an explanation. It may surprise some readers that I should be so much further ad-

* The common southern expression is eh? or what say? pronounced almost like one word.

vanced in correct speaking than Richard; but southern children, who have good models in their parents, and who associate with the intelligent, will almost involuntarily correct themselves of inaccuracies. I was much more with my parents than the boys were. I have never felt any more apprehension at having my children associate with negroes, lest their dialect should be permanently injured, than I should have at their listening to the broken English of a foreigner; and though, at the time of which I speak, I preferred to talk to the negroes in their dialect, I never used it to the whites.

"Be so *obleeging* as to tell me what your brother says, miss," said Mr. Bates.

"He says," answered I, "that John has *mashed* his hand on the *dray*."

"Dray, miss? What is a dray?"

"That thing, sir, with wheels, out by the potato-field."

"No, no, miss," said Mr. Bates, "that is a *truck*."

"We call it a dray, sir," said I.

"You mustn't call it so no more then. The *Borston* folks call that a *truck*," insisted Mr. Bates.

"You should say, Master Richard, that John has *jammed* his hand on the *truck*."

Richard and I stole a glance as each other, but of course we could not dispute Boston phraseology.

"You must *git red* of these curious ways of talking," continued Mr. Bates, "as rapid as possible."

Thinks I, what does *git red* mean? I have since found that many well-educated persons in a city, which is acknowledged to be the most enlightened in the United States, use this expression; and ladies, very intellectual ones too, say, "I wish I could *git red* of my *bunnet*."

Let me at this point protest against the word *get*, as not only of selfish origin, but a miserable expletive. There is no sentence that is not better without it, and when it gets to *git*, it is intolerable.

I was called up to read a part of "Collins's Ode on the Passions," and commenced with,

"First *fare* his hand its skill to try—"

"*Fare!*" said Mr. Bates, "how do you spell it?"

"F-e-a-r *fare*," said I.

"How do you pronounce these words?" said he, pointing to *appear*, *ear*, *tear*, &c., in the spelling-book.

I answered, *appare*, *are*, *tare*, &c.

With equal impropriety I pronounced the words *day*, *play*, &c. almost like *dee*, *plee*, and my southern brethren must excuse me when I tell them, ay, very intellectual ones too, statesmen and belles, that many of them pronounce in this style unconsciously, and not only so, but often call fair *fere*, and hair *here*.

For instance,

> "The *tare* down childhood's cheek that flows,
> Is like the dewdrop on the rose."

Or,

> "Wreath'd in its dark brown curls, her *here*
> Half hid Matilda's forehead *fere*."

At the close of our lesson Mr. Bates told me that papa wished me to take a ride (*anglicé* drive) with him. Jim, who rarely left us, was standing with an inquisitive look at the door.

"Young man," said the teacher to him, "you may go to the *barn* and *tackle* the horse and *shay*."

"I no been hear wha' Maus Bate say," said Jim.

Mr. Bates repeated his direction. Jim was confounded, and we were all in the same predicament. At this moment, papa, who felt some curiosity to know our progress, entered, and Mr. Bates stated his difficulty.

"Oh, I understand you," said papa laughing. "Jim, go to the *stable* and *harness* the horse and *chair*."

I might proceed in this *exposé* of both parties, but if this little sketch leads us to more attention to our own defects, and more charity for sectional differences, it is enough.

It was difficult for papa to *git red* of our teacher, though we felt hourly his deficiencies and faults. His own knowledge of his unfitness for the task prevented his enforcing his requisitions with any firmness; the only alternative was for him to descend to be our playmate, to coax us, and even enlist Jim as a companion. Several odd incidents occurred, but the two I am about to record tended at last to sever the unnatural alliance between a good-tempered but ignorant teacher, and gay but intelligent children.

If those who were engaged in the occurrence I am about to relate ever glance at these pages in these their soberer days, they may excite a smile.

Papa and mamma having gone on a visit to the city, we were left entirely under Mr. Bates's control. Unfortunately, several lads from the neighborhood came to stay a few days with us, and John and Richard were resolved not to pursue their studies, claiming the visit of the boys as a holyday. I confess that they were exceedingly provoking; and Mr. Bates, finding them incorrigible, locked them in their bedrooms, on bread and water, for twenty-four hours. They had fairly roused the lion; he was seriously angry.

For the first part of the day we heard the boys drumming, and marching, and whistling, and saw them at the windows making odd gesticulations. As the dinner-hour advanced, they became more silent. I felt pretty sure that Jim would stand their friend; indeed, he said to me,

"Neber mind, Miss Neely, Jim can play cootah* to da buckrah."

About ten o'clock in the evening, when we had retired for the night, Mr. Bates fancied he heard unusual noises; and looking out, he saw a large basket hoisted by a rope to my brothers' window and descend again; he then observed one of the young visitors enter the basket, which was raised as before. On its descent, Jim alighted from it, saying in a whisper,

"So now, don't draw 'em up till I come back again," and then ran off to the servants' apartments.

Mr. Bates left his room silently, went through the piazza on tiptoe, and tried the strength of the rope. It seemed made of stout double line; and as the height was not very great, and the piazza, pillars, shutters, &c., were at hand to steady himself by, his passions, too, being excited, he determined to pay the boys a visit. My brothers, feeling a weight in the basket as he entered, called in a whisper, saying, "Ready, Jim?" "Ready," said Mr. Bates, squeezing himself into the basket, and feeling for the first time a little tremor.

"By George," said John, "if this is not a cargo; help us, Dick; all of you lend us a hand. Jim is heavier than I thought for. Quick, Ingols, fasten the rope to the bedstead; so there, now pull."

"Softly," said Richard, "or the *black crane* will hear us," a cognomen with which they generally honored Mr. Bates.

By the time Mr. Bates had risen half-way on his aerial excursion, he repented his temerity; a sort of sea-sickness came over him, and he was fain to cry out,

"John, I say, John, Richard, be easy now, *I'm* in't."

The boys were for a moment ready to let the basket drop in their amazement. It vibrated fearfully.

* Alluding to the deception of the turtle, which draws in its head previously to snapping at anything.

'Haul me up, haul me up," roared Mr. Bates, in an ecstasy of terror.

John called to the boys to hold on, and fastening the rope with another tie to the bedstead, went to the window.

"Who are you?" said he, in an angry tone.

"My—dear—John," said Mr. Bates, catching his breath, "*I'm* in't, Mr. Bates; my dear John, for mercy's sake, hoist me up."

The boys saw their power, and held a consultation. At length John, returning to the window ready to burst with laughter, said, "Who is this thief coming to rob us of our bread and water?"

"My dear young gentlemen," said the terrified man, "I want nothing but to get out of this *tarnation* basket. I calculate that my heft will be too much for it. Every time it knocks agin the house it jounces my life out. I shall be particularly obligated to you either to let me up or down. I an't particular which."

The boys whispered.

"Up or down," shrieked Mr. Bates. "You don't ought to keep me here."

"Mr. Bates," said John solemnly, "if we will let you in, will you let us out?"

"I wish I could reach you the key aforehand," said the poor man; "but it is in my pantaloons pocket, and sartin as I go to move for'ard, the basket will fall whop."

"You are in a bad fix," said Richard, gravely.

"Oh, I'm in an awful situation," cried he; "I wish I was in Connecticut! I feel so squeamy-like at my stomach; I don't know what to do! Pray be spry and take me in."

The boys retreated to the bed, and stuffed their handkerchiefs into their mouths to conceal their laughter. The shaking of the bedstead moved the basket, and they heard another ejaculation.

Richard was the first to pity him. "Come, boys, let him out." It was a prodigious tug to get him up. Jim, with his eyes as big as saucers, stood below, wondering to see "Maus Bate" go up instead of himself and a plate of ham he had been frying.

Few men ever felt less of the dignity of human nature than Mr. Bates when he alighted from the basket. The boys had partaken of an excellent supper, which John had procured, together with their hunting tinder-box and a candle. He walked to the door with a very solemn step, unlocked it, and returned to his own apartment.

This incident really seemed to sober us. It was an outlet for cherished mischief, and we studied for some time with considerable diligence. Mr. Bates never referred to it again. We told our parents, but their just reproofs did but little good when we saw that they laughed until the tears ran down their cheeks, and papa, holding his sides, begged we would stop if we had any pity on him.

Thus we worried along through the winter. Mr. Bates was a thorough teacher as far as his knowledge went; but our contempt for him was so great as to prevent his having any moral power over us. He was uncomfortable enough, and the thought of his simple and warm-hearted Prudence, his affectionate family and cheerful home, often stole over his mind and shaded his brow with gloom.

We had been upon good behavior for some time, when the first of April, that day of "quips and cranks," and more than "wreathed smiles," drew near. Mr. Bates himself seemed animated by the reminiscences of April-fool-day, and detailed to Jim and us the exploits of his youth.

The jokes passed round. Occasionally he was to be seen unconsciously trailing a dirty rag at his back, or a ridiculous motto; nor was he at all backward in retaliation.

He was very fond of bottled cider, but very nervous at drawing a cork. John and I filled a bottle with weak molasses and water, and placed it, with the corkscrew, in the accustomed place. At the usual hour Mr. Bates approached the slab. He held the bottle far off, and drew cautiously, while John stood ready with a tumbler, Mr. Bates being in his usual tremor. The cork came out with difficulty, and his countenance looked as vapid as the diluted mixture. But he had his revenge. He made in secret something to imitate a short remnant of candle out of a raw sweet potato. In New-England, he told us afterward, they use the parsnip for this trick. The imitation was perfect, particularly the wick, which was simply the potato cut small at that point, slit in fine shreds, and touched with coal. This secret he communicated only to me. About twilight, when we were together, he rang the bell for Jim, and, giving the candle to him, told him to light it quickly. Jim went to the servants' hall, where there was a fire, and Mr. Bates, pretending to hurry him, followed, calling us after him. Jim took up a coal with the tongs and began to blow, his great mouth enlarging and closing like a dying shark's. Mr. Bates's impatience increased. "Blow harder, Jim." Jim puffed like a porpoise, but in vain.

"He obstinate like a nigger," said Jim, in a passion.

John snatched it from him, and went through the same process, until our restrained laughter broke forth. Mr. Bates rubbed his hands, and looked like an elephant in a frolic.

I have a very great objection to offer to this April trick, which is this. I have heard two gentlemen, who never used an oath on any other occasion, swear at it

It was but too obvious that our connection with Mr. Bates must be terminated.

Papa opened the matter to him, and gave him a generous remuneration. Mr. Bates received his dismissal quietly, and papa's gift gratefully, saying, "He reckoned he should make a better fist at farming than edicating."

We parted in friendship; and John, the last person in the world I should have suspected of such sensibility, shed tears

CHAPTER VI.

PARENTAL TEACHING.

"*Mrs. Page.*—Sir Hugh, my husband says my son profits nothing in the world at his book; I pray you ask him some questions in his accidence.
" *Evans.*—Come hither, William; hold up your head, come."

After the departure of our Connecticut teacher, Mr. Bates, papa resolved to carry on our education himself. We were to rise by daylight, that he might pursue his accustomed ride over the fields after breakfast. New writing-books were taken out and ruled, fresh quills laid by their side, our task carefully committed to memory, and we sat with a mixture of docility and curiosity to know how he would manage as a teacher. The first three days, our lessons being on trodden ground, and ourselves under the impulse of novelty, we were very amiable, he very paternal; on the fourth, John was turned out of the room, Richard was pronounced a mule, and I went sobbing to mamma, as if my heart would break, while papa said he might be compelled to ditch rice-fields, but he never would undertake to teach children again.

A slight constraint was thrown over the family for a day or two, but it soon wore off, and he returned to his good-nature. For three weeks we were as wild as fawns, until mamma's attention was attracted by my sunburnt complexion and my brother's torn clothes.

"This will never answer," said she to papa. "Look at Cornelia's face! It is as brown as a chinquapin. Richard has ruined his new suit, and John has cut his leg with the carpenter's tools. I have half a mind to keep school for them myself."

Papa gave a slight whistle, which seemed rather to stimulate than check her resolution. "Cornelia," said she, "go directly to your brothers, and prepare your books for to-morrow. *I* will teach you."

The picture about to be presented is not overwrought. I am confident of the sympathy of many a mother, whose finger has been kept on a word in the lesson, amid countless interruptions, so long, that her pupils, forgetting her vocation, have lounged through the first interruptions, and finished with a frolic.

One would suppose that the retirement of a plantation was the most appropriate spot for a mother and her children to give and receive instruction. Not so; for instead of a limited household, her dependants are increased to a number which would constitute a village. She is obliged to listen to cases of grievance, is a nurse to the sick, and distributes the half-yearly clothing; indeed, the mere giving out of thread and needles is something of a charge on so large a scale. A planter's lady may seem indolent, because there are so many under her who perform trivial services; but the very circumstance of keeping so many menials in order is an arduous one, and the *keys* of her establishment are a care of which a Northern housekeeper knows nothing, and include a very extensive class of duties. Many fair, and even aristocratic girls, if we may use this phrase in our republican country, who grace a ball-room, or loll in a liveried carriage, may be seen with these steel talismans, presiding over store-houses, and measuring, with the accuracy and conscientiousness of a shopman, the daily allowance of the family, or cutting homespun suits, for days together, for the young and the old negroes under their charge; while matrons, who would ring a bell for their pocket-handkerchief to be brought to them. will act the part of a surgeon or physician with a promptitude and skill which would excite astonishment in a stranger. Very frequently, servants, like children, will only take medicine from their superiors, and in this case the planter's wife or daughter is admirably fitted to aid them.

There are few establishments where all care and responsibility devolves on the master, and even then the superintendence of a large domestic circle, and the rites of hospitality, demand so large a portion of the mistress's time, as leaves her but little opportunity for systematic teaching in her family. In this case she is wise to seek an efficient tutor, still appropriating those opportunities which perpetually arise under the same roof to improve their moral and religious culture, and cultivate those sympathies which exalt these precious beings from children to friends.

The young, conscientious, ardent mother must be taught this by experience. She has a jealousy at first of any instruction that shall come between their dawning minds and her own; and is only taught by the constantly thwarted recitation, that in this country, at least, good housekeeping and good teaching cannot be combined.

But to return to my narrative. The morning after mamma's order, we assembled at ten o'clock. There was a little trepidation in her manner, but we loved her too well to annoy her by noticing it. Her education had been confined to mere rudiments, and her good sense led her only to conduct our reading, writing, and spelling.

We stood in a line.

"Spell *irrigate*," said she. Just then the coachman entered, and bowing, said,

"Maussa send me for de key for get four quart o' corn for I .m bay horse."

The key was given.

"Spell *imitate*," said mamma.

"We did not spell *irrigate*," we all exclaimed.

"Oh, no," said she, "*irrigate*."

By the time the two words were well through, Chloe, the most refined of our colored circle, appeared.

"Will mistress please to *medjure* out some calomel for Syphax, who is feverish and onrestless?"*

During mamma's visit to the doctor's shop, as the medicine-closet was called, we turned the inkstand over on her mahogany table, and wiped it up with our pocket-handkerchiefs. It required some time to cleanse and arrange ourselves; and just as we were seated and had advanced a little way on our orthographical journey, Maum Phillis entered with her usual drawl,

"Little maussa want for nurse, marm."

While this operation was going on, we gathered round mamma to play bo-peep with the baby, until even she forgot our lessons. At length the little pet was dismissed with the white drops still resting on his red lips, and our line was formed again.

Mamma's next interruption, after successfully issuing a few words, was to settle a quarrel between Lafayette and Venus, two little blackies, who were going through their daily drill, in learning to rub the furniture, which, with brushing flies at meals, constitutes the first instruction for house servants. These important and classical personages rubbed about a stroke to the minute on each side of the cellaret, rolling up their eyes and making grimaces at each other. At this crisis they had laid

* Uneasy.

claim to the same rubbing-cloth; mamma stopped the dispute by ordering my seamstress Flora, who was sewing for me, to apply the weight of her thimble, that long-known weapon of offence, as well as implement of industry, to their organ of firmness.

"Spell *accentuate*," said mamma, whose finger had slipped from the column.

"No, no, that is not the place," we exclaimed, rectifying the mistake.

"Spell *irritate*," said she, with admirable coolness, and John fairly succeeded, just as the overseer's son, a sallow little boy, with yellow hair, and blue homespun dress, came in with his hat on, and kicking up one foot for manners, said,

"Faything says as how he wants Master Richard's horse to help tote some tetters* to tother field."

This pretty piece of alliteration was complied with, after some remonstrance from brother Dick, and we finished our column. At this crisis, before we were fairly seated at writing, mamma was summoned to the hall to one of the field hands, who had received an injury in the ankle from a hoe. Papa and the overseer being at a distance, she was obliged to superintend the wound. We all followed her, Lafayette and Venus bringing up the rear. She inspected the sufferer's great foot, covered with blood and perspiration, superintended a bath, prepared a healing application, and bound it on with her own delicate hands, first quietly tying a black apron over her white dress. Here was no shrinking, no hiding of the eyes; and while extracting some extraneous substance from the wound, her manner was as resolute as it was gentle and consoling. This episode gave Richard an opportunity to unload his pockets of groundnuts, and treat us therewith. We were again seated at

* Potatoes.

our writing books, and were going on swimmingly with "*Avoid evil company*," when a little crow-minder, hoarse from his late occupation, came in with a basket of eggs, and said,

"Mammy Phillis send missis some egg for buy, ma'am; she an't so berry well, and ax for some 'baccer."

It took a little time to pay for the eggs and send to the store-room for the Virginia weed, of which opportunity we availed ourselves to draw figures on our slates: mamma reproved us, and we were resuming our duties. when the cook's son approached, and said,

"Missis, Daddy Ajax say he been broke de axe, and ax me for ax you for len him de new axe."

This made us shout out with laughter, and the business was scarcely settled, when the dinner-horn sounded. That evening a carriage full of friends arrived from the city to pass a week with us, and thus ended mamma's experiment in teaching.

Our summers were usually passed at Springland, a pine settlement, where about twenty families resorted at that season of the year. We were so fortunate as to find a French lady already engaged in teaching, from whom I took lessons on the pianoforte and guitar. The summer swiftly passed away. Papa was delighted with my facility in French, in which my brothers were also engaged, and we were happy to retain Madame d'Anville in our own family on our return to Roseland.

In the middle of November a stranger was announced to papa, and a young man of very prepossessing appearance entered with a letter. It proved to be from our teacher, Mr. Bates. The contents were as follows:—

"*Respected Sir.*—I now sit down to write to you, to inform you that I am well, as also are, sir and mar'm, my sister Nancy, and all the rest of our folks except aunt Patty, who is but poorly, having attacks of the rheumatiz, and shortness of breath. I should add, that Mrs. Prudence Bates (who, after the regular publishment on the church doors for three Sundays, was united to me in the holy bands of wedlock, by our minister, Mr. Ezekiel Duncan) is in a good state of health at this present, though her uncle, by her father's side, has been sick of jaundice, a complaint that has been off and on with him for a considerable spell.

"The bearer of this epistle is Parson Duncan's son, by name Mr. Charles Duncan, a very likely young man, but poorly in health, and Dr. Hincks says going down to Charleston may set him up. I have the candor to say that I think him, on some accounts, a more proper teacher than your humble servant, having served his time at a regular college edication.

"I have taken to farming, and lot upon seeing the Carolina seeds come up that you gave me. Our folks say that I speak quite outlandish since I come home; and when I told neighbor Holt tother day about *growing corn*, and spoke about somebody that was *raised* in a certain place, he as good as laughed in my face, and said it sounded curious.

"I have tried a heap to make our folks bile the hommony Miss Wilton give me as they do at Roseland; but it is the very picture of swill, and I must say the hogs eat it a nation faster than we do. When I told Aunt Patty that Southern folks ate clabber, she rolled up her eyes, and wondered I could abide to sit at table with such critters; and though I told her that it was genteel, and that I stomached it very well, she can't no how git over it, and makes me feel very curious by telling everybody that happens in how they eat hogs' victuals down at Charleston.

"Sister Nancy was very much obligated by the fans and basket Miss Neely sent her, and was in a great maze at niggers doing anything so tasty; and they were all astonished when I told them how the white folks buy what the niggers make, and what a laying up they can git if they have a mind to, jist from knick-knacks, and eggs, and potatoes, and so on.

"Mrs. Prudence admires the Thomson's Seasons Mr. John sent her. She has kivered it with a bit of blue homespun, and put it up safe.

"I didn't say nothing to none on you about a keg of shrimps that I brought on here from Charleston. When I got here, Mr. Wilton, they were a sight for mortal eyes! Nobody could tell which was head or which was tail. A perfect regiment of critters had took hold on 'em; and when I told our folks how much nicer and delicater they were than lobsters, they began to twit me, and I an't hearn the last of it yit. I only wish I could have preserved the live-stock for a museum.

"I send by Mr. Duncan some long-necked squashes and russet apples of my own raising. The folks here stare like mad when I tell them you eat punkins biled like squash.

"I have writ a much longer letter than I thought on; but somehow it makes me chirpy to think of Roseland, though the young folks were obstreperous.

"Give my love nevertheless to them, and Miss Wilton, and all the little ones, as also I would not forget Daddy Jacque, whom I consider, notwithstanding his color, as a very respectable person. I cannot say as much for Jim, who was an eternal thorn in my side, by reason of his quickness at mischief, and his slowness of waiting upon me; and I take this opportunity of testifying, that I believe, if he had been in New-England, he would have had his deserts before this; but you Southern folks do put up with an unaccountable sight from niggers, and I hope Jim will not be allowed his full tether, if so be Mr. Charles should take my situation in your family. I often tell our folks how I used to catch up a thing and do it rather than wait for half a dozen on 'em to take their own time. If I lived to the age of Methusalem, I never could git that composed, quiet kind of way you Southern folks have of waiting on the niggers. I only wish they could see aunt Patty move when the rheumatiz is off—if she isn't spry, I don't know.

"Excuse all errors.

"Yours to serve,

"JOSEPH BATES."

I detected a gentle, half-comical smile on Mr. Duncan's mouth as he raised his splendid eyes to papa while delivering Mr. Bates's letter; but he soon walked to the window, and asked me some questions about the Cherokee rose-hedge, and other objects in view, which were novelties to him. I felt instantly that he was a gentleman, by the atmosphere of refinement which was thrown over him, and I saw that papa sympathized with me, as with graceful courtesy he welcomed him to Roseland.

CHAPTER VII.

CHARLES DUNCAN.

"A spirit urging onward and still on
To some high, noble object to be won;
And pressing still, through danger and distress,
Regardless of them all,
Till that high object, whatsoe'er it be,
Friendship, or virtuous fame, our country's liberty,
The improvement of our race, the happiness
Of one poor individual,
Or of unnumber'd thousands be attained."

S. G. BULLFINCH.

"And as a bird each fond endearment tries,
To tempt its new-fledged offspring to the skies,
He tried each art, reproved each dull delay,
Allured to brighter worlds, and led the way."

GOLDSMITH.

THERE is no moral object so beautiful to me as a conscientious young man! I watch him as I do a star in the heavens: clouds may be before him, but we know that his light is behind them, and will beam again; the blaze of others' prosperity may outshine him, but we know that, though unseen, he illumines his true sphere. He resists temptation not without a struggle, for that is not virtue, but he does resist and conquer; he hears the sarcasm of the profligate, and it stings him, for that is the trial of virtue, but he heals the wound with his own pure touch; he heeds not the watchword of fashion if it leads to sin; the atheist who says, not only in his heart but with his lips, "There is no God," controls him not, for he sees the hand of a creating

God, and reverences it; of a preserving God, and rejoices in it. Woman is sheltered by fond arms and guided by loving counsel; old age is protected by its experience, and manhood by its strength; but the young man stands amid the temptations of the world like a self-balanced tower. Happy he who seeks and gains the prop and shelter of Christianity.

Onward, then, conscientious youth! raise thy standard and nerve thyself for *goodness*. If God has given thee intellectual power, awaken it in that cause; never let it be said of thee, he helped to swell the tide of sin, by pouring his influence into its channels. If thou art feeble in mental strength, throw not that poor drop into a polluted current. Awake, arise, young man! Assume the beautiful garments of virtue! It is easy, fearfully easy to sin; it is difficult to be pure and holy. Put on thy strength, then; let thy chivalry be aroused against error—let *truth* be the lady of thy love—defend her.

A review of the character of Charles Duncan has led me to this expression of feeling. I was thirteen years of age when he arrived at Roseland, and became our teacher in conjunction with Madame d'Anville. I ought to describe his appearance. I wish I could. I can say that his form was the perfection of manly symmetry; I can tell of his clear, dark, intellectual eyes, where softness and vivacity seemed living in friendly rivalry; I can paint the rich clustering hair thrown away from his noble forehead, and that forehead rising in its white mass like a tower of mind; I can give some conception of the rich glow that colored up a complexion of such transparent hue, that it would have seemed effeminate but for the strong character of his frame and features, that glow, too fallacious, too burningly bright, which spoke of a fire consuming the vase in which it was kindled; but his voice it is impossible for me to describe. He never spoke without silencing others, not by noise or vehemence, but with a slow, musical emphasis, that went straight to the heart; nor was the voice low or whispered; but, without a tinge of vanity, it seemed to say, *I must be heard.*

Why are not such individuals on thrones wielding sceptres, or pouring out their talents before senates, or, aided by wealth and power, lifted up to the high temples of literature and science? Why must sickness and penury be thrown over souls which God has made of his purest essence? Thank Heaven, we know that this question will be well answered when we see them in their white robes hymning strains the first and richest among the heavenly choir!

It was well for me that Charles Duncan instructed us. *Madame* was a conscientious teacher, but her conscience only embraced externals. I practised two hours daily my musical tasks, and delighted my papa by addressing the French consul, on a visit to Charleston, with a mixture of pertness and bashfulness, in his native tongue. Papa was satisfied if he paid round sums of money for my education, and mamma was easy if my teachers seemed busy. Until Duncan came, my mind was the only instrument exercised, and that was swayed by earthly hands. True, my heart was open, and many a kind breeze of nature swept over its chords; but he tuned them both to harmony, and brought out those tones which liken us to angels, and yet fit us for the world. His searching but frequent question was, Are you acting from duty, from principle, as in the sight of God?

Papa was at first opposed to the full cultivation of my mind in the branches studied by my brothers. He laughed and said, "The girl would consider herself more learned than her father."

"Why should she not," said Duncan, "if humility be so wrought in her as to make her feel her own inferiority to the true standard of mind? Fear not, Colonel Wilton! Intellectual women are the most modest inquirers after truth, and accomplished women often the most scrupulous observers of social duty."

"Well, well," answered papa, "only do not spoil her eyes and shoulders, and let her be ready for my morning ride on horseback, and you may teach her the remainder of the day. By the way, Cornelia, are you never going to hold your whip-hand steady; you jerk it like a cracker* woman! Your head should be a little higher too, though it is pretty well. The Wiltons are not often accused of that fault." Then, whistling to his dogs, he left me to my studies.

Whatever may be the difficulty of parental instruction on a Southern plantation, none is experienced by the judicious private teacher. Here is no copying of others, no meretricious ambition from the struggle after pre-eminence.

> "The native heart bursts through, and scorns disguise."

In these far woods, breathing space is given for the young pulsation of the opening feelings. There may be the danger of the aristocracy of solitude, but the little irritations, the paltry rivalry of schools is unknown.

It was not merely in hours of recitation that we were taught; and I can recollect now, though then perhaps I did not observe it, that my teacher associated every object with some elevated motive. I never saw a mind so inwrought with heaven, and yet he was sportive, and no laugh rang more clearly than his, awakening the very echo in its joy. He taught me to be a happy early riser, and pointed out to me the glories of kindling morning; I gathered and dissected wild flowers by his side; we watched the stars in their silent courses together, until I could

* Appellation given to the back country people, who use long whips with their wagons, which they crack to stimulate the team.

welcome each like familiar eyes. Once I shrank from a storm, but he pointed out to me God's hand issuing in love, not anger, from the tempest, and I was calmed. He sang with me, taught me to distinguish what was false in sentiment in my songs, and by some poetical change brought a pure spirit into this court of folly; he read to me, and the breathings of the muse went down into my heart, calling up from unknown depths new creations of sentiment; he selected tales of romance, until I could discriminate between the fallacious and the imitable. Even history in his hands was a medium of pleasure; he never read to me the fatiguing details of war; connecting events by interesting associations, and drawing characters in strong contrasts, or singling them out like so many pictures, he brought before me the warriors and statesmen in their respective eras, until they stood as living things in my imagination.

Unable to follow my brothers in their rambling amusements, we were thrown constantly together, and the whole aim of his being seemed to be to train me like some tender plant, and not only to shed sweet dews around me, and keep every weed from my side, but to prop me with truth, and preserve my upward tendencies unswerved. With him I breathed the very atmosphere of piety; the study of the character and words of the Saviour seemed like sunshine to his soul—Cornelia, he said, drink deep at this fountain, it is a well of life.

Two years passed away with the customary change between Springland and the plantation; Duncan was still with us, and an addition was formed to our circle by the daily visits of Lewis Barnwell, a youth of eighteen, and the son of a neighbor. He had returned from college, for private reasons, to pursue his studies at home previous to graduating. He applied to Duncan for instruction, and thus was an almost constant inmate of our residence.

A change was gradually wrought. If I entered a pleasure-boat, it was Lewis, not Duncan, who sat at my side; if I rode with Duncan, Lewis was soon seen galloping through the avenue, and, without any effort of mine, chatting of everything at my elbow, while Duncan silently dropped behind; every question apart from my studies, and every expression of my thoughts which Duncan had been accustomed to answer, seemed wrested away from him. At table, Lewis anticipated every wish and motion as if it were his *right* to make me happy, and this was so gradual that *I* scarcely marked the difference. Had I been older I might have noticed an abstraction of manner steal over my dear tutor, with sometimes a deeper flush and sometimes a sudden paleness on his cheek; I should have observed him precipitately retreating when Lewis and I jested over the playful topics of youth, and as precipitately returning, to notice without mingling in our mirth.

One morning, however, my attention was effectually drawn to him. As we were standing in the piazza after breakfast, a servant came from the Elms, Mr. Barnwell's residence, with a bunch of flowers, with Master Lewis's compliments to Miss Cornelia. Duncan took them, looked a moment at the collection; a contortion like one in deep suffering passed over his face; he turned deadly pale, and sank on a seat, while the flowers dropped from his hand. I hastened to him, and Richard brought me some cologne water, with which I bathed his forehead. He bore it for a moment, the same expression of suffering again passed across his countenance, and he said with a stifled voice, "Take away your hand, for God's sake, Miss Wilton!"

Miss Wilton! Richard and I looked at each other with surprise.

"He is very ill," said I, innocently; "call mamma"—but, with an effort, he recovered, saying he had been liable to sudden faintness when at college, and he thought it was returning upon him.

"I fear, in my absence of mind," continued he, "that I spoke harshly to you, my dear Cornelia—shake hands with me and forgive me."

I gave him my hand; and as it rested a moment in his, I gazed on him with an affecting presentiment of evil totally undefinable. Again a shade crossed his expressive countenance, not so deep, but of the same character as before; and sighing as if the very fount of feeling were loosened, he resigned my hand.

I took up the bouquet which had been neglected on the floor. To a *forget-me-not* was attached my name in Lewis's handwriting. I glanced at Duncan, and blushed intensely, while he regarded me with a penetrating gaze, from which I gladly turned away. I hurried to my own apartment, and sat and mused for some time with the flowers in my hand; and, though without any fixed impressions, I separated the *forget-me-not* from the bouquet, and placed it in my hair.

How difficult is it for growing age to recall the emotions of that period of life, when on a look, a word, a touch, may rest the history of years! What a tale was told by that little flower, how many feelings unfolded! Lewis joined us in our evening stroll, and a bright glow lighted up his features as he recognized the flower in my hair.

The morning after this little development, which after all, I scarcely understood or dwelt upon, Mr. Duncan was requested by papa to accompany me in my ride.

"I have never showed you my magnolia," said he; "the warm spring has developed its blossoms unusually early. If you will bear a slow ride among the bushes, we will visit it." I assented; and, preceded by Toney, a little crow-minder who was off duty, and who ran in front to part the bushes, we commenced our excursion, scattering the dew-drops at every step. I had entirely forgotten the excitement of yesterday; and, as we walked our horses, I poured forth all the thoughts of a happy confiding heart, while Toney, who was often my attendant on such excursions, began his task of gallantry, and gathered flowers for my herbarium.

After a ride of two miles we reached the magnolia. Mr. Duncan had caused the brushwood to be cleared from beneath it, and it stood alone, except that a vine had clung (as they seem to do by magic in our woods) to one of the outer branches, and, rising and descending again and again to an incredible distance, formed with its intertwining arms a giant trunk. The magnolia, the queen of the Southern forest, stood with her large white blossoms resting on her polished leaves, sending out afar her delicious perfume.

"I must have a blossom, Mr. Duncan," said I, as we alighted, "to remember your tree by."

With one of his bright smiles, he went to an opposite branch where a flower seemed attainable, while I attempted to draw down another which was above me with my whip. At this moment I heard Lewis's voice in a gay "good-morning;" and carelessly turning, at his salutation, while springing to gain the blossom, I fell with violence to the ground.

My head had struck against a fallen tree, and I was insensible. In my first consciousness, I uttered the name of Lewis. I perceived myself lying in the arms of some one, who gave me a momentary but shivering pressure. I then felt myself gently placed in the arms of another. I opened my eyes, Lewis was supporting me, and Mr. Duncan, pale as a marble statue, leaned against the magnolia.

"Is Mr. Duncan ill?" I said, as a breeze sweeping across my brow gave me sudden consciousness.

"He loves you," said Lewis, in an agitated whisper. "He would willingly die for you. Which of us shall *live* for you, dearest?"—and, with a renewed recollection of my danger, he pressed his hand on my forehead as if to assure himself that life was there.

Duncan looked on. It was in vain that he struggled with his excited spirit; without uttering a word, he stood until Lewis lifted me to my saddle, and then, heart-struck, alas! I saw it, I saw it, he turned towards home.

CHAPTER VIII.

CHARLES DUNCAN.

"By solemn vision, and bright silver dream,
His infancy was nurtured. Every sight
And sound from the vast earth and ambient air,
Sent to his heart its choicest impulses.
The fountains of divine philosophy
Fled not his thirsting lips, and all of great,
Or good, or lovely, which the sacred past
In truth or fable consecrates, he felt
And knew.—SHELLEY.

"He needs not glory's wreath
To keep his memory from the blight of years."
MRS. HALE.

FROM the day of our visit to the magnolia, Mr. Duncan's manners were marked by a series of respectful attentions, and a nice deference to social forms. But while devoted to every duty, he became a lonely rambler in the woods, or secluded himself in his study, and a light was visible in his apartment when the latest member of the family retired. The bright spot on his cheek grew brighter, his hands became thin, and we could see their blue veins as they lay in languor at his side. At length a short restrained cough followed every exertion; he clung to the balustrade in ascending the steps, and looked with an eager eye to a resting-place after his walks, which were daily more circumscribed. An enemy, which perhaps answered sympathy would have longer lulled, was roused, and consumption revelled through his frame. Sometimes it was exhibited in deep and silent despondency; sometimes his eye was illuminated with unnatural lustre; and occasionally his fine intellect jarred with the breaking of his corporeal powers.

He began to speak of his childhood—of his home, of the old elm that shaded the sloping hill at his father's door, and to long for a draught of water from the well beneath its shade. Then a deadly heaviness and debility came over his frame, and light fancies floated on his mind. He talked of the vessel that was to bear him away, and I was to be his companion.

"Cornelia and he," he said, "would gaze on the wide ocean together; he would show her God's power on the deep—he would carry her to his native home, where the wild flowers sprang up, and the birds were bright as here; his father's hand should rest on her sunny curls, and he would love the tenderness in her bright eyes—they would listen to him in the old meeting-house, where the prayers were purer and the hymns sweeter than aught in the wide world. He was not rich, but what were riches to true love? Cornelia and he could live together beneath his father's roof—the old man would be kind to them, and his hearth was warm."

Then a change came over him, and he talked of fame. "They shall hear me," he exclaimed (and his thrilling voice rang upon my ear, while his arm was stretched forward with graceful energy). "Think you that strong thought can be chained? You may restrain a torrent in its course, but mind will on, on with its master impulse. You think me weak, Cornelia" (for I was gazing with deep commiseration at his panting chest); "but you know not what can be done by *will*. I will advocate truth—I *will* crush error—I *will* lift up the feeble, and bring down the haughty, and to God shall be the praise."

It was now that mamma's quiet virtues shone beyond the

glare of intellectual accomplishments. She attended him devotedly; prepared luxuries for his taste; watched his looks with untiring but delicate assiduity; made every arrangement for his contemplated voyage; and when I, melted by unaffected distress, retreated to weep in silence, she nursed him like the son of her bosom.

Nature was still beautiful to him, and he held his hand eagerly for the garden bouquet which was my daily gift; while a smile (it lingers yet like a sunset glow on the mountain height of memory), a grateful, gentle smile, lighted up his features, as, with a few murmured words, unheard by me, he bent his lips over the blossoms.

Lewis was full of kind attentions, and Duncan received him with a look of welcome; but we observed that it increased the nervous wandering of his thoughts to see him.

"Father knows the spot where I am to be buried," he said one day after an interview with him, "just beside my mother's grave, where the barberry bushes rise over the stone wall. The graveyard is large enough for us. Just beside my mother—my mother—my mother," he continued, in almost a whisper—"what a small hand was this when she pressed it for the last time—smaller than Cornelia's!" Then he gazed on his thin hand, until, wearied with thoughts, his head reclined on his arm-chair, and he slept.

This excitement yielded to medical aid; and the contrast of his clear and energetic mind, as his fever subsided, in the view of his probable death, was singularly affecting.

We removed to the city with him in order to facilitate his departure home. It was one of our bright May mornings the day before he sailed, and mamma and I were sitting beside him. He looked around at the various testimonials which were collected in his room from our kind acquaintances—those affecting, spontaneous exhibitions of hospitality, which almost invariably soothe the sick stranger in Southern cities, who feels, when far from the domestic relations which once comforted his desponding moments, that these slight attentions are the most exquisite recompense he can receive.

A servant brought a choice collection of flowers from the garden of a florist—on one of the blossoms was pinned a note, written with a delicate hand—" A stranger's kind wishes for the invalid."

Duncan smiled. " This is the way you win our hearts," said he; and after gazing for some moments on the flowers, he continued mournfully, " These are the last *southern* flowers I shall ever see, Mrs. Wilton."

Mamma was silent; I laid my face on the arm of his chair, and my tears trickled down on his wasted hand. " Be calm, Cornelia," he said. " I have done little, if I have only educated you for life. My aim has been higher; but if some of my teachings have been lost on one so young, I hope that my death may be an impressive lesson. This composure of mine has not been attained without a struggle, without prayer, without the severance of ties that have bound me with a grasp of iron. But I am calm. The sunshine which looks so brightly upon us is faint compared with those views of heaven that break at times on my imagination—these flowers, fresh and gorgeous, and cultured though they be, are almost colorless to an eye that looks forward to celestial bowers. Mrs. Wilton, may I tell Cornelia a story to teach her not to place her affections too strongly on earth, or, at least" (and he glanced upward), " to give her a resource if earth should fail?"

Mamma gently smiled her acquiescence.

" I knew a youth," he said, " whose temperament led him to extremes; one who, though untiring in energy, sank under disappointment; if he lost a bird or a flower that he had trained and loved he wept passionate tears; and if thwarted, his will rose in angry defiance. He lost his mother just at the period when her control was most valuable to him. He had never been parted from her before; she had awoke him every morning with her smile; and every evening, though half ashamed at the indulgence, he stole to her side, laid his head on her knee, and felt her gentle fingers twining his hair, or pressing his sleepy eyelids. She died; it was his first sorrow, and it cut his soul as the strong axe of the woodman severs the sapling. He threw himself on her cold stiffened form, and when that was wrested from him he tore up the soil with his young hands, and sought to bury himself with her. A mind like this required gentle training, but it also required strong motives to virtue. His father guarded him with tender yet vigorous care, and watched him as we watch the pulse of fever, and administer to its wants or check its excitement. He found that, for such a temperament, a high and ennobling example must be held up, and a fair and glorious hope. Earth, Cornelia, affords no spot where such spirits can rest; it quenches not their thirst—they must drink at an inexhaustible fountain, or they die.

"The father of the youth pointed out this fountain in the gospel of Christ, and with dexterous art directed him how and where to find it. Under these influences, which levelled his impetuous feelings to their true standard, he pursued his collegiate studies. Can I call them studies? He played with the deep things of science as a child wields its toys; mastered them while others were conning their first lessons, and bore off honors as easily as the wind carries clouds. But he was poor; and when his ambitious hopes were winging their flight to future fame, that cold conviction came and struck them to the earth. He toiled night and day for a pittance which the rich man expends on a bawble, but he toiled in vain; a feverish flame was consuming him; it would have consumed him quite, had not religious patience whispered quietness to his excited spirit and burning frame. Sickness came on, that cloud out of which speaks a voice of mercy, and he was ordered to a Southern climate; the climate of generous and tender hearts, my friends (and he clasped our hands in his). Under the soothing influences of this change he recovered; his nerves were new strung —he trod on flowers—hope lighted up his way, and a thought came over him again, that by high intellectual exertion he might rise to a level with kindred minds.

"A young pupil was intrusted to him in the fresh morning of intelligence; blessed with such a growth of mental luxury that he scarcely knew where to stop in training her powers, and making them worthy of the form which enshrined them. Nay, start not, Cornelia; I speak as a dying man to dying men. I have never before told you you were beautiful; had your mind been less lovely, your person, perhaps, would have attracted me more; but your intellect and your young affections were all to me.

"I had a dream of hope, wild and unfixed I am aware, but it beguiled me into happiness. I meant to have shut it up in my own breast, gone abroad into the world, won a place among men, brought back a name and laid it at your feet, and asked you of your father; but another came. I saw your eye kindle for him when it was only kind to me. I saw you blush at his name when my voice was scarcely heard. I knew these indications too well; my heart echoed the truth they told at every throb—for a while I knew them in bitterness of spirit.

"Think not that I am dying of love," he continued, as my sobs interrupted his narrative. "The dart of disease was long since lodged in my system. Had I been in health, my vaulting ambition for earthly distinction, and those religious influences which kept it in check, would have enabled my mind to recover its tone even in witnessing your preference for another. Now, in the prospect of the grave, I can give up this precious hand almost without a sigh—my hopes rest elsewhere."

Duncan sailed on the following day, and it seemed to me that the world was a wilderness. I lingered on the spot where I had heard his last words; I visited his apartment, touched his books with reverent grief, and when I saw passages marked by his hand, my gushing tears fell in renewed tenderness.

Many years afterward I visited the northern section of our country. I saw its glowing orchards, its lofty hills, its cultivated vales; I enjoyed all that is high and intellectual in its society; I admired its institutions, supported by combined generosity, rising in perfect harmony; I beheld commerce whitening its seas, and agriculture busy with its soil: I lingered breathless and awe-struck before the great Niagara, and gazed with calmer joy on the placid lakes that lie like quiet faces on the cultured bosom of New-York; I stood in the clouds on the summit of the White Mountains, and gathered flowers in the meadows below; but when was my heart most thrilled and softened, when did I feel that all that is gorgeous and lovely on earth is but a trumpet note that sounds for heaven? It was when, leaning on the arm of a venerable man, whose gray hair and trembling step was mocked by the living lustre of a smile. that spoke of undying mind, I visited the burial-place of ——, and read the inscription,

"SACRED TO THE MEMORY OF

CHARLES DUNCAN.

AGED 24.

Blessed are the pure in heart for they shall see God."

CHAPTER IX.

THE BOAT-SONG.—TRIALS.

"I would not enter on my list of friends,
(Though graced with polish'd manners and fine sense,
Yet wanting sensibility) the man
Who needlessly sets foot upon a worm."—*Task.*

"Play the fool on Sundays—
If he the tinkling harpsichord regards
As inoffensive, what offence in cards?
Strike up the fiddles, let us all be gay!"
Progress of Error.

DUNCAN'S departure was indeed an impressive lesson, for I knew that he must die; and this event, more than any other, served to create the vivid impression which I have always felt of the close connection between mortality and immortality. Perhaps, had I seen the pangs of dissolution, and witnessed his form laid in its narrow house, and heard the winds rush over his grave without chilling his repose, and seen the sun shed down its light upon it without unclosing those eyes which had so often sparkled in its rays, I might have dwelt on his materiality; but from the moment that he pressed my hand in parting, and gave a last melancholy smile as the carriage drove from the door, I connected him with heaven. I said, *His mind cannot die.*

Early in November we departed for the plantation. Lewis, who with his family had been residing at Springland through the summer, hastened from the Elms after our temporary separation to welcome us. His feelings were touched by the loss of our friend, and his sympathy made him doubly welcome. I soon found, however, that the force of Duncan's example, which had evidently been a check on his manners, wore away, and occasionally he uttered an oath, or a sentiment forbidden in the Christian school of love and purity. The elasticity of sixteen did not conceal from me that this was wrong; for the principles implanted by Duncan forbade my contemplating the indulgence of *trifling error* with complacency, and his departure made me revert to his lessons as a sacred gift committed to my care. I observed with sorrow, that whoever did not reach a certain standard of taste and fashion, were subjects of Lewis's ridicule; goodness seemed to him nothing for its own sake; he cared not for the warmth of the sun without its glare. Generous, and even lavish in his habits, he was penurious in that best of all charity that studies the feelings of others. Yet he was our guest, and commanded my courtesy; and there was, besides, a fascination about him that won my favor. It is impossible for a *young* girl to see a discriminating man assume the most deferential deportment to her, while ridiculing others, without some vanity; and as I trusted that his *heart* was right, I enjoyed his humorous satire, hoping not to compromise my sense of rectitude by it; and the bright intellect of Lewis, his playful manners, his devotion to me, and the sympathy of youth, would probably have taken my affections captive at once, had not the character of Duncan, and the peculiar circumstances of his departure, created for me an elevated standard of manly virtue, and rather turned the romance of early feeling towards his memory.

My parents' sincere respect had been awakened by Duncan's character. How delightful is it to think that goodness multiplies itself, and that, in the ocean of wrong, one little point of truth may move circle on circle almost indefinitely! Papa rejoiced, as all men, even the profligate, will rejoice, to see his daughter's mind trained to piety; and mamma, in her faithful attendance on Duncan's wants, perceived a purer atmosphere created around her earthly path. New ties were awakened between us, and I soon found an echo in her heart unknown to me before.

The time was rapidly approaching for Lewis's return to college: those delicate and frequent attentions, which tell the tale of the heart, were certainly not without their power in softening mine, and I lost my sadness at the thought of Duncan.

One fine afternoon my brothers and myself visited the Elms in a row-boat, and Lewis returned with us by the light of the moon, which looked down on the silvery waves of the Ashley as if refreshed with its own fair image. The foliage of the trees was pictured like sunken forests of verdure in the pellucid stream. The call of a night-bird to its mate, a boat-horn waking the echoes, and the mysterious talk of solitary nature, were the only sounds abroad, and these were drowned in the plash of our oars, and the bursts of laughter from our merry group.

"Come, Juba," said Lewis to the head oarsman, "sing us a song; the boys* will help you."

"How you been ax me for sing, Maus Lewis? Me an't got no voice for sing," answered Juba, who, like many of his brethren, required as much urging as a city belle.

After delaying until we had almost forgotten our request, Juba commenced a tune, the oarsmen striking in with a full but untaught counter at the last word of every line.

"Hi de good boat Neely?†
She row bery fast, Miss Neely!
An't no boat like a' Miss Neely,
Ho yoi'!

---

* *Boys*, a term used to negroes even of a mature age.

† Plantation boats are often named for members of a family. The chorus of one of the prettiest boat-songs I ever heard, was *Eliza*.

"Who gawing to row wid Miss Neely ?
Can't catch a' dis boat Neely—
Nobody show he face wid Neely,
Ho yoi' ?"

As Juba concluded this verse he paused; a sly expression passed over his face; he put an additional quid of tobacco in his mouth, and went on—

"Maybe Maus Lewis take de oar for Neely,
Bery handsome boat Miss Neely!
Maus Lewis nice captain for Neely,
Ho yoi'!"

The verse was welcomed with shouts of laughter, and called for again and again, until the echoes of the Ashley shouted "encore!" but all the solicitations of the young men were ineffectual with Juba, who looked the personification of composure.

It is not remarkable that my thoughts should have been occupied, in a lonely stroll on the following day, with the subject of Juba's song, nor that I should turn my steps to a footpath which had been trodden by the negroes from Mr. Barnwell's residence to ours. Not, of course, to go there, for it was two miles off, but it was a sweet romantic walk, and for half the distance branching trees knit by clustering vines formed a secluded and delicious arbor. I strayed on, animated by those thoughts and reveries that lift the form along like a bird's. At one point the scenery was so lovely that I stopped to gaze on it, and my elastic feelings were about bursting out into song, when I heard a groan. I started; it was repeated; I knew from the accompanying ejaculation that it was from a negro, and, as a planter's daughter fears none but white men, I hastened to discover the object. I was surprised, on turning from the path, to find among the bushes a servant of Mr. Barnwell's disabled.

"What is the matter, Bill?" said I to the boy, who was about sixteen years of age. He looked sullenly, and gave no reply.

"Are you hurt?" said I. "Can I do anything for you? I can go home, or even to Mr. Barnwell's, and get help. Master Lewis will come to you in a moment."

"Bill no want Maus Lewis," said the boy, bitterly, shaking his head. "If *old* maussa come, bery well, but Maus Lewis—" I could not distinguish the remainder of the sentence.

I was perplexed to know what to do, and was turning homeward, when another groan arrested my attention, and I saw Bill attempt to rise, in evident pain.

"You are foolish, boy," said I, "not to tell me what troubles you, and let me call Lewis."

Bill's eyes glared fiercely for a moment, and, turning down the collar of his jacket, I saw the blood streaming from his neck, while he uttered through his shut teeth, "Maus Lewis!"

I started as if a voice of thunder had sounded on my ear. Papa's and Mr. Barnwell's plantations, like most others at the South, were regulated with almost military precision. No punishment was ever inflicted but by an authorized person, and if he overstepped the boundaries of mercy in his justice, he was expelled from his authority. From my infancy, I had never seen a gentleman forget the deportment of a gentleman to our slaves. Deliberation was the leading trait of papa's character as a master, though his feelings were in other respects ardent; and he was never wearied in ascertaining the circumstances of any case which required it. Slaves on plantations are not shut up in prisons, but a strict superintending hand is necessary to maintain that discipline without which not even the social hearth can be preserved free from strife.

I gazed on the boy with commiseration—he might have been guilty of wrong, but Lewis's was not the hand to chastise him and I could not check the mental inquiry, if one who could yield to his passions with an inferior, would not be an imperious companion with an equal.

As I stood thus, I saw Lewis approach; he did not perceive Bill, and advanced gaily. I presume the expression of my face was unusual. As I looked from him to the boy, his eyes turned in the same direction, an angry flush kindled on his face, and for a moment his ratan was lifted as in threat. Another glance of my eye changed his expression, and he began the story of his offence.

No matter what it was—a charm was lost to me—one of the golden threads that had linked my imagination to the beautiful and good was snapped asunder, nor was it united when Lewis, with a look of sorrow, threw from his purse a pecuniary compensation to the boy.

But youth is full of hope and forgiveness; Lewis was sorry, Bill as cheerful as before, and it was not many days ere the former was replaced in my confidence; besides, he was about to leave us; and though he had never said he loved me, and my happy temperament cared not for the declaration, yet I felt that his absence would leave a chasm in our little circle.

One Sabbath evening, just before his departure, as I was playing some sacred melodies, he took up a song-book.

"Cornelia, this is a very *sacred* air," said he, turning to a popular song. "I am sure it has elevated my feelings more than half the psalm-tunes that people sing through their noses. Do sing it!"

I looked at him with surprise. "Cornelia," continued he, laughing, "don't look so solemnly. I suppose you would stop the mouth of the mocking-bird that is singing his every-day song on the catalpa-tree, because he has not a Sunday tune; or shut up the flower-cups for dressing too gaily!"

"The birds and flowers have had no *revelation*, Lewis," said I, "to tell them to reverence the Sabbath."

A look that I scarcely understood, and yet could not but disapprove, and a short whistle were his answer.

"Just sing *this* song for me, Cornelia," persisted he, "and I will not ask for another. I am sure it is solemn enough; and what if it is a love-song, are we not commanded to love one another?" and he looked at me so earnestly, that I blushed and knew not what to say, but shook my head disapprovingly.

"Then play me this overture," urged he, "and I will give up the song. What can be more sublime than this opening?" pointing to the notes.

"I cannot play anything, Lewis," said I, "but what is consecrated by the original intention of the composer, or by sacred use. What can you wish for more exquisite than these pieces of Handel and Haydn, which are not only perfect in themselves, but have the charm of holy associations; and what melody is finer than the old English psalmody? Here are the three tunes mentioned in the 'Cotter's Saturday Night,' which Mr. Duncan loved to hear on the Sabbath twilight. Shall I sing *them* for you?"

"Duncan! forever Duncan!" said Lewis, in a suppressed voice. "I wish you had never known that Puritanical Yankee;" but seeing me look offended, he continued, humbly, "You will not play what I wish you to?"

"No, Lewis," I answered, effectually brought to self-possession by his sarcasm on one so dear to me.

"But, Cornelia," said he, "this is altogether a matter of prejudice. One of the most sensible girls, and the most exquisite singer in ——, does not hesitate to sing and play popular airs on Sunday evening."

"Tell her, then, when you next meet her," said I, rising and leaving the pianoforte, "that she does not deserve the gift which God has given her; that the higher her voice rises in the scale of harmony, the lower sinks her sense of moral and religious duty. Ask her if it is indeed *too much* for one whom God has endowed with such powers, to devote them one day in seven to Him? And never dare, Mr. Barnwell, to use a name so sacred as that of Charles Duncan disrespectfully in my presence—the name of one" (and my eyes filled with tears) "who is perhaps now looking on me from his spiritual throne, anxious to know if his pure example sustains me in temptation."

It is rarely that a girl of sixteen reproves seriously. A pretty sullenness, a pettish retort, or a gay badinage are her weapons; but when the light of a just indignation does dart from a youthful eye, when with an elevated form, a kindling glance, a crimson cheek, and a voice half tremulous, half authoritative, she denounces error, sages may bend before her.

Lewis felt it was no longer safe to trifle; he knew, as most men do, when a woman is sincere, and, bidding me good-night, he retired.

CHAPTER X.

THE DEPARTURE.

"Poetry and song,
Music and books led the glad hours along;
Worlds of the vision'd minstrel, fancy, wove
Tales of old time, of chivalry, and love;
Or converse calm, or wit-shafts sprinkled round,
Like beams from gems, too light and fine to wound;
With spirits sparkling as the morning's sun,
Light as the dancing wave he smiles upon,
Like his own course—alas! too soon to know
Bright suns may set in storms, and gay hearts sink in woe."

J. R. DRAKE.

"How happy is he born and taught,
Who serveth not another's will;
Whose armor is his honest thought,
And simple truth his utmost skill!
Whose passions not his masters are."

SIR H. WOTTON.

"I HAVE come to bid you good-bye," said Lewis, the second morning after our stormy interview, as, pushing aside the clustering vines at the window with his riding-whip, he lightly tapped my shoulder. "Am I forgiven?"

It is a happy part of my temperament to forget offences, and the severest punishment ever inflicted on me for being angry at all, is to feel, after the first irritability is over, the necessity of studying the curve of a courtesy, or the precise point to which a finger must be extended in shaking hands. I could never be drilled into these calculations. I have had *preferences*, warm ones too; but ice upon ice in the manners of others has been necessary, before my innate love of human beings, as brethren, could be chilled. Old as I am, I am a novice still in this. Nor am I sorry; for by this token I feel that God has given me a heart to love his creatures.

Lewis was the last person in the world against whom I could have harbored anger; and as he inserted his handsome face among the leaves, glowing with exercise, and kindling with excited sensibility and doubt unusual to him, and which the little bravado of his manner could not conceal, he saw at once, by my smile, that he was forgiven.

"I am afraid to come in till you bid me," said he, putting his hand before his face boyishly.

His eyes were not so much hidden as to conceal my extended hand, which he seized, and, leaping through the window, in a moment was surrounded by our little ones, who loaded with caresses the absentee of two days.

No shade was left on any brow. Who has not felt the electric magic of a smile? Delicious good-humor! Bright gift from Him who giveth sunshine and flowers—blessed fireside partner—brightest soother of care—most delicate grace of youth—fair lingerer by the side of serene old age—I dedicate myself to thee! What though the wrinkle gathers on my brow, and the chestnut curls of youth are fading to the gray of gathered years, give me but the reflected lustre of thy smile, and I shall charm even yet the eyes that love me!

Lewis lingered; he had been successful in hunting, and he must stay to taste Maum Nell's cookery of the venison he brought us; Robert had some new fishing-tackle from town, and Lewis must certainly wait to test it; papa was trimming fruit-trees, and Lewis had lately seen his father's mode, and must help him; John was to get his opinion of a new saddle for his mare Jenny; and, lest all these things should be insufficient to fill his time, Lewis drew from his pocket the newly-published poem of "The Lady of the Lake," and offered to read it to mamma and me. He was a glorious reader, and his eyes helped him on with their full expression. "The longest summer's day would have seemed too much in haste," while, with a perfect imbodying of the author's sentiments in his voice and looks, he read to us this delicate inspiration; how then must our winter daylight have flown! Yet, let the truth be confessed, neither Malcolm Graeme nor Ellen Douglas prevented our discussing the venison at dinner, nor our enjoying a dance after supper, for we possessed the usual plantation luxury of a fiddler. I do not feel bound to say how many tunes Diggory played, nor how well a few visits to town had initiated his quick eye and ear into the tunes and figures of some newly-introduced cotillions. It is amusing to observe how soon a pretty air is appropriated, in Charleston, by the negroes, by their quick musical organs. You hear the mason's apprentice whistle it as he handles his trowel, the chimney-sweep sings it between his technical cry, the nurse warbles it forth to her charge, and, almost before you know it yourself, you hear it trilling from the lips of your dressing-maid.

Mamma was dragged from her seat like a martyr by one of the boys, and I, as usual, was Lewis's partner. Diggory's air of importance was exceedingly ludicrous; his whole identity seemed changed by the stroke of his fiddle. Poor mamma had never been much of a dancer; all her early associations were connected with the minuet and contra-dance; and when Diggory called out with the voice of a Stentor,

"Fore and back two, ole missis—ladies change—turn you partiner at de corner—shasha all round," she was nearly beside herself; while Diggory, sometimes stopping short and rolling up his white eyes, exclaimed, "My lor! my ole missis spile eberyting!"

Diggory, alas! in his musical science and dancing oratory was but a specimen of our city ball-room performers. Unacquainted with the science of music, though gifted with decided natural powers, they play antics with the "high heaven of sound," while sawing violins, harsh clarionets, jingling tambourines, crashing triangles, with the occasional climax of a *base* drum, make up in quantity what is deficient in quality; and then, overtopping even that climax, comes the shout of a voice with the negro dialect, calling out the figures, which, to a stranger, makes "confusion worse confounded." The South is certainly far, far behind the civilized world in music of this character, and there seems little hope of a remedy.*

But, fortunately, youth is not critical anywhere, and we were not critical at Roseland. Diggory's fiddle, like the horn of Oberon, was a potent spell to set us in motion; and as for his harmony, we knew not the folly of being too wise, nor cared for the luxurious adaptation to modulated sound, gliding

"Softly sweet in Lydian measure."

Our dancing was all spring and impulse, like the step of childhood when it chases butterflies to the piping of fresh winds.

"I shall leave the Elms to-morrow," said Lewis in a low tone to me, when we had "tired each other down." "Get your cloak and walk with me in the piazza; do, Cornelia."

I appealed to mamma, who consented, inserting another pin in my cloak, and wondering that we could leave the bright lightwood blaze on the hearth for the cold moonlight. She was sure papa and herself would not be such fools.

The night was beautiful, and the waning moon revealed the "lesser glories." They brought Duncan to my thoughts, and my lips spake from the fulness of my heart.

* In 1849, I am happy to say that this evil is thoroughly remedied.

"I am not surprised, Lewis," I said, "that the ancients should have imbodied the stars in forms of life. I could weave an image of Charles Duncan with every constellation. The diamond which helps to form Delphinus reminds me of his beautifully-proportioned character; Sagitta of his thoughts, which flew like bright arrows to every mind; the Crux of the elevated faith which lay along and illuminated his path, like that on the Galaxy; and Corona of the glowing crown which ought in life and in death to encircle his noble brow."

An impatient motion from Lewis checked me, and I looked at him for his meaning.

"I did not come to prate about the stars, Miss Wilton," said he, bitterly. "I must soon leave you, and they will be all darkness to me; but you," continued he, sarcastically, "will be comforted in their beams, for Charles Duncan is their hero."

"Unkind Lewis," said I; but, wishing to soothe him, I added, "Suppose I make you the head of my system; 'there is a glory of the *sun*' as well as of the moon and stars."

"I am not in the mood for trifling, Cornelia," interrupted he, impetuously. "I asked for a few moments' intercourse with you, to lay before you the collected love of my early years. I know we are young, but I am going from you. You will visit Charleston, and a thousand fools will linger near you, and catch your smile, and listen to your voice, while I am distant and unremembered. I wished to tell you, that from the first moment of our childish frolics to the present time, you have been my heart's choice; and to offer you that heart in its truest devotion; but no; your form is near me, it is true; but, though you know that this is your last interview with me for months, perhaps forever, you gaze on the stars and sigh for Charles Duncan."

I was puzzled for a reply; half frightened with the abruptness of the declaration, and the unreasonableness of his views, I knew not what to say, and fairly laughed outright. He became furious; called me coquettish, heartless, and many names that love should not even know how to spell.

"What do you require of me, Lewis?" said I, anxiously.

"Your whole soul," was his answer. "My day-thought and night-dream will be only of you, and I demand the same returns. I will not *accept* a love doled out of the heart's treasury like gold from the purse of the miser. True affection knows no *meum* and *tuum;* it is poured forth like a flood from two souls, and those two become one. But I am a fool to frighten you with my vehemence. I will be more gentle. I will sue you as the south wind courts the flowers. I will be as gentle as Charles Duncan, if you will only promise to keep your heart until my return, if you do not give it to me."

"You have done well for me, Lewis," said I, "to repeat that name; it is a talisman. Mr. Duncan, who studied my temperament, often warned me never to connect myself either in friendship or love with one who knew not *self-control.* Stormy passions terrify me. Besides, I do not deserve the language you have used to me. I love Charles Duncan as I love my own brothers—no farther."

"But he has biassed you," said Lewis, moodily; "you confess it;" and he drew his arm away from mine rudely.

"He never breathed your name disrespectfully," answered I, warmly; "he was too high-souled for that."

"If it is true, then, that you do *not* love Charles Duncan," said he, throwing himself on his knees before me, his eyes flashing with emotion, his teeth shut, and his breast heaving, "swear to me that you will enter into no engagement with him or others until my return. You will never break a vow. Swear it to me, in mercy, Cornelia."

"I will not make such a vow," said I, resolutely, withdrawing the hands he was clasping in his; "my heart is not to be taken by storm; and as for swearing, I have been taught by too gentle a master."

"Curse him! curse him!" muttered Lewis, with the bitter gush of overwrought passion. I started from his side with a scream of terror, ran through the piazza as if pursued by a fiend, burst open the door, and threw myself weeping into mamma's arms. The next day I heard that Lewis was gone.

CHAPTER XI.

JACQUE'S FUNERAL.

> "The earliest summon'd, and the longest spared,
> Are here deposited, with tribute paid
> Various; but unto each *some* tribute paid."
>
> WORDSWORTH'S *Excursion.*

LET me pause to bestow a parting notice on one who is still associated with the happiest and tenderest scenes of my youth. Jacque's labors, as is customary with aged slaves, had been gradually suspended. He still performed a few voluntary duties, and might be seen on sunshiny days propping a failing fence, clearing an encumbered hedge, drying nets, making baskets of rushes or oak, attending to his pigs or poultry, or, with a characteristic eye to his master's interests, tottering to the field, and shaking his head if he detected any symptom of waste. Still retaining a feeling of authority, he was angered by idleness; even the young negroes, whose greatest toil was to turn somersets, and dance to their own whistling, tried to look busy or grave when his eye was on them, long after his corporeal and mental powers had ceased their activity. But the time drew near when old Jacque must die. It was in vain that mamma gave him her personal attendance, sent him daily luxuries, and anticipated his wants with almost filial tenderness; the golden chord of his life was loosened, and we were told one morning that he had died, breathing a prayer for his master's family.

Mamma had asked him, many years before, if there was anything she could do for his comfort.

"Tank you much, my missis," he answered; "Jacque hab everyting him want in dis world, 'cept he shroud, praise God."

Mamma gave him money, and he expended it on grave-clothes. He had taken them out and aired them from year to year; now they were indeed to enfold his venerable remains; and we were a mourning family; true, we were not clad in weeds, but a tender tie had been riven, and it was riven with tears. None but those who live under our peculiar institutions can imagine the strong bond existing between faithful servants and the families with whom they are connected.

I was informed by Maum Nanny, Jacque's sister, that he had left something for me in the *sill* of his chest as his dying bequest. An old pocket-book was found there, which I opened, and discovered several bills of continental money carefully wrapped in paper.*

Plantation negroes prefer to bury their dead at night or before sunrise. Neighboring plantations are notified, and all who can obtain tickets from overseers attend. A spot of ground is allotted for their burial-place, and simple monuments of affection may usually be found in them. The ceremony of interment is commonly performed by a class leader, a pious colored man, who is the spiritual teacher of the neighborhood, and prepares his brethren by an examination into their belief, and a watch over their conduct and feelings, for communion.

The "pomp and circumstance" of the burial, for it is not less among slaves, in proportion, than in palaces, delayed the funeral

* It may scarcely be necessary to repeat that this incident and others in the Southern Matron, like those in the Northern Housekeeper, are founded in truth.

until midnight. As the visitors assembled, they crowded the hut of the deceased, and when that was full, stood around the entrance near the coffin. At short intervals some among the group commenced a hymn, in which all joined; refreshments were then decorously distributed.*

The death of Jacque was particularly affecting to me, for I had been his especial favorite. I went with the boys to see him after his decease; and though I did not feel the faintness which came over me at witnessing the remains of grandmamma, yet I had that dizzy sensation which youth often experiences at the immense difference between a bright intellectual glance and the glazed eye or moveless lid, between the warm touch of affection and the stiff, cold hand that returns no pressure.

The night of his interment was mild, and I sat at my window by the starlight, watching the approach of the negroes as they crossed the fields or came through the avenue. Torches were seen glowing in the range of whitewashed huts, and a bush-light† was flaming near Jacque's habitation, which was so brilliant that I perceived the coffin and the groups gathering round it; while occasionally strains of their hymn came floating with a softened cadence on the breeze. The procession was formed; six women dressed in white, preceded the coffin, and the pall-bearers, bearing torches, were on each side. Their path lay near the house, and nothing was to be heard but an occasional ejaculation of "Lord Jesus!" "He knows!" "God have mercy!" "His will be done!"

* This solemnity is usually styled by the negroes "a setting up." When a funeral occurs at too great a distance from the city to procure tea, coffee, &c., or the owners do not provide them, the body is interred, and the friends afterward celebrate what is called a "false burying," where religious ceremonies are performed, and refreshments provided.

† A fire of light wood kindled on a small mound of earth.

The burial-place was near the river, and a huge oak threw its arms over it as if protecting the dwelling of the dead. I could see them as they wound down the slope and stood in a circle round the grave, distance still softening their sacred song. It was one which I had heard from infancy in their devotional exercises, but never had it touched my feelings as now, when it rose over poor Jacque's last dwelling-place. The leader spoke; at first his voice was low, then rising to that declamatory shout which often carries the feelings captive, it reached me where I sat. He described the tomb of Lazarus, and said that Jesus wept, and that they might weep, for a good brother was gone, and there was no Jesus by his grave to bring him back; he dwelt on the character of Jacque, and on their duty in imitating his example; told them to be grateful for their religious blessings, for, while the heathen were in darkness, a great light had shone upon them; dwelt long on their sinfulness and God's anger, and taxed his imagination to paint the torments of hell unless they repented and accepted the Gospel.

Familiarity with his dialect prevented with me all that might have been ludicrous to a stranger. He prayed for his master and mistress, that God might reward them for all their goodness to brother Jacque. "Oh Lord Jesus," he cried, "bless my young maussas. Gie 'em good counsel, and let 'em drink of de water of life, and bless my young missis; may she know de Lord dat bought her, and may she bring her alabaster box of ointment and pour it out for the love of her maussa, Christ."

As these words reached me, I could not restrain my tears; I laid my head on the window-sill and sobbed aloud. Another hymn was sung. The words of Watts, the sweet singer of the Christian Israel, whose tender notes fall like gentle dew on the heart of monarch and slave, rose in the quiet midnight under that starry heaven.

"Why do we mourn departing friends,
Or shake at death's alarms?
'Tis but the voice that Jesus sends
To call them to his arms."

As they ceased, the waving lights passed away. I was again alone with night in its silent beauty. I threw myself on my bed, the sounds still vibrating on my memory; and, as my eyes closed in sleep, a vision of the mansion whither the spirit of Jacque had risen came before me, and I heard cherub voices welcome him to his heavenly home.

A plain marble slab may be seen at Roseland, on which is inscribed,

SACRED TO THE MEMORY OF
JACQUE,
A FAITHFUL SLAVE.
His master bears this testimony to his worth.*

* A similar monument is on a plantation a few miles from Charleston.

CHAPTER XII.

THE COUNTRY CHURCH.

> "Encincture small,
> But infinite in grasp of joy and woe!
> Hopes, fears, in never-ending ebb and flow—
> The spousal trembling—and the 'dust to dust'—
> The prayers—the contrite struggle—and the trust
> That to tho Almighty Father looks through all!"
>
> WORDSWORTH.

ONE would have thought, by the lathering and scrubbing on Sunday mornings at Roseland, that we were laborers through the week, and had but this holiday. All the little ones came forth from their ablutions with wry faces and blue noses, looking like anything rather than tranquil young Christians; and mamma had that stiff air which a determination to keep new clothes for Sunday is apt to produce. She was frequently belated, for the church was eight miles distant, and it really was an effort to get children, servants, horses and carriages ready for such a drive. We suffered a country inconvenience with regard to clothes. Mamma's new bonnet, on its arrival from the city, was liable to contract, and stand upon the top of her head like a funnel; or little Ben, our hero of six years, was squeezed into a new jacket, every button of which remonstrated; or papa's boots would give an unaccountable pinch on his corns, though the pattern sent to town was of ample dimensions. But these incidents were not always occurring. Often did mamma's bonnet fit, and Ben's little fat figure roll on in easy rotundity, and papa's face beam out a cornless smile, and the little race of Wiltons, with their plump, mottled bare arms and necks, and curling hair, and unfretted cleanliness, come *tottling* down from their baths the very pictures of happy childhood; while the babe, Patsey, looked redolent of smiles, spite of the pink satin hat and the three rows of lace which lay with its checkered shade on her soft brow, confining her one thin lock of silky brown hair, and spite of her satin-lined cloak fettering her dimpled feet as they played a tattoo against her nurse's ribs.

Mamma, when she could find time, madame, when she could find inclination, Mr. Duncan and I or the other children, usually occupied the carriage; my brothers rode their own horses, while papa preferred a little buggy, in which he could cross and reconnoitre two or three fields on his way.

Many of these drives Mr. Duncan and I had taken alone. He told me that not on one mountain only is God worshipped in spirit and in truth, but that the woods and skies are a temple, in which, as in earthly fanes, we may commune with the Deity, and I soon realized this truth. Nature seemed more still on the Sabbath than at other times in our lone and lofty forests; the birds checked their chattering joy, and poured out hymns of praise; the woods waved in calmer reverence, and there was a hush of solemnity in the floating clouds, as they canopied the throne of the Invisible.

Nor were these emotions disturbed by the view of our country church. It rose in simple architecture, discovered by its white walls amid the clustering green; and though it was sometimes thought that a sufficient care was not taken to prune the wild growth around it, particularly in the graveyard, where affection could scarcely read the record of its love, yet the wildness of the spot seemed to me to suit the mood of revery which falls on the thoughtful rambler amid forest graves. The burial-place was not large, for most plantations have their own; but it was capacious enough to tell the usual tale of infancy withered in its early bud, of manhood cut down in its prime, and of old age seeking its last repose. The birds, scarcely restrained by winter, poured out their songs over the dead; the gray moss hung floating from the falling walls; rose-bushes, unchecked and untrained, waved in the winds; and a tame deer, which no one claimed, resorted thither, loving the Sabbath communion of human beings. It was a simple scene, and where was its charm? I have heard that those who have crossed the ocean, and seen the tombs of buried intellect in England's great metropolis, and gazed on the ruins of fallen greatness in luxurious Italy, and pondered on the Eastern Pyramids towering over a handful of dust, in the midst of the lofty speculations incident in such scenes, would revert to the place of their early worship, and the thought of it would come like the gushing of a cool stream over the soul. What is this charm? Answer, simple, untaught Nature, for the voice can only rise from thee!

But, with all this sensibility to external objects, I had listened to the ritual and preaching of this church almost untouched; for our minister, and may God forgive him, was cold himself, unkindled with that sense of his high vocation which lends ardor to prayer and power to exhortation. How could his audience feel zeal in services where they saw no heart? It is praise to them that they performed their duty. How could he expect the soul to hover on the lips of his hearers when reading a prayer in a style which a school-boy would be corrected for using?

And *can* a clergyman, indeed, become cold under an office of mediation between God and man? Can *he* enter the sacred desk unprepared, stammering, and absent, who has to plead a cause high as heaven, wide as eternity? I know not but I might, as a fallible being, become chilled by repetition; but I feel that, were I a man placed under the wide responsibility of guiding souls, and *choosing* that sacred position in society, I would cultivate every power; even external attractions should not be beyond my care; I would make pure eloquence my study, that the voice God gave me might call his children to know him; I would cultivate personal purity and grace, that men might be attracted by God's image; I would plead with them as a hungry man pleads for nourishment, and pray with them as myself expecting to share their doom. I would be ingenious in plans to draw them to heaven.

Our pastor was one of whom it is said, Oh, he is not a fine preacher, but he is a good man! Perverted term—when given to one dragging a paralyzed mind. The atmosphere of religion is materially affected by these sleepy heirs of ten talents, who should be working up the whole to all possible perfection. Yet when, on opening his sermon, our pastor would sometimes find a leaf of his well-tumbled discourse missing; when he even mistook the order of services; when an ill-written word was slurred over with a cough, it was still said, "Our minister *means* well, he is only careless." Careless! a minister of the gospel careless! Then may Gabriel be careless, as he stands with veiled face to receive the orders of his king.

Alas for our poor little church. Prayer was offered up with cold monotony. Our singing was reduced to the fine squeak of an old lady, who would utterly have failed but for the aid of a few ancient negroes, whose ear was more true than hers. The number of gentlemen around the church till the commencement of the sermon was greater than the occupants of the pews within, and the subjects of conversation were of the most worldly nature. It seemed to me that old Mr. Guildstreet always kept his best joke for the last, and its effects were seen on the partially-composed features of the gentlemen as they entered, just before the giving out of the text. John once asked a searching question—" Papa, are the church prayers only made for ladies and children?"

"Oh, no, my son," said papa, and I saw a reverential shade of thought steal over his brow; "*men* feel the need of prayer."

There was probably more excuse for these worldly discussions at our country church than elsewhere. Good friends were parted for a long summer, and amid winter business met but seldom. Tying their horses under a sheltering tree, they began with the compliments of the day; then followed an inevitable comparison of the state of crops, then a discussion of public news, and he was the most sought who had seen the last newspaper; again the great agricultural interests of the country were brought forward, until every man approached nearer his neighbor's button, when the last strain of the hymn reminded them that something else was going on, and they entered with whispering answers or remarks almost on the floor of God's temple. The deportment of the ladies was generally different. They preserved a serious air on entering church and throughout the service. After the blessing was pronounced began *their* exchange. I do not speak of this in blame. It is a part of the social intercourse of Southern life, necessarily arising from our widely-separated estates; it preserves us from coldness, and I am glad of an opportunity of stating this, as strangers have frequently complained of our habit of conversing after church. Ladies from the Northern States bow almost with solemnity to a near neighbor, and retire, while Southern ones, with a cordial shake of the hand, testify their pleasure at the interview. I have sometimes said to myself in a New-England church, Can these Christians *love* one another? So different are the impressions produced on the two parties, that we here think it cold-hearted not to greet each other with expressions of cordial interest.

I cannot well extend the same excuse to the gentlemen, who encroached, at the period of which I am speaking, on the short hour of religious service; they may meet often or earlier; and even when the pressure of pecuniary or political interests calls for communication on the Sabbath, let them pause when those services commence, which, if worth anything at all, are worth ten minutes of preparatory prayer.

Such *was* our country church; but a brighter chapter remains to be unfolded; prayers soon arose, on which the young wing of devotion poised itself for heaven; hymns where the music of the heart and voice struggled in harmony; and exhortations, which, while they warned us of the consequences of neglect, taught us our glorious destination, and bade us faithfully prepare for it.

CHAPTER XIII.

THE STRANGER.

> "Let not those
> Whose homes are bright with sunshine and with love,
> Put on the insolence of happiness,
> Glorying in their proud lot; a lonely hour
> Is on its way to each, to all."
>
> MRS. HEMANS' *Siege of Valencia.*

IN January I was to leave my country home for the city; my beautiful home, which rose in solitude like a white bird amid the green forests. Papa was at infinite pains to justify the name of Roseland. It was his delight to bring strangers from the town to visit us; and, without describing the place, drive them through the pine woods; then enter the avenue where the Cherokee hedge shut out the view; then, by a sudden turn, bring Roseland before them; and here Thomson might have perceived, at midwinter, perhaps with more truth than in an English spring,

> "A shower of roses on our plains descend."

They formed a carpet beneath, bowers above; the most common hedge and fence was enlivened by them; and in a sunny winter morning there was a bright, airy freshness about their pink leaves, for frost gives additional vigor to this lovely flower, and deepens its hue. Mamma and I kept up the character of the place within doors. Vases of roses were placed in the bedrooms, and a few strewn over the pillows of strangers.

A little sentimentality lingered in my heart connected with Lewis; but it will easily be discerned that my preference for him had arisen rather from the sympathy of youthful tastes, than that deep-rooted feeling which outlasts change and absence. I learned by letters to our friends at the Elms that he too was undergoing the same curative process, and regaining his heart's freedom; and let not my romantic readers be shocked, but think whether the actual experience of life does not agree with these fluctuating impressions of early youth.

My brothers had entered college, and papa was visiting his planting interest on Edisto, when mamma and I were aroused one evening, from a game of chess, by the cry of fire. This sound, so dreadful in a populous place, is fearfully appalling in the country, where the willing though inexperienced negroes are our only assistants. We rushed to the piazza door, and strained our eyes through the darkness. Nothing was to be seen but the graceful wave of the trees, and the stars looking down in their nightly walks above; but soon the glossy branches of an orange-tree shone with a sudden glare, and the flame burst from the servants' hall, a room on the back piazza.

The people came running from their houses in every direction. Their first thought was of our children; mamma had already darted to their rooms, and they came around us wringing their hands in sudden fright and wonder at the scene. With a kind of instinct, we rescued papa's papers and valuables, aided by the servants, some of them showing a presence of mind which seems to belong more to character than station; most of them, however, being paralyzed by fright.

The back part of the building was now entirely in flames; they rushed like devouring monsters, and mamma and I retreated from the increasing heat.

A sudden thought struck me. The portraits of my grandparents had not been preserved; and it seemed to me as if dear friends were consuming.

"Oh, Hector," I cried to the driver, "you know where the large pictures are in the hall; the beams have caught at the piazza door, but you can force the windows—save them, my good fellows, for your master's sake."

"Ay, ay," shouted the men, "we fetch ole maussa and ole missis. Don't cry, Miss Neely," and they hurried through the piazza.

How many reflections crowded through my mind as they disappeared! My youthful sports; the hours I had passed with Charles Duncan; my parting with Lewis; my father's fond attachment to this residence; my brother's grief; all rose in rapid succession.

At this moment a horseman rode up the avenue at full speed, attended by a servant. He saw our group by the flames, and, leaping on the ground, offered his assistance. Mamma was engaged in soothing the children, and I, looking at the building, shook my head in hopelessness, as the ruin spread far and wide. A moving object arrested my attention, waving its arms at an upper window illuminated by the flames; and, as a portion of the roof fell with a crash, I fancied I heard a scream. Darkness settled for a moment over the building; and then a fresh light looming up revealed the figure again. It was old Nanny, Jacque's sister. It seemed to me like a nightmare, as she stood tossing her thin arms wildly in the flames, her dark form in contrast with the lurid light. A momentary faintness came over me at the thought of a fellow-creature perishing thus before my gaze. It passed away, and I felt a frantic desire for her safety. "I can go," I cried—"I know the passage; one way yet remains. For Heaven's sake, let me go. I will perish rather than see her die."

"I will save her," said the stranger, in a voice whose low, equal tones came with a singular power over my feelings. "Explain to me in a few words the situation of the apartment." I did so.

"Ned, give me the hatchet and follow," said he to his servant.

As he departed, Hector and the men arrived with the portraits. They seemed a presage of good. I kissed the inanimate faces as if they could recognize my tenderness; and it seemed to me that, with a pitying melancholy, their eyes were turned to the ruin of their early love.

But for a moment, however, could I dwell on them. Life, human life, is the fibre running through God's creation with supreme power; that poor, struggling being, tottering on the edge of natural decay, without ties of consanguinity—my father's slave—that helpless being was more to me at that moment than worlds at my feet. She was human, and she lived. The stranger had disappeared, but there she stood, her shrivelled form expanded with terror, her dim eyes dilated, and her broken voice uttering the piercing shriek of desperate agony. In my dreams I sometimes see that figure still.

My brain whirled with intense expectation. I heard another crash of falling timbers, and she was gone! I hid my face in horror, but a voice, the calm voice of the stranger, thrilling and elevated with emotion, was heard, "Safe, safe, by Heaven! Forward, Ned!" and they appeared bearing the exhausted form of the old woman, and laid her on the bank where we stood.

The eyes of the portraits seemed now turned on their rescued old attendant, and opening her own, a wild expression crossed them, as she encountered those familiar faces of manly and feminine beauty. She rose slowly from the bank, then made a low obeisance before them, and, turning to the burning building from which she had been borne, fell on her knees in prayer and wept.

And my beautiful home was a ruin! The flames leaped from point to point like fiery serpents; the wide amphitheatre of woods was tinged with the glow; the Ashley mirrored the flaming pile; and the stars seemed to shrink far back in their darkened concave. All now was as a dream to me; true, I heard the stranger's quiet tones giving directions suited to the emergency, and I felt that a form of no common elegance, and a face of sweet and serene expression was near. I heard mamma's soothing voice addressing the servants and children, and my baby-sister's joyful shout in her nurse's arms, at the brilliant toy of her burning home; but my thoughts were all garnered up in that one image, the scene of my childhood. I was aroused by the arrival of our friends from the Elms, with offers of assistance. Amid their sympathy and congratulations at our escape, the stranger rode unthanked away.

How often afterward did I gaze through crowds in the hope of being recognized by him, offering those thanks that lay like a hidden treasure, kept for him in the depths of my soul!

CHAPTER XIV.

NEGRO SUPERSTITIONS.

The New Preacher.

> "Late, late yestreen I saw the new moone,
> Wi' the auld moone in hir arme;
> And I feir, I feir, my dier master,
> That you will com to harme."
>
> SIR PATRICK SPENCE.—*Old Ballad.*

> "Oh, sweeter than the marriage-feast,
> 'Tis sweeter far to me,
> To walk together to the kirk
> With a goodly company!
>
> To walk together to the kirk,
> And all together pray,
> While each to his great Father bends,
> Old men, and babes, and loving friends,
> And youths and maidens gay!"
>
> *The Rime of the Ancient Mariner.*

MISFORTUNE is not required to develop kind neighborhood at the South. A system of attentions is going on in prosperity so tranquilly, that, when adverse circumstances befall one, no surprise is excited at a great benefit. Not a day had passed for years without some friendly act between the Elms and Roseland. The question was not asked, Have they this preserve, or that flower? would they like to read this book, or copy that pattern? But the preserve or the flower, the book or the pattern, were sent as testimonials of good-will. Remembrance was our simple watchword.

The Elms was to us now as another home. Lewis's temporary estrangement had caused no coldness, for we had so long regarded each other in our sports and quarrels as children, that we were still thought of in the same light by our respective families.

On the evening after the burning of Roseland, brother Ben and I visited the ruins. The sun had not set, and the laborers, retiring from their tasks, stopped to speak to me. We soon formed a group by the still smoking walls; while a shake of the head, or an ejaculation with upraised eye, testified their sympathy with me, and their acknowledgment of the Power who holds the elements in his hand.

I must ask indulgence of general readers for mingling so much of the peculiarities of negroes with my details. Surrounded with them from infancy, they form a part of the landscape of a Southern woman's life; take them away, and the picture would lose half its reality. They watch our cradles; they are the companions of our sports; it is they who aid our bridal decorations, and they wrap us in our shrouds.

"Miss Neely," said the driver, approaching me with an air of solemnity, "you been hear sister Nelly dream?"

"No, Hector," I answered; "what was it?"

"He berry awful for true," said Hector, and his voice fell to the key of mystery. "When sister Nelly put Maus Ben to bed de night o' de fire, Maus Ben ax 'em for sing one hymn for 'em, cause *he eye clean;** den sister Nelly begin for sing till Maus Ben and him fell asleep, *all two.*† Den sister Nelly dream dat de devil was stand on de edge o' de big hominy-pot, and stir de hominy wid he pitchfork; and while he stir de hominy, and sister Nelly right scare, he stare at she wid he red eye like fire, and he wisk he tail, and fire run roun he tail like it run roun one dry pine-tree."

* Watchful. † Both.

Hector had scarcely concluded when an old woman claimed my attention. She had been sitting on a charred log, her hoe laid by her side, her elbows resting on her knees, and her body rocking to and fro; but, when Hector paused she stood up, and, courtesying with a very dismal tone and seesaw motion, said—

"He no for notting, my young missis, dat one screech-owl been screech on de oak by Dinah house *tree* night last week. When he didn't done screech, Plato took one lightwood torch, and light 'em, and fling 'em into de tree, and den he gone. We all say something gwine happen!"

"Miss Neely," said a lad, bustling up with great importance, "if dat dog Growler" (pointing to him) "an't got sense! All night before de fire he been creep roun and roun wid he tail between he leg, and look up to maussa house, and gie such a howl, ki! how he howl! and I say to marmy, 'Someting bad gwine for happen, marmy, sure!'"

As the boy spoke, I observed the hair on the crown of his head tied closely up to a piece of stick an inch long, so that his mouth and eyes stood almost ajar.

"Why is your hair tied so tight, Bob?" said I; "it makes your eyes stare."

His mother, who was near, came up and answered for him.

"Him palate down, Miss Neely. He catch one cold at de fire, and I been tie he hair up for fetch up he palate. Make your manners to Miss Neely, Bobby, son."

The communication of the negroes was interrupted, for papa was discovered coming up the avenue. I hastened to meet him; a look of apprehension wrought on his features, as, alighting, and glancing at the ruins, he pressed forward with a struggling whisper—"Your mother?—the children?"

"Safe, papa, all safe!"

"God be thanked!" he exclaimed; and, leaning against the

fence, he shaded his eyes with his hands. I did not interrupt him. His strong and ardent mind was realizing its dependence. God was receiving the tribute which, sooner or later, awaits his power from every heart.

When he raised his head, tears were in his eyes. He took me fondly in his arms, kissed me again and again, called me his own, his blessed one, and then proceeded with me to the ruin. The sun was throwing his last bright rays over the blackened walls; to some it might have seemed in mockery of the desolation; but as they fell on papa's face, lighting up its look of tenderness and gratitude, I felt as if Nature was welcoming him still.

"Hector," said papa, extending his hand to him, after I had rapidly sketched the events of the conflagration, "Cornelia tells me you were a brave fellow. I must reward you for saving the portraits."

"Ay, ay, maussa," said Hector respectfully touching his hat, "bless God for all his mercy. Please de Lord, while nigger have hand for work, ole maussa and ole missis an't gwine for burn up."

The next morning was the Sabbath, and we prepared for church. Accidental circumstances had prevented my attending for several Sundays; and though I had heard of a change in our preaching, I had not given much thought to the subject. Service had commenced on our arrival, and I perceived no scattered individuals, as usual, outside. Even Mr. Guildstreet had retired. On entering the church, I heard some one reading the liturgy in tones of singular sensibility. He seemed pleading for some good which earth could not bestow. An attitude of devotion prevailed throughout the congregation; and, for the first time, excited by gratitude and kindled by sympathy, my heart went up fully with *public* prayer. But my devotional thoughts were suddenly startled by a voice in the pew behind me, repeating the responses; it was low, but I could not mistake it. I had heard it under circumstances too exciting to be lost to my memory. It was the voice of the daring, generous stranger. I should have recognized it amid a multitude. "Now!" thought I, with a glow all about my heart, "I shall have an opportunity to thank him!" but not for worlds could I have turned towards him.

A hymn was given out, and I was recalled to my higher duties. There was a pause of a moment, until a sweet female voice commenced the tune, trembling, but with true harmony. Like a leading bird, it fluttered a while alone; then came gathering voices, sustaining and surrounding its upward flight, until the church was filled with melody.

The concert of our lips ceased, but we felt a sacred joy in the depths of our souls. The speaker arose to read from Scripture. Was it really the same volume to which I had been so often a weary listener? There was life in every word; and, as I saw the speaker turn his eyes on me, on *me*, I felt a new and living interest. Why is that expressive organ so often denied its legitimate power in the pulpit? One glance which says, "I am addressing *you*, you are the being to whom God sends his message," makes doubly touching an illustrated truth.

Again the congregation united in petition and praise, and the preacher began his discourse with animated solemnity. His voice would have been too powerful had it not been for the variation of its cadence; and his manner might have been thought overwrought, had not a native modesty, a face of most benignant expression, and a simplicity of style fitted to the unlearned by its clearness, softened their enthusiasm. It was not the gathered inhabitants of a few plantations he seemed addressing; one would have thought, from his earnestness, that the world was his audience. He stood soul to soul with his hearers, and rested not until he felt his victory.

I had forgotten the stranger while my heart was struggling with this thought, "What shall *I* do to be saved?" Holy resolutions were bursting like unsealed fountains within me; and, with a gush of joy, I raised in that sanctuary a new altar, and wrote upon it, *Holiness to the Lord!*

But man was made for mingled sympathies; inspiring and lovely as these were, they were soon interrupted. Who has not felt the power of the ocean, leaping in its giant might, and been touched by all that is beautiful and bright in the sunshine on its waters, and fancied a living language in the clouds rising and rolling like another sea above? Yet, in this princely display of Nature, when the mind seems not to belong to earth, let a little skiff approach on that broad expanse, with one human being, and a train of associations come rushing around him, concentrating themselves in him, and the vast and beautiful are for a time forgotten. Thus were my thoughts won back to earth, when the voice of the stranger in the closing hymn sounded on my ear, and my grateful heart again began to frame words expressive of its feelings. The service was concluded, and I turned, modestly struggling with enthusiasm. There he stood, calm and graceful, *the same!* I felt a glow rush over my face, my eyes met his fully, and I was about to address him, when a glance told me that *I was not recognized!* I shrank back with a sense of mortification even painful, as, with a bow of graceful acknowledgment to the occupants of the pew, he quietly retired.

"Who *is* that?" at length said I, in a whisper to Bell Wilson, my neighbor, as he disappeared.

"I cannot say, Cornelia," was her reply. "Papa saw a stranger at the porch, and asked him to our pew. He is a handsome fellow!"

I did not join in her admiration. I was offended, I knew not why; and went pouting into the chair with papa with an air of uncommon dignity.

CHAPTER XV.

THE STRANGER.—COUNTRY CHRISTMAS.—MORTIFICATIONS.

> "The household stir
> Warned me to rise—
> A stir unusual, and accompanied
> With many a tuning of rude instruments."
>
> ROGERS' *Italy.*

> "'Tis merry, 'tis merry, in good green wood
> So blithe Lady Alice is singing,
> On the beech's pride and oak's brown side
> Lord Richard's axe is ringing."
>
> SIR WALTER SCOTT.

MY frowns were quite unnoticed by papa, who solaced himself for my silence by singing St. Martin's. This is one joy of the woods; freedom to sing or shout in the overflow of feeling, or even in the glory of vacuity. It was not for me at my age to muse long; my head was too full of the young hero.

"Papa," said I, "did you see that stranger at church?"

"Yes, my love," he answered, resuming an interrupted strain of St. Martin's.

"Did you not think him handsome?" said I, pulling an overhanging branch of bay-tree as we passed it.

"I can't say I did," replied he.

"Oh papa! But you will acknowledge that he has a very refined and noble air," said I, with earnestness.

"You must be in love with him, Cornelia," said papa, "for love is blind, they say; that is the only excuse I can make for your thinking him noble-looking and all that."

"In love, papa!" said I, blushing to the eyes, "with a person I never saw but once?" and I twisted one of the bay-leaves into twenty pieces. After a pause, I rallied my forces for another attack.

"Did you observe how peculiarly glossy and clustering his hair was?"

"I observed that he had a long queue," said papa, laughing.

A girl of sixteen cannot bear a joke. I drew up in a very dignified style for two minutes, and meant to be silent, but my thoughts came to the end of my tongue again.

"I suppose, papa," said I (rather tartly), "that you do not even think his eyes good looking?"

"My child," answered he, peeping under my bonnet, "what are you talking about? His eyes are as rheumy as an old woman's."

This was more than I could bear. I had intended to have told papa who he was, after having heard, as I expected, some volunteer admiration of his appearance; I only said, pettishly, "I wish, at least, I could learn his name."

"His name?" said papa. "It is Gribb, Silas Gribb, of the firm of Gribb and Kendall. I intend to negotiate with him as my factor, and Mr. Barnwell has asked him to dine with us to-day."

My romance was cut up by the roots. As for falling in love with Mr. Silas Gribb, it was out of the question; nevertheless, my heart beat at the thought of an interview; and by the time I reached the Elms I flew to my apartment, spouting with Juliet, "what's in a name?" adjusted "each particular hair," placed a japonica of priceless worth in my waving curls, deliberated which would suit best my excited complexion, peach-bloom or celestial blue, gave a lingering look of satisfied vanity at my glass, decided on pale yellow, and descended to the dining-room, busying myself with rolling up the edge of my pocket-handkerchief with my thumb and finger, and trotting my feet after I was seated as if they were urging a spinning-wheel.

I could not forgive papa immediately for his badinage, and did not approach near enough to hear his conversation with Mr. Barnwell, in which the name of Gribb seemed the key-note, and harshly, I confess, with all its sweet associations, it sounded.

At length a vehicle was seen rolling along the avenue, and in a few minutes Mr. Gribb was announced. I gave an uncontrollable jump of astonishment as I saw in him a stout, square man of forty, with rheumy eyes, as papa had said, and a queue that, as he moved his head, stuck out every way like the spear of Milton's angel guarding paradise. My first impulse was to pull out the green-house japonica from my hair, and preserve it in a glass of water.

As papa had evidently not seen *my* stranger, I forgave him for his unintentional jests, while at the same time an awkward consciousness prevented my returning to the subject again.

And now arrived Christmas eve. It would have stimulated a manufacturer to see the rows of stockings, of all sizes and hues, that were hung in the capacious corners at the Elms, to receive the tribute of St. Nicholas. Long did the children delay, speculating on their probable contents for the morrow; then bid us good-night, in order to awake early; then return to adjust them more conveniently; and then, weary of speculating, retire.

Who does not remember his youthful Christmas; the reiterated charge to his *maumer* to awake him *first;* the scramble to dress in the dim morning twilight; the rush through the entries to the respective sleeping-rooms, ending with the merry shout? These movements are alike in all children, but the mode of approaching the stocking varies according to the character of the individual: some dart upon it with eagerness, give a rapid survey of the contents, and swallow the *bonbons* selfishly; others examine deliberately, and lay a plan of arrangement and distribution, thus shadowing forth the principles and habits of after-years.

The family at the Elms were effectually roused even before the shouts of the children had been heard. From time immemorial, a small field-piece had been kept solely for Christmas; and it was the privilege of their negroes (for there is some little peculiarity on every plantation) to place this cannon in the piazza of the dwelling-house, and fire it at early dawn. Mighty were the shoutings that followed this martial detonation.

The people at Roseland had no cannon; but, as a substitute, they commenced a salute with the combination of every noise they could make by the agency of tin and brass, aiding their rude music. One set of people would have been sufficient to drive Morpheus in a panic from our pillows; but from both plantations united, the clamor was prodigious.

Dancing commenced in the piazza and on the lawn soon after the firing of the cannon, nor was it suspended a moment by the presence of the whites.

Mamma and I and our friends had been busy the day previous in cutting the turban-handkerchiefs, and arranging the woollen caps and other articles which were to be presented.

After breakfast the people withdrew from the piazza, and we took possession while they came up in *gangs* to receive their gifts. As we had each several hundred to supply, the Barnwells and ourselves stood on opposite sides. The women almost universally twined their handkerchiefs about their heads as soon as they received them, with an air of grace that would have surprised a stranger. The men flung up their new woollen caps, and stopped to make two or three flourishing bows, while the women dropped a courtesy with a pleased look, turning up one eye, and showing their beautiful teeth.

A few seemed to realize the sacredness of the day even then; a feeling which has greatly increased with the religious observances and facilities of late years. This prevented any violent outbreak of joy; but on the two succeeding days this restraint was removed, and there were scarcely any bounds to the exuberance of their spirits.

Warm punch or egg-nogg circulated freely, and at least a dozen large clothes-baskets of gingerbread were produced for each plantation. A beef of their master's was killed, and the stores of weeks or months from their own savings were produced for the occasion.

The festival lasts three days, and as no tasks are imposed, it is a favorite time to visit the neighboring plantations. The New-Yorkers on the New-year are not more hospitable than these light-hearted communities on this occasion.

But the glory of our country Christmas was Diggory as chief fiddler. A chair from the drawing-room was handed out for him on this occasion, where he sat like a lord in the midst of his brethren, flourishing his bow, and issuing his dancing decrees. Behind him stood a tall stout fellow beating a triangle, and another drumming with two long sticks upon a piece of wood. All the musicians kept their own feet and bodies going as fast as the dancers themselves. One movement was very peculiar. A woman, standing in the centre of a circle, commenced with a kind of shuffle, in which her body moved round and round, while her feet seemed scarcely to stir from their position. She held a handkerchief before her, which she occasionally twisted round her waist, head, or arms, but mostly stretched out in front as if to ward off assaults. After a few minutes an old black man leaped into the circle, and knelt before her with gestures of entreaty; the lady turned her back and danced off in an opposite direction. Hector started up and began dancing after her, holding out his arms as if he would embrace her, but still keeping at a respectful distance; again he ventured to solicit her hand, but the coy damsel still refused. At this crisis Jim sprang forward, and his petitions, commenced in the same manner, were more kindly listened to. Hector rushed from the scene, clinching his fist and striking his forehead in the true Kemble style, and the damsel spread her handkerchief before her face as if to hide the blushes. The favored suitor gave her a salute, and a brisker measure succeeded, in which, one by one, many others joined, until it ended in a kind of contra-dance, and this lasted five hours.

Christmas departed; gifts of affection were exchanged, and there was proffered

> "Many a courtesy,
> That sought no recompense, and met with none,
> But in the swell of heart with which it came."

The old year, gathering its flowing mantle, wrought in varied forms by hands animated with joy or trembling with sorrow, swept off to render its silent testimony to heaven of what had been. As I write this, I recall the change of age upon my soul. In their accounts with the Deity, days are now as years were then; and every sun as it rolls off in setting splendor, and every morn that wakes on the path of duty, like a new year, tells of my nearness to the mysterious future.

* * * * * * *

The morning before we left the Elms, I rode on horseback, accompanied by Jim, to bid farewell to my favorite haunts. Jim liked nothing better than this service, for he could then talk to me of the probable return of his young masters from college, and indulge in speculations about them.

After riding several miles, I struck into a by-path of a retired and romantic character, and a musing mood came over me. It was a path which Duncan had loved. I felt that of late I had forgotten his teaching; that I was becoming more a victim of feeling, more a being of impulse than formerly. Why, thought I, this fluctuation between religious and worldly hopes? I knew not then how necessary is trial to character, and how even gold is comparatively valueless until it is purified, and weighed, and stamped.

I began to ask myself if Duncan would not have been interested in the stranger. I have seen him but twice, thought I, once as the preserver of a helpless negro, again in the solemnity of prayer. Duncan *would* have liked these things, and a delicious serenity stole over my thoughts, and the heavens looked brighter, and my heart beat lightly, and my lips burst forth into song.

I was interrupted by perceiving that a fence which had formerly enclosed the land of a neighboring planter was about being removed, while laborers were working in a ditch adjoining.

"What is going on here, Jim?" said I.

"Ole Maus Osborne dead," was his answer, "and one buckra* been com for mak de bounds of de land."

As Jim said this I myself perceived the *buckra.* He was stooping to examine a landmark, his hat suspended on the standing fence, and his servant near bearing a case of tools. He was habited in a round jacket of workman's shape, adapted to display a graceful figure, and of that cut and quality which betrays

* White man.

to the most casual observer that a view has been kept to appearances even in this simple costume. He held an axe thrown over one shoulder, in the other hand a rule. It did not take many minutes to inform my heart who he was; with a sense of agitation perfectly uncontrollable, I jerked the reins in a manner to which *Jenny*, my brother's mare, was not accustomed. She turned, and sprang, and, before I could recover myself, I was thrown into the ditch face downward.

Hope not for romance, gentle reader, but imagine me scrambling in the wet slippery clay, grasping handfuls of mud. I soon felt a strong but gentle arm aiding Jim in my release, who cried,

"Don't be scare, young missis, tan't nottin hurtful. Help hoist she up dis way, maussa."

Chagrined beyond expression, I could only mumble through a mouthful of mud, "Thank you, sir," as I was placed on Jenny by the stranger. Jenny, the brute, who had been checked in her flight, looked the picture of unconcern at my predicament.

It seemed my duty to give one parting bow to the stranger. Glowing with exercise, the winds waving his rich hair, he stood erect, the image of manly beauty; but, while he bowed, a smile, which I fancied to be partly comical, played on his lips, awakening in my thoughts the apprehension of what might be my appearance. Stung again with renewed mortification, I lent Jenny the reins and cantered towards home. I could not resist stopping, however, to ask Jim how my face looked.

"He berry dirty, for true, Miss Neely," said he, with a sympathizing tone. "He tak plenty of soap and water for clean 'em."

Fortunately, I encountered no one; but, in passing the large mirror in the parlor on my return, I saw myself at full length.

My best friends would scarcely have known me. My bonnet was soiled and twisted awry, a mixture of red clay and black mud from two combined strata caked my dress, and lay in patches on my face.

I could not bear the spectacle, but ran up stairs, and girlishly burst into tears, the channels of which rather added to my ferocious aspect; and catching another glimpse of myself in the glass, my appearance seemed so grotesque, that my mood changed, and I fell into long and uncontrolled laughter.

Composing myself at length, I commenced my ablutions. At the dinner-table I discovered for the first time the loss of a valuable ring from my finger; and an undefined sense of mortification prevented my mentioning it, or referring to my accident.

CHAPTER XVI.

ADIEU TO ROSELAND.—THE STRANGER.—THE RACES.

"How now, Master Brook? Master Brook, the matter will be known to-night or never."

Merry Wives of Windsor.

"If you had known the virtue of the ring,
Or half her worthiness that gave the ring,
Or your own honor to retain the ring,
You would not then have parted with the ring."

Merchant of Venice.

"Come, wilt thou see me ride?
And when I am o' horseback, I will swear
I love thee infinitely."

Henry VIII.

I SALLIED to Roseland in the evening, to bid farewell to the people, and visit once more my favorite arbor at the foot of the garden, where it slopes to the river. The oaks shone green and crisp in the winter sun, which was rolling down rapidly to the western trees; the river glowed beneath the kindling clouds; a few birds, animated by the softened temperature, cut the clear atmosphere with happy wings, and careered and darted from shore to shore. The echo of the hammer on the new-raised walls of our dwelling-house was the only sound that broke on the stillness, except the laugh or shout of my little brothers and their attendants, who were fishing at the landing, and whose figures were clearly defined as they bent over the almost waveless stream. As my heart, in the softness of approaching separation, opened keenly to sight and sound, a chorus of a hymn was heard, and a flat, well-manned with negroes, turned the bend of the river, gently moving on the flooding tide. They were singing the beautiful words—

"When I can read my title clear
To mansions in the skies,
I'll bid farewell to ev'ry fear,
And dry my weeping eyes."

The crew joined with a full chorus; and, as they floated by, their notes of Christian hope lingering on the air, I felt the blessed adaptedness of that religion which thus bends down to dwell with the lowly. I have since listened to the full burst of orchestral harmony, seen the white arm of beauty lie like a snow-wreath on the harp, calling up its strains of melody, and heard the rich strife of rival voices from coral lips, now gushing like a fountain of sound, and now dying off like a dream of music, but I have never forgotten that hymn upon the Ashley. As it slowly receded, I mused on heaven until the happy past and the airy future stole in, and mingled with my thoughts like the earth and sky before me.

But the lengthening shadows reminded me that I was to visit some infirm negroes: as I advanced towards their houses, a little regiment of blackies, more willing and less ragged than Falstaff's, came marching towards me, with the pride of childhood, to excite my attention; the drummers were substituting their piggins for a more appropriate instrument; and a rag surmounted a waving reed for a standard. On seeing me they halted and turned, forming an escort to the huts.

What a blessed thing to childhood is the fresh air and light of heaven! No manufactories, with their overtasked inmates, to whom all but Sabbath sunshine is a stranger, arose on our plantation. What a blessed thing to *all* is it to enjoy that light, and bathe in that air, whatever may be their deprivations!

Long before the manufacturer's task in other regions is closed, our laborers were lolling on sunny banks, or trimming their gardens, or fondling their little ones, or busy in their houses, scarcely more liable to intrusion than the royal retirement of a Guelph or a Capet.

The expectation of my departure increased my sympathy with the children who were sporting about their houses; and I lingered to observe their shouts, songs, antic tricks, and ingenious devices for amusement.

The adieus of the negroes were mingled with salutary advice for my future conduct, and various commissions for city purchases; nor was the word fashion unknown in that humble group. A wide or narrow check was all-important in a turban-handkerchief or apron, and the hat of a man "*must sure be ship-shape.*" An observer may easily detect here, too, the peculiarities which distinguish higher society. The belle of a plantation is, in some sort, the same airy creature who treads the boards of a city ball-room; the respectable matron of the field has a similar range of influence with her who presides and dictates in polished circles; the sable beau has the dandy's air of conscious exquisiteness; and the intelligent lead the mass, as elsewhere.

Leaving the huts and crossing towards the new building, I perceived Chloe, mamma's waiting-maid, speaking with a gentleman on horseback, who rode away before I reached the spot. I inquired who he was.

"The gentleman, ma'am, what saved aunt Nanny, ma'am," said she. "He is very pretty spoken, ma'am; quite a genteel person, ma'am. He 'quired very particular after missis and master; quite assidious like, ma'am."

"Did he say nothing about any one else, Chloe?" asked I.

"Yes, ma'am," said Chloe; "he 'quired after the baby, Miss Patsey, ma'am; hoped she wan't no how worsted; and he made me sensible that he was sorry to be so dilantory in asking, ma'am."

"Chloe," said I, a sudden thought occurring to me, "how was I dressed the night of the fire?"

"I can't particularize no how about the frock, ma'am," said she; "but, just as you was racin' out higglety-pigglety, ma'am, missis bid me throw your old cloak and her wadded calash over you, to s'cure you from the djews, ma'am."

I saw through the matter. Mamma had been quite in the back-ground with the children, except little Patsey, who was near me in her nurse's arms; while I, concealed by my cloak, and that most frightful of all head-dresses, a calash, was mistaken by the stranger, in that agitated moment, for Mrs. Wilton.

"Miss Co'neely," said Chloe, "there's one thing I can't no how 'count for, ma'am. I can take my Bible oath that I saw your ring on the gentleman's little finger, ma'am. Old mistress used to say there wan't such a waluable as that this side of Ingland. How come so?"

"I must have dropped it in my ride," answered I, "and one of the *daddies* probably gave it to the stranger."

And thereupon I fell into a pleasant dream; and a bright castle rose in the air, and hope fluttered over it with a smile that colored up its gems and flowers with hues from heaven; and it was not the less fair that it floated in misty clouds beyond me.

Go, youthful visionary, enjoy thy flitting happiness! No cold philosophy shall trammel the power, which a kind Providence has given thee, of happy creations. I see thine eyes sparkle, and thy cheeks glow in the sweet illusion! Gaze on the airy building while thou mayst; reality will come full soon, and for light and hope thou wilt see darkness and sorrow, until that better light appears which comes by God's revelation, and which shines out from eternity.

When I returned to the Elms, extra lights were ordered in the servants' hall for a wedding, which was about to take place between two of the field-hands, who had requested the family to be present. The ceremony was to be performed by Friday, their religious *leader*. This man had been, many years before, suddenly converted while ploughing, and the evidence seemed satisfactory by the number of followers he obtained. He lived up to his profession for a considerable period, but the hour of temptation came; a theft in the smoke-house was traced to him, and he was immediately deserted by the people, who chose a leader of more consistent practice. Subsequently Friday repented, reformed, and got religion again, as he said, at the plough, at the same spot where the first call had been given. Being reinstated in his office, he was invited to unite the happy couple.

The bride and her attendants appeared with the little finery that we could gather from our country toilets.

Friday, nothing daunted by our presence, commenced a prayer, which was followed by an exhortation to the pair before him on their duties; then, turning to the groom, he said—

"Bacchus, you been guine marry dis woman for lub or for money?"

"For lub, sir," replied Bacchus, bowing, half to the propounder, and half to his bride.

"Sheba," said Friday to the lady, "you been guine for marry dis man for lub or for money?"

"For lub, sir," replied Sheba, courtesying modestly.

"Den," said Friday, "I pernounce you man and wife, and wish you many happy return! Salute de bride!" Upon which the lips of Bacchus resounded on the lips of Sheba like the

Christmas cannon. W eall shook hands with her, and a dance in the kitchen, under Diggory's direction, concluded their evening's amusement.

It was a harsh, dark morning when we left the Elms, the beginning of one of those periods peculiar to our climate, whether of great heat or cold, which rarely lasts over three days. With the sensitiveness of human nature, we are always alarmed at the first day, in despair on the second, and, by the end of the third, the medium temperature is restored. The negroes received us, as we passed Roseland, with chattering teeth and long faces, and none of them were "*so bery well.*"

And now came the realization of what is *termed* pleasure, in that city whirl from January until March, which shatters the constitution and confuses the brain. I was soon drawn into the vortex; and, when once entered, nothing but the voice of conscience or the sobering tie of matrimony brings us back. It is, however, surprising to observe how soon Southern wives fall into the habits of quiet domestic life, whatever may have been their previous tastes. Long may this be the boast of America, though foreign travellers ridicule and wonder; and while the unmarried woman tastes the exhilarating cup of fashion, let the young wife and mother seek her dearest charm at home, kindle up into smiles for *one*, and tune her sweet voice, no longer lavished on the crowd, to infant lullabies.

A new charm was added to my existence in the friendship of my cousin, Anna Allston, who had just completed her education at a Philadelphia seminary. I was struck at once by her exquisite beauty, but I soon forgot it was beauty, in the surpassing loveliness of her character. It was not the finely-turned head, and glossy hair, and melting eyes, and rosy lips, that made her Anna Allston; it was heart and mind shining through them all. One would have said, in gazing on her thoughtful brow, that she was born for the aristocracy of life, until her humility, her patience under reproof, her cheerful attendance on the wants of others, betrayed her as belonging to God's whole creation, not to a clan.

As two streams, that rise in different sources on a mountain, roll on a while in their separate course, and meet and mingle at the base, so we became one in taste, habits, and affection. Anna was soon an inmate of our family, and was unto me as a sister.

Papa's interest with regard to my appearance in society was quite unexpected to me. When dressed for a party, I was turned to the light this way and that; the satin shoe and the kid glove, and the pearl sprig in my hair were examined; and, if all was *comme il faut*, he patted me on the cheek and said, "That will do." And let me pause and record gratefully his judicious instructions on dress, on which subject he was uniformly serious.

"Do not imagine, my daughter," he said, "that you are agreeable or attractive when your person is exposed, or when you aid nature by artificial means. Two classes of persons may gaze on you, to be sure; the immoral and licentious with familiarity, the reflecting and serious with sadness. Will you consent to such scrutiny? Follow fashion no further than fashion follows propriety. Never let your mantuamaker dictate to your morals."

It is one of the quiet joys of memory, that I never disobeyed his injunctions.

Anna and I had attended no public assemblies, papa not being able to accompany us. We had his promise for the race-ball. He was something of a jockey, and had a direct interest in the races of the season. It was with no small care that he fitted out his equipage for the races, mamma having no interest in such things. It was in perfect taste; not so conspicuous as to excite attention, but, when attention was called, fixing it by an air of perfect fitness. Anna's dress and mine were his choice too. Most of the ladies appeared in dress bonnets and gay costume, scarcely appropriate to the season and the amusement. We were habited in close, dark riding-dresses, with hat and feathers. Nothing could look prettier than Anna's light figure. The fresh breeze, too, tinged her delicate cheek and brightened her placid eyes as we drove along.

Papa rode on horseback; and our only companion was a city belle, an experienced one, who dared to laugh when she wished to, and sometimes oftener and louder than was necessary. She seemed to know everybody, and staked sugarplums and gloves by the dozen with every challenger, without looking at the horses.

We were delayed on our arrival by papa, who could not immediately wait on us to the stand. Anna and I shrank back timidly, half envying Miss Lawton's nods, and smiles, and ready words to her passing acquaintance.

"Look, girls, at that splendid equipage of Captain Redding, there on the right, with the outriders in yellow! Heavens! what a fright of a hat Bell Wilson has on! How can her mother let her make such an object of herself! Ah, cousin Edward, how are you? Miss Wilton—Miss Allston—Mr. Simons. New housings for the occasion, I see. Who are you for? don't ask me to bet; I have risked all my pocket-money now on Colonel Wilton's Psyche. For mercy's sake, look at the Farwells! what has brought them out? Heaven keep Psyche from a look at those girls! she will certainly sheer, and I shall lose my gloves. Ah, Arthur Marion returned? Move away, Edward," continued she, as a young man rode up and extended his hand to Miss Lawton. There was a glittering ring on that hand. It was *mine.*

"Mr. Marion," said Miss Lawton, "we are all for the Wilton interest here. Let me introduce you to—" At this moment the pressure of the crowd forced him on. He kissed his hand and bowed, and a sunbeam fell on his jewelled finger as he disappeared in the throng.

Papa came and conducted Anna and myself to the stand; while Miss Lawton, laughing in pretended perplexity at whose arm she should select among her many beaux, lightly followed.

It was droll enough to hear the changes that were rung on Psyche's name as she was led forth; even the newspaper was resorted to to spell it. One called her Pyke, another Syke, another Switchey. A countryman who had bet upon her called out, "Hurra for Pikery!" A gentleman, quite at fault, made a practical pun by sneezing instead of pronouncing her name, while another cried, "Physic! Physic forever!"

Those who doubt the morality of a horse-race, or who have never witnessed one, will scarcely be able to understand the feelings of a young girl who has been brought up in a kind of companionship with these noble creatures, under circumstances like mine, as the bugle sounded the preparatory note; and it may excite a smile in those who regard the sport as low and vulgar; but, from the moment papa's beautiful Psyche started, at the tap of the drum, my breath seemed suspended, and my eyes followed her as if she were the only living thing in existence. Darting like a sunbeam, she pressed on; as she approached in the first heat in advance of her rival, I unconsciously stood up to urge her on her way; and when, unflagging and triumphant, she bounded to the goal, I shouted aloud, though unheard amid the cheers, and tears, I must confess it, started to my eyes.

CHAPTER XVII.

AN ALARM.—RETURN FROM THE RACES.—JOCKEY CLUB BALL.

"Grim-visaged vice with all her hydra race,
And antic folly with her rude grimace,
And all the arts that cunning gamesters know,
And all the practice of the fiends below,
Here yield a theme that *other bards* may try."

CRAFT'S *Raciad.*

"A heav'nly image in the glass appears,
To that she bends, to that her eyes she rears,
The inferior priestess at her altar's side,
Trembling, begins the sacred rites of pride."

POPE.

"Some with the ladies in the ball-room ply
Their bounding elasticity of heel,
Evolving, as they trip it whirlingly,
The merry mazes of th' entangled reel."

Anster Fair.

THE races were over; papa led us to our carriage; and Miss Lawton was counting her triumphs, on her fingers, to the beaux who, with prancing steeds, lingered by her; when, on looking in idle curiosity at the throng, I perceived Jim, near where our carriage was stationed, with my little brother Ben by his side.

Negroes love the excitement of any public spectacle; and they are indulged so much as to become almost a nuisance in pressing around military and other displays. They often carry a white child for more perfect security; and there is in a Southern crowd a curious contrast between the fair, careless faces of infants held high in their nurse's arms, and the bronzed, eager countenances of those who attend them. Now and then a guard appears; and they dodge, and scamper, and disperse, for a few moments, like a flock of sheep, with shouts, and often laughter; but only to return again with the same eagerness as before.

Jim, with a new cap set a little on one side, was, at that moment, one of the most glorified beings in existence. His eyes seemed to drink in the scene; his wide mouth developing a set of teeth as expressive as any features; and while he held Ben in one hand, he was beating time with the other against his thigh to the music of a distant fiddle. Ben was equally enraptured; forgetting his fine new clothes, in which he had been trammelled in the morning, he trotted along by Jim's side, asking and answering eager questions. They caught a glimpse of us, and were hastening to the carriage, when the horses that were attached to a vehicle behind started, plunged, reared, and pressed on the alarmed crowd. Instead of retreating, Jim attempted to cross to us. I saw the horses dash on—I saw Ben fall, and my eyes closed in a kind of despair. I was roused instantly by a shout of joy and approbation from the crowd; and in a moment perceived Ben clasping, with a strong and almost convulsive energy, the neck of Lewis—our dear Lewis Barnwell.

Leaving his horse with his servant, he sprang into the carriage; and in a moment his joyous, careless spirits, free as if nothing had occurred, were illuminating every object which they glanced upon.

"Heart-whole, Cornelia," said he, knocking on his breast playfully. "Those red-cheeked Connecticut girls cured my wounds in a month. I visited poor Duncan, too," continued he (while a tender sadness, that made him doubly handsome, shaded his happy eyes), "and I learned lessons which only the grave teaches. Do you know that I almost envied him that melting away to death, and that quiet rest where the snow-flakes are lying in coldness and in purity? I fear my spirit" (and he spoke almost prophetically) "will wrestle fearfully with the destroying angel. But how you have improved, *Miss Wilton*," he exclaimed, not minding a blush that rose and covered even my forehead with the glow—"I suppose I must read—for a fawn-like, romping country-lassie, a graceful, polished city belle! Miss Lawton, do not let her be spoiled, if you are her friend. I hate a regular belle as I do a green persimmon. Calculating all night, and dressing all day, their hearts get beaten up by the world like grist in a mortar; and when a man marries a woman, he gets a body without a soul, and sometimes a dress without a body. Miss Lawton, I am sure you are not a professed belle, or you would not blush so becomingly; and Miss Allston"—he paused—there was something too spiritually soft in those full eyes for trifling. Lewis gave her one long, earnest look, longer than propriety warranted; as if to read through those beautiful windows the volume of her soul. Her sweet tranquillity was undisturbed; no alarm or consciousness was on her brow; yet, as she quietly withdrew her glance from his, her cheek faintly glowed, like the surface of an unruffled lake when the twilight sky looks down without a cloud.

And now rolled back that varied throng; and the waters of Canonsborough reflected the gay housings of returning steeds, the richly-panelled carriages, and the floating veils of beauty; while the earnest voice of the gesticulating negro—the oath of the sailor—the prattle of childhood—the ambitious crack of the coachman's whip—and the shrill laugh of the fair, mingled and floated on the wind.

I did not ask myself then, as I now do, if all this *seeming* was true; I did not speculate on the pouting lip of disappointed beauty, which had been, perchance, slighted and forgotten; I did not perceive, in some dark and moody individual, the loser of thousands, nor detect beneath a gayer tone a fiercer pang; I did not return in imagination to the ground, and trace the votaries of debauchery and drunkenness, in their unholy pleasures, nor follow the revellers to homes where anxious wives and hungry children awaited, but without hope, their return.

* * * * * * *

The dress for the first ball! Who shall describe its infinite importance? As Flora laid mine, article by article, on the bed after dinner, and Cely, Anna's maid, with laudable rivalry, did the same, how admiringly we gazed; how we folded every plait in the silky gauze, smoothed every wrinkle in the glossy satin, and measured the little slipper, until, wearied with the completeness of preparation, we sank into *ennui* until evening.

Perhaps there is nothing more ridiculous than the pains bestowed on the arrangement of an article of dress compared with its effect.

"Bring another light, Cely," said Anna to her maid, as she stood before her toilet, in an important tone.

It was placed beside the other, near the dressing-glass, but my grave cousin was not satisfied.

"Another, Cely."

It was brought, and arranged anew, before the focus of rays was right for the true development.

"Now, Cely," said she, with a business voice, "put this *last pin* in my sash." It was done—*the last pin!* and Anna Allston stood before her mirror the image of youthful beauty; and Cely looked at her mistress with a satisfied gaze, and folded her arms, for her task was done.

We went down stairs, not, as usual, with springing steps and interlacing arms, whispering sweet confidence, but stiff and conscious, followed by Flora and Cely. As we passed two of the negroes in the dining-room, one of them said,

'Ki, Miss Neely look more prettier dan Miss Anna, for true!"

And, for an instant, as I passed the mirror, and saw the heightened glow on my cheek, contrasted with her paler hue, I thought so too; but, as I looked at her again, the vanity passed away; for how could any combination of flesh and blood compete with the refined loveliness that floated about and around her like a silver-edged cloud?

Mamma was dressed, for papa had insisted on her introducing us in public. I scarcely knew my dear, quiet, comfortable mother in the plum-colored satin dress, exalted turban, and waving feathers, with which she was arrayed. Chloe stood looking more important than ever behind her chair. We were dressed too early, and were beginning to feel the weariness consequent on such a circumstance, when Lewis Barnwell was announced. Such a companion is a golden treasure—a half-hour before a ball.

The carriages began to roll through Broad-street. Neither Chloe, Flora, nor Cely would allow Lewis to wrap us in our shawls, but laid them with peculiar caution on our shoulders. He entered the carriage, and went with us to the hall, where, with a tragic gesture of regret, for he was not a member of the Jockey Club, he left us to the care of the managers.

Shy and fluttered, we followed mamma up the broad stairs, and half shrank back as the light of the chandeliers burst upon us; and the seats looked a mile off as we trod over the chalked horses on the floor; and a thrilling joy woke up in us as the band struck a full accompaniment.

When seated in such a scene, one gradually finds one's own

relative importance. Mamma's plum-colored satin and feather no longer seemed to me the *ne plus ultra* of dress, when I observed the row of brilliant-looking ladies who lined the room; and Anna and I shrivelled up into almost nothingness, as peeping, without partners, from behind a cotillion-set, we saw the easy, graceful, practised forms of the city belles.

Papa brought up several *oldish* country gentlemen to speak to us, who joked about their dancing days being over! and the managers, after a while, succeeded in obtaining two strangers for our partners in a cotillion. Anna's nearly tore her gauze frock in his ambitious leaps; and mine, not knowing the figures, raced after me like another Theseus following his Ariadne, and breathed a puff of self-congratulation when the order "*partner round*" gave him an acknowledged right to seize me.

Anna and I glanced at each other with a smile as the gentlemen retired; but we had danced, and that was something.

"Take your partners for another cotillion," said the managers; and partners were taken, but not Anna and I. Another and another was called, and everybody seemed conversing except us. Where were Anna's and my long, long talks, when words came out quick and gay like the song of birds. Mamma was half off in a dozy slumber, and the *oldish* gentlemen had gone to the card-room.

"Oh, dear," said I to Anna, with a sigh, "if we were only at Roseland with Diggory's fiddle!"

"I never will come to another ball," said Anna, with more acrimony than she was wont to show.

At this crisis a set was forming directly in front of us; and leading a graceful girl, who listened and smiled as he spoke, came Arthur Marion. I saw him glance at our group like one who did not feel quite assured of knowing the individuals there; and then, as if decided in the negative, turn away to his partner.

A doubtful expression once crossed his face as he met my eyes in dancing; but it passed off and did not return.

I had sat so long neglected that my nerves became excited. I felt as if I was mocked; the sensation of anger which had agitated me at church returned. The music sounded harsh and grating—I would have closed my ears; I felt as if I should scream, or weep, or grasp at something violently, and yet I sat like a statue. How often have such scenes of light and joy shone on aching hearts? Mr. Marion's partner dropped her handkerchief, and as he drew off his glove to present it to her, the blaze of the chandelier fell on my ring. A reaction took place; I became, I know not why, tranquil; but the forms in the dance were dreamy, and I seemed to be in another sphere.

The supper-hour arrived. No Adonis of my imagination, but old Mr. Guildstreet, waited on me. Mamma revived from her drowsiness as we seated ourselves beneath the evergreen arbors at the table, which was spread with every luxury. The cotillion-set of Arthur Marion had preceded us; his fair partner was by my side. What a contrast was that brilliant, easy, talkative coterie to ours! I evaded Marion's eye irresistibly whenever it sought mine.

"Marion," said a youth on his right, "Miss Saunders has challenged me to remember her gloves to-morrow; lend me your ring as a talisman."

I started as if a pistol had been fired off.

"No, no," said Mr. Marion, laughing; "none but the owner of this ring shall take it from my finger."

"Miss Saunders," said the first speaker, "do you know the history of that ring?"

"No," said a sweet voice beyond; "pray tell it me."

"I protest," said Marion, "against Elliot's relating it; if it must be known, I will tell it."

"No," said the sweet voice, "Mr. Elliot shall tell the tale. He looks ripe for it."

And Mr. Elliot began, with infinite humor, to describe the adventure.

In vain Marion again protested, and grew grave in his tone, and once spoke almost in anger; Elliot went on in his irresistible drollery; and when he imitated "Hoist she up dis way, maussa," and described my mud-caked face, as I turned to make my parting bow, even Marion's gravity was conquered; and such a peal of laughter rang out from the group, as made papa and Mr. Guildstreet, who had heard none of the conversation, push aside their plates of oysters for a moment ere they returned to the onslaught.

I could have cried outright; my head throbbed; my heart beat as if it would have flown from my bosom; my ears tingled; and that laugh seemed multiplied to an infinitude. I could not divest myself of the idea that I was known and ridiculed; and I entreated papa, with an earnestness that surprised him, to hurry home.

I was obliged to climb over the seat, which was not removable; and Marion, in common courtesy, offered his hand. He perceived my extreme agitation (for I trembled excessively, and almost thought I should have fallen); regarded me with an expression of interest and sympathy; and when a servant brought my shawl, respectfully placed it on my shoulders, while my *thank you, sir*, was as indistinct as when my mouth was full of mud.

"Allow me to forestall the manager, and accompany you to your carriage," said he.

But old Mr. Guildstreet bustled over the seat, and offered his arm—Marion retired.

* * * * * * *

"Undress me, Flora," said I, pressing my hand to my throbbing head as we reached our bedroom, where our maids were waiting for us.

"Miss Neely," exclaimed Flora, "how you been trow yourself down on de chair so hasty! You been marsh you frock all up to nottin."

"And jus look how Miss Anna flung down she bracelet, like it an't wort,"* cried Cely, picking up the jewel and depositing it in its case.

* Worth anything.

CHAPTER XVIII.

MUSIC.—ESSAY AT HOUSEKEEPING.—FORTUNE-TELLER.

"Is Rosaline, whom thou didst love so dear,
So soon forsaken? Young men's love then lies,
Not truly in their hearts, but in their eyes."

Romeo and Juliet.

"First loves are not necessarily more foolish than others, but the chances are certainly against them. Proximity of time or place, a variety of accidental circumstances, more than the essential merits of the object, often produce what is called first love."

MARIA EDGEWORTH.

"I sat
And took my coffee with my guest."

GOETHE'S *Hermann and Dorothea.*

It is pleasant to watch the opening of young and pure affections. Anna's heart was hanging like a bud on its stalk; petal after petal expanded, till it lay with its rich developments beneath the eye of love; the sun warmed, the breeze fanned, the dew nourished it, and Lewis was to her the sun, the breeze, the dew.

Borne away by his intense admiration of female beauty, he was irresistibly attracted; and, day after day, Anna's loveliness and simplicity beguiled him almost unknowingly into stronger sentiments. We were soon in each other's confidence, for the habits of our childhood were renewed, and he often playfully reverted to the past. He retained the same virtues and faults as formerly. High-souled and generous, but thoughtless and passionate, he was governed by the most sudden impulses to right and wrong, yet ever repenting heartily of excesses. As I perceived Anna's affections gradually, though unknown to herself, leaning towards him, I trembled for her; but when I saw her delicate will turning by a look the course of his passions, I was comforted, and I said to him—

"Oh, Lewis, thus may it ever be! Let that small fair hand lay on the helm, and trust your bark to her."

The eyes of Lewis never wandered from Anna as she stood at her harp, or played the guitar, or gave to a few simple chords on the pianoforte a charm and tenderness peculiar to her touch; and well might he gaze, for she realized the dreams of poesy; well might he listen as a mortal would listen to the tones of a tuneful cherub. Besides the charm of grace and native harmony, Anna excelled in what may be termed *intellectual* music, giving force and beauty to melody by distinct pronunciation. When she closed her songs, no one had to ask, as is often the case, What song is that? The words had gone down to the hearts of her listeners, and told their own story. She seemed determined to do justice to the poet as well as to the musician, and every sentiment was brought out like a beautiful picture.

Persons who pronounce distinctly rarely sing ridiculous words, and this just taste is rewarded by eager and delighted listeners. Ballad-singing on this principle affords exquisite pleasure; if poetry and music are each so charming in themselves, how delicious the marriage of poetry and music!

There is as much difference in hearing the following line from the lips of two different singers, as there is in the printed arrangement:—

"To shield thee, to save thee, or perish there too."

Toshieldtheetosavetheeorperishtheretoo.

Correct pronunciation is equally important with distinct emphasis. When Moore's song, "I knew by the smoke," was in fashion, I was puzzled to know what a singer meant by

"An art that is umble, might ope for it ere."

A lady, on one occasion, after Anna's bewitching performance, displayed the most singular perversity in her pronunciation of *v* and *w;* the song, unfortunately, was the very *ne plus ultra* of *v* and *w-ism*—the exquisite Vale of Avoca. She sang—

"There is not in the *v*ide *v*orld a *w*alley so sweet,
As the *w*ale in whose bosom the bright *v*aters meet!
——Sweet *w*ale of A*w*oca, how calm could I rest
In thy *w*alley of shade with the friend I love best,
*V*ere the cares *v*ich *v*e meet in this cold *v*orld should cease,
And our hearts, like thy *v*aters, be mingled in peace."

Music and romance were partially interrupted, for mamma was obliged by pressing business to return to Roseland, and inhabit the finished apartments of the new house. She was not sorry at heart; she longed to be once more gazing on the ducks and turkeys, and superintending her dairy, with the range of other country occupations, and thus I was left in the town establishment. The division of servants caused some embarrassment. Mamma's fixed habits and liability to visitors rendered it necessary that she should retain many of them. Papa had always one or two employed; the consequence was, that, though amply supplied with new recruits from the country, there seemed to be great doubt about their quality.

That I might feel perfectly easy on one point, papa bought a professed French cook, who was advertised in the papers, and according to his frequent custom, brought home two gentlemen to dine the very day mamma went away. There had been so much regularity in our family heretofore, that I should as soon have thought of interfering with the solar system as with the routine of the kitchen, and I felt perfectly at ease when summoned to the dining-room.

As I dipped the ladle into the tureen, and saw, instead of the usual richly-concocted turtle-soup, a few pieces of meat in a thin reddish fluid, sailing about like small craft in an open bay, my mind misgave me; but, knowing little of such matters, I helped round.

"What is this?" said papa, as he elevated a spoonful, and let it drop back into his plate.

No one spoke.

"In the name of common sense, Mark," said he, in a louder tone to one of the servants, "what have we got here?"

"Cuffee call 'em French bully, sir," said Mark, bowing, and trying to keep his countenance.

"French fire!" shouted papa, dislodging a mouthful into the grate; "my tongue is in a flame! Gentlemen, for Heaven's sake, put down your spoons, and don't be martyred through politeness. Mark, tell Cuffee, with my compliments, to eat it all, or he gets no Sunday money."

The soup was taken away, and the covers removed, when, lo! there stood before papa a pig on his four feet, with a lemon between his teeth, and a string of sausages round his neck. His grin was horrible.

Before me, though at the head of many delicacies provided by papa, was an immense field of *hopping John*;* a good dish, to be sure, but no more presentable to strangers at the South than baked beans and pork in New-England. I had not self-possession to joke about the unsightly dish, nor courage to offer it. I glanced at papa.

"What is that mountain before you, my daughter?" said papa, looking comically *over* his pig.

* Bacon and rice.

"*Ossa* on Pelion," said Lewis, laughing, and pointing at the almost bare bones that surmounted the rice.

* * * * * * *

Have housekeepers never found that conversation has often taken a turn which seemed doubly to aggravate after misfortunes?

The subject of coffee was discussed at dinner in all its various bearings; our guests were Europeans, and evidently *au fait* in its mysteries. One contended for Mocha, the other for Java; one was for infusion, another for decoction. The greatest traveller had drank it in Turkey, and seen persons employed in watching it while it was parching on tin plates, who took out each separate bean as it became brown enough; he argued that it should be pounded, not ground.

The other thought, and he thumped the table to add force to his assertion, that the French must have arrived at greater perfection than the Asiatics in this delicious beverage; and his eyes sparkled as if he were under its influence, as he described its richness and flavor when taken from the hands of a pretty *limonadière* at the *Café des Mille Colonnes* at Paris.

Papa threw down his gauntlet for home-made coffee, and boasted (papa sometimes boasted a little) of his last purchase of Mocha, and the superior skill with which it was made by Kate, who usually superintended it.

The conversation was prolonged throughout the sitting; indeed, until the beverage appeared in the drawing-room to assert its own claims, with its rich brown hue, its delightful perfume, and the vapor curling in beautiful wreaths from the gilt cups. As papa dipped his spoon in his cup, a glance told him that the chemical affinities were all rightly adjusted to the palate. It was tasted—augh! There was a moment's silence; Lewis looked ready for laughter; Anna and I were distressed; papa was angry; and our guests, with their eyes fixed on the carpet, were doubtless ruminating on Turkey and France. The taste was so utterly abominable, that papa was alarmed, and summoned Kate.

"Kate," said papa, "what have you put in the coffee?"

"Me an't put nottin 'tall in 'em, sir. He mak like he always been mak."

"Did you grind or pound it?"

"He de poun', sir."

"In what?"

"In de mortar, sir."

"Go and ask the cook what was in the mortar."

Little was said during Kate's absence; we sat as solemn as members of the Inquisition. Kate entered.

"De cook say he spec' he lef *leettle* bit pepper and salt in de mortar."

Our visitors soon departed, probably minuting on their journals that Americans season their coffee with pepper and salt.

The cook was then summoned to his trial. Papa eyed him sternly, and said,

"You call yourself a French cook, do you?"

"No, sir; maussa and de 'vertise call me French cook. I follows de mason trade, but didn't want to disoblige nobody."

In the sequel, Cuffee repaired our dilapidated chimneys, while a less pretending cook performed her duties better.

The distance of the kitchen from the house at the South often repulses housekeepers, both in cold and warm weather, from visiting it frequently; indeed, a young woman often feels herself an intruder, and as if she had but half a right to pry into the affairs of the negroes in the yard. In my rare visits, I was struck by one mode of fattening poultry. Two fine-looking turkeys were always kept tied to a part of the dresser, and fed by the cook, who talked to them by name, partly as pets and partly as victims, as they picked up the crumbs at her feet. On another occasion I found her applying a live coal to the tail of a turtle; I exclaimed against her cruelty.

"He too stubborn, Miss Neely."

As she spoke he put out his head, which was her object, and a sharp knife being near, terminated his troubles by decapitation.

Some of the mistakes that occurred in mamma's absence were as ludicrous as mortifying.

One day, as a field-boy was scrubbing the entry leading to the street door, I heard his voice in pretty strong remonstrance. Supposing him to be talking with a fellow-servant, I took no notice of it until I heard him roar out at the foot of the stairs in a tremendous passion—

"Miss Neely, one buckra woman want for track up all de clean floor."

I ran down as rapidly as I could, and found the elegant Miss Lawton on the off side of his tub of water, held in abeyance by Titus's scrubbing brush.

The social and agreeable habit of calling at tea-time is almost peculiar to Charleston. One evening, having several extra guests, Titus was summoned to carry the cake-tray. Long acquaintance and Lewis's jocose manner made him feel on particularly easy terms with him; and as Lewis was helping himself, Titus called to me—

"Miss Neely, if Maus Lewis tak two piece of cake, he an't lef enough for sarve all."

Passing from Lewis he came to a gentleman who was occupied in looking at the paper to ascertain a point of intelligence; and seeing him thus engaged, Titus took up a piece of toast carefully with his thumb and finger, and laid it on a plate in the gentleman's lap.

Having served us all, he deposited the tray on a table, and stood still.

After due time, I said, "Hand the cake round, Titus."

Titus approached the table, took hold of the cake-basket with an air of importance, and deliberately turned it round, almost wrenching his arm in his attempt to do it thoroughly; and then with a satisfied air, retreated.

* * * * * * *

Before Lewis left town, a discussion about some stolen articles, that had been restored to the servants through the influence of a fortune-teller, inspired him and me with a desire to visit her; not with faith, for we were aware that when one assertion of the witch was true, a hundred misled the negroes, who spent their money on a shadow; ours was the true spirit of fun and curiosity; and one evening, when we were going in full dress to a party, unbonnetted as usual, Lewis, with his accustomed impetuosity and decision, ordered the coachman to —— street. Gay and laughing, he speculated on our fate.

Anna became reluctant to go. "The very thought frightens me," said she. "We have no right—"

"Right! Miss Allston," said Lewis. "You speak as if we expected to see a sibyl instead of an ignorant pretender. I am simply curious to meet a woman who operates so powerfully on so many minds."

Our fortune-teller was surrounded by none of those associations that usually lend a fascination to the mysteries of the craft. No cave with wild and repulsive entrance concealed her; no lofty trees whispered and sighed as she delivered her oracles; not a wrinkle was stamped on her brow; there was even something of beauty in her regular profile, and her large black eyes threw forth a lustrous ray; still, as we entered her small apartment, where one candle glanced with dim and yellow light on the individual who pretended to the awful power of knowing those secrets which belong only to the Eternal, our laugh was checked, and Anna's fair cheek was paler than its usual delicate hue. She trembled so much that I half regretted her presence.

I advanced first. The woman looked at me with her penetrating eyes; and pouring some tea into a cup, waved it gently until the grounds were scattered and settled; then, pouring off the liquid, she examined them with an air of deceptive earnestness. I believe my whole heart was in my face as I bent eagerly forward to this singular dispenser of destiny. What a war of feeling and reason!

"Here," said she, peering at the cup, "is a young man on horseback, and there—do you see something shining there?" and she pointed with a bodkin to the centre of the cup, looking full in my eyes—"see, there is a *ring*—and—"

I was silly enough to forget that a young man and a ring would probably be the very first things that a fortune-teller would speak of to a girl of my age: and putting my hands to my ears I screamed out, "No, no; not another word! I will not hear another word!" while Lewis clapped his hands and shouted, "Excellent, go on, good woman, go on!"

But I was resolute. I felt as if the walls had ears and eyes, and that too much had already been told, and sheltered my burning face behind Anna.

"Now, Miss Anna," said Lewis, as with gentle force he drew her towards the woman.

How beautiful she was at that moment in the struggle to conquer her reluctance! Perhaps the contrast of the tall commonplace figure of the fortune-teller made her spiritual loveliness more striking. She grasped her little fan almost convulsively; her eyes shunned the dark orbs that were fixed upon her; and as the lips of the fortune-teller uttered a sound, she caught Lewis's hand, and looked up to him beseechingly, while tears started to her eyes.

Lewis could trifle no longer—he retained her hand—throwing at the same time a double *douceur* to the woman, and said earnestly—

"God forbid that my boyish whims should give you a moment's pang!" And drawing her arm in his, he whispered, as we descended the steps,

"Let *me* read your fortune, sweet trembler, and its first and last oracle shall be *love, love.*"

It was the only time he had spoken thus.

Anna was silent through our drive; once she sighed so deeply that we started, and I felt a warm tear drop on my arm!

We reached the hall, and were separated a while by the dance.

The next time I saw her her cheek was glowing, her eye sparkling, her step light as a fay's on a moonbeam, and her smile all radiance and joy; while Lewis stood, not dancing with her but gazing on her, and she knew that it was so.

CHAPTER XIX.

COUNTRY GUESTS.—A MORNING WALK.—NEW TRIALS.

"Show not to the poor thy pride,
Let their home a cottage be;
Nor the country-dweller hide
In a palace fit for thee.
Better far his humble shed,
Humble sheds of neighbors by,
And the old and scanty bed,
Where he sleeps and hopes to die."

CRABBE.

"I WISH your likeness had been taken last night," said I to Anna, as, walking through King-street on the morning after the ball, I glanced at her placid face. "You will never look again as you did then, with that Shakspeare expression between tragedy and comedy. How could you fit those gloves at Madame ——'s store so quietly, with Lewis at your side? If my heart's wishes were in such a train as yours, I should have jumped over the counter."

Anna looked at me with an arch expression, which seemed to say, "If you could see down far into my heart, you would not find any trying on of gloves there."

Gentle creature! Why was she not spared for a riper friendship! How rich, how golden would have been her maturity! But Heaven calls such spirits to minister at its eternal altar, while we of coarser mould are left to struggle with the world.

When we returned from our walk, the servants told us that

a *cracker** man and woman were in the drawing-room, waiting for papa. On reaching the door, which was partly open, I perceived a tall, sallow-looking countryman, with a blue homespun dress, which hung loosely about him, standing with his hat on, his arms akimbo, speaking to a young girl almost equally sallow, also dressed in homespun, with a *cracker* or cape bonnet of the same material.

As he addressed her she rose, and they stood before one of the small convex mirrors at that time in fashion.

"Now, Susy," said he, "just see what a *smart chance* smaller it makes us."

So speaking, they walked backwards, gazing at their diminishing size; exclaiming, "If that an't despert curous! Well, anyhow, that's droll!" until they nearly fell over Anna and me as we entered. Recovering themselves, they nodded at us, the man keeping his hat on still.

I should have been embarrassed had not papa entered, and, instantly recognizing his visitor, cordially shook hands with him.

"And who is this?" said he, turning to the girl.

"Well, that's Susy, my sister," was the answer.

"Miss Susy is very welcome, as well as yourself," said papa. "Cornelia, I hope my friend Mr. Slute will stay with us, and you must do all you can to make him and his sister comfortable."

I fear there was an inhospitable look of astonishment in my face, for papa immediately addressed me, with a look to call my attention.

"I do not know that I ever informed you," said he, "of a circumstance which occurred to me last spring, in my journey.

* Wagoners, so called from the snapping of their long whips, to stimulate their team.

An accident happening to my horse, I was obliged to hire one of the little animals called 'marsh tackies' to carry me over a creek. They are usually very strong and sure; but, as my luck would have it, this little wretch began to plunge instead of swimming. In this style I reached the opposite shore, where, so far from stopping, he set off at full speed, knocked me against the projecting limb of a tree, and deposited me among the cypress-trees in the swamp. This not being enough, he cut sundry capers, and kicked off my saddle-bags: satisfied with that, he allowed me to catch and tie him to a tree, while I waded down the creek to recover my property. Mark, appearing with my own horse, mounted the *tackie*, and we rode to the nearest habitation, which, fortunately, was Mr. Slute's, who lent me a clean suit of homespun, entertained me with every kindness, without accepting any compensation, and has complied with my request, to come to us when he should visit Charleston."

While papa made this statement, which was evidently given for me to recover my self-possession, Mr. Slute still stood before the mirror, with a mountain of tobacco in his cheek, now and then retiring and advancing, and nodding at Susy. No other decorations of the room seemed to excite their interest, though they had probably never seen any furniture but coarse oak chairs, seated with hickory shavings, or deer, or alligator skins, pine tables, serving various purposes, and perhaps a wooden clock, a luxury to which most country people aspire.

It required a prodigious struggle for me to seem at ease with our new guests; but I conquered, and felt that satisfaction which results from the determination to make others happy.

The first moment we could gain together, Anna and I vented our ohs and ahs, and gave keen feminine glances at awkward possibilities.

The Slutes were to pass but a few days with us, and Susy's

perfect innocence soon won on my regard. The third day after their arrival, Lewis was to dine with us and bring a friend. He frightened as much as he amused me by his manners to our guests, catching at once their peculiar dialect, and addressing them in their own style. I saw Mr. Slute look keenly at him the first evening, but his flexibility and winning tones soon dispelled all doubt. He was entirely devoted to Susy, rattling on about country matters, while she sat staring and laughing at him in a kind of surprise that was exceedingly amusing. I trembled lest he should go too far, and trespass on the bounds which some minds, the most open to the ludicrous, often preserve so kindly.

On the day the gentlemen were to dine with us, after consulting Anna, I decided to give Susy a little advice, as she seemed so gentle and amiable.

"You must not be offended," said I, looking away from her, "if I speak to you frankly about something. It is not considered perfectly polite to pick bones at the dinner-table, in the city, particularly with both hands."

"Why, do tell!" said she.

"I expect Mr. Barnwell and another young man to dine here," continued I, "and I wish, if it does not make any difference to you, you would not pick your bones to-day at table."

"Well, I don't know," said Susy, "I an't a grain set upon pickin bones, no how, but I reckon I mout forget it."

I mused a moment, and then said, "As you sit next to me, if I see you putting a bone to your mouth I will just touch you with my foot, and that will make you remember."

"Sartain," said Susy, good-naturedly; "that's mighty reasonable."

The dinner-hour arrived, and, as ill luck would have it, Susy preferred a rib of roast pork to anything else: however, I felt quite secure, as I perceived her assiduously cutting the meat off. As the conversation became more animated, my attention was withdrawn; at my next glance, I saw her with both hands up, tugging at the bone in her mouth. I touched her foot—with a wild kind of stare she let her hands drop, leaving the long bone between her teeth!

Among the articles at the dessert were whips and jellies; Susy eyed them keenly, and Lewis handed her a whip. As the pure white bubbles stood high in the glass, she inserted her spoon into the froth, and then introduced it heaping into her mouth, expecting to taste a solid and tangible morsel. Susy started, set down the glass, shook her pocket-handkerchief, looked in her lap, pushed back her chair, felt of her frock, examined the floor, and then said, in a low tone—

"Well, if that truck an't gone mighty curious."

I hope it will be understood that not a particle of contempt is intended in this sketch; for, while aiming to present a picture of manners, it is as unphilosophical as ill-natured to view local relations with so narrow an eye. The class of persons whom I describe are everything they should be in their own sphere; they maintain in the duties of domestic life simplicity and honesty, and, should danger threaten our country, none would be more forward than they to protect and defend her. No foolish ambition carries them voluntarily into society unsuited to their unsophisticated habits; and, when circumstances throw them into such circles, they preserve their own individuality. Nor does this sketch touch that class of persons at the South who, though removed from cities, possess the cultivation of the metropolis without its cares and vanities.

If it were not too obvious that Providence has balanced the pleasures and evils of every grade of human beings, I might say that this latter class are the happiest in the world. With wealth to procure means of education, and to enjoy it when obtained, they live in a little region of their own; nor are they in solitude and ignorance; though secluded, their hospitable doors are open to friends, and the frequent traveller brings to their tranquil abodes the softened echo of the world.

The following morning Miss Slute requested me to accompany her brother and herself to make some purchases in King-street. I could give no excuse for declining, but consented with as good a grace as possible; and beseeching Anna to accompany us, I ordered the carriage, though for so short a distance. What was our consternation to see Susy come down stairs with a stiff new white lace veil, reaching nearly to her feet, tied over her cracker bonnet. Anna and I entered the carriage in silence, shrinking back as our friends, in their eagerness to see everything, leaned from the windows. In King-street we alighted, Susy and her brother taking hold of hands and walking in front of us. On entering a shop they perceived that they had lost the memorandum for their purchases, and disagreed about the articles and the quantity. Anna and I gave ourselves up in despair for a while to their erratic movements, and then proposed returning to the carriage; but alas! in darting from shop to shop the coachman had lost us. Fashion and business began, as usual, to throng King-street; and many a glance was cast at our guests, as, hand in hand, they preceded us, frequently speaking our names aloud. At length Lewis discerned us; he smoothed down his face with a comical look and joined us.

"Can you think of no way," whispered I, "to get us out of King-street?"

Lewis laughed at my perplexed look, and answering "Oh yes," turned to Mr. Slute, reminded him that he had promised to show them St. Michael's steeple, and asked him if he would like to go now.

"Well, I don't know," said Mr. Slute, "I don't care if I do."

We left King-street, Susy and her brother taking hold of hands, and Lewis following with Anna and me. Not far from St. Michael's corner sat a black woman, with a stock of ginger-cake, molasses candy, &c. to sell, over which she waved a fly-brush of palmetto. In front of us was a group of young men, among whom I started at distinguishing Arthur Marion. At this moment we were hailed from behind by Mr. Slute and Susy, who had bargained for a large square of the gingerbread, and were asking us to partake of it. They had joined us, and were pressing it on us, when Marion and another gentleman, advancing from the group, passed us. It was in vain for me to see as though I saw not; I felt the blood rush to my face, and saw a glow of recognition kindle up on his, although there was no other movement of acquaintanceship.

Mr. Slute resumed his walk, munching his cake, and, as I glanced back, I saw that Marion and Mr. Elliot had turned and were following us. As we stopped under the portico of St. Michael's, while Lewis went opposite to the guard-house to procure the key of the church door, they passed us slowly, and another full glance told me that I was recognized, but whether as the lady of the ditch or the lady of the ball I knew not. Marion and Elliot suppressed a smile as they saw the gingerbread-eaters, while Anna and I stood like two victims, blushing to the eyes. They passed on; but, as the guard-man opened the door for us to enter the church, I ventured one more look. Marion and his companion were turning towards the building, and, as we commenced ascending the stairs, I heard his mellow voice and Elliot's gay laugh below.

CHAPTER XX.

A VISIT TO ST. MICHAEL'S TOWER.

"St. Michael's spire! St. Michael's spire!
How fair thou risest to the sight;
Now, glittering in the noon sun's fire,
Now, softened by the 'pale moonlight.'"

Lewis, accustomed to the way, with Anna under his protection, rapidly preceded us. We followed more slowly, and were soon in utter darkness on the spiral stairway. I was not aware that there was only room enough for one person to go at a time, neither had I given a thought to the steepness of the ascent, nor to the excessive gloom and solitude, exciting, in almost every inexperienced visitor, a peculiar sensation. My agitation was not unmixed with terror, and yet I was disposed to laugh, as a relief to the apprehension that lay like a weight upon my senses, as we wound round and round, feeling our way at every step.

Lewis and Anna were soon far beyond our hearing and observation, and the scene suited well his eccentric nature. He heeded not the darkness, and Anna soon forgot it too. Love held a torch brighter than sunbeams; and, as he supported her slight figure, he almost fancied the blush that mantled on her cheek, and he fancied not, but he felt, the trembling of her hand as he urged his hopes.

"Speak to me, Anna," whispered he; "let me hear your voice

now, alone and solitary, before the world comes between to break the spell! Speak, dearest! Let me hear you in this darkness say, that in the darker walks of life I shall be your companion. Say that I may aid you on your way, and that you will soften mine with your tenderness. Speak but one word, now, now; that word will be a light to my soul."

Anna did murmur a word, and the light broke from the belfry windows, and revealed a look that spoke still more.

"Blessed augury!" said Lewis; "so shall your love shine out on my existence."

No one can imagine, without actual experience, how long appears the really brief period of darkness in ascending the first flight of that tower. Mr. Slute and Susy were just in advance of me, and my own expressions of excitement were soon suspended by her more violent alarm. At length she burst forth in hysterical shrieks, and came to a complete stand.

"I an't a going a grain farther," sobbed she; "you mout as well a' put me in my coffin at once't as to bring me to this pisonous hole."

"'Tan't no use to talk about it now, any how," said Mr. Slute. "It won't help you none to stay there squealing like a stuck shote. If you don't choose to let me tote ye up, you must let it alone." So saying, he ascended the stairs, still calling on Susy to follow.

But Susy, frightened beyond all control, spread out her hands helplessly in the darkness to feel for me, crying out—

"Poor, poor Susy Slute's buried alive! Poor me! What shall I do?"

I spoke to her as soothingly as possible, but without effect; she would neither advance nor return, but seemed in an ecstacy of terror.

At length I heard a voice close behind me. "Can I be of

any assistance here?" it said. "If my name is any pledge of my good-will, it is Arthur Marion."

"Thank you, sir," said I, exceedingly embarrassed at the preposterous predicament in which I was again placed, and bewildered with the darkness.

"What is the lady's name?" asked Marion.

"Miss Susan Slute," I replied.

"Miss Susan," said he, encouragingly, "you have only about fifteen steps to go to reach the platform, where it will be light; let me count them for you as you ascend. One—that is right," continued he, as he heard our dresses rustle; "two—three—you are going on bravely now"—and he spoke as a tender parent would address a timid child, until the glimmering light above stimulated her to more exertion, and we reached the bell-room, where, throwing herself on a seat, she recovered from her alarm. But nothing would induce her to proceed; and, stating to the gentlemen that I preferred remaining with her until her brother's return, they left us and ascended another flight.

The delicacy of Marion's manner was not lost on me. What refinement, what goodness was in every look and tone! Again my heart whispered, "Charles Duncan would have loved him!"

It was not long before Mr. Slute returned. Susy's entreaties to go home were too earnest to withstand; and, as he stated that the next flight of stairs was lighted throughout, I parted from them in pursuit of Lewis and Anna, whom he had left in the second balcony.

Though no longer in darkness, the excitement was intense from my loneliness, and it appeared to me that I should never reach the first balcony. When I had attained the spot I resolved to wait for Lewis and Anna; and, as I turned to gaze on my own fair city, a thrill of astonishment and delight ran through me at its beautiful proportions.

On either side, the Ashley and Cooper, gently swelling tc the sea, or twining off in silvery streams to the woodlands, shone in the sunbeams; the blue sea rocked the masts at the wharves, or extended its broad surface for vessels that stood with their spread sails, like eagles plumed for flight; the flag of Fort Moultrie waved in the distance; and nearer, Castle Pinckney sat like a swan upon the waters. I looked below; a map seemed spread before me. I felt like a being of another sphere; like something apart from the human machines who were moving noiselessly and voicelessly to me, reduced by distance to a speck amid their own creations.

I sat quietly expecting Lewis and Anna, until their delay startled me; and then I smiled as I thought of the absorbing character of their intercourse, and perhaps I smiled the more as a glance at the Ashley reminded me of former scenes upon its banks, when I was Lewis's heroine.

I now resolved to ascend another flight of stairs, and meet them on the highest balcony. I had taken but a few steps before my heart began to beat violently. I could almost hear its throbbing, the stillness was so profound. I was confident, however, that they awaited me there, and quickened my steps, though dizzy with the increasing height, and agitated by undefinable alarms. I reached the second balcony, certain that Lewis and Anna would spring to meet me. They were not there. I called their names; I ran with the steps of a frightened fawn around the pilasters, with a faint hope at my heart that they might have hidden themselves in a frolicsome humor They appeared not; again, in agony of spirit, I shouted, " Lewis! Anna! for mercy's sake come to me!" My voice melted in that vast height, a hundred and twenty feet from the earth, like a snow-flake on a stream.

How the feelings color objects! There shone the heavens in

their broad sweep of majesty, calmly, beautifully blue, looking down upon the earth; there lay the earth, with its green bosom open to the sky; the rivers still wound to the sea, like loving children to a mother's arms; the sea expanded its broad surface, while near and remote sails stiffened in the breeze; the city slept in quiet distance below, and man moved there still, the lord of the creation. I heeded them not; they even seemed to mock my growing terrors; while the winds, as they swept round the tower, brought shrill and terrific voices to my ear, and, as they died away fitfully, my pulses sank, and my limbs trembled.

My last resource was to ascend the spire. There again was deep darkness. I shrank back; and yet the hope that, ignorant of my separation from my companions, Lewis and Anna were secreted there, urged me on. I took a few upward steps, and my brain reeled in the felt gloom. Again I cried, "Lewis! Anna!" but not even echo returned a sound. At length the thought flashed through my mind that they had gone down without perceiving me in the first gallery, which, from its extent and octagonal form, they could easily have done, and, presuming that I had descended with Mr. Slute, had probably left the tower. At this idea my brain snapped with the intensity of my alarm; strange lights seemed to dance in the obscurity. Once more I screamed "Lewis! Anna!" No sound replied to my cries; my voice grew hoarse with my efforts; seconds seemed like years. I attempted again to move forward; I groped about with a wild impulse, beating the air in the horrible uncertainty, and fell.

When Marion and Elliot descended the stairs from the pigeon-holes, they found me insensible at the entrance of the balcony. On recovering I perceived Marion supporting me, while Elliot stood fanning me with his hat. I must have been stunned with the fall, for I could not immediately comprehend my situation, or feel power to move. I afterward recalled their looks of terror and perplexity, but it was many minutes before my consciousness was fully restored. When it was, I started from my position—they had taken off my hat, while my hair was loosed and fell around me. In a moment I perceived the embarrassment of my situation, and the blood seemed to rush in tingling torrents through my frame. From extreme faintness I felt my cheeks suddenly flushed with a glow of shame, and, in a reaction from the silence of insensibility, I began to pour forth a torrent of excuses, and thanks, and explanations: nor was this all; nature claimed the tribute she so often calls from the young, and I burst into tears.

Elliot was about to speak to me.

"Hush!" whispered Marion; "tears will relieve her."

I wiped my eyes and advanced to the stairs.

"Allow me," said he, without offering his arm, "to precede you one step, to guard against dizziness as you descend."

I followed passively; he said little, but occasionally turned his head towards me with a look of the most respectful inquiry, while Elliot, his usual *dégagée* manner quite subdued, followed us.

At the last flight, however, when we were in total darkness, they both questioned me frequently, that they might know if my strength failed me.

It was a singular circumstance, that in the previous descent, as Marion kept his hand on the balustrades and pillars for support, my diamond ring, glittering on his finger, seemed to me a guide and comfort. It was now no longer visible. I felt again sudden oppression; my voice faltered, my limbs seemed to give way beneath me, and I should have fallen, had not light and air broke in from the portico and restored me.

Marion requested to see me home safely, and I went on, debating with myself how to thank him. Nothing but monosyllables could I muster, though my heart was so full. That night, on my pillow, how many delightful things I thought of which I might have said.

We reached the door, and I stammered out the very thing I did not mean to say—"I must thank you for the past and the present together, Mr. Marion. You seem to be destined for my knight-errant."

He looked surprised, but smiled.

"I am not aware," said he, "of any past claim on my chivalry; but, if you will allow me one for the future, I shall feel honored."

He bowed gracefully, and I saw by his manner that I was still unknown except as the girl of the ball-room.

The door opened. Anna, with a look of surprise and joy, flew to me and kissed my cheek, while Mr. Marion walked on.

CHAPTER XXI.

THE WEDDING.

"Canst thou love me, Kate? A good leg will fall; a straight back will stoop; a black beard will turn white; a curled pate will grow bald; a fair face will wither; a full eye wax hollow; but a good heart, Kate, is the sun and the moon, or rather the sun and not the moon; for it shines bright, and never changes, but keeps its course truly. If thou wouldst have such a one, have me."—*Henry V.*

"I saw her from the altar led,
With silvery veil, but slightly swept aside,
The fresh, young rose-bud deepening on her cheek,
And on her brow the sweet and solemn thoughts
Of one who gives a priceless gift away."
MRS. SIGOURNEY.

A GAY group of bridesmaids were assembled in that sunny month, the month of April, around the toilet of Anna Allston, fitting the slipper's neat proportion, or twining orange-blossoms in her soft hair, or adjusting the floating veil; and, as the jests of their light hearts went round, a dimple would play in the delicate fulness of her cheek, or a sigh, sweet and gentle as a summer breath floating over roses, escape from her veiled breast, or a glance of such mingled pleasure and reproach as rather excited than checked her merry attendants, stole from her deep blue eyes.

Around her were kind manifestations of friendship—the pure satin cushion, where pins, arranged in finished letters, told "*joy to the bride;*" the beautiful vase, through whose transparency light came like thoughts through an ingenuous countenance; perfumes, not needed by her whose breath was fresh as infancy;

books, sweet mementoes of intellectual sympathy; jewels, glittering on her small fingers, save that on which was to be placed the golden circlet, touching emblem of the love which owns no termination; and flowers, those fair and frail gifts which were to tell to-morrow the moral of beauty and decay.

When all was done that nature, whose dowry was so rich, and art, which even dares to tint the bosom of a shell, could do; when no jealous eye might detect an imperfection in the snowy robe, or floating veil, or braided hair, Lewis was summoned. He cast one proud, triumphant glance upon Anna's moonlight loveliness, but withdrew it, for the crimson flood rushed to her cheek and brow, and thrilled her taper fingers, and made the white rose which she held still paler.

Amid that brilliant group were two persons watching the motions of the lovely girl with no common interest. Cely her maid, and her old nurse Binah. A china toilette cup and saucer, of classical proportions, with Anna's name in gilt letters on the outside, were brought in as a gift from one of Lewis's connections. As old Binah took the cup from the servant, she approached her young mistress with a solemn courtesy and an upward look, and said,

"May God Almighty grant my young missis for drink out such a cup like dis in heaven."*

Cely's thoughts were less spiritual. She evidently deprecated the well-meant assistance rendered to the bride, and whenever we interfered with any part of her dress, quietly but instantly re-arranged it.

The bridemaids presented the white favors to the groomsmen, and we were summoned to the apartments below. They were decorated with branches of magnolia, wild-orange, holly, and other evergreens of our woods, while the graceful and

* This touching prayer was heard by the writer.

odorous yellow jessamine was entwined with their firmer foliage, and many a spring blossom peeped between the glossy green.

The atmosphere seemed to breathe of Anna's presence; the bright-wreathed flowers kindled up anew, and the light softened as she moved onward. There was no eye but for her.

The wide semicircle of groomsmen and bridemaids was formed; there was a hush—the solemn words were uttered, and soon the parents of Lewis embraced their daughter; and as she felt their twining arms and loving kiss, she whispered, "I am no longer an orphan."

As first bridemaid, I was called upon to cut the cake, which contained a ring. Many an eye was turned towards me, for she who finds the ring in her portion will, it is said, be the next bride. The girls eagerly took their share, and shade after shade came over their smiling faces. I broke my slice, and the ring fell on the floor. There was a gallant scramble among the beaux who threw themselves at my feet to find it. Did I *fancy* that he who was successful lingered a moment in his kneeling attitude while presenting it to me? Was it in mere gallantry that he bowed his lips to the ring? Was there not something of reality in his gay address? Perhaps it was imagination, but the youth was Arthur Marion, and two weeks' acquaintance does wonders with young people.

"Will you exchange rings with me, Mr. Marion?" said I, as we were promenading the piazza, in the pauses of the dance, and jesting of my success. "I have taken a great fancy to that diamond ring on your little finger."

He blushed like a girl.

"You will think me romantic, Miss Wilton," said he, "but I have made a resolution never to part with this ring, except to the owner. I had not seen *you*, remember, when I made this vow."

"And who is the owner?" asked I. "I have a right, in my office to-night, to take some liberties."

He paused a while, and then said gravely,

"I am afraid you will laugh at me as Elliot does, but your authority is not to be resisted."

After a little hesitation, he related the adventures of the ditch. It was amusing to see the difference between his and Elliot's representations. Marion even threw a shade of romance over his heroine, but I could not preserve my gravity. Marion looked graver still.

"You are amused, Miss Wilton," said he, "at this detail, and laugh almost as wickedly as Elliot; but, I assure you, his ridicule has only stimulated me to shelter that lady from the shafts of his wit."

"I know," said I, "that it would be too romantic in these days to expect our heroines to come out as pure and unsullied from a ditch as Una and her milk-white lamb; but you must confess that your heroine was not in a very interesting predicament."

"Every woman is interesting to me who requires my protection," rejoined Marion.

"Should you know your heroine again?" said I.

"I am confident that I should know her person anywhere," he replied. "Her face was concealed by her bent hat and soiled veil; but her figure which I gazed on until she was out of sight, I think I should recognize in a crowd; and on horseback I could not be mistaken in her. I have seldom seen so symmetrical a form, at least not until *very* recently," and he bowed and smiled.

"How was it that the negroes did not know the lady or her attendants?" asked I.

"They were new hands," he answered, "and could tell me nothing of them."

"What was the height of your lady of the ditch?" said I, laughing.

"She was not as tall as you are," replied he, "but rather nearer Mrs. Barnwell's size."

I started at the name. It sounded almost gratingly. I felt half jealous that my friend should no longer be Anna Allston, as she stood bowing to the various salutations, graceful as a fringe-tree, whose white tassels wave in the clustering forests.

"You are determined, then, not to exchange rings with me?" said I, twisting my gold one on my finger.

He looked embarrassed.

"You cannot, I perceive," said he, "enter into my feelings on this subject. I confess that they are foolishly romantic; but my imagination has been so long enlisted, that it is impossible for me immediately to divest myself of its influence. If any one *could* wean me from the unknown lady of my vow—" a few more words were said in a low tone, but they were words of mere gallantry, and convinced me that his heart was with his vow, and not with me.

I escaped to the drawing-room with some light jest, such as often comes up, like the vapor of Niagara, from a woman's heart, when a wild and struggling current is rushing below. The ceremonious courtesy, the gay farewell, the presented cake, soon occupied me, until each had received their proper gift, and the last negro, with his written pass, was treading the quiet streets of the guarded city.

Dreams are odd things. I was dreaming that night that the Cham of Tartary had ordered his kingdom to be searched for a lady whose great toe should be small enough to fit a gold thimble. His chief governor, with his staff of office, was superintending the thrusting of mine into its shining prison, when the merciless city negroes, with their fiddles and tamborines, came to salute the married pair with their customary daybreak music. I roused Cely to throw them their fee, and they departed; but I had lost the Cham of Tartary's gold thimble.

I will make no lamentations over papa's old wine, nor reflections on the conduct of young men who, forgetting the sanctity of private life, think that a wedding, instead of presenting a scene of solemn, and tender, and elevated thought, must be a signal for intemperate revel; nor hint at the frowning glances of those who were overlooked in the invitations, nor at the petty scandal of those who were there; it is sufficient that the morning sun rose brightly on Anna, the heroine of the hour, and that her heart folded its fluttering wing, and reposed in joy in her husband's love.

The bridal party left town that day for the Elms. Nature was too in *her* bridal robe, and glittered in April smiles and tears, like her who was welcomed in tender gaiety to her new home.

At twilight music was heard approaching, and a large party of negroes came with their instruments, singing a welcome. They walked three times round the house, playing, "Joy to the bride," "Come, haste to the wedding," and other tunes. As they passed the door, some of them peeped at us, but they were too bashful to enter; at length one old woman gained courage to come in, and, dropping a courtesy, handed Anna a calabash of eggs. Anna shook hands with her, and, at Lewis's suggestion, who told her that the people would not retire until they saw her, she went to the piazza.

They were delighted with her appearance; eggs were handed her in all directions, and they renewed their songs and dances.

Among the number, though a little apart, stood a young woman with an infant. She appeared not to notice the departure of the others, but lingered by the steps, dancing her infant in her arms, uttering unintelligible sounds; while as she pointed now to Anna, now to her infant, her face wore a pleasant smile,

"Poor Bella!" said Lewis, "she is deaf and dumb."

As Bella turned to go, some wild boys among the people who had been excited by the music and dancing, came to her and threatened, half playfully, to take her child from her arms.

A howl, wild, long, and fearful, burst from the dumb creature as she clasped the baby more closely to her bosom.

It was not the last time that I was to hear that cry.

CHAPTER XXII.

MY POOR COUSIN ANNA.

"My flower, my blighted flower; thou that wert made
For the kind fostering of sweet summer airs,
How hath the storm been with thee! Lay thy head
On this true breast again, my gentle one!
And tell me all."

MRS. HEMANS' *English Martyrs.*

A WEEK had flown as weeks will flee with the young and happy, when Lewis was summoned away on business, to return, however, the following day. I need not describe the parting caress, the laughing delay, the half-bashful recall, hand lingering in hand, the jest mocking the sigh, and the smile struggling with the tear. Who has not loved? Who has not parted?

At length, with spirits elastic as boyhood, he sprang over the balustrade, gathered a sweet rose, and, shaking the dew from its petals, passed it between the railings to Anna, and said,

"Put it in your hair, dearest; there is another on the stem which will bloom to-morrow; come here in the morning, and gather it for my return."

Anna smiled as she placed the rose in her hair, and her blush was as richly tinged as the flower; yet even for this short parting her heart was full, and the smile of her lips was subdued by the sudden sadness of her eyes.

Lewis mounted his horse, and his gaze said, as plainly as words could do, that she was all the world to him—and this is no faint test of a woman's power; for if there is a moment when a youth forgets everything in creation but himself, it is when, standing before an admiring group, he pats his noble steed, leaps to the saddle, sits erect as Olympian Jove, and then springs away before the free air of heaven.

* * * * * * *

The sight of his parting glance lingered long upon my thoughts; and often, in after-years, has it risen to me, its brightness sadly contrasted by his fate, like sunshine on a ruin. I have since dwelt until thought became agony on the probable circumstances of that day. I have fancied the full stream of joy that gushed up in his heart, as he rode cheerfully along the avenue of his paternal home, where the oaks, throwing their vast arms from side to side, their mossy drapery waving in the air, rustled a kind farewell; while the Ashley, with its clear waters, looked from its wooded banks, and bade him God speed; and the far sky that blesses all pierced the thick boughs above, and smiled upon his way. I have fancied the older negroes (for he was their pride) greeting him with respectful salutations, and the younger ones (to whom he was both a terror and a playmate) turning up their white eyes with a smile of familiar recognition as they sought the sunniest bank. I have fancied him communing with his own heart (for his feelings were as strong in good as in evil), pondering schemes of benevolence, in which Anna was to be his dear assistant, and looking forward to a sphere of usefulness and happiness.

I have since dwelt on the terrific change in this dream of joy. I have imagined, until the figures stood before me with a reality that made me shudder, his encounter with an enemy. I knew too well the whirlwind of his passions. I had seen him, when a boy, dash himself on the ground and clinch the grass, when his will was thwarted—I had seen his hand raised in sudden impulse against an inferior—I had heard him in manhood curse one of the purest and best beings that ever walked in the likeness of God, and I felt that such passions, if not restrained by the gentle teachings and strong inward power of Christianity, might work his ruin. I have mused on these things painfully, fearfully. I have fancied a death-struggle on that day in the forest without an observer, save the lofty trees in their cold grandeur; a cry unanswered but by the moaning winds.

Poor impetuous Lewis! a moral rises from your nameless grave—the Ashley murmurs it in its gliding current, once perchance tinged with your blood; and the forest-breeze whispers in the thoughtful ear a warning to *ungoverned passions.*

* * * * * * *

On the morning after his departure, Anna gathered the fresh rosebud, and twined it in her hair. As I saw her beaming eyes turned to the avenue, I felt that her loveliness was not for the crowd, but for retirement; that retirement where the student should sometimes sojourn to pour out the breathings of unnamed hopes; where the worldly should look a while at what God has done; and where romantic youth should still its volatile pulses, and feel in nature the nerving presence of Divinity.

The day passed—twilight approached, and Lewis came not. Anna walked the piazza with a restless step. She touched her guitar, its notes were sickly; her kitten rubbed its silken fur against her ankle, Anna gave her no answering caress; she sang a few notes of a song, they sank into a sigh.

"Let us go and meet him," said she, impatiently.

Followed by our attendants, we strolled arm in arm through the avenue. We reached its termination, and strained our eyes through the increasing gloom. No moving object was visible but the cattle gleaning the springing herbage. Darkness settled quietly over the heavens, unconscious of the saddened hearts it shaded; star by star looked down from above; the owl sounded from the distant thickets; and the nearer whip-poorwill uttered her sad lament. Anna and I returned in silence. Was there a presentiment of evil? She burst into tears, and Anna rarely wept. I cheered her, and twined my arms around her, and told her of the thousand causes that might delay our Lewis, and kissed her precious forehead, and wiped her tears, but still they flowed.

Days rolled on, and no tidings were gained of the wanderer. The forest was searched while a ray of hope remained. Its picturesque loneliness was broken by friends straining their eager eyes for a relic of their lost favorite; by mercenaries, who sometimes forgot the promised reward in interest for the noble youth; by Indians, fleet of foot and keen of sight, who were employed in the pursuit; and not seldom were seen in those gloomy woods two females, whom once the hare on its track would have startled, but who boldly braved that solitude for him.

Poor Anna! she ceased to eat, to sleep; her only relief was in exploring the untracked woods. A feverish restlessness wrought on her soul and body. The voice, the footstep of a messenger sent the blood with an electrical rush to her face, which melted away again to paleness. Her eyes were wandering, and her words few, as we rode on horseback through the forests for hours, attended by Selim, a faithful family-servant. Often, wearied out with penetrating the gloomiest spots in silence, I besought her to return; but her cheek kindled and her voice rose in anger, and I had not the heart to thwart her.

A few days passed thus, and I was terrified by the increasing eccentricity of her movements; at length, one day, when a few miles from home, she called me to her, with a mysterious but fixed look, and I guided my horse close to hers. It was a bright, clear morning, the birds were singing among the trees; our woods were glowing with flowers, and yet she said, whispering,

"I am weary of looking for him in this darkness. I see chattering faces peeping from behind every tree, mocking me; but I have a voice left; I can call him, cousin." Then straining every nerve, she began to shout the name of Lewis in long, piercing, unsuspended accents. The echoes took up the shrill and fearful sound, and the woods were vocal with his name. I entreated, commanded her to be silent; she heeded me no more than the winds among the pine-tops; still went up the cry, and echo still shouted back the name.

I dismounted, and called old Selim to assist me in taking her from her horse; she was passive, but still her shrieks rent the air, and curdled my inmost soul. I sat on the grass, and took her in my arms; I reasoned with her; I called her by every endearing name; I laid her head on my bosom; I pressed my hand gently over her starting eyes, and smoothed the glossy waves of her beautiful hair; it was useless; still rang the cry—then my tears fell fast upon her face, and old Selim, kneeling by her side, prayed aloud.

At length, a sudden instinct prompted me to bend my lips to her ear and sing the name of Lewis. I chose a plaintive Methodist air, in which he had often joined with us on Sabbath evenings, uttering only his name. Gradually her voice lowered—sank to a murmur—she was still—she slept.

From this day she sank, oh how rapidly! It is fearful to trace decay in one so young, and who had been so fair. No bright hectic lighted up her cheek; no light brightened in her eye; the destroyer laid his hand cold, hard, and sudden upon her frame: her form shrivelled; her feet shrank in her small slippers; her lips were pale; her eye became glassy and dim;

her fingers stood out lean and blue from her white robe; and when her wedding-ring fell, she was too feeble to regain it; a harsh contraction gathered on her polished brow; she spoke but little, and then gasped forth hurried words, hoarse and thick; oh how unlike the silver tones of her happier days!

She daily tottered to the spot on the piazza where she parted from her young husband, and broke buds and leaves from the bush whence he gathered his last rose. It had risen in spring luxuriance, and thrust its foliage through the paling. When too feeble to visit the piazza, her easy-chair was drawn to the window, where she could gaze on it; and there she sat, uncomplaining and unenjoying, except when a rose was brought to her, and then her white lips would open with a piteous smile as she placed it in her neglected hair.

We talked to her of heaven, of her duty. Alas! her mind was a wreck; the golden bowl was broken! Her look was never upward; it was still, still on the summer rose-bush.

We removed her to Springland as the sickly season advanced. It was heart-breaking to see her look back to the rose-bush as she was lifted to the carriage.

One day a stranger came and presented me unexpectedly with Lewis's pocket-book. He had found it when hunting by the river's bank, at some distance from the main road. He stated that the bushes were crushed near the spot, and deep indentations, as of struggling footsteps, in the soil.

I gave it to Anna; she uttered a thrilling scream of joy, grasped it with her poor hands, and looked wistfully in my face.

"Open it, dearest," said I; and the tears fell fast from my eyes. "It is our own Lewis's."

She unfastened the strap with her feeble fingers, and taking out each paper, one by one, glanced at them as if they were familiar to her, until she saw one written in pencil. It bore the date of his departure, and was evidently a romantic burst of his thoughts in the solitude of the forests.

Anna began to read the following stanzas aloud; her voice, broken and husky at first, gradually strengthened with the unusual effort, until it resumed something of its natural sweetness; and had it not been for her ghastly paleness, there would have been something too in her eyes of that expression, which once melted every beholder.

THOUGHTS IN A SOUTHERN FOREST.

"Cheerless to me ye do not seem,
Tall pines, that hide the solar beam,
And stand in close array;
Nor when, like warriors stern and tall,
By the swart woodman's axe ye fall,
Still ponderous in decay.

How proudly soars each stately head,
With clouds for crowning plumage spread,
And helms of living green!
I love to see the solemn bend
To which your lofty forms ye lend
When breezes wake unseen.

Fit music are the rushing sounds
With which the lonely wood abounds
For your majestic file,
When autumn winds, with rushing swell,
Urged on by ocean's mighty spell,
Tell you to stoop a while.

Fit death for you the fearful crash
Which, at the lightning's dazzling flash,
Lays your green honors low!
And fittest dirge the wood-bird's cry,
When to their frighted young they fly,
As the tall branches go.

Not here, I own, not here arise
Tall spires, that, pointing to the skies,
Uplift the thought sublime!

Not here the orchard bursting bright,
Gives flowers and fruitage to the sight,
As in some distant clime.

Yet, mistletoe, not sad to me,
Thy gathering clusters wander free,
Crowning the old oak's brow!
Not with the Druid's timid eye,
I see thee raise the banner high,
Which woke his mystic vow.

Nor mournful floats the mossy veil,
Waving when forest breezes wail,
Within the cypress grove;
It floated on my boyish sight,
And now its tendrils, swinging light,
Win my familiar love.

And see, from yonder wooded gloom,
The jasmine opes its yellow bloom,
By odors sweet betrayed;
Thus, Anna dear, thy loveliness
Will bloom, with gentle power to bless
Amid life's light and shade."

"I did not know that my Lewis was a poet," said Anna; and one of the sad smiles she gave only to her roses passed over her features as she laid the paper next her heart.

Slowly her reason began to gather; large tears rolled down her cheeks, and sighs, so deep that her frame shook with the effort, rose from her breast.

She spoke little; but her eyes were upraised, her hands clasped as if in prayer; and from this moment a secret communication seemed established between herself and Heaven.

She never smiled again. I am wrong—the night before her death she beckoned me to her, and taking from her bosom Lewis's stanzas, she showed me his withered rose in the paper's folds, and smiled.

Death had little to do to crush her shattered frame; he

checked the last blue veins that lingered on her temple; he severed the almost imperceptible clasp with which she retained my hand; he cast a film more dense over her azure eye, which, with its last look, sought mine; and the throbbings of one of the softest hearts that ever ached under the burden of earth's woes were still.

She only whispered—

"I wish I could have shared his lonesome grave."

That midsummer's sun shone on hers.

CHAPTER XXIII.

THE PINE-LAND VILLAGE.

"Death is beautiful—not as the end of man, not as the extinction of a noble and wonderful being, not as the final result and close of existence, but beautiful in its time, as the momentary passage to a fairer land; the extrication of the soul from its temporary dwelling-place, the resting of the no longer needed body; the free ascent of the delivered spirit to its new abode."—G. PUTNAM.

IT is a solemn thing when death passes over our homes. Let who will depart, whether it be the infant, whose faint eye scarcely opens on the creation which it is so soon to leave, or the old man, whose orbs, weary and dim, are closed on familiar objects, or the maiden, with the rose bursting on her cheek, and her careless step treading lightly on the earth which is so soon to receive her, or the young man, with vigorous frame and active mind, looking thoughtfully into the mysterious and the true; whether it be the father, towards whom his family turn like flowers to the sunbeam, or a mother, whose smile, like daylight, was scarcely felt in its constancy until it was withdrawn; no matter which of life's varied relations is broken; no matter if it even be a stranger, who, without claim but that of hospitality, comes to your threshold and gives up his lonely spirit to God's higher household, away from his own hearth-stone, still it is death—there is its stillness—its shroud—its fixed and pale repose; the voice tells not its wants—the eye knows not. We bend over the stiffened form, and turn away, and come not again, for it is death; perchance we lift the bloodless hand, or smooth the straying hair—but only once, for it is death, and we are chilled. We tread lightly—yet the dead hear not. Why does the boy stop his whistle as he passes that door? Why does the housemaid quicken her step and shade her eyes just there as from a phantom?

Is there no way to render death less dark and unlovely? Were it for me to draw its image, the fleshless bone and the darkened skull should no longer image forth its horrors, nor the hourglass and the scythe be its emblems. It should be sad, for death is sad—not horrible. It should be dressed like night, with dark and flowing robes, and solemn, perhaps uncertain step; but, like night, with the new moon lighting up her sombre mantle, and distant stars, images of far-off life, looking down on her brow. Sin is unlovely—is monstrous; but death should only be unlovely when allied with her.

And yet I felt its bitterness. Anna was gone. My heart stretched forth its tendrils and they fell, unsupported by her sweet sympathy. Her voice, so gentle in its youthful joy, was hushed; her eye, so full of the deep revelations of love and truth, was closed forever; her step, light as the motion of an elastic flower, was arrested; and thus it fares, one by one, with all whom we love: but it is well for us; "the branches are lopped from the tree, that the trunk may fall more easily."

I was sitting, a few evenings after Anna's death, in the piazza, musing on her fate. This had been a favorite spot and favorite hour with Duncan. Throwing aside books, he taught me from the great book of nature: he had anticipated such moments as the present for me; he had told me of the probability of crushed affections and blighted hopes. He drew morals from surrounding objects; for, even from the vacancy and barrenness of a pine-land settlement, his mind extracted instruction—his rich mind, whose spiritual chemistry could convert earth's vapors into heaven-tinged clouds; and now those clouds, hidden to my eyes by the recent glare of worldly fashion, came rolling back in their mellowed brightness. Beautiful force of virtue, which, though sunk beneath life's horizon, throws up its rays long after its orb has disappeared! and let not the good spirits who labor on the ground of the human heart be discouraged; the seed *will* take root, some blessed words *will* shoot down into the soil of the affections, and spring up in after-years.

There is something picturesque in the evening hour at a pine-land village. A few trees are cleared away, affording just sufficient room for a house, whose white-washed palings contrast prettily with the dark hue of the pine; from ten to thirty of these constitute a village, where planters reside during the summer months. A fire is kindled at twilight, of brush or light-wood knots, near every house, which, while it drives away insects gives a cheerful illumination to the scene.

These lights had just begun to blaze, one by one, in the growing shadows of night, while the paler hue of summer lightning broke in fitful lustre between the trees. Here and there might be seen a negro, his dusky form in full relief against the glare of the blazing light; or young ones, dancing and singing around the fire, presenting grotesque images of thoughtless happiness; or a procession of neighbors, preceded by *linkboys*, passing for a festival or a religious service; while their cheerful human sounds broke pleasantly the song of the night-bird, or the unwearied talk of the winds in the pine-tops.

As I mused deeply, with my head resting on the window-sill, a string of Anna's guitar broke within. How trifles sometimes touch the soul! I lived an age in the little time until its awakened vibrations died away in silence; but they did die, and grief gathered up its unexhausted stores, and I wept.

An approaching step made me dry my tears, but they flowed again, for it was Marion's—he who had seen our Anna enthroned on love's temple, breathing the atmosphere of hope and joy.

And Marion, God be thanked, destroyed not the precious lesson of affliction which the Father wisely sent for his untutored child; no light or careless word from him won me back to earth; the glow of religious thought was in his eye—a holy consolation in his reasoning. He drew me away from Anna's grave—from its loneliness and decay, but not to the world; not to that broken cistern, but to the spiritual fountain of Christian faith.

Let young men be careful of woman's highest interests. In those moments of prepossession when her heart and mind instinctively turn to model themselves on his, whom God has made of stronger fabric, let him not sap those foundations of religious trust which may hereafter be dearer to him than her young loveliness, and which, when that loveliness has faded in the dust, will bloom and ripen in a better world.

Marion breathed not a word of love or preference, but I felt elevated by his sympathy, by the thought that he considered me worthy of it; and when he departed that evening there was a rustling as of happy wings unfolding in my inmost heart, and I was comforted.

But still my spirits and health failed under the immediate influence of Anna's loss, and papa, believing that our retirement rather increased than softened my regrets, proposed a change to Sullivan's Island. Springland was but too obnoxious to the common charge against pine-land settlements, extreme dulness or extreme dissipation. There were there, as there are everywhere else, well-tempered minds preserving the equilibrium of virtue, but it is almost impossible to secure a community from dangerous habits in a territory, realizing in its monotony the satirical description of an American poet:—

" Where to the north—pine-trees in prospect rise,
Where to the south—pine-trees assail the skies,
Where to the east—pine-trees obstruct the view,
Where to the west—pine-trees forever grew."

The planter misses the wide range of his fields, and his wife and daughters the bustle of the city. Happy they, under these circumstances, who shun, on one hand, the unhallowed amusements of associated pleasure-hunters, and the chilling influence of seclusion on the other.

How often have I blessed my needle for rescuing me from the temptations which assail the other sex.

Bright and innocent little implement, whether plied over tasteful luxuries, or gaining the poor pittance of a day, thou art equally the friend of her whose visions tend to wander amid the regions of higher abstractions, and of her whose thoughts are pinned down to the tread-mill of thy minute progress. Quiet rescuer from clubs and midnight revels, amid the minor blessings of woman's lot, thou shalt not be forgotten! Still come, and let thy fairy wand shine on her; still lend an ambitious joy to the playthings of the girl; still move unconsciously under the glittering smile of the maiden planning thy triumphant results; still beguile the mother whose thought roves to her boy on the distant ocean, or the daughter watching by the sick-bed of one who has heretofore toiled for her; still soothe the long, dreary moments of faithful love; and, though a tear sometimes fall on thy shining point, it shall not gather the rust of despair, since *employment* is thy dower.

CHAPTER XXIV.

SULLIVAN'S ISLAND.

"Thus, thus the sunny day went by,
And night came brooding o'er the seas,
A thick cloud swarthed the distant sky,
And hollow murmurs fill'd the breeze."

S. G. Goodrich.

"A whirling ocean now fills the wall
Of the crystal heaven, and buries all;
And I, cut off from the world, remain
Alone with the terrible hurricane."

Bryant.

There are no two scenes more widely different than a pine-land settlement and Sullivan's Island. The hum of business or pleasure now sounds at the Cove, but the more remote part of it is lonely in the extreme. A plantation is solitary; shut out from the noise of the world, surrounded by a vast amphitheatre of trees, its occupants see little but the wide fields around, the graduated foliage in the distance, and the over-arching sky; but then the large negro family is there, claiming and giving, in a thousand ways, human recognition. A pine-land village is secluded; files of trees shut out there even the sky; the world is heard not; the resident rises to a monotonous routine, and sleeps but to rise for the same quiet duties, or thrice-told pleasures; but still the habitations cluster in comparative nearness: the night fire blazes cheerfully; and oh, how faithfully does kind neighborhood come forth in sickness, and tell the sufferer he is *not* in solitude. But there is little to soften the loneliness of the more remote residences on Moultrieville. Our dwelling stood alone, on a sandy eminence, with the broad beach in the front distance, and wild myrtles scantily rising as a dwarf shrubbery behind. Nothing was to be heard but the dreamy dashing of the waves, or the curlew's cry; nothing seen but what the ocean offered—the porpoise raising its unwieldy form in the waters, the passing sail, whose distance rather adds to the feeling of separation from human ties, and the sea-bird winging its unwearied flight.

Yet in this solitude I breathed a free spiritual, as well as physical atmosphere. I communed with the winds, and the waves, and the stars, and they gave back answers to my heart, thrilling, yet sobering. It was a joy to stand on the beach, and see the setting sun with its glow of glory lighting up sky and sea; to note the stars, as day declined, marshalled in their shining courses, at first singly, then in countless numbers; to watch the light-house beacon, man's faint competitor with those higher watches; to see the young moon rising with faint crescent, beautiful as growing youth; to note its progress night by night, until it burst in silvery radiance, making the dark waves glorious. And it was a joy to feel in my inmost soul a capacity to appreciate what was great and fair, to rise in bright abstractions, and throw from me all that was earthly, and feel that my higher powers would thus brilliantly light up, when the mortal part should moulder in the grave; to clasp my hands in unuttered prayer, to weep tears of sacred happiness. This was the privilege of my new solitude, and my soul grew in the process; it was part of the heavenly training by which, I trust, God is leading me to a more spiritual existence. This is not romance; it is the feeling of youth, and will be understood by minds not yet fettered by the world.

There were other pleasures at the island not so elevating, but more social and almost defying solitude. I loved to see my brothers and the young negroes revelling in the waves, as Rover, intoxicated with delight, now dashing into the water, now shaking his dripping sides, seemed to feel himself the monarch of the scene, while little Patsey, carried by her *maumer*, dipped her dimpled feet into the shallow wave; then, clinging to her nurse's neck, uttered a cry, half fear, half joy; then grew more bold, until, with a shuddering delight, she permitted the coming waves to dash her limbs, gleaming through the element like a rose-tinged shell.

Then what joyous shouts went up from the beach from the boys' games, the skipping rope, the bounding ball, the kite, while I searched for shells, or wrote, in idle musings, names on the level sands, or rode on horseback on the sea-washed plain, where the fresh breeze in my face inspired health and spirits.

But life's pictures are not all sunny; clouds *will* gather, storms must rise, and whirlwinds sweep over our path.

There came occasionally from town to visit us an old military friend of my grandfather's. It was a great pleasure to us to hear Captain Hyam's stories, to stroll about the island, as he painted out scenes of historical interest; and it was a touching sight to see an old man, on that spot sacred to so many patriotic associations, leading the boys' young minds from their sports to their country's story.

One afternoon we strolled to the cove to observe the arrival of the packet-boats, bringing from the city their customary motley group. There were reclining invalids, with their eyes shooting a sudden brilliancy, as the sea-breeze swept over their languid brows; sickly infants, seizing the first relished morsel; the happy and healthy, who would fain add another tinge to a blooming cheek. There was the mechanic, generously recreating his industrious family, the professional man escaping from the stifling court-room, the chamber of disease, or the secluded study, to feel the Atlantic breeze, untainted by human breathing, and gaze on the clear heavens and unfettered sea. I will not enter on this innocent catalogue those whose motives are gross and impure; the sensualist and the gambler, who dare to sojourn where God's mercies rush by in purifying love, and whose stagnant souls are untouched with sensibility by the wave or the breeze.

The younger passengers, scattered in various parties, shouted in the fulness of excitement as they gained the front beach; shoes and stockings were doffed, pantaloons rolled up, and, followed by their colored attendants, they sang and danced in the coming and retreating waves.

How happy were they all; true, there were no hills rising in magnificence to meet the sky; no sloping fields winding gracefully to the shore; no rocks stationed like guardians round the coast; but there was enough that was beautiful and glorious for the old, exciting and cheering to the young. Generous boys and gentle girls in innocent joy resorted there, gathered rough shells, and threw them in the dark waters; greeted their conscious dog as he came dripping, with some prize, from the surge; wrote sweet names on the beach; ran and shouted in careless laughter against the breeze, or mused on those thoughts which come even to childhood from the bounding sea.

Captain Hyam was one of the passengers, and our boys engaged him for a shooting ramble to the curlew-ground, while I wondered how they could have the heart to disturb the flight of the birds in their aerial processions, now mingling as if for consultation, now extending in a pencilled line, lengthening, until lost in the viewless air. I remonstrated against destroying them, and won my cause, by attaching to the captain's watch a riband, on which I had wrought, in gold letters, 28th June 1776.

Our good old friend consented to remain with us, and we lingered on the beach, so delicious in its coolness after a sultry day. Nature was as bright as our feelings. A few large, pillowy clouds rested beneath the heavens, softening, but not obscuring the declining autumnal sun; the city, with its spires, rose in the distance; the light-house, beautiful emblem of hope and safety, towered on one side; and on the other the main, with its level verdure, seemed like a fringe of green on the azure horizon. Pleasure-boats were darting from the cove, the rocking skiff of the fisherman lay easily on the waves, and the majestic merchantman passed through the channel with its freighted stores.

Some there were who, on that day, had looked with prescient fear on the clouds and fancied evil, and the accustomed ear detected the roar of a distant swell upon the ocean.

The clouds rapidly deepened at twilight, and the wind rose, but we closed the shutters, and gathered round our evening lamp without alarm. As we sat chatting at the table, a sudden gust shook our dwelling, and a drizzling rain began to fall; it increased; in an hour it poured in torrents, and the building rocked like an infant's cradle. A sudden silence prevailed, among our circle, and we spoke low, or uttered strong ejaculations. I was fearfully alarmed; and as each gust came, with its roaring accompaniment of angry waves, I could scarcely restrain my cry. I felt the blood rush to my heart; my eyes seemed starting from their sockets, and I covered them with my hands to shut out, if I could, the threat of nature.

Suddenly the recollection of Charles Duncan's teachings of God in his providence came to my mind. I remembered how he had once gently drawn my hands from my eyes, and told me that Heaven's best messages were sometimes heralded by storms. I remembered this, and the spirit's prayer was awakened, and a trust in God followed like a brooding wing, spreading itself over my fluttering heart, and though I trembled, I was calm.

A knocking at the door was heard in a pause of the wind, and two individuals hurried in drenched with rain.

"How fortunate," exclaimed one, advancing, and panting with his efforts, "to find you. My friend and I were seeking his house in vain, and your piazza light guided us here."

It was Marion, and for a while I forgot the storm. But it approached, and rose and rose like some living monster preparing itself for a death-struggle, until the waves lifted the piazza. It was no longer safe, and we looked abroad in desperation, while our voices could scarcely be heard amid the roar of the elements. Moving masses of ruins were seen floating on the white foam; beyond, all was intense darkness. Collecting the servants, we resolved to leave the house by the back entrance, as yet not reached by the tide, and attempt to gain the fort. Our dear little Patsey, still sleeping in the arms of her nurse Binah, a strong and active woman, was in the centre of the group. The darkness seemed supernatural, and we soon approached a gully, where the tide was rushing on to intercept our way. For a short time a shout, a word of encouragement, a faint jest had been heard, but this was now hushed; there was an awful pause, too, in the elements; it seemed that nature was preparing a nervous heave; and clinging to each other, we thought to die together. It came—the gale rushed with ten thousand voices, thundering on, roaring and raging over bursting waves; we clung to each other still more firmly, but we were parted as easily as gossamer tufts in the south winds of summer. One arm I still felt grasping mine with a nervous force, one voice was left to me, and it said, "We must think of death—it is at hand; prayer is not new to us, my dear Miss Wilton; God will hear us now."

We groped in the darkness, but rather sought to return than advance, for we could see by the moving foam that water was before us. We reached a building and ascended the steps; it was my own home, and no longer in danger, for the wind had changed, and to the waves had been said, Thus far shall ye go and no farther. But I felt bereaved and desolate; there stood the remnant of our evening meal; and the candles, lighted in so much mirth, glimmered dimly in the wind that still rushed through the crevices. I wept, I prayed, and the night passed by, oh, how slowly!

The morning rose, and the sun shone down on that scene of desolation. One servant never was found, but the other members of the family had been variously preserved. Some fishermen, at the early dawn, in ascertaining the fate of their craft, perceived one of their boats high on the sand, capsized, and resting on some timbers. They raised it, and there lay Patsey, our little cherub, wrapped in her nurse's apron, and sleeping in her arms.

But our venerable friend was gone. Amid the sad revelations of that day, his form was recognized, but *his* sleep was the sleep of death. Grasping his hickory cane, his gray hairs wet with surf, lay the veteran on the beach. We looked at him with tearful eyes; and as the soldiers of the fort raised him in their arms, the sun shone on his watch-chain, and the date of 1776 renewed our tears.

A mournful and respectful train wound its way, with military honors, by the curlew-ground, to the myrtles; the muffled drum mingling with air and sea, and the minute guns with sad precision told the tread of death.

Fit was the burial. Let the worldling be laid amid the city's hum, let the babe and the maiden rest beneath the green turf, and flowers blossom over their grave, but the heroes of the South—where can they find a better monument than those hallowed sands, or a holier dirge than that which sweeps over the spot sacred to our early fame?

CHAPTER XXV.

THE PEDLER.

"*Servant.*—Oh, master, if you did but hear the pedler at the door! He hath ribands of all colors of the rainbow; he has the prettiest love-songs for maids!

"*Autolicus.*—And you shall pay well for 'em. [*Aside.*

Will you buy any tape,
Or lace for your cape,
My dainty duck, my dear-a?
Any silk and thread,
And toys for your head
Of the new'st and fin'st wear-a?
Come to the pedler;
Money's a meddler,
That doth utter all men's wear-a.

Winter's Tale.

ROSELAND once more assumed an air of elegance and comfort; we resumed our old habits, brushed up and re-gilt like the portraits of my grandparents, which were again suspended from the walls; the friend was welcomed, the stranger sheltered. I must confess there was a little less ease than formerly, for everything was *new.* Who has not in his life been checked and restrained by the constantly-recurring exclamations, uttered in a tone of tartness,

"My dear, take care of that paint! My love, don't touch those *clean* things! My *sweet* child, pick up those groundnut-shells! My darling, why *will* you let Rover track the clean floors?"

This state of bondage to cleanliness lasted not long, however, at Roseland. Gradually the children were seen eating their sweet-potatoes at all hours; the sight of Ben's powder-horn and fishing-tackle excited no nervous alarm; my music-books were allowed to be in angular instead of parallel lines, and I was permitted to romp out of the nursery with Patsey, while the house assumed that delicious position, where an air of general neatness prevails, without a slavish attention to minute wants, or a perpetual dread of doing or touching something wrong.

I was amusing myself, one morning, by seeing Patsey's efforts to get her big toe into her mouth, as she lay upon the floor, for her figure was too rotund to admit of walking. Puckering up her red lips with as intense an interest as if the world depended on the effort, she at length succeeded, and smacked them with a flavorous relish. As I began to frolic with her, she showed her teeth, white as rice-grains, and her round, fresh laugh rang out in musical peals; at length I jumped over her. Binah, her nurse, caught me by the arm in anger, exclaiming,

"What for you ben walk over *my child*,* Miss Neely? Just go back same fashion, or my child an't gauin for grow no more agen."

I was really obliged to skip back to pacify her, but I soon offended anew by snatching her from her nurse's arms through the open window, as I stood on the piazza.

"My lor, Miss Neely," cried her nurse, "how you ben do sich a ting! Put Miss Patsey straight back; if you carry him trou one door fore you ben put 'em back, he just keep *leetle* so!"

It would be interesting to know the origin of these and other superstitions. Perhaps they have some more rational begin-

* This appellation is constantly given by negro nurses to the white children under their care.

ning than is dreamed of in our philosophy. No nurse at the South will allow a child to be carried to a looking-glass before it is a month old, and its infant sneeze must never be unanswered by "God bless you."

A little incident soon occurred to break the retirement of Roseland.

Every man has some peculiar taste or preference, and, I think, though papa dressed with great elegance, his was a decided love of his old clothes; his garments, like his friends, became dearer to him from their wear and tear in his service, and they were deposited successively in his dressing-room, though mamma thought them quite unfit for him. He averred that he required his old hunting-suits for accidents; his summer-jackets and vests, though faded, were the coolest in the world; his worm-eaten but warm *roquelaure* was admirable for riding about the fields, &c. In vain mamma represented the economy of cutting up some for the boys, and giving others to the servants; he would not consent, nor part with articles in which he said he felt at home. Often did mamma remonstrate against the dressing-room's looking like a haberdasher's shop; often did she take down a coat, hold it up to the light, and show him perforations that would have honored New-Orleans or Waterloo; often, while Chloe was flogging the pantaloons, which ungallantly kicked in return, did she declare that it was a sin and a shame for her master to have such things in the house; still the anti-cherubic shapes accumulated on the nails and hooks, and were even considered as of sufficient importance to be preserved from the fire at the burning of Roseland.

Our little circle about this time was animated by a visit from a pedler. As soon as he was perceived crossing the lawn with a large basket on his arm, and a bundle slung across a stick on his shoulder, a stir commenced in the house. Mamma assumed an air of importance and responsibility; I felt a pleasurable excitement; Chloe's and Flora's eyes twinkled with expectation; while, from different quarters, the house servants entered, standing with eyes and mouth silently open, as the pedler, after depositing his basket and deliberately untying his bundle, offered his goods to our inspection. He was a stout man, with a dark complexion, pitted with the small-pox, and spoke in a foreign accent. I confess that I yielded myself to the pleasure of purchasing some gewgaws, which I afterward gave to Flora, while mamma looked at the glass and plated ware.

"Ver sheap," said the pedler, following her eye, and taking up a pair of glass pitchers; "only two dollar—sheap as dirt. If te lady hash any old closhes, it is petter as money."

Mamma took the pitchers in her hand with an inquisitorial air, balanced them, knocked them with her small knuckles—they rang as clear as a bell—examined the glass—there was not a flaw in it. Chloe went through the same process; they looked significantly at each other, nodded, set the pitchers on the slab, and gave a little approbatory cough.

"They are certainly very cheap," said mamma.

"They is, for true, my mistress," said Chloe, with solemnity, "and more handsomer than Mrs. Whitney's that she gin six dollars for at Charleston."

"Chloe," said mamma, "were not those pantaloons you were shaking to-day quite shrunk and worn out?"

"Yes, ma'am," said she; "and they don't fit no how. The last time the Colonel wore them he seemed quite *onrestless*."

"Just step up," said her mistress, "and bring them down; but stay—what did you say was the price of these candlesticks, sir?"

"Tish only von dollars; but tish more sheaper for te old

closhes. If te lady will get te old closhes, I will put in te pellows and te prush, and it ish more sheaper, too."

Chloe and mamma looked at each other, and raised their eyebrows.

" I will just step up and see those pantaloons," said mamma, in a consulting tone. " It will be a mercy to the colonel to clear out some of that rubbish. I am confident he can never wear the pantaloons again ; they are rubbed in the knees, and require seating, and he never *will* wear seated pantaloons. These things are unusually cheap, and the colonel told me lately we were in want of a few little matters of this sort." Thus saying, with a significant whisper to me to watch the pedler, she disappeared with Chloe.

They soon returned, Chloe bearing a variety of garments, for mamma had taken the important *premier pas.* The pantaloons were first produced. The pedler took them in his hand, which flew up like an empty scale, to show how light they were ; he held them up to the sun, and a half-contemptuous smile crossed his lips ; then shaking his head, he threw them down beside his basket. A drab overcoat was next inspected, and was also thrown aside with a doubtful expression.

" Mr. Pedler," said mamma, in a very soft tone, " you must allow me a fair price ; these are excellent articles."

" Oh, ver fair," said he, " but te closhes ish not ver goot ; te closhesman is not going to give me noting for dish," and he laid a waistcoat on the other two articles.

Mamma and Chloe had by this time reached the depths of the basket, and, with sympathetic exclamations, arranged several articles on the slab.

" You will let me have these pitchers," said mamma, with a look of concentrated resolution, " for that very nice pair of pantaloons."

The pedler gave a short whistle expressive of contempt, shook his head, and said, " Tish not possibles. I will give two pisher and von prush for te pantaloon and waistcoat."

Mamma and Chloe glanced at each other and at me; I was absorbed in my own bargains, and said, carelessly, that the pitchers were perfect beauties. Chloe pushed one pitcher a little forward, mamma pushed the other on a parallel line, then poised a decanter, and again applied her delicate knuckles for the test. That, too, rang out the musical, unbroken sound, so dear to the housewife's ear, and, with a pair of plated candlesticks, was deposited on the table. The pedler took up the drab overcoat.

" Te closhesman's give noting for dish."

Mamma looked disconcerted. The expression of her face implied the fear that the pedler would not even accept it as a gift. Chloe and she held a whispering consultation. At this moment Binah came in with little Patsey, who, seeing the articles on the slab, pointed with her dimpled fingers, and said her only words,

" Pretty! pretty!"

At the same moment, Lafayette and Venus, the two little novices in furniture-rubbing, exclaimed,

"Ki! if dem ting an't shine too much!"

These opinions made the turning point in mamma's mind, though coming from such insignificant sources.

" So they are pretty, my darling," said mamma to Patsey; and then, turning to the pedler, she asked him what he would give in exchange for the pantaloons, the waistcoat, and the coat.

The pedler set aside two decanters, one pitcher, the plated candlesticks, and a hearth-brush.

" Tish ver goot pargains for te lady," said he.

Mamma gained courage.

"I cannot think of letting you have all these things without something more. You must at least throw in that little tray," and she looked at a small scarlet one, worth perhaps a quarter of a dollar.

The pedler hesitated, and held it up so that the morning sun shone on its bright hues.

"I shall not make a bargain without *that*," said mamma, resolutely. The pedler sighed, and laying it with the selected articles, said,

"Tish ver great pargains for te lady."

Mamma smiled triumphantly, and the pedler, tying up his bundle and slinging his stick; departed with an air of humility.

Papa's voice was soon heard, as usual, before he was seen.

"Rub down Beauty, Mark, and tell Diggory to call out the hounds."

There was a slight embarrassment in mamma's manner when he entered, mingled with the same quantity of bravado. He nodded to her, tapped me on the head with his riding-whip, gave Patsey a kiss as she stretched out her arms to him, tossed her in the air, and, returning her to her nurse, was passing on.

"Do stop, colonel," said mamma, "and admire my bargains. See this cut glass and plate that we have been wishing for, to save our best set."

"What, this trash?" said he, pausing a moment at the table —"blown glass and washed brass! Who has been fooling you?"

"Colonel," said mamma, coloring highly, "how can you—"

"I cannot stop a minute, now, wife," said he. "Jones and Ferguson are for a hunt to-day! They are waiting at Drake's corner. It looks like falling weather, and my old drab will come in well to-day."

Mamma looked frightened, and he passed on up stairs. He

was one of those gentlemen who keep a house alive, as the phrase is, whether in merriment or the contrary, and we were always prepared to search for his hat, or whip, or slippers, which he was confident he put in their places, but which, by some miracle, were often in opposite directions. Our greatest trial, however, was with mamma's and his spectacles, for they had four pairs between them—far-sighted and near-sighted. There were, indeed, *optical* delusions practised with them; for when papa wanted his, they were hidden behind some pickle-jar; and when mamma had carefully placed hers in her key-basket, they were generally found in one of papa's various pockets; when a distant object was to be seen, he was sure to mount the near-sighted, and cry "Pshaw!" and if a splinter was to be taken out, nothing could be found but the far-sighted ones, and he said something worse: sometimes all four pairs were missing, and such a scampering ensued!

We now heard a great outcry up stairs. "Wife! Chloe! Cornelia! come and find my drab coat!" We looked at each other in dismay, but papa was not a man for delay, and we obeyed his summons.

"Wife," said he, beating aside the externals of man that hung about his dressing-room, "where is my old drab coat?"

Mamma swallowed as if a dry artichoke was in her throat, as she said, slowly, "Why, colonel, you know you had not worn that coat for months, and as you have another one, and a *roquelaure*, and the coat was full of moth-holes, I exchanged it with the pedler for cut glass and plate."

"Cut devils!" said papa, who liked to soften an oath by combinations; "it was worth twenty dollars—yes, more, because I felt at home in it. I hate new coats as I do—"

"But, colonel," interrupted mamma, "you did not see the scarlet tray, and the—"

"Scarlet nonsense!" shouted papa; "I believe, if they could, women would sell their husbands to those rascally pedlers!"

Beauty and the hounds were now pronounced ready. I followed papa to the piazza, and heard his wrath rolling off as he cantered away.

CHAPTER XXVI.

THE DUEL.

"Some fell for wrong and some for right,
But mony bade the world gude night."

ROBERT BURNS.

"Such I hold to be the genuine use of gunpowder, that it makes all men alike tall. * * *

"With respect to duels, indeed, I have my own ideas. Few things in this so surprising world strike me with more surprise. Two little visual spectra of men, hovering with insecure enough cohesion in the midst of the *Unfathomable*, and to dissolve therein, at any rate, very soon, make pause at the distance of twelve paces asunder, whirl round, and simultaneously, by the cunningest mechanism, explode one another into dissolution."—*Sartor Resartus.*

IT is a lovely tie that unites brothers and sisters, when the little jealousies of childhood are past. My brothers were expected from college, and my heart beat with curiosity and love. I practised the tunes they used to prefer, decorating their bedrooms with such trifling articles of taste as the country-house afforded, ran again and again to the window to watch their approach through the avenue, and glanced at the mirror to see what they would think of me. They came—John was unaltered, though of firmer fabric. His chestnut curls still lay clustering on his head; he still idly thrust his hand through them; they fluttered as they were wont in boyhood, when the winds lifted their rich masses, and shook as mirth and laughter stirred his frame. His saucy eyes still looked archly into mine; his old jests were renewed, and his laugh went round like a spell, while his teeth, in their glittering whiteness, fairly fixed our eyes. The hounds knew his whistle, the servants gathered around him to receive the cordial shake of his hand, and every *uncle* and *aunty* on the plantation was remembered. There was a mixture of good-will and vanity in all that he did; one could scarcely say which preponderated.

But Richard—one could see the growth of soul in his whole exterior. His forehead had enlarged, and seemed bleached by pure intellect; his light thin hair floated back as though nothing should come between his mind-lit brow and heaven. He was taller than John, and at the same time more graceful and yielding. When his brother laughed he only smiled, and the smile seemed in sympathy for John, and not the ruffling of his serious spirit. There was a repose about him that called one away from his external beauty, of which he seemed unconscious, to his spiritual nature, the sense of which appeared ever present with him; not that power which the world calls talent, and which sometimes leads to vanity, but that sense of a connection with a higher order of hidden creation, which leads to a holy confidence in the Supreme Good. He said little; but when he spoke we paused, and our eyes lingered on him as his thoughts played on his lips after the voice had passed away.

I could not be weary of looking at the manly growth of my dear brothers, of twining John's rebel curls on my finger, or parting the silken locks from Richard's thoughtful brow. As evening approached we sat on the sofa, hand clasped in hand, while mamma looked on us all in love; or I felt their arms encircle me as they gave me a renewed look of approving curiosity, or we listened to John's list of college troubles and college exploits, and I glanced into Richard's eyes to know if they were true. Papa too, his old reminiscences brightening up, gave them his bygone experience, and they chatted together of batterpuddings, whose affinities could scarcely be conquered by a rebound from the floor to the ceiling; Indian puddings, faithful as the sun in their daily return; rank butter, which disclosed, in its almost interminable kegs, every evil of the palate, with scarcely the benefit of hope at the bottom; milk, which, from its color, seemed to be under "skyey influences" rather than vegetable; coffee, whose geographical experience never reached further than the beet-bed of a Yankee garden; and tea, whose solutions would not have agitated the sensitive nerves of "Fine-ear, who could hear the grass grow." Then came the stale jokes of a jest-book substituted for the president's Bible; of the diffusion of hellebore by some mischievous wight in the recitation-room, which occasioned the whole class, tutor and all, to burst into fits of inextinguishable sneezing; of the rolling of hot iron balls down entry stairs, to be taken up by some poor unsuspecting martyr proctor; of all sorts of fantastic excuses offered by idle and ingenious scholars for their neglected lessons, disturbing even the gravity of the instructors; of strange mistakes committed in recitation, some intentional, and some unintentional, but all equally adapted to provoke the shout of irresistible laughter; of hairbreadth escapes and impudent subterfuges on the visits of tutors to noisy rooms; of the summoning of two or three frightened freshmen to a government meeting of sophomores and juniors, dressed up in their gowns, and the awful sentence of suspension or rustication passed upon the trembling and believing culprits; of the two, three, four, or five dollars, according to the merit of the composition, given to indigent but talented scholars, for writing themes, and forensics, and commencement parts; of a thousand other exploits, more adapted to a volume than a chapter; and "thrice they slew the slain."

John fell naturally into his old pursuits; club dinners, fishing-parties, and the chase soon occupied his leisure moments, while Richard devoted his time to books and to me. I soon perceived that the name of Randolph, a classmate and neighbor who had returned with them, was painful to Richard. Gradually, as we read together, or penetrated our old haunts on horseback, or strolled at sunset, kindling up our common sympathies at the altar of nature, he opened his heart to me. Randolph had insulted him on the voyage. John, in his ardent and careless way, had tried to effect a reconciliation, and thought he had succeeded, but Richard could only be satisfied by an apology. It had been demanded privately since his return and refused, though with explanations, and thus the beautiful repose of his spirit was broken. In John's case it would have been decided by "a word and a blow;" but Richard's mental and physical temperaments were both different from his; and while John entered into his favorite pursuits, Richard gave himself up to sensitive and jealous misery.

The subject of duelling had been frequently discussed in former years by papa and Duncan. Duncan thought it an outrage on the law of God, and an impatient interference with the political code of our country, which aims to provide for the rights of its citizens. He argued that the grievances between two private individuals ought not to be placed in the scale against the nuisance of throwing whole families and communities into terror, agitation, and unspeakable distress; that it is full season for an enlightened age to put down one of the most savage and foolish relics of barbarous times; that a spurious and animal bravery is the very highest sentiment which the practice promotes, while a lofty moral courage is exercised in refusing, not in accepting a challenge; that the most valuable lives are now exposed to destruction whenever an unprincipled bully sees fit to offer an insult; that, so far from the stain of dishonor being effaced by duelling, it is generally engrained more deeply, as is evinced by the fact that nothing is considered more uncivil than to allude to a particular duel in the presence of the survivor, or of the friends of either party; that, according to the present practice, virtue, vice, honor, infamy, truth, falsehood, are all made to depend on the most factitious and contingent principle in the world, viz., the event of a combat—the lottery of the pistol; that the conduct and the passions which are thus fostered seem natural to wolves, not to human beings; that the most valiant men of antiquity, the Cæsars, the Catos, and the Pompeys, never dreamed of avenging their personal injuries by private combats; that, since the most brave, enlightened, and virtuous nations on earth have been entirely ignorant of duelling, it is not essentially an institution of honor, but a frightful and barbarous custom, worthy of its ferocious origin; that, by a principle of false shame and the fear of reproach, it transforms the best of men into hypocrites and liars, and drives them out to murder the friends of their youth and their bosoms, for an indiscreet word which they ought to forget, perhaps for a merited reproach which they ought to endure; that the duellist, by a horrible refinement and reduplication of crime, unites at once in his own person the character of a murderer and suicide; that the practice is not necessary to vindicate one's reputation from the charge of cowardice, since every brave man has opportunities to expose his life for the sake of his country and of humanity; that no man of true sensibility can ever expect to be serene and happy after having killed his antagonist; and, finally, that genuine honor lies in ourselves, and not in the opinion of the world; that it is neither defended by sword nor buckler, but by a life of integrity and irreproachableness; and that this combat is more glorious than any other.

Papa, on the contrary, advocated it as a check on the violence of human passion, as well as on the meanness of dishonor, and a salutary substitute for imperfect laws, particularly in a thinly populated country, where arbitration is difficult, and the laws slow in their operation. He maintained that the agony of enduring an insult, and especially the scorn and contempt of society, are more intolerable than all the evils arising from the practice of duelling, and that the refusing to fight is an ambiguous action, since cowards may pretend principle to shelter themselves from a danger they dare not meet.

I had often listened with intense interest to these discussions, and found myself leaning to what seemed to me the heroic side of the question, when papa said one day to Duncan, after a long argument—

"Could you, sir, condescend to bear an insult tamely?"

I felt my cheek flush as Duncan replied, calmly, "I would trust to the laws of my country for redress, and never violate what I think to be the will of God."

As papa gave the slightest possible whistle and turned on his heel, I blushed deeper, but it was for Duncan; nor could his calm and dispassionate arguments with me ever separate the thought of cowardice from his views. Alas! I knew not then how my lofty feelings would be tested!

"What shall I do, Cornelia?" said Richard, as we struck into a retired footpath, after pouring out our souls to each other as we were wont to do. "I feel the sting of this insult rankling like a serpent's fang within me through the day, and at night I see it branded in burning characters, in waking darkness, and yet more hideous dreams. I see it in every man's face calling me coward, and women seem to me to shrink from one who cannot defend them. I have tried to look all round this subject calmly, but it comes to me like a nightmare."

We were thrown together in the company of Randolph. I glanced at Richard, and soon saw a deep red spot gather on his cheek; his lips were compressed, and his manner stately. Randolph asked an introduction to me. I received him like ice, for my heart was my poor Richard's, who sat silent and reserved. Randolph became particularly gay; his wit flashed out, and shone the brighter over Richard's clouds. In the playfulness of his feelings he said things which a jealousy like ours was not slow to misinterpret. We left the circle abruptly.

"I can bear this no longer," said my brother, as he walked on with rapid strides, and pressed his hand to his forehead. "Randolph scoffs at me. I must have the satisfaction of a gentleman. Even you despise me for my abject submission."

I was silent for a while, and then said, "I can bear anything better than your disgrace, brother."

How little did it occur to me that I might have been a medium of reconciliation instead of a desperate adviser! If the right string had been touched in my brother's mind, all would have been tuned to harmony; but my preconceived views of physical courage overbalanced the claim of high moral duty. Poor Richard! we went home; he threw himself moodily on the sofa, buried his face in his hands, and, rising, poured out his feelings anew in words of burning anger.

Oh, woman, beware how you aid in inflaming the passions of man! The courtesan of classic times won her judges by a display of her personal charms; let your manifestation be only of the bright and tender virtues; let not your influence, either of person or mind, swell the tempest of unlawful excitement. It is not my object here to argue for or against duelling; that is the province of abler minds; but I may venture to show how *female* influence may "ride on the whirlwind and direct the storm" of masculine feeling for good or for evil; how the genius of Christianity, or even worldly philosophy, quietly exhibited in woman's gentle tones, may come with their enlightening power, not for the avoidance of mere physical pain, but with a serious regard to man's true dignity and ultimate destiny. I warn my sex against inflammatory expressions. Beautiful and graceful to the eye, can they be hard and unforgiving? We wonder not that the coarse nettle leaves its sting; but, when the flower that we carry to our lips ejects its poison, grief and surprise are added to the pain. Had I but given those "soft answers that turn away wrath," had I thought of how many good feelings in man's nature may be operated upon—instead of stimulating the evil, I might have been the blessed means of reconciling two noble spirits. But I did not; my haughty soul would not stoop to the thought that my brother should even inquire into the motives of an aggressor. Stoop! mistaken term! The peacemaker stoops not, but rather rises to a high moral elevation, and looks calmly down upon the angry passions that are floating beneath him.

A challenge was sent, unknown to any of our domestic circle but myself. The meeting was to be on the following morning, in a field two miles distant, at early dawn. Papa and John were in the city.

Richard and I sat late in the piazza on that evening. We spoke but little; we did not, as we were often, in the fulness of our confidence, accustomed to do, clasp each other's hands. The voices of our family seemed to me like dreams and echoes rather than realities; *to-morrow* was spoken of—it was as a vague image for a moment—then the thought of its probable results swept over me like a coming tempest. The family retired to their quiet repose. Richard gave the little ones no kiss, as usual, and answered not their childish prattle; they all went, and we were left alone. Then came the agony; I could not let him go; I clung round his neck and petitioned him to stay. I felt already like a murderer. I offered to mediate—to do anything rather than expose a human life to risk the untried possibilities of a future state of being. Richard was affectionate, but firm.

"It is too late, my sister," he said. "Had I been a little more patient" (alas! what duellist has not had a moment like this?) "I might have prevented this result. Perhaps, after all, I have exaggerated this affair; but it is too late—to stop now would be infamy. And now, Cornelia, for my last charge. I have endeavored to write to-day, but in vain. I leave the commission to your tenderness."

As he said this, he handed me an unframed miniature of a full-length figure, on which was written "Eliza." He had showed it me before, but now it struck me with tenfold interest. It was feminine almost to childishness, except the eyes; but there beamed forth from those dark orbs a full-formed soul, thirsting for intellectual food. The figure was slight, symmetrical, and waving—one of those that seem formed to lean on man's stronger arm: but the gazer on that portrait turned, as by a spell, and rested on those large dark eyes, beaming in glittering softness, until his heart said, "I love thee, gentle one!"

"Those beautiful eyes," said Richard, mournfully, as he leaned over my shoulder, while the moon shed its rays upon the picture, "must they weep for me—for me, who vowed that the tears of our parting were the last that they should shed? I wiped them then, and Eliza stood like a trusting child as I did so; and when I said I could not leave her till she smiled, she did smile a radiant smile of hope and trustingness. Oh, God! have I not deceived her young heart? And my poor mother, she who has but just begun to reap the labor of maternal love, should I not have borne more for her? Randolph, too, do I hate him? do I wish his death? Would I not heal him if he were wounded, give him drink if he thirsted, and stand with him hand to hand against a common enemy? Strengthen me, Cornelia, I am bewildered; weep not thus, my sister, for God's sake; strengthen me."

I could not; and we yielded in each other's arms to one of those long and passionate bursts of agony that sweep along life's paths, and make the heart and body grow old.

At twelve o'clock we parted. I listened for his tread in the adjoining room; all was still. I would have given the world to hear his footstep. I could not bear the silence, but went to his door and whispered his name. He answered instantly, and calmly—

"Go back, my sister. I cannot see you."

"Only one word, Richard—one look more."

"No; go—go!"

I went to my bedroom. The moon was at full. Everything looked gigantic; the shadows lay in grotesque masses; the trees waved their arms like living things; the whippoorwill's note was like a shriek in my ear. Twice in that long night I went to Richard's door, and sat there; once I heard the click of a pistol. Still his only answer to my petition was,

"Go, go, Cornelia," in his calm, sweet tone.

I laid myself down by the door, with my face upon the boards; their coolness was fresh to my burning cheek. I saw figures in the darkness—wounded forms—gashes—streaming blood—and Eliza was there—unconscious, with her glittering, moonlight eyes.

The door opened. I would have caught and held my brother, but, seemingly aware of my design, he stooped, and, holding my hands tightly in his, laid a long kiss upon my lips, and escaped rapidly down the stairs. I would have screamed to him to return, but my voice failed me. I was dizzy—faint; it was but a moment, but he was gone; then a ferocious horror came over me like madness. I clinched my hands and teeth, and a shivering went through my frame. It was insupportable. I rushed to mamma's apartment, and told her the horrid tale. Then was all the mother roused: then a throe deeper than birth-struggles tore her heart. It was fearful to see my calm parent thus moved. "We must go to him," were all the words she uttered, but such looks, such piteous, piteous groans! Will they ever leave my memory, or the reproaches of his nurse, who, wringing her hands, shrieked out—

"Miss Neely, Miss Neely, how you been let my young maussa do such a ting? God have mercy on he soul."

We hurried on in silence, as if a word might delay us. The moon had gone down, and that melancholy moment, melancholy even to happy hearts, arrived—the breaking dawn. How is it that awakening nature is thus sad? Does not the analogy of all human feeling tell us to sympathize joyfully with such scenes? How is it, then, that the moon and stars, which play as in jubilee around the form of midnight, look, before the gray dawn, like sad travellers journeying a lonely way?

We hastened on, nor thought of the stars as they sank, one by one, to shine on other worlds, nor of the purple glow that rose in rich coloring on the eastern sky. We were near the place of meeting—human figures were seen. A flash—a sound—we reached the spot—the cries of our attendants pierced the air. Mamma received her unconscious son in her arms, and I clasped, with a breaking heart, his pulseless hand.

CHAPTER XXVII.

MARIA ALWYN AND HER MOTHER.

"And thou, sad sufferer under nameless ill,
That yields not to the touch of human skill,
Improve the kind occasion, understand
A father's frown, and kiss his chastening hand.
To thee the day-spring and the blaze of noon,
The purple evening and resplendent moon,
Shine not, or undesired and hated shine,
Seen through the medium of a cloud like thine."—COWPER.

"Nous nous aimions tous-deux dès la plus tendre enfance,
Et j'avois sur son cœur une entière puissance;
Je trouvais à lui plaire une extrème douceur,
Et les chagrins du frère étoient ceux de la sœur."—RACINE.

As I saw the face of my brother, on which death seemed to have stamped an instantaneous seal, and heard his nurse's groans and lamentations, and mamma's piercing words of love, and the physician's inquiring voice, it seemed to me as if some wild and fearful tragedy were enacting. Still I felt an awful testimony within me, which declared, "You have made this ruin—your words, which should have stilled the tempest, have given it force; you, who call yourself the gentle and tender Christian, have held the torch and spread this ruin."

Randolph approached; pale as death, he gazed silently for a moment on his fallen victim, and then, with a suppressed voice, said—

"Would to God that society required not this sacrifice! It

is a fearful thing to go thus before one's Maker and Judge.' With a half-unconscious shudder he was then led away.

Life was not extinct, but it fluttered almost to dissolution. Richard was borne home, and we followed—a sorrow-struck train. His nurse wrung her hands and wept audibly; Bella, the dumb woman, met us with her wild howling; and Jim looked anxious and subdued.

Life struggled fearfully for a few days with the destroyer. Mamma, by his bedside, and I, lying on his pillow, watched his pallid face; it was indeed like death; his silky hair was parted from his noble forehead, and his dark lashes lay on his marble cheek; one could not see that he breathed; to my excited imagination, the fluttering pulse often seemed to stop, his hands fell nerveless, and only now and then a quivering sigh stole from his breast.

Slowly, at length, his eyes unclosed, and a faint smile, as they met our gaze, like the shadow of an infant's dream, parted his lips. Oh, my heart! I was faint with joy. Again came the blessed testimony of life and love; he whispered *Mother!* She bent over to his pale lips, clasped his clasping hand, laid her face on his pillow, and wept. It was a moment for the heart's prayer. His old nurse, with upraised eyes and trembling hands, stood by and uttered hers aloud. Jim looked on anxiously, for he was frightened by mamma's tears.

"He will live!" I whispered to Jim; "he has spoken and smiled."

A little sustenance was given him; he smiled again, and Jim caught the beautiful glance of coming life as it beamed even on him.

"Ki!" said Jim, in a tone a little over a whisper, and snapping his fingers, "dead an't gwying for catch Maus Dick yet!"

So saying, he opened the door softly, slid down the balusters, cut a few somersets through the yard, and proclaimed the good news to the people. Poor fellow! it was the first time he had voluntarily left his young master's room. Night and day he and Richard's old nurse had taken their stations there unbidden; when asleep, a word aroused them; when waking, they watched with active kindness. What Southern family has not this testimony to give of some faithful dependant who thus creates a tie of gratitude?

Richard's recovery was rapid, and the busy kindness devoted to a Southern convalescent was soon discernible. Custards and preserves, and the niceties of the season, decorated with bouquets of flowers, were sent by the neighbors; while the colored people brought eggs in little baskets, with young poultry from their own stores. One old woman came to the door and asked "just to look in."

His nurse brought her humble offering, and said, with a courtesying apology—

"I an't raise but one chicken dis year, but I fetch 'em for my child's soup."

The first night that I retired to my own apartment, with a heart weighed low by gratitude, I threw myself upon my knees by the window where the moonlight scene had been so appalling. The stars, from their abodes of darkness, threw down their glimmering rays and lighted my weeping eyes. I felt like one who had been rescued from a precipice, and looked back with trembling on the chasm below. Did I feel that a great duty had been performed, and that noble approval which gives us strength to bear and wings to fly? No; *escape* was the only cause of triumph; and however men may vindicate duelling on grounds of expediency, will they not find this the predominant feeling when they survive? Not the reward of bravery, not the elevating testimony of high moral courage, but a simple relief from some dark and overhanging necessity, is the best result of this horrid and unnatural violation of social peace.

John returned with papa, and, after the first strong emotions were over, laughter and jest echoed through our mansion; but Richard and I for a while dwelt on higher things. He had been too near the unknown abyss of a future world not to feel a cast of solemnity over his soul. We reasoned together of sacred things—of death and a judgment to come.

"It may be a vain speculation," he said to me, "but I delight in anticipating the future state of disembodied spirits. What are your thoughts on this subject, Cornelia?"

"It is my favorite idea," I answered, "that 'we shall all be changed,' spiritually as well as physically. The world has been more bright to me than to many, but I have no wish to carry away any of its recollections. Young as I am, I am tired of its struggles. I hope for a butterfly transition—a change from this headaching and heartaching scene to a bright and God-sunned atmosphere. I love to think that when I have done weaving (faithfully) my earthly envelope, I shall spring from it, gorgeous and beautiful, and flit away, forgetful of the coarse chrysalis that falls, as I ascend in joy to my heavenly Father's spiritual kingdom. But one thing I must require in my flight" (and I pressed Richard's hand to my cheek), "that brother butterflies shall go with me."

"I would prefer annihilation," said Richard, "to a forgetting of my individual self. The spirit must be able to look back, and compare, and judge; it must feel its growth, to be happy. Accession in knowledge is the only test of spirituality. I cannot imagine even the Supreme Mind *at rest;* it must be experimenting, creating still."

Thus we discoursed together, or I read to him; a soothing quiet stole over us, and the spirit of prayer was around us.

This is the worth of sorrow. Before we suffer, words are said, but the spirit prays not; it is mere form; but, when affliction has struck the rock of our hearts, and its religious waters gush forth, *we pray always;* that is, a conscious presence of divinity is within us, and our thoughts are prayers.

But this holy influence is not felt by all, and wretched are those who, having tasted these waters, feel not that the Lord is gracious. While Richard was convalescent, a neighbor, a widow, lost her only child, a daughter. We were not in the habit of visiting her; but, hearing that she was in distress, and without domestic friends, mamma commissioned me to go to her, with such offers of service and sympathy as our own softened feelings dictated. In my own equestrian excursions, I had seen Mrs. Alwyn riding about her fields. Her appearance was remarkable; tall, masculine in her proportions, with full, flashing black eyes, she gave directions to her people, not "with a low voice, that excellent thing in woman," but in coarse tones of encouragement or vituperation. It was said that the love of gain and fear of her neighbors were all that restrained her from positive cruelty. She arose at the dawn of day, and even used agricultural implements herself, to stimulate her negroes. She denied herself rest and relaxation, and spent a life of unmitigated toil, and for what? That she might educate and accomplish her daughter; and Maria "grew like a living flower beneath her eye." With her mother's commanding height, she possessed a wavy delicacy of figure; her mother's dark and flashing eyes were, in her, softened by modest sensibility; she touched with taste and skill the piano which her parent's hard labor had earned, and around her apartments were hung, in expensive frames, trophy after trophy of her conquests with the pencil. While Mrs. Alwyn reconnoitred the fields, a terror to idlers, or attended to the drudgery of the house, Maria lived secluded, her soft hands embroidering tasteful attire, or her dark eyes dropping tears of sympathy over fictitious sorrow. It was sufficient happiness to her mother to glance at her white-robed daughter, as she sat apart like an idol in its shrine. Maria often expostulated with her, and wrought tasteful caps and kerchiefs, and playfully arrayed her mother in them, but with little effect. Mrs. Alwyn strode about in her soiled and tattered dress, not hesitating, as occasion demanded, to test the strength of her hand on the ears and shoulders of some unhappy loiterer. I had met Maria at church, and occasionally in my rambles, and had thought of knowing her further, as I heard details of her situation and character, when I learned that she was suddenly withdrawn from this living and moving scene. I willingly hastened to her bereaved mother.

I was ushered in by her frightened-looking servant, with that light and solemn tread which we see where death is. I was shocked to observe the body of the deceased laid out on a table in the parlor, in order to be near, as I learned afterward, to her mother, that she might see her while she prepared the house for the funeral. A white shroud and sheet inwrapped the body, and there seemed to be a supernatural extent in the tall figure, as the pointed toes stood up beneath the thin covering. Over the beautiful eyes, now but partially closed, lay pieces of metal. Was this indeed Maria, thus cold and pale as new-fallen snow?

Mrs. Alwyn sat where she could watch the corpse and gaze upon its countenance. She held a plate in her hand, and a towel, as if she had been wiping it. A stern coldness was mingled with her grief, and she rocked to and fro in her chair, with the motion which sorrow loves.

I entered; she regarded me with a slight motion of the head. I took her hand—it was passive. I spoke, but there

10

was no answer, and I sat down in silence. At length, with a look in which distress and anger were strangely blended, she said—

"There she is, Miss Wilton! see what it's come to! a beautiful corpse she is! That girl an't done a thing to trouble her mother's heart since she came into the world, a stark baby, till now. Do you see them pictures?" (and she pointed with her soiled dark fingers from one to the other.) "I have toiled night and day, I've worked like a nigger, and more than any nigger, I've been up early and abed late, to get that girl a genteel education, and what has it all come to? Look at that piano—I put the hay into the loft with the pitchfork with my own hands, to let the niggers have time to bring that here. Didn't she sing sweetly? I worked my fingers most to the bone for them pictures and music, and what has it all come to? Just look at her and see. Where's her voice now? What has it all come to? Wasn't she a pretty-faced girl, with her white hands, that I wouldn't let so much as wash a cup? Look at them now, stiff and still!" (I turned and shuddered as I looked at Maria's long, straight arm as it lay in her shroud.)

"Miss Wilton, it don't seem to me as if I can bear it, or as if I *ought* to."

I ventured to suggest a reliance on a higher Power, who afflicts only in mercy.

"It tan't no mercy," said she passionately. "I wouldn't treat a dog so. If you had a garden full of seeds, and saw them come up and blow out beautiful, and their stalks grow greener and bigger every day, while you was watering them, do you think it would be merciful if anybody was to come and tramp them all down and pull up your pretty flowers by the root? There wasn't a prettier flower in all creation than that," continued she, pointing to the lifeless form, "and now see what she is."

"She *was* a lovely girl," said I, "and you had reason to be proud of her. I have often observed her tall, graceful figure as she came into church. I am glad to hear that she was kind and dutiful; that, at least, must comfort you."

"'Tan't no comfort," said Mrs. Alwyn, bitterly. "If she had been cross and ugly, she might have gone and welcome. What is the use of having a person about you that an't pleasant? But I'll tell you what is a mortal hard case; to have something taken away that was the delight of your eyes; one who used to be the first object you loved to look at in the morning, and the last at night. In the morning, when I came from the field, I used to go to her bedroom and wake her. How pretty she was on her pillow, with one cheek all red like a rose, where she had laid on it, and the other like a lily! and when I said 'Maria!' how she rubbed her eyes like a child, and half pouted and half smiled as I waked her. Where is the rosy cheek now?"

My heart thrilled as I saw its paleness.

"And then," continued her mother, "she sat so lady-like at table, as if she had been born and bred genteel; her frocks like snow, and her cambric handkerchiefs in her lap. At night I used to go in and tuck up her bed; she was always at her books, or her work, or reading her Bible, or on her knees at prayer, for she was a pious child."

"You must at least be grateful that her mind was so pure, and pious, and prepared for death," said I.

"Grateful!" replied she, angrily. "What good will it do me? I shall be none the better for her hymns and her prayers. If she had stayed, I could have heard her sweet voice. Now, I've worked my fingers to the bone just for that dead body. I can't bear it, and that's an end of the matter. I don't think it's fair that she should die. Well, I must go to work and bury her," muttered she, in a lower tone, and retiring into the next apartment, where she could still glance at her lifeless child.

I stood a while and meditated on the early dead. Her image came before me as I had often seen her enter church, dressed with exquisite care, and a reference to the changing shades of fashion. Her head had a gentle bend or wave, from a consciousness of her height, which, as she did not stoop, was rather graceful, while her cheek, usually pale, was lighted up by the thought of public observation. She often rested an ungloved hand on the side of the pew, which, as it was delicately white, and glittering with jewels, I sometimes thought was for display; but her modest eyes seemed to deny it; and her voice, rising in rich and earnest tones in the hymns and chants, and her air of devotion in prayer, showed an engagedness that comported not with vanity.

Now I saw her stretched on her hard resting-place, death giving that supernatural length to her tall form; those glazed eyes, that were so lately lit up with intellectual glory, but partially closed by the heavy metal on the starting lids; those feet, which had trod the aisles with light and graceful movement, stiff and prominent under the white death-clothing; that fair hand, whose sparkling gems had glittered to the observer, dazzling in whiteness still, but with the unrosy paleness of the grave.

Her wretched mother's unbelief saddened still more this painful picture. Could she have looked on her with Christian trust, and fancied that spirit translated to the garden of heaven, where blight, and frost, and tear-dews fall not; could she have fancied her upward-soaring, and retained but a fold of her garment to aid her own flight, how would her cold heart have felt the change! But alas! the grave was to her the end of all this sweetness and truth; faith stood not by that grave, with patient eye and folded wing, ready to spread, at God's command, either over the path of earthly duty or spiritual joy.

But grief will be busy. The miserable mother decorated the cold corpse with all that custom and fashion demand; the finest cambric enshrouded it, the sheerest muslin lay on that pale forehead; the coffin glittered with funeral-ornaments; ceremony lingered in the well-ordered procession; and in a few months a pompous monument proclaimed to the world the death and the virtues of Maria Alwyn.

This picture (literally true) is a startling representation of an irreligious, uncultivated mind; but are there not many who secretly carry out these sacrilegious feelings when God lays their earthly blessings in the dust?

CHAPTER XXVIII.

MY BROTHER BEN'S EDUCATION.

"He saw whatever thou hast seen;
Encountered all that troubles thee:
He was—whatever thou hast been;
He is—what thou shalt be."

We were at this period made unhappy by my brother Benjamin's abrupt return from school; and it may not be unprofitable to relate his reverses before and after this time, independently of my narrative.

Why are there no more ripe and accomplished scholars among us? The secret, I apprehend, will be partially understood, if the progress of his education is examined. It will probably awaken the sympathetic groans of many a young man, who has to mourn over a similar experience. I fear we must look forward to an indefinite repetition of similar consequences, until Charleston shall provide one grand and uniform institution, or system of institutions, for the education of her youth, that shall be unaffected by the death or change of teachers, or the boundless variety of text-books; and until parents shall co-operate cheerfully with the rules of such a system.

At the age of nine years, Ben was placed at one of the best schools in Charleston, and boarded in a private family. He was a lad of excellent abilities; rather more fond, indeed, of his play and horses than of study, but never wilfully backward at his lesson. His teacher, besides superintending the usual branches of his English education, put him early into the Latin grammar. Ben was punctual at school, and learned two or three of his lessons every evening at home. When we were in town, I gave him what assistance I could, though now and then a hearty cry took place over the difficulties which neither he nor I could comprehend. His troubles at school were of the ordinary description—sometimes a detention till long after the dinner-hour—sometimes a severe chastisement for noise or carelessness—and sometimes a station far below the middle of his class. Yet he was evidently making an improvement in most of his studies; and could his present opportunities have been continued, Ben might have become, in time, a very respectable scholar. Unfortunately, however, his teacher, at the end of the year, abandoned his occupation for a profession, and Ben was thrown loose on the scholastic world.

After some time, another teacher was procured for him. On entering his new place of instruction, he was examined in all his studies, and pronounced to be miserably deficient in every respect. The fact is, this gentleman made no allowance whatever for the perturbation of the poor boy's mind; when suddenly brought before a strange teacher, his attention being distracted by a new and noisy school, and that, too, after a month or more of entire interruption in his studies. The learned gentleman found particular fault with Ben's ignorance of the multiplication table and Latin grammar, and took occasion to express some doubts of the capacity of his former instructor to teach in those departments. I need not say how very unjust was such an inference. Be that as it may, my brother was ordered to begin all his books again, and was stationed in a class inferior to that which he had left at the other school. He came home completely discouraged and mortified; disgusted alike with learning and with his new instructor.

May I be permitted, with due modesty, to suggest, that much mischief is occasionally inflicted in this way on ingenious and well-intentioned youth, in consequence of an examination, which can only be superficial and imperfect? Would it not be more proper to take the word of the parents and of the former teacher as to the progress already made by the pupil? It would be found, in a short time, that he could easily revive his former knowledge, without being necessitated to lose his standing for a whole year, or to suffer a mortifying degradation.

But the feelings of youth are elastic. It is one of the blessings of that period of life, that its mortifications are not attended with enduring bitterness. Ben accommodated himself to his new situation with tolerable grace; and by the close of another year he had just about regained that point in his progress at which he had been left by his former teacher. In consequence, however, of falling into some untoward scrape, he was chastised with undue severity by his tutor, who was a man of violent passions. Papa's temper was equally violent, and the affair terminated in an abrupt withdrawal of my brother Ben from his present school, and his transference to another.

From the precipitancy with which this exchange was effected, papa had no opportunity to institute any minute inquiry as to the merits or studies of Ben's new school. The boy trotted off with much cheerfulness on the first morning of his attendance, and with his satchel full of his old school-books. But papa was not a little surprised and mortified in seeing Ben return home at about ten o'clock, with his heavy satchel on his arm, and a note from his new teacher, requesting that the boy should be furnished with an entirely new set of books, since those which he had brought with him to school were now quite out of date. Pike's arithmetic was to be exchanged for Daboll's; Morse's Geography for Cumming's; Ruddiman's Latin Grammar for Adam's; Webster's Spelling-book for Carpenter's; Bingham's English Grammar for Murray's; the American Selection for the English Reader; the New Testament for the whole Bible; while one set of copy-slips was to be substituted for another; a single-ruled writing-book for a double-ruled one, which Ben had just begun; and the gentleman had even the thorough-goingness to request that my brother's large, stout, new slate might be exchanged for a recently-invented tablet, which would come in requisition at certain times when the blackboard should not be used.

In general, papa was very liberally disposed as to pecuniary matters, and was always particularly willing to encourage suggested improvements in education. But it so happened, that this year his crops had been lamentably cut short, and the prices of rice and cotton were very much depressed. This, added to the irritability under which he was still laboring from his difficulty with the preceding teacher, excited him, in a moment of self-forgetfulness, to exclaim that he would not procure a single one of these newfangled books, and that he did not care whether Ben attended any of those vexatious schools or not. I knew it was hopeless to attempt to change this unhappy mood immediately, and the result was, that poor Ben ran about the streets for a full week unoccupied, gathering large stores of boyish experience no doubt, but sadly falling behindhand in point of literary cultivation.

It was now time for me to interfere; indeed, I was conscious that papa, having gotten the better of his temper, and opened his mind to the influence of reason, was only waiting for a word or two from me, in order to enter upon a more praiseworthy course. One morning, therefore, at the breakfast-table, I ventured to express my regret that Ben should continue in his present unhappy state of idleness, and suggested that he might possibly have been fortunate in making an exchange of teachers; for it was to be supposed that improvements must be going on in school-books as well as in everything else. It cost me but a few words to obtain permission to go out that very morning in pursuit of the whole appointed list.

I searched every book-store in the city, finding one book here and another there, but was unable to procure more than half the prescribed number. I was assured, that if I had called but two or three days before, I might have obtained some of the most important of those which were wanting. But it was now too late, and we were obliged to await a new importation from the North. Steamboats, in those days, arrived not with weekly punctuality; and, therefore, Ben was compelled to run wild nearly another month before he could enter the wished-for school, equipped, externally at least, with all the educational improvements of the age.

My brother, who had now arrived at an age of some reflection, found himself, somewhat to his astonishment, at the foot of the hill of science. The preceding years appeared to his view like a vacant dream. Young as he was, he could not help inquiring what had become of them; but supposing that Heaven and parental guardianship had ordered all things aright in this matter, he resolved to dismiss unavailing regrets, and begin anew, with commendable diligence and ardor, the study of numeration, and of the definite and indefinite articles, and of the astronomical introduction to geography.

We could find no fault with Ben's present teacher. The lad made a satisfactory progress in his studies, and all things flowed along in peace until August of the next year, when his preceptor, who happened to be a native of New-England, was fatally attacked by the yellow fever, and died, leaving his school involved in sorrow and confusion. There was no more study for that season; and we were obliged to wait until late in the autumn before a gentleman could be procured to undertake the school on his own account. My brother was, of course, injured by this unfortunate intermission in his studies. He lost somewhat in his power of application, and gained as much in his inclination for all kinds of youthful amusements. His new preceptor, not only desirous of making up the recently lost time of his school, but being one of those teachers who are over-stimulated by the ambition of advancing his pupils with wonderful rapidity, heaped lesson upon lesson, and even required several new branches and books to be learned, in order that he might surprise the parents and the committee, at the succeeding annual examination, with the unequalled result of his labors. Ben humorously requested his father to furnish him with a horse and dray to transport his books between the school and the house. It was indeed no small physical labor for him to carry his little library backward and forward. His satchel, though of large dimensions, could not contain the whole, and he was obliged to carry several books under his left arm. Groaning and perspiring, grumbling and bantering together, he lugged to and fro his heavy loads for a few days, until papa purchased for him a small, strong white horse, with tail and mane closely cropped. I manufactured for him a new sack, resembling more a clothesbag than a satchel. Putting into this the whole of his school furniture, and placing it on the neck of his favorite pony, he mounted and rode off with a lighter body at least, if not with a lighter heart, than he had lately enjoyed.

He was now beginning to be ashamed of the backwardness of his learning, compared with his age. He conceived a new and passionate fondness for study. He arose every morning at dawn, and retired not to rest until near midnight. He even refused to devote any hours to recreation, so determined was he to realize the whole system of his present teacher, and to accomplish every one of his lessons in the most perfect manner. But this was more than the powers of nature could bear. He pursued the present course about three months, and found his health and constitution rapidly giving way. The family physician being consulted, directed that he should quit school and books altogether for some time, and reside with mamma in the country. Thus, by making too much haste, poor Ben, as well as his teacher, rather retarded than accelerated his progress. He passed a few weeks in the country, entirely abandoned to amusements, and returned to town in perfect health. On again attending school, he experienced the immense disadvantage of being far behind his class. The studies which he had missed were indispensably necessary to a right understanding of his present lessons. This circumstance, added to the sufferings he had already endured from over-application, threw Ben into complete despair. Finding it impossible to accomplish all his tasks in a tolerable manner, he grew indifferent and inattentive. He was contented to remain at the foot of his class, and was proof against any species of degradation and punishment. He frequently played the truant. He protracted his holydays in the country till near the first of February and the middle of May. His afternoons in town were devoted to riding on his little horse, whose flesh rapidly disappeared by racings on the battery and gallopings through Meeting-street, at the peril of all the negro children in his way.

It was now full time to try a new experiment with my unlucky brother. A school happened to be opened near our residence; and as it was but too manifest that Ben was wasting away his precious youth by his present career, we determined on seizing this opportunity to make an exchange, and give him another chance for improvement. Accordingly, he became a pupil of our new neighbor, whom, if I were devising characteristic names for the teachers enumerated in this chapter, I might call by the appropriate title of Mr. Easy. If Ben was before oppressed with the multitude of his tasks, he had now far too little to accomplish. When a lesson was assigned him to be learned at home, which was but seldom the case, he might attend to it or not, as he chose, for it was never exacted from him. His teacher was all indulgence; going nominally over the common branches of learning with his pupils, but leaving it to their own genius and good sense whether any of them should become scholars or idlers. Now Ben had not quite sufficient independent energy to make much progress under a system like this. He was naturally docile, and would have lent himself kindly to the influences of any good and effective method. But being somewhat of a victim to circumstances, he could not resist the thousand temptations of a city life, when opposed to the feeble prescriptions of an indulgent preceptor. Accordingly, he was in a fair way of being ruined. His talk was of horses. His companions were idlers. He commenced playing on the guitar. He was a precocious dandy. His thoughts were overmuch given to dancing, and gallantry, and all those other arts by which the precious sands of time are irrevocably wasted. Fortunately, the school which he now attended died a natural death. It had not sufficient stamina to keep itself alive. One after another of the pupils dropped away, and the incapable teacher emigrated to Alabama, leaving my brother Ben, with only two fellow-students, to seek for better places of education.

Just about this time, advertisements appeared in the daily prints, announcing a new institution, to be conducted on a highly improved and refined plan. The public were told that appeals would be made entirely to the good feelings of the pupils—that everything like corporeal chastisement would be banished—that the memory and other inferior faculties of the mind would be very little cultivated—while almost exclusive attention would be paid to the development of the reason and other higher powers. Dazzled by these brilliant promises, papa and Ben conceived that all former disappointments were now to be cancelled; and that nothing but the happiest career was opened before the sanguine and ambitious young man. He was one of the earliest candidates for the benefits of this improved and refined system. For a time, everything flowed on smoothly and sweetly in this paradise of academies. The millennium of education seemed to have arrived. The teacher was a man of polished and plausible deportment, and fascinated my brother's imagination and good-will. But before long, Ben discovered that he could make no progress in the classics without a considerable tax on his memory—the declensions and the rules of his Greek and Latin grammars were not always ready on his tongue—and on such occasions his teacher was apt to fret, and assign my brother pretty heavy tasks to commit to memory at home. Those long conversations and processes of reasoning, too, which were to develop the youthful mind, and which were so charming to Ben in the outset, grew at length to be somewhat fatiguing—his attention would too frequently lag, and thus incense his preceptor—and he would sometimes doubt the cogency of his arguments or statements, instead of assenting to them with that beautiful docility which was at first equally agreeable to both teacher and pupil. One day, especially, when all these various grievances had swelled and festered to an outbreaking point, Ben very rudely questioned some position or reasoning of his preceptor. The latter replied indignantly. Ben followed up his insubordination. The teacher, forgetting his own maxim respecting personal chastisement, gave Ben a severe blow, which was immediately retorted by the fiery lad, and a downright engagement between them ensued before the whole school. The consequence was, that my brother appeared at dinner-table that day with black and blue marks on his countenance, and was soon after expelled from the institution.

He was now sent to an academy at the North, where he passed another year. But the previous habits and fortunes of his life had poorly fitted him to sustain the duties of this new situation. With shame and regret, he found himself far behind his companions and equals in age, and knew no other way to obtain the notoriety of which youth in general are so fond, than to launch out into a life of brilliant extravagance and dissipation. This course soon exhausted not only the very liberal allowances transmitted by my father, but also the copious remittances secretly forwarded by my mother; and at the end of a year he was recalled home, with an unsettled character and disposition.

A succession of struggles enabled him to enter a Southern college, and, after many suspensions and fines, bring us home a diploma and a blue riband.

The question now again to be asked is, Where is the remedy for this imperfect education—for evils which so many of both sexes have felt, in common with poor Ben? The most obvious mode that occurs to me is, to convert schools into places for *teaching* instead of *recitation*. As the present plan operates, every parent would willingly change offices with the teacher; that is, if a master would superintend the committing a lesson to memory, with the requisite explanations, the parent would very gladly hear it recited.

Would it not be practicable for masters to teach, and explain, and *see* that a lesson is committed one day, and hear it recited the next? A few parents might complain that the boys and girls were idle at home, merely from habit; but they would soon find their gain in being able to cultivate some *favorite* study, in exercise, &c. I am confident that if Ben had been taught his lessons at school, it would have changed the whole habit of his mind.

How ill suited is a bustling parlor for the studies of children, and how few parents know how to teach!

I do not mean, in these remarks, to say one disrespectful word of teachers. A more conscientious, self-sacrificing, enlightened class of persons than they cannot be found, and they but comply with the customs around them in their present system; but, to justify my remarks, I have only to state, that the evil referred to has reached such a height, that some parents have been under the necessity of *hiring* instructors at night to teach their children the school lessons for the following day. If the system continue as it is, the name of *teacher* should be changed to *lesson-hearer*.

CHAPTER XXIX.

MARION.—DUMB BELLA.—THE INDIAN.—A WEDDING.

"But who is she, retiring and alone,
That makes her thoughts by sign and gesture known?
No voice escapes those lips in accents dear,
'Tis one dead silence all from year to year.
Yet let not pity too officious rise;
Nature compensates that which it denies.
The expressive look—the motion fraught with grace—
May rival language and supply its place:
And for that senseless ear perchance are given
Ethereal sounds, and intercourse with heaven."

S. GILMAN.

Is Marion forgotten? asks some young girl to whom love is the Alpha and Omega of a story. No, not forgotten; but I never proposed to write a love-story in these simple details, whose object is to show the habits of Southern domestic life.

I must confess, however, that an expecting look was cast up the avenue as strangers approached, and a tremor felt when *he* actually came. There was a slight abstraction, too, in his manners, which the students of love-thermometers might have supposed a suspicious circumstance. Whenever he saw me on horseback he looked wistfully, and his face reddened. My dress was entirely different from that in which he had seen me at the time of my *bouleversement;* my height and manner were altered, and I always began to jest on trifling topics, for I was frightened at the thought of a disclosure after what had passed. It seemed to me as if feminine pride called on me to keep my secret, since Anna and Lewis, who alone could have revealed it gracefully, were gone.

Marion was preparing himself for usefulness. Inheriting a large estate, he did not feel authorized to enter on its duties without some personal discipline. He attended medical and surgical lectures, that he might supply with advice the accidental wants of his people; and interested himself in mechanics as a means of saving labor on his plantation. His fine person never looked more noble to me than when in his workman's jacket, with his tools in his hand, he superintended, and even aided, the works of his people. He felt the responsibility of his situation, and looked with a steady and inquiring eye on his duties, removing evil where it was practicable, and ameliorating what was inevitable. It was not gain only that he sought; he was aware that he controlled the happiness of a large family of his fellow-creatures. He neither permitted himself to exercise oppression, nor tolerated it in others. Happy human faces were his delight, and the blessings that followed his footsteps were like angel voices crowning his cares. He felt how much a planter has to answer to man and to God in the patriarchal relation he holds, and he shrank not indolently from the arduous demand. High responsibility exalts the character of a good man, and I could not but perceive the growth of *principle* in Marion's words and actions, while I heard among some of the young men who visited us a tone of frivolity that sadly contrasted with his earnest dignity of thought and expression. I insensibly prized him for this difference, and felt how much safer would be the happiness of a wife in his keeping than in that of a mere idler.

The moral education of Southern youth should be directed to their peculiar duties; indeed, there are passages in the teachings of the New Testament which apply peculiarly to our institutions, and which, though almost negative elsewhere, are exquisitely beautiful in the classification of relative duties here. "Masters, give unto your servants that which is just and equal, knowing that ye also have a master in heaven." "Ye masters, forbear threatening, knowing that your master is also in heaven, neither is there respect of persons with him." "Servants, obey in all things your masters according to the flesh." "Let as many servants as are under the yoke count their own masters worthy of all honor." The temptations of power should be diligently pointed out, passion repressed, purity enforced, and then the young Southerner will rise like the sun over the wide sphere of his duty, diffusing light and warmth around him. As Mentor dwelt with eloquence on the expected legislation of Telemachus, so should every father prepare his son, at the South, for the little kingdom over which he is to reign in wisdom and love.

It would seem, at the first glance, that one of the most difficult offices of the planter would be to restrain the tempers of the uneducated beings under his care; but daily occupation and systematic routine are favorable to harmony, and God has seemed wonderfully to have balanced human passions. There are few Zelucos among fathers. The subject of surprise is, the escape of so many from injury, under the hand of passion, in all communities. Who has not seen a mother of the laboring classes shake a child with her strong arm, until one would suppose dislocation would follow, and the child come out from the operation rather strengthened, as from a Calisthenic exercise? How many shoes, aimed at the head of a culprit, have missed their destination! It is curious to observe how seldom they nit. As far as I have observed, the poorer classes in New-England shake their children in a sudden impulse of anger; while negroes throw something at theirs. There is that which is tremendously exciting in a shake—the chatter of one's teeth, the impotence of one's nerves and sinews, and the trill of the voice as one begs pardon. I would rather, of the two, run my chance of a missile, and take to dodging, if I were a child.

How difficult is it for us, who have time to reason with children, to enter into the feelings of parents hurried by a thousand cares. The poor mother standing at her wash-tub, burning over the fire, or delving at her needle, must be summary in her punishments, and the little rebel takes advantage of her limited minutes. Even the dark closet, the resort of leisurely people, consumes too much time for her; and when she thinks her urchin is well seated on a bench in the corner, to which he has been banished, he has slipped off and gone to some new experiment. The poor soul can neither stay to administer a dose of castor-oil, as one of my friends does, for bad temper, nor apply a cold bath, nor bind a strip of paper on the forehead, with the offence designated, nor condemn the child to the bed all day—an admirable prescription, by-the-way, for those who sleep too late in the morning. These are all punishments of leisure, and the laborer cannot exercise them. Is it not wonderful, then, that, as correction is necessarily so brief, it is not often more calamitous? Scientific discipline has adopted the cat-o'-nine-tails and the ferula, so that the operation can be carried on without maiming; but the poor woman cannot deliberately apply even these. She must take the first tangible thing, and, luckily, the natural implement is her own hand; luckily, too, that very hand relishes not a too potent tingling, or too dislocating a shake, and the child is safe. But while I have been throwing off these rambling thoughts, my little Clarence has been fishing my best cap from a bandbox; and, as he swings it on his hook, his Lilliputian waiting-man follows him, crying,

"Buy fish, missis? buy any fish?" Shall I use my *natural implement* on the rogue?

My personal experience supplies me with but one example of passion leading to fatal consequences in our own neighborhood, but it was a most aggravated case, and related to Bella, the deaf and dumb girl, and to her mother, the Zeluco of my story. I have never seen anything more affecting than Bella's attachment to her infant. It was one of God's holy compensations for infirm human nature; she felt no want with her babe in her arms; and language—oh! the language between these two creatures—the twining of arms, the gaze of the eyes, the pressure of the lips; and, when any attempt was made to take the child from her, how that strange howl thrilled the soul! She was faithful in the discharge of her duties; the family at the Elms treated her with peculiar tenderness, and the child was the pet of the household. But her passions, like those of most mutes, were violent, and her mother, so far from pitying, treated her with brutality. One day when I was visiting at the Elms, we heard a cry wilder than I had ever known from poor Bella. Her mother had attacked her in anger, and levelled a blow with a stick of wood, which laid her and her infant on the ground. In a week that smiling baby was a corpse by Bella's side, and she was fast journeying to the same sad bourn. Even in death she could not let her baby go, and her wild cry sounded fierce and long when any one attempted to remove it. It was laid in its shroud by her side; she felt its little forehead and cold hands, and moaned over its unmoved lips. Poor Bella was tenderly cared for by her mistress, and her pious colored friends stood around her and pointed upward, as if to God. She shook her head, and clung to her dead infant. It was forced from her, and placed in its humble coffin and peaceful grave, and two days after Bella was laid by its side. It is a sad, though humble story. I have long since laid it to my heart; and when passion has threatened to shake me in my intercourse with those around me, the image of that wrathful mother, though comparatively irresponsible, has arisen to my view, darkly pointing at Bella's grave.

Little that was interesting occurred at this time at Roseland; but one incident may show a feature of our life. We shall not long have such to record, for the Indian race, like the noble trees of our forests, are disappearing—the axe is laid at their roots. As I was playing the piano one morning, I heard a light footstep; and, turning round, saw an Indian in full costume, standing, with folded arms, against the entrance of the door, his eyes bent directly on me. I was so startled that I could not proceed in singing. I made two or three ineffectual attempts, and then preferred passing out of the room close to him rather than remain. As I rose from the instrument his eyes followed me, though his attitude was unchanged, and he made a gesture for me to return and play. I went to mamma, who decided that I must do so. She, like most Southern ladies, had no unnecessary fears. She was in the habit of passing months with her children on the plantation, without any other protection than her servants. The Indian had remained in the same erect attitude, as if he expected our return; and, as mamma bowed in passing, he returned her salutation. I sat down and played several tunes, glancing occasionally at him; his eyes were still fixed on me. At length, as I passed, he uttered a sound like "*thank*," and retired as silently as he came. I have never since seen so perfect and interesting a specimen of his race. There was something inexpressibly lofty and graceful in his air.

On our next visit to the city, Flora asked me, with almost apparent blushes, "if she could take a partner;" and I was made to understand that Kit, a stevedore, had solicited her hand. Of course I could make no objection, though losing some valuable services by the plan; and preparations were made for the wedding, which she chose to have performed in the wash-kitchen instead of our parlor. The floor was nicely scrubbed, seats placed around, and the tin candlesticks on the wall ornamented with sprigs of green. When all was ready we were invited out with the clergyman, who, as usual, was chosen by the bride. The room was lined with guests. As we entered the bride and groom rose, attended by six groomsmen and six bridemaids, the latter dressed in white, with flowers, riband, or tarnished silver and gold sprigs in their hair. The minister proceeded in the ceremony, and at length told them to join their right hands. The handmaidens were pretty expert in drawing off Flora's glove, as her hands were soft as mine; but Kit was the very image of helplessness. He looked as if he longed to give the glove (it was clinging white cotton) a pull, but etiquette forbade. His arm was extended, and his palm open, in a kind of spasmodic motion, as the head groomsman tugged at the forefinger. By degrees his aids came up, until there was one at each digit, while a sixth directed; but, the more they pulled, the more the glove "would not stay pulled." The bridemaids began to titter, and Flora, losing her patience, said, "Pull it off yourself, Kit;" but the superintendent of the ceremony waved her off solemnly, and, after picking a while upon the thumb and fingers, the tenacious glove yielded, and by "a long pull, a strong pull, and a pull altogether," Kit's brawny hand was laid bare, and grasped that of the more delicate Flora. The ceremony proceeded without further impediment, and, shaking hands with the bride, we returned to the house. As we left the threshold of the wash-room, the whole party shouted forth a Methodist hymn. It was a solemn and affecting sound, and I felt it to be a rebuke to the vapid jests that so often circulate after more imposing ceremonials. Wine and cake were sent us immediately after, and a whole iced cake presented to the minister the following day, according to the usual custom among the colored people in the city. Mamma and I were introduced to the bride's chamber, which was neatly set off with white curtains and toilet cover. I have sometimes seen the apartments of colored brides decorated with evergreens.

CHAPTER XXX.

THE DEER HUNT.

"Hark! from yon covert where those towering oaks
Above the humble copse aspiring rise,
What glorious triumphs burst in every gale
Upon our ravish'd ears! The hunters shout,
The clanging horns swell their sweet winding notes.
The pack wide opening load the trembling air
With various melody; from tree to tree
The propagated cry redoubling bounds,
And wing'd zephyrs waft the floating joy
Through all the regions near!"

The Chase.

WINTER in Carolina comes with no stern aspect; she loves the merry dance by the lightwood knots thrown on the spacious hearth, and sunny nature woos us from without, where flowers scarcely blighted and the huntsman's horn are kindly substitutes for glittering frostwork and noisy sleigh-bells. Often, in childhood, when I had heard the stir and preparation for the chase, I had longed to take a part; and when, on a bright winter morning, I saw parties move off, I was almost tempted to spring on my own good steed, and follow through the avenue. As I advanced in years, and felt perfect confidence in my own skill in horsemanship, I frequently urged papa to allow me to accompany him; but he objected on the score of the dangerous character of our woods for one in female attire on horseback. In the holydays of this season, Bell Wilson (who, by-the-way, had attained the rare accomplishment of being able to discharge a fowling-piece) and I rallied our forces for a last attack, and one evening, seconded by my brothers and Marion, we succeeded in obtaining an unwilling consent from papa to accompany his party the following day.

Jim, who was, in his way, the soul of the hunting enterprises at Roseland, awoke us early, and we soon heard papa's horn on the piazza, the notes of which were answered by the joyful tongues of the beagles, and by the horns of the neighboring sportsmen.

We ran down to breakfast, scarcely able to eat from the excitement of the scene, as my brothers and our friends came in equipped for the hunt. The usual dress of a hunter is composed of a cap, a frockcoat, reaching half-way between the hips and the knees, with breast-pockets for carrying ammunition, &c., boots, spurs, and blowing-horn. This last appendage is suspended from the right shoulder, the horn itself hanging under the left arm. But dress is altogether a matter of fancy, and comical indeed are some of the figures which sally forth to enjoy the sport of the woods.

The first person who entered was our neighbor, Mr. Plumer, an eccentric but intelligent man, tall, excessively thin, and sharp-visaged, his spare legs being inserted in military boots to protect him from the mud of the swamps. He addressed us with his usual joke of,

"Good morning, young ladies. You see I prefer hunting a *deer* to hunting a *dear*. Ha—ha—ha!"

Next came Mr. Prentiss, a real townsman, with spatterdashes, his hat on one side of his head, a fresh cravat, and his white shirt-cuffs in full sight over his Limerick gloves. Then followed Dick Bradford, his broadcloth leggins fastened from the ankle to the knee with gilt buttons, accompanied by Captain Rogerson, with woollen ones tied above the knee and around the ankle with flannel list. Marion and my brothers wore their usual plantation dress, with hunting-coat and cap. They threw a horn round Bell's neck and mine, exacting the promise that we should not use them.

Mr. Plumer, whistling to his dogs, and blowing his horn, gallopped off to secure the best stand. Papa followed, attended by Jim calling his hounds, and sounding his horn, to announce to the sportsmen that he was under way. The gentlemen followed, leaving Bell and me with Richard and Marion.

Collected at the ground the hunt was arranged. Mr. Plumer, counting our forces, exclaimed,

" Let me see, six of us without Marion and Richard, who are ladies' men—very good—very good; more than that mars the sport—mars the sport. They must mind the *dears*, while we hunt the *deers*, ha—ha—ha!"

The *boys** were directed how to *drive*. They were to commence by driving the swamp, the gentlemen and ourselves taking up our stand at the head of the swamp, while they were to put in below, and drive through to us. If the dogs started and ran back, the boys were to stop them; but if they ran to the head of the swamp, they were to scream behind them, and force the deer out to the standers. We accordingly proceeded to the head of the swamp, and took our stands every one at his post. The boys then commenced driving by whooping and riding about in the swamp, every now and then speaking to and encouraging the dogs. It was wonderful to me to see the sympathy of the hounds, their diligence and docility. After driving about for some time, Bounce, a cold-nose dog, struck a trail, while the boys encouraged him, rode to him, brushed through the briers and bushes, occasionally shouting and clapping their hands to stimulate the industrious animal. After working cold

* Common epithet for negro men.

scent awhile, Bounce was joined by Diamond, Ringwood, Music, Dash, Killbuck, Rock, Luna, and Trimbush, who alternately dropped in, working the trail of an old buck into the drive. And now a chorus of music burst forth from the anxious pack, which momentarily expected the jump of the deer, while the boys continued encouraging and urging them on.

Presently up bounced the old buck, the dogs burst forth into full cry, the boys shouting "Mind, mind ahead!" to apprize the sportsmen that the deer was up and coming. The hunters then, every man at his stand, drew themselves up to a point behind some large tree or bush, waiting with breathless anxiety the approach of the deer. The dogs came bearing down to us, roaring it in the swamp, giving their tongues at every jump. Presently the old buck broke cover, and came dashing by John with the speed of lightning. My heart leaped to my mouth. John sprang forward, raised his gun, took his aim, and blazed away both barrels one after the other. The old buck faltered a moment, but kept his course. My sympathies were stirred for the noble animal, and, as I saw him bound on, I uttered a shout of joy. The dogs came dashing after in full cry, and were with difficulty stopped by John, who blew his horn and collected the party; each man came galloping up to the post with the eager questions,

"Is he shot? What have you done?"

"I don't know," said John; "I think I hit him. I am sure I saw him flounder at my last barrel; let us look for blood. Give me time to reload, and if there is blood we will hustle him."

By this time Jim, who came first after the dogs, had dismounted, and was walking on the track of the deer looking for blood.

"Here blood, Maus John, for true," said Jim, dashing away

the brushwood, and grinning from ear to ear; "but he an't too much."*

John having reloaded, the boys were ordered to stick close to the dogs, and if they jumped the buck, to catch him, knowing that, if badly wounded, he would not run far before lying down. The hunters then screamed to the hounds, who broke off in full cry, while we followed in the chase. I strained my sight onward, and again my sympathetic joy was roused as the deer once more, apparently unhurt, disappeared in the swamp. Our broken forces were now rearranged. Marion, Richard, Bell, and I were stationed in a cross-road leading from the swamp, where the boys, having galloped round, had again commenced driving. Mr. Plumer was at the next stand higher up the road, the others nearer the swamp, but all in sight of each other. We had not waited long when we heard once more the hounds bearing down in full cry directly towards our stand.

"What music! what music!" cried Marion, in raptures, as the pack set up a renewed yell.

I could not but smile as I remembered the remark of a city gentleman, who once said, "Where is the music? I hear nothing but the barking of dogs." The deer continued to approach, and now we heard the crackling of the bushes, and now the fine creature sprang in sight; but as he came within gunshot of John, he turned and took the direction of the stand at which Mr. Prentiss was stationed, when lo, quick as thought, we saw him on the other side of Mr. Plumer, having escaped the shots, and come out considerably beyond the road.

"On," shouted Marion to the hunters; "if the old buck gets to the creek we lose him."

Mr. Plumer had already dashed on, as if for life, and we followed up the road. The hounds then came out in the distance,

* This in negro dialect means *there is very little.*

followed by the drivers in a complete Gilpin race, whooping and screaming; two were on mules, the rest on horses. One had dropped his red cap, another his venison-bag.

"There goes Jim's luncheon," said Richard, as something else was seen to fall; "that fellow never stirs without his hoecake."

"Young ladies," exclaimed Marion, whose whole soul yearned for the chase, though comparatively restrained by our presence, "you must canter briskly, or we shall lose the sport." And as he said this, Richard and Bell turned into a cross-road.

Unfortunately, as I loosed my rein, I touched the horse with my whip. I had been warned that he was an old hunter, but forgot it, until he sprang forward and left everything behind. I had sufficient presence of mind to guide him aright, and, obedient to the rein, he kept the road. The sound of approaching hoofs made him quicken his speed; he appeared to fly, and I became giddy with the wild dread of consequences; but Marion was soon by my side, seizing the bridle, panting, and crying,

"Hold fast, Miss Wilton, hold fast! We will stop gradually. I knew my horse had the speed of yours. Be firm, be firm."

We rode on at a furious rate some short distance before he succeeded in stopping the excited animal. When this was effected, he assisted me to dismount, and exchanged his gentler though spirited steed for mine. In the midst of this little transaction I perceived that the sport was forgotten. His eye was bent on me with such an air of perplexed attention that, blushing and agitated, I shrank from his gaze. He glanced at the ring on his finger, then again at me; some associations seemed rushing through his mind, and lent a melting brightness to the half smile that played upon his lips, while I, with the most awkward consciousness, urged on my palfrey. He seized the bridle.

"Stop, Miss Wilton," he exclaimed eagerly. "One word before you go. It must be so. I feel an intuition of the truth. Withdraw not your hand until I try this precious ring on your finger. Oh, stay, dearest Cornelia," he continued, as, conscious and embarrassed, I hesitated for a reply. My hand was in his, the ring sparkled in the sun; but before he could measure its little circlet Richard and Bell rode up briskly, calling out,

"The deer has been turned, we hear the dogs coming this way."

"Oh, let him go, pray, let him go," I exclaimed; "he has won his life. I cannot bear to have him killed."

"Perhaps he will turn to the river," said Bell; "it is on our way, and we will see him foil these mighty Nimrods."

We cantered on, the dogs apparently not far distant. On turning into the public road we beheld the deer coming directly towards us. Marion and Richard reined up, and raised their guns, but Bell and I screamed, "Don't shoot, for mercy's sake, don't shoot!" and they reluctantly lowered them. The deer, thus pressed by ourselves in front and by the hunters and dogs in pursuit, stood still, looked about him, and seemed to hesitate for an instant. How beautiful, how majestic his appearance in that attitude of reflection! Turning suddenly, he bounded over the fence into papa's oakery, and, quick as thought, made his way towards the river. Baffled in their aim, the hunters swept round to endeavor to arrest him at the lower entrance, while we quickly entered a private and shorter access. Crossing a field to the yard and garden, we reached the river's edge, which bordered it, just as the deer, swimming for life, was making his way across the current. The dogs rushed on, the hunters firing ineffectual shots in the distance, while Bell and I, beneath a sycamore, waved our handkerchiefs in triumph, and shouted our congratulations as the noble animal sprang, apparently unhurt, from the water, and was lost in the thickets on the opposite bank.

"Not scathed, by George," said papa: "not grazed by a single shot; he has won his life nobly!"

"Look at Diamond and Trimbush," cried mamma, running from the house down the garden-path, in an agony of trepidation, as the dogs came back, wet and whimpering, from their ineffectual chase; "they are trampling my carnations, and Luna is making a bed of the wall-flowers."

Our attention was drawn away by Jim, who advanced with the boys, and whose appearance, now that the excitement was over, made us shout with laughter. He was half as large again as usual, with white cotton oozing out of divers apertures in his dress, and the tail of his fox-skin cap flapping up and down as he rehearsed with various gesticulations, to his companions, his share of the adventures.

"Jim," exclaimed Richard, "what a figure you cut."

"No cut 'em, Maus Dick, only stuff 'em," said Jim, looking complacently on his strange attire, while, taking off his fox-skin cap with the pendant-tail, he scraped his foot to the company. "You see, maussa, you see, sir, de brier bery bad, and I jist been put one nudder breeches on top o' tudder, tie him tight at he foot, and stuff 'tween em wid cotton; den de brier just lick de breeches, and an't hut me none at all."

Our shouts were scarcely over at Jim's statement, before Mr. Plumer came up, and, knocking his muddy military boots against his gun, said to me, "Ha, my dear, we've paid *dear* for the *deer*, ha—ha—ha!"

CHAPTER XXXI.

AN ERROR IN JUDGMENT.

"Sleep like a lover woo thee,
Isabel!
And golden dreams come to thee
Like a spell."—N. P. WILLIS.

"If thou remember'st not the slightest folly
That ever love did make thee run into,
Thou hast not loved."—*Midsummer Night's Dream.*

MARION had no opportunity for private conversation with me on the evening of the hunt, but the excitement of his feelings was obvious enough to the coolest eye. I saw his gaze following me as I moved; his very silence, too, was a language until, on departing, he whispered the hope that I might permit him to see me the morning following. Shall I describe my night of tumultuous waking thoughts and busy dreams? What young heart has not thus throbbed as the life-decision hovered near, when it could count the hours before the time which must decide its future destiny? How hope colors up that destiny until not a shade is left on its kindled horizon! Amid the glow of feeling on that night, Duncan rose to my memory. I fancied I could see the sweet approving smile which had sometimes followed my girlish efforts in duty; again I lingered in thought on his last looks and words, calling up his rich monitions, his practical excellence, and realizing anew, in my love of virtue, the touching truth that good seeds are not planted in vain in the young heart, but spring up vigorous and beautiful in after years. Mingled with these thoughts came the sad, pale form of my Anna and her lost Lewis; and though my tears had long since ceased to flow for them, they were still pictured to me as dim stars struggling with tempestuous clouds. Amid these thoughts I laid my head on my pillow, and soon a brighter image rose, and Marion's form, the model of manly beauty, was before me, and his eyes, with their soft sunshine, beamed on me, and his voice uttered its words of "truth and soberness," and my heart seemed like a song in its lightness, and all pleasant things were before me; I knew that I loved, I felt that I was beloved again, and so I slept.

How rich and bright was that following morning!—there was gladness in everything. The birds fancied that young spring had come; and, as one of our native poets has beautifully sung,

"In russet coat
Most homely, like true genius bursting forth
In spite of adverse fortune, a full choir
Within himself, the merry mock-bird sate,
Filling the air with melody—and, at times,
In the rapt fervor of his sweetest song,
His quivering form up-sprang into the sky
In spiral circles, as if he would catch
New powers from kindred warblers in the clouds."

The sun lay in a yellow glow on the earth, where a few blades still struggled with wintry frosts, while the roses, crisp and mottled like a bright girl's winter-cheek, sparkled in the dew. And the toilet of that morning, why was it so agitated and yet so lingering? Why did my half-combed hair hang in its waves, while I, forgetful of its braids, looked out on sky and field, and knew not that I looked? Why did I clasp my hands upon my heart as if to soothe its tumult, and yet garner up thoughts that set its full tide flowing? Why did the riband that Marion had praised seem like a relic, while the sigh that rose over a faded flower which he had given me was as warm as the devotee's in her most rapt devotion? Oh, gentle genius of youthful love, floating in clouds of light and beauty around the trusting heart, thou canst tell!

Let me receive all praise that I committed none of the alleged crimes of lovers at the breakfast-table. No spilled coffee can be laid to my charge. I did not put butter instead of sugar into papa's tea, or say yes, madam, when I should have said no, sir. Having a little of the pride of good sense, I did not depart from social usefulness, but assisted mamma in washing the cups, brushed papa's hat, arranged the flowers, and went through my little routine of household duty without a mistake. At length, all was done. Papa and my brothers went out on their various errands, mamma walked to the river-side to her dairy, and I was left alone. Then I began to feel an unwonted tremor. I could not read or sew; I shrank from walking in the piazza, because there I should first see Marion; I would not go into the garden, because it would look like avoiding him. A sudden thought struck me. With a mixed feeling of frolic and agitation I ordered my horse to be saddled, and ran up stairs to a remote closet, where my riding-dress and hat had been banished after my fall in the ditch. There they were—the same splashes of mud on the habit, the same dangling black feathers, the same crushed wire and stiff veil. Dressing quickly, I rang for Jim, whom I made partially my confidant. All Jim's politeness could not prevent him from laughing out at the appearance I exhibited.

"Ki!" shouted he; "Miss Neely look more worser dan she did when she tumble head over heel. De jacket too leetle, and de sleeve an't fetch to de wrist. Miss Neely been scare de crow!"

I asked Jim if he was certain that Mr. Marion always took the private path across the fields fron our avenue; and having ascertained this fact, I threw a large shawl over my shoulders, put a fresh veil above the soiled one, mounted my horse, and, followed by Jim, with a beating heart cantered down the avenue.

Jim was very eloquent respecting the events of the day previous, but I scarcely heard his details; and when I had fairly reached the cross-road my mind misgave me.

He will think me forward and bold, thought I, to come and meet him thus; there is something too farcical in this attire, ill-suited to maiden modesty. And thinking thus, my whole heart began to sink within me at the bare idea of forfeiting his esteem by indelicacy.

"I must turn back, Jim," said I, hastily; "I feel faint, and must go home."

"Wha fo you been go, Miss Neely?" said he. "See Maus Marion be here. He'm jis been tak de short cut round de corner. You no be want for shee um?" And he showed all his teeth in laughing as he surveyed my dress again.

"Not for the world, Jim," cried I, "would I have him see me. I shall die if he does," I continued, in uncontrolled agitation—and turning my horse, I urged him to a gallop.

If I can only get home one minute before him, thought I, and change my dress. And I screamed, "Go on, Jim, and open both the gates. Quick! quick! I am frightened, I am ill! Oh, what a fool he will think me!"

Jim, frightened himself at my violence, readily obeyed.

But the same good steed with which Marion once before overtook me was speeding on. My head snapped, my face was in a blaze, and, as if to complete my trials, the shawl and veil which I had put on loosely in order to remove them quickly, caught in the bushes. I sprang from the horse and let him pass on, hoping that Marion might pursue him while I hid in the shrubbery near by; alas, he had seen me; with the speed of lightning he approached and dismounted, and I, foolish girl that I was, hid my face upon a stump of a tree that was near, and burst into tears.

"Good heavens!" exclaimed Marion; "what can this mean?"

I could not answer, and I was ashamed to look up. He scarcely knew what to do—at length he said, in a low voice,

"This is a singular vision! Can it be Miss Wilton?"

"Yes," said I, sobbing. "Oh, it is so silly! I am so ashamed!"

In a moment he was by my side, and kneeling there, he laid aside my bonnet, and wiped away my tears, and I did not forbid him.

"Fear not to weep before me, dearest," he said. "It is the privilege of love to wipe tears—smiles are for the crowd; but you have no need of tears, Cornelia; I would rather see this" (and he took my soiled hat from the ground and kissed it reverently) "than the tiara of a princess."

My hand lay in his; he gently transferred the cherished ring to my finger, and pressed his lips one moment on its glittering surface. There was no need of explanation; heart whispered to heart its own story, and so thought Jim; for, galloping back with my horse, he put his head among the bushes, and seeing the posture of affairs, tied him to a tree, and rode quietly away.

CHAPTER XXXII.

A DEPARTURE AND AN INTRODUCTION.

> " A mother's love !—oh ! thou knowest not how much of feeling lies
> In those sweet words ; the hopes, the fears, the daily strengthening ties ;
> It lives ere yet the infant draws its earliest vital breath,
> And dies but when the mother's heart chills in the grasp of death."
>
> EMMA C. EMBURY.

> " Mother, whatever griefs may fret,
> Cares entangle, sins beset
> This thy daughter, and with tears
> Stain her cheek in future years,
> Heavenly succor, not denied
> To the babe, whate'er betide,
> Will to the woman be supplied."
>
> WORDSWORTH.

MUCH has been said of the manœuvring of mothers to obtain settlements for their daughters ; but the class is infinitely larger of those parents who feel as if their girls were still in childhood, and who wake up as if from a dream, on finding that the beings who have lain in their bosoms, and walked the path of opening life, and surrounded the household hearth, and been close as the very air they breathed, are suddenly wrenched from them by a stronger tie, the love of years torn up by the very roots, and transplanted to a stranger's heart.

Such was the shock that mamma received in her tranquil routine of duty. The possibility of my belonging to another was like an earthquake to her. I had been cherished like a tree of her own planting, beneath which she was to repose; it was strange to her that other hands should gather its blossoms and fruits. My dear mother! she took me to her arms and wept—she to whom tears were so rare! All that day she drooped in her duties; her brow was thoughtful; she sighed often, and seemed like one struggling with a burden. But Marion soon reconciled her to love's destiny by tender assiduities, and she felt that she had gained a son in the partial loss of a daughter.

Papa was equally astonished at a result which might have been foreseen with much less acuteness than he possessed; but the effect on him was to produce a volley of jokes, that sent the blood rushing to my cheeks, and disconcerted Marion, upon whose plate, at dinner, mamma, in compensatory kindness, piled a mass of food like a Grecian hecatomb. Was it wonderful that Marion should gain my consent to escape from this notoriety to a secluded *tête-à-tête* on the evening of that eventful day, where, unobserved, the "course of our true love" might be traced from its first slight fountain of preference?

"My mother must see you, Cornelia," said he. "I feel like a miser until I have revealed my treasure to her, and Ellen too, and my father. I thank Heaven, dearest, that you will be appreciated in my home!"

So an early day was appointed for a visit to Winnapee, Mr. Marion's plantation, situated in one of the eastern parishes.

We left Roseland in a row-boat for the city, where a carriage was to meet us on the following morning, to conduct us on our remaining way. The followers of Columbus would have been glad of the provisions with which mamma supplied us for this half-day's excursion. I cannot say much for the animation of our party, notwithstanding Richard and John were with us. A first love, a new joy, are serious; and a tender and solemn moral seems to spring from this peculiarity of the human temperament. What philosophy would ever portray happiness with laughing eyes and dancing movements? Beautiful happiness! I own, a smile is on her lip, but it is like the lining of a sable cloud; her eyes are bright, but they look forward to hope or back on memory still; she shuts up her bosom's thoughts, with a presentiment that they may fly if the door of their cage is loosed; her foot treads carefully on the flowers at her feet, lest she should crush them; over those very flowers a tear sometimes glances (for happiness has tears), and their petals heave in the throbs of the heart, near which they are enshrined.

Alas for those who are condemned to a companionship with lovers! John and Richard talked over their hunting experiences, discussed all the characters in the parish, predicted the crops, sang snatches of tunes, partook of mamma's dainties, and yawned. As for me, I saw a transparency in the waters that pictured the wintry boughs along the shore, lending them a charm unseen before; I saw a purer blue in the sunny sky, and the white clouds that were reflected in the river were like rich pillows for reposing angels; the couching birds, that sprang up at the dash of the oars, seemed painted with new colors, and their flight was airy as if they followed the bidding of a loved one; the oarsman's stroke dwelt on the silent air like music; there was harmony in the crackling bushes, when, as we neared the shore, some startled animal bounded away, and all nature was to me like an infolding mantle of love and tenderness.

I had often before this day been sheltered from the winter breeze by some kind hand; my cloak had been wrapped around me with equal care, and others had sought my eyes to know their faintest wishes. Why, then, was all thus bright and fresh to my vision? What made the circumstance still more unaccountable was, that John and Richard wrapped themselves in their boat-cloaks and fell asleep.

A shower came on before we reached town, but even this was not altogether to be deprecated. There were so many opportunities to show a kind, considerate attention, and to make one feel as if one was all the world to a loving heart!

On the following morning we proceeded in Mr. Marion's carriage. Vegetation on the Cooper river varies from that on the Ashley. Instead of wooded banks, long tracts of land are devoted to rice-culture. In the winter these appear dreary enough, except to the planter, who sees a promise hidden to common eyes, and to the sportsman, who detects game in ditches and on banks. At some seasons of the year, those immense fields are very attractive. More extended than the domains of many a feudal baron, arranged with almost military order and neatness, in spring the rich green of the rice-blades lies, as far as the eye can reach, in velvet softness, while in autumn its golden grains wave to the winds beneath the untiring sunshine.

My brothers were on horseback. There is something very animating in this style of companionship: the sudden gallop by the side of the carriage, to tell a joke or make a remark on the scenery; the picturesque air of the riders, as they recede from sight or check their spirited steeds to be overtaken; the conscious air of a horseman, as he wields the bridle and makes a graceful curvet—these things give life and spirit to a country drive; and my brothers, glad to be relieved from the monotony of the boat, added to the interest by the glee of unobserved retirement. The inclemency of the previous day was followed by a mild and balmy atmosphere, which, in some moods of physical temperament, sends a revery over the soul. Marion and I glanced from subject to subject, testing our new sympathies; mused upon unexpressed thoughts, gazed together upon the woods, or traced the Etiwan* through their openings. How

* Indian name for Cooper river.

happy is that intercourse where no *obligation* is felt to converse; where the heart breaks forth from the lips in unfettered exclamations of joy and tenderness, then sinks back to realize its joy, and fosters its tenderness in silence, and looks again to nature for sympathy!

The buds of a mild February (which belongs to a Southern spring) were struggling with the stiffened leaves of winter, which the frost had tinged, but not severed from their branches; the soft gray of the floating moss prevailed in its hue over the yet sheathed foliage, and a misty atmosphere, shading down the sunbeams, suited well this sober livery of nature; the scanty foliage revealed the squirrel and the red-bird, as they sprang from branch to branch; the Etiwan, playing like a truant child, wound brightly in eccentric turns, so abruptly, that the shores often looked like clustering islands; the broad rice-fields lay ready for the genial moment when the planter should sow his grain, and their trimmed banks spoke of agricultural care; the crows clustered in the old oaks with their social cawings; the blackbird chattered near, and then, startled by our approach, swept off like a light cloud on the heavens; now a solitary crane on the marshes stretched up its long neck to listen, and then, with flapping wings, soared away; while the small gray sparrow, with tripping steps, and irregular flight, ascended and descended on the plains.

The course of our journey brought us to a ferry. There is something infinitely more romantic in crossing a ferry than in rumbling over a bridge at full speed; and, whatever utilitarians may say, I cannot but enjoy the loitering half-hour when the negroes, with lazy movement, ply the oar, while the lumbering boat, yielding to the current, like a good manœuvrer, but to obtain the mastery, nears the shore. Yes; let us lovers of leisure gaze up and down our placid streams, in thoughts perchance listless, perchance wise, soothed by the plash of the oar or the ripple of the wave—and who knows but we shall gain as much in the end as they who glide over space like lightning, and before whom objects appear as the shadow of a flying bird in the sunshine.

Feeling the necessity of refreshment, we alighted for a while beneath a tree by the roadside, for a *maroon.* While the men-servants spread a table-cloth on the ground, Flora withdrew from their concealment mamma's cold fowl and ham, and the gentlemen laid their cloaks for seats. We were soon, despite of sentiment, reclining on them, with good appetites and merry faces; the dogs wheeled round us in antic gambols, or looked, with eager eyes, at the morsels we threw them; the birds hopped almost to where we sat; the stealthy squirrel peeped as he climbed the neighboring tree, and the changing lizard ran on the old Virginia fence unscared.

The merry meal was over, and we resumed our drive. There are few girls, however self-possessed they may be, who are not somewhat abashed, under circumstances like mine, with the expected introduction to strangers; but I had prepared myself for the occasion. As we approached the residence of Arthur's parents, a glance told me that there was a study of elegance and form in its proprietors. I sat unconsciously more erect when the gray-headed, liveried porter, with a subdued welcome, and a bow which would not have dishonored Sir Charles Grandison, held the gate for us to pass through to the court. I thought, for the first time, how often I had seen Jim, in an old jacket, displace the regular servant, and saunter or rush to the gate to admit visitors, perhaps attended by three or four dirty little urchins, while the harangue which he gave them on manners drew but the more attention to their dishabille. I remembered how his unceremonious box on their ears had sent them off roaring with a noise quite disproportioned to their pain, and I resolved, on my return, to reform abuses, and to restore the régime of my grandmamma, who had been a great lover of form, and who used to say that the affections were never crushed by being clothed in good manners, and that respect for others produced self-respect.

I was soon folded in the arms of Arthur's family. If anything, the embrace was too soft and measured; too much like the porter's bow, the gravelled walk, the trimmed shrubbery; but I afterward found, as grandmamma had said, that this polish crushed no actual warmth of the heart.

I retired quickly to dress for dinner, and found that Flora had unfolded a new frock which I had taken from the mantua-maker in the city. I perceived that it was too showy for the occasion; but it was too late to look for another, and, to add to my troubles, it did not fit; Flora's strength and skill were called in requisition to make it meet, and she at length succeeded. Fluttered and vexed, I heard the summons to dinner, and, pulling on a pair of new gloves, descended to the drawing-room, where Ellen Marion was seated in the most simple and elegant repose. I am sure of the sympathy of my female readers, who, whatever may be their station in society, have, I doubt not, been over-dressed at least once in their lives. Who can forget the first pang at the suspicion of the fact; the furtive glance around the company, to ascertain some companionship in finery; the earnest gaze at every new-comer, in hope that some extra ribbon or lace may be displayed; and then the settling down into the conviction that one is altogether *out of taste*, while the blush that began on the cheek spreads and deepens, till the forehead glows and the fingers tingle?

Arthur's father waited on me to the dining-room (I used to hate these *handings-in* when I was a girl), and seated me with my back to a blazing fire. My gloves were not yet fairly on, but looked like extra joints at every finger, and my silk rustled like a patch of corn-broom in a breeze ; I felt as if I were all gloves and silk ; and longed for our home voices to break in on the soft and measured cadence of the Marions. I allowed myself to be helped to everything I did not like, and, to complete my despair, tipped my well-filled plate into my lap, where I had neglected to lay a napkin, and was obliged to have it spooned up from my new silk. So much for first impressions on my lover's relations, and so much for my late boast of self-possession !

CHAPTER XXXIII.

THE RETURN.

"He raised his veil—the maid turned slowly round—
Looked at him—shriek'd—and sunk upon the ground."
MOORE'S *Veiled Prophet of Khorassan.*

A CHANGE of dress, and the delicate attentions of the Marions, soon restored my self-possession; and the reaction produced in me a degree of vivacity that awoke to unaccustomed tones the Chesterfieldian echoes of Winnapee. A few delicious days with Ellen supplied to me again poor Anna's loss. How quickly young thoughts leap to each other! We talked the long nights almost through; topics growing as we lifted the veils of our hearts, and revealed their fresh hopes and memories. We had marked the same passages in books; we preferred the same songs; we walked the piazza with interlacing arms, loving the same glow and the same shade. It was sweet to lavish on Ellen the treasures of tenderness I dared not bestow on Arthur; to look on her as his softened image, while I turned my eyes from him, and to hear her unwearied praises of his goodness and beauty, each imparting a glory to the other.

"I shall call you my *own* sister, soon," said Ellen, with a whisper that sent a blush of joy to my cheeks, as with embraces, such as dear friends give, we parted.

On reaching the close of our journey, we observed a field adjoining our avenue on fire; this common and necessary occurrence in agriculture at the South did not surprise us; but, on entering the avenue, we were startled and terrified at finding the Cherokee rose-hedge, which in winter is very combustible, in flames. I have mentioned this hedge, I think, before. Nothing in nature could exceed its beauty when in bloom in the month of April. For three miles the long feelers of the vine lifted themselves up or athwart, from five to six feet in height and breadth; and the eye knew not whether most to admire the glossy green of the leaves, or the white blossoms which reposed on them like wreaths of snow. Here and there its long arms reached to a neighboring tree, and seemed to revel while enfolding it. Everywhere they stretched themselves out like living things, waving to catch support in their luxuriance. Amid this sheet of white, the accustomed sight could detect the lingering blossoms of the yellow jasmine, the opening scarlet woodbine, struggling with its fair but overpowering rival, while the shrub honeysuckle threw out its perfume beneath, amid the lower foliage.

The piercing thorn of the Cherokee rose renders it impenetrable by cattle; but it harbors reptiles; and being somewhat unmanageable in its growth, is not a favorite with the planter. No mere feeling of utility, however, would induce papa to displace his, while it extorted a burst of admiration from every beholder. Through an unpardonable carelessness in the negroes, they had not guarded it from the flames at the two extremities, where it had caught, and was raging furiously; thus shutting them out from all hope of escape, except through the hedge, which, in many parts, was totally inaccessible. We heard their cries for help without the power to aid them. Fortunately for us, our plantation adjoined another, the avenue of which ran parallel with our own; the hedge on the left had not yet thoroughly caught; a slight embankment separated the two, with ditches between, and the wind blew onward, not across the road, thus giving us comparative security in proceeding. Arthur himself, taking the reins, struck at once into this avenue and drove at full speed. The wind increased, while the crackling and roaring sound, the flying cinders, and the growing heat, gave us a new motive for flight. The hope of escaping the flames was soon more faint, for Frank, the coachman, cried out, "Fire ahead, maussa!" Marion checked the horses; it was true, the flames were about to meet on the right-hand hedge of papa's avenue; still the left was but partially ignited, and the current of air continued to blow from the path we had taken. In the momentary pause of deliberation, we heard a shriek from the enclosure on the right. Merciful Heaven! it was Binah's voice, raised to a yell of horror, crying—

"Help, help, God Almighty! help Binah, for Christ's sake! Help little Miss Patsey! We guine for burn up; help, help!"

Arthur hesitated not a moment, but I saw that he turned deadly pale.

"You can remain here a few minutes in safety," said he; "the wind still favors us. I will soon return." And scarcely allowing himself a look at me, he threw Frank's cloak over his head as a protection against the briers, leaped the ditch, ascended the bank, with his strong arm forced a passage through the hedge, and disappeared.

I scarcely remember what next occurred; but a frantic violence took possession of me, and I would have followed but for Frank's restraining arm. I watched the flakes that rose and sailed off in the distance, or caught some neighboring tree. I saw the young trees fall, and the flames curl round the old; the sound seemed like the hissing of serpents' tongues in mockery, and I chattered and mocked at them in return. Those moments seemed to concentrate ages of feeling. At length I heard a voice, Arthur's voice, calling for aid, but so strange and unnatural! Frank had been industrious in making a clearance through the hedge, whose top began to burn in various directions. We climbed the bank, sprang through and found him. He had rescued Patsey, and protécted her with Frank's cloak; Binah had clung to him as long as life lasted; but there she lay, a withered corpse, while he staggered forward and fell. I took Patsey in my arms; the frightened child clung sobbing to my neck, while Frank bore Arthur to the carriage. The flames were now around us, but love and fear gave us power. Frank drove furiously. Poor Arthur spoke not; blackened by the smoke, and torn with briers, he lay helpless across the seats. We were near home, but the seconds seemed hours. I could not caress my poor little Patsey, who pressed her cheek to my bosom in silence, and trembled like an aspen leaf. The rushing smoke stifled, the heated air oppressed me; and the silence was only interrupted by Arthur's groans. On entering the court I made one more effort to arouse the sufferer.

"Speak to me, Arthur," I said; "one word, only one," but his parched lips attempted utterance in vain.

On our arrival he was carried to bed, and medical aid called; mamma, in the meantime, prescribing for him, and allowing me to sit by his side with her. He could not bear a ray of light, and I attended him in darkness. Alas, I could not press his dear hand, nor cool his brain, nor touch his parched lips; all was agony, burning, restless agony.

Who has not at some moments of their lives felt willing to lie down and die for a beloved one? At such periods the grave has seemed a sweet bed of repose, and death a precious minister of love.

For many days I saw not the face of my dear Arthur. I

retired with mamma while the physicians dressed his wounds, and returned again to sit by his side. Gradually he began to utter words, and called my name. I wept with joy at the blessed sound; then one poor hand could press mine faintly, and bear the soft language I reciprocated. Slowly the light was admitted, and I saw him; but—oh, my heart—how changed! The beauty of which I was so proud was gone! The rich hair no longer lay on his noble brow; and that brow, once so serene, was furrowed by deeper lines than age or sorrow can engrave. *I should not have known him!* God forgive me, but I thought him hideous. I felt my blood curdle, and my head swim with an indefinite terror. The poor sufferer did not heed me, for his eyes were closed to the light. I thought my heart would have burst, and rushed to my own apartment. I traversed it with rapid steps; I crushed my hands upon my bosom to stop its beatings, and pressed my forehead to the wainscot to cool its burnings. I stamped in a kind of vindictive wrath, and uttered words of impious fury. I think I was going mad, but I grew faint; slow tears came to me; I was not left to blaspheme; I was softened; they fell like rain, and my spiritual triumph prevailed.

What, I thought, is this perishing clay to an immortal? His frail beauty would at best have lasted but a few years. Who knows but I should have loved too fondly those dark eyes, whose intellectual brightness struggled with their mellow tenderness; that mouth chiselled to the most perfect turn of manly symmetry? My poor Arthur! I have sometimes feared that your grasping intellect and exquisite person united placed you too much above me, that I must worship you like a bright, distant star; it is not so now. I shall not fear to lay your aching head against my heart, to smooth the lingering curl on your fevered brow, and call you mine only.

With these thoughts I kneeled in prayer. Earth seemed a vain thing to me; duty and Christian hope my birthright.

"Arthur," said I, cheerfully, as I sat by his bedside a week after, with his hand in mine, parting the scanty hair on his scarred forehead, "you are not aware how much you are altered by this sad accident. You asked yesterday for a glass, you must be prepared for a change."

He started, hesitated a moment, and said, in a low tone, "I feared this. Can you endure me?"

"If I had loved your beauty only," I replied, "I might not have borne its loss so well as I do; but while God spares your intellect and heart, I have still enough to be proud of."

He looked thoughtful, and said, "Is it really come to this? I have had fearful suspicions of it." His hand shook in mine with sudden tremor. "I have frequently desired to introduce the subject," he continued, mournfully, "but had not courage. You are not aware that vanity has been my besetting sin. I can recollect the earliest praise of my beauty. I remember ladies taking me in their arms when I was a child, and bestowing on me extravagant expressions of endearment and praise; I remember my power over young girls, who flattered me with their eyes, when their lips were too modest to speak; my quick ear has caught voices in public, even of rude boys in the street, pronouncing me beautiful; and, yes, I will confess all, I have lingered over my own miniature with a kind of idol-worship. I struggled with this weakness, and thought it mastered; God's will be done if this dispensation is sent to punish me."

"Not to punish you, Arthur," said I, fondly, as I perceived the nervous irritability of his feelings, "but it may be to try you, to perfect you, and to reveal to you my true love, which asks for nothing in return but yours. Oh, if you knew the warm and brooding tenderness that has settled on my heart since your misfortune, you too would say, it is enough for me it is worth more than external charms can buy."

Arthur improved in his appearance and health. I kept the mirror from him, telling him that every day diminished his disfigurement; and he cheerfully assented to my wishes, while his mind appeared to be regaining its tone.

"You will be almost what you were, dear Arthur," I said to him one day when he began to despond; "indeed, I forget that you are not the same. Judge me by yourself: would you look at me with less of true love's preference, if I were to be altered by misfortune?"

He shuddered, and exclaimed, "Do not mention it; I cannot bear to think of it." (I repeat his language, not with vanity, but to show his intense love of what he thought beautiful.) "Let me gaze on you;" and he fixed his melancholy eyes full on mine, "lest some awful power should change you. So long as those fringed orbs beam in their speaking sweetness; so long as I can trace the rose-tints on your cheeks, and the deep brilliancy of your lips; while your braided hair lies thus in its glossy folds; while these soft hands are white as sun-tinged ivory; while your step glides around me, and I can catch the fine proportions of your modest form; while your voice falls in sweet modulations on my ears, stirring up love's echoes, I will bear God's dispensations on myself; but pray, pray that they may stop before they reach you."

Arthur was at length able to walk a few steps, though in great weakness, about his apartment. In my earnestness to assist him one day, I forgot that he might approach the looking-glass; he did so inadvertently, glanced at himself, exclaimed, "My God!" and fell senseless.

He was removed to his bed, requested his room to be darkened, and the curtains drawn around it, while, without repulsing my attentions, he seemed to prefer communing with himself in silence. I saw that a violent struggle was going on, rendered more overwhelming by his physical weakness. This lasted some days.

"Cornelia," said he to me at length, in a tone of bitterness, "I intended to have surprised you with a gift from my poor Ellen—a likeness of Arthur Marion; do you remember *him?* Look in my writing-desk and bring it to me."

I went and presented it with a trembling hand, not daring to glance at it. He told me to open a shutter; I did, and the bright light burst in on the miniature and on him.

"Come here," said he, sternly; "come and look." I obeyed; the likeness was perfect. The girl who dreams of Endymion never pictured anything more beautiful. I glanced at Arthur's face, it was disfigured with conflicting passions. I perceived that this was his last great trial, and braced myself for the result. He sat up in the bed, to which he had been confined since his fall, gazed long and earnestly on the picture, then, clinching it with upraised arm, dashed it against the ceiling. He watched it as it was shivered to atoms; then, drawing the bed-clothes over his face, wept and sobbed aloud.

I kneeled beside him, clasped his hands in mine, laid my head on his pillow, and moaned as a mother with her suffering child. I prayed to God to comfort him, and the prayer was accepted. It *was* his last great struggle, and he rose from it like a man and a Christian.

CHAPTER XXXIV.

CHANGES.—WHITE SERVANTS.

"If obliged to attend to some household affair,
I have scarce so much time as to say the Lord's prayer;
This gives me no trouble; my dutiful part
Is obedience to him, whom I have at my heart
As well at my work as retiring to pray;
And his love does not suffer in mine a decay.
He has taught me himself, that a work which I do
For *his sake* is a prayer very real and true."

Poems of JOHN BYROM. 1691.

I KNOW of no purer or more sacred pleasure than to watch the recovery of a beloved valetudinarian, to see the eye light up from day to day, and the grateful smile play round the lip; to note the growing relish of the delicate appetite; to support the footsteps of the feeble one a little farther, from effort to effort; to see the glance rest soothingly on a fresh flower; to hear the exclamation of joy at the first view of nature, as leaning on our arm, the invalid looks abroad; to note the strengthening mind yield itself up while words of sacred truth or lighter amusement are read; to take the first drive, and mark how the breeze and sunshine come to the languid spirit as to a drooping plant, lifting up its leaves of hope and joy.

It was delightful to me to be the minister of comfort to Arthur, and to see the shadows pass off from his clear thoughts. He was a religious being, and it was his comfort to throw his cares on Him "who cared for him." The sight of Patsey was at first painful to him, but the dear child soon won her way to his confidence; she laid her little head on his knees, climbed to his arms, and told him, in childhood's winning tones, her pleasures and troubles. Her grief for Binah's loss was exceedingly affecting. She went about the house and grounds calling for her *mauma*, or sang in low tones the hymns she had taught her; and when the hour arrived when she had been accustomed to lay her flaxen locks against Binah's sable cheek, while she soothed her to sleep, for several nights a restless and plaintive sound murmured on her lips, and an eager watching, as for something lost, dwelt in her troubled eye.

Marion regained with health much of his original symmetry. The radiance and softness of his dark eyes were unquenched, and the long lashes gathered lovingly below them; the curled lip regained its fulness and richness, and even the deep scar on his brow was hidden by the lock of hair whose pliant curl I loved to adjust, when he, forgetful of the defect, carelessly brushed it aside.

There was no obstacle to our marriage. The whole clan of Wiltons and Marions met at Roseland, where mamma, revelling in housewifery cheer, moved as in a native element. Strange to say, there were but two offences given—one to a maiden cousin of Arthur's, who had commenced making a nightcap for me the day our engagement was announced to her. It was cut in mathematical forms of every shape and size, embellished with inserting trimming, and finished with two frills; yet, notwithstanding this token, she was omitted in the invitations. I sent her an extra slice of cake to conciliate her, but it was returned unopened, and she has never spoken to me to this day. The other individual was a colored confectioner in the city, who expected to make my cake. The first time I met her after my marriage she *cut* me, tossed up her head, and passed on; but we were reconciled on my bespeaking my entertainment at my first city party from her.

Our summer was passed in journeying, and we realized the rich experience of happiness shared by individuals who sympathize in taste and feeling. We felt a thrill in common while traversing the wild passes of Trenton Falls; the mutual prayer burst from our lips beneath and above Niagara's torrent; we clasped each other's hands on the brow of the Green Hills, and gazed upward together in awe-struck homage at the White Mountains; and it was with my own Arthur that I wept, his old father standing by, over Duncan's grave. Unwedded love has its jealousies, and wills not that even a flower should be prized too highly; but wedded confidence is pure; knowing that all is possessed of the heart's deep treasures, it gives and shares with sober joy. Arthur stood silently by my side while memory lent its tribute to true and tender friendship; and afterward, folding me in sympathy to his heart, prayed that he might be worthy of such tears.

The strong local attachment of negroes was developed in a most interesting and amusing manner on our journey. Four years previous to my marriage, a patroon, by the name of Ormsby, belonging to one of papa's schooners, was carried away under mysterious circumstances, with another negro, a simple, half-idiot fellow, belonging also to papa. When their loss was announced and finally confirmed on the plantation, it was received by Ormsby's wife with an apparent calmness singularly contrasted with the usual obstreperous grief of her class. It was observed, however, that as day passed away after day, she never smiled; and, though still attentive to her duty, wasted away without any symptom of disease. Love had been the sun of her existence as it had been to poor Anna's more refined affection. The vase, though colored differently, glowed by the same light from within; when that light was extinguished, creation seemed dark to both. She went to her daily tasks heedless of the jests of her lighter-hearted companions; the cloud still hung around her face and over her soul, and in a year and a half she died, broken-hearted.

Arthur and I were attended in our journey from the South by papa's coachman, and in a Northern city he unexpectedly encountered Ormsby. The poor patroon sprang towards his fellow-servant, wrung his hand, and burst into tears. He was conducted to me, and no sooner recognized me than he fell on his knees at my feet, clung to my garments, burst into tears anew, and thanked God that he lived to see one of our family again. He had been carried to Calcutta, had worked his way back to America, and was endeavoring to return to Carolina. I told him that he was at liberty to remain where he was, but he said his only wish on earth was to live and die in his master's service. The idiot fellow, who was with him, manifested his feelings in an uncouth style, and all his affections were riveted on the schooner from which he had been forced away. On our return, papa told them that they were at liberty to dispose of their own time as they pleased. The idiot rushed to his schooner, hugged the mast, kissed the rigging, tossed up his hat in the air, hurrahed; then lying down complacently with his face to the sun, swore he would live and die there; and he kept his word. Through the winter he served as a sailor, and in summer, when the schooner was lying by, made her his home. Ormsby continued an exemplary servant, devoted to papa's interests. Less romantic than his faithful wife, he married again, as he said, to be comfortable, but not until he had raised a simple slab, in the negro burial-place at Roseland, to the memory of the broken-hearted one.

This local feeling was also manifested in our coachman while we were at Niagara. After the silent and overwhelming joy which ravished his spirit had passed away, Arthur said to Mark—

"Did you ever see anything so fine as this, boy?"

"Eh! eh! massa," said the indignant fellow, snapping his fingers, "dis here can't show he face to Couter Bridge!"

Couter Bridge consists of a few planks thrown over a muddy spot in the suburbs of Charleston, a spot sacred to the truant frolics of many an errand-boy.

Amid our plans for the future we resolved to engage a white female housekeeper. A young woman was recommended to us, and her unfortunate circumstances decided us to take her to the South. Her parents were both intemperate, and appropriated to their sensual wants her daily earnings. Saddened and disheartened, unable to support, and without the hope of reclaiming them, she resolved to accompany us. Accidental engagements prevented our meeting until we were on board the vessel, and I was somewhat startled to find my housekeeper Miss Lucilla Hall, in a cloth riding-habit, and straw bonnet fresher and better than my own. There was a flash of self-respect in her large dark eyes, and her dress was fitted to her person with a precision that showed a determination to compete in appearance with those above her. She was not actually graceful or elegant, but how could I think of ordering such a person? I was really embarrassed, said *ma'am* to her in my incertitude, and used as much form, and perhaps more, than I should to a distinguished stranger. Southerners must necessarily experience this awkwardness from the different mode in which servitude exists in other portions of the country. Lucilla's discretion and good sense soon, however, determined her level. She began superintending my baggage, and sat at that unobtrusive distance where she could be summoned without seeming to be a companion. The only attempt at refinement on board the vessel which did not sit gracefully on her, was a conversation with a passenger, which I accidentally heard, on Walter Scott's *last novel!* How *can* I ask her to bring me a glass of water? thought I; and my difficulty in placing her in the right position at home again occurred to me.

On the evening of our arrival I showed her her apartment, and paid her every attention in my power, which was rewarded by her air of happiness and content. I bade her good-night cheerfully, and left the dependant stranger to her busy dreams. The next morning, as I opened the parlor door, I found her standing with a newspaper in her hand. A deep red spot shone on her cheek; her eye flashed a moment; then, dropping the paper and covering her face with her hands, she burst into tears, and left the room.

I took up the paper, and saw the secret of her wounded feelings in the announcement of the arrival of Arthur Marion, Esq., lady, and *servant!* Poor Lucilla, a dark cloud rested for several days on her countenance; nor were her social relations, though I studied her feelings in every mode in my power, calculated to make her happy. She seemed to hang in an unbalanced sphere between me and the servants of the household. By-and-by, however, a love-passage came in to throw a little light over her heart.

A young carpenter in the neighborhood, whom she had never seen, sent her a brace of birds and a water-melon, upon which she came, blushing with surprise, and asked my advice. I told her it was probably a piece of neighborly attention, and she had best accept them. The following day another watermelon came, with the initials of both parties carved on the rind; and on the third, as Lucilla stood in the piazza, two hands pushed a huge one through the partially-opened street-door; it rolled towards the excited girl, and she saw in large letters on the green rind:—

"J. M.
to
L. H.
"'If you love me as I love yon,
No knife shall cut our love in two.'"

Lucilla had not a spark of coquetry, and was evidently affected by this novel courtship; my advice ceased to be asked, and I lost my pretty housekeeper, who soon headed an establishment of her own.

It was about this time that the first great impulse was given to the temperance cause in Massachusetts. An individual, who may perhaps read these pages, made the parents of Lucilla his especial care; they signed the pledge, reformed, and have since gone down to peaceful graves, leaving their blessing and God's smile on their benefactor.

The history of Lucilla's successor, which I will give in her own language, illustrates some of the difficulties of servitude, and is a beautiful picture of the every-day struggles of the conscientious poor. It will be seen by these two cases how difficult it is to study the wishes of white dependants among us who have any refinement; the vulgar we cannot tolerate. Though strictly attentive to her duties, I perceived that her feelings were laboring under some excitement; and while seeking my presence under various pretences, her manner was never serene and composed.

One evening when I was alone in the country, waiting Arthur's return from a club, I sent for Betsey from her own room to sit with me. A cheerful fire blazed on the hearth; and as we sat sewing together, I asked her some questions about her early life, expressed my surprise at her correct language and manners, and by degrees drew from her her simple story.

"I do not recollect my father or mother," said my humble companion; "but at seven I was bound by the overseers of the poor to a lady in Boston, who promised to keep me until I was eighteen, and provide for me, at the end of my service, a situation where I might learn a trade. A child of seven years is very young to be cast out on the world, and many were the sufferings I endured. Mrs. Granby was very kind to me; but she had several young children who were badly managed, and I was made the sport of their ill-humors. If they broke a plate, it was immediately said, Betsey has done it; if the sugar was eaten out of the sugar-bowl, the theft was laid to me; if one of the children cried, it was Betsey who teased her. Sometimes when I was sent into the nursery to watch them, we all played happily together, and then I forgot my troubles. Mrs. Granby was opposed to punishment, and therefore the children were allowed to do as they pleased. I have often gone to bed and wept myself to sleep at the injustice that was done me. One little girl, about four years of age, was afraid to go to bed alone; and it was my task to lie down by her until she was fast asleep. Many a cold evening I have laid shivering on the outside of the bed, hoping every moment she would drop asleep; and just as I imagined I could get away, she would bounce up, and cry, 'Betsey, Betsey, you shan't go away!' Sometimes I would drop to sleep myself, and then, when it was time to lay the table for supper, I was obliged to rouse myself, and go down half awake. I did not have any very hard work to do, but I was called on for every purpose; if anything was lost, Betsey must find it—if wood was wanted, I must bring it. The grown-up servants in the kitchen, as well as the children in the parlor, laid every blame on me, so that I hardly knew what was right or wrong. If I told the truth, I was an impudent hussy; and if I tried to conceal anything, I was a deceitful child. I was willing to work, but was liable to so many interruptions that I accomplished nothing.

"I lived in this family until I was ten years old, when Mrs Granby died, and I was released from that service. I had been very much neglected, and scarcely knew right from wrong; but God watched over me, and I was kept from sin. I had a little Bible, which had been my mother's; and although I could not read in it, I always kept it under my pillow, and I thought it would help to make me good.

"After the funeral, I seemed to be left alone; for although Mrs. Granby had done little for me, still she was kind, and fed and clothed me; I had, besides, become attached to the little girl by whose side I had lain so many nights; and when I saw the carriage drive up to the door which was to take them all to their grandmother's in the country, I thought I should die with grief.

"It was soon spoken of in the neighborhood that little Betsey wanted a place, and a lady came for me. In this new situation there were no children. The lady was very sickly, and wished me to wait on her, and to be constantly in the room with her. The change was very great, from one of noise, and disorder, and merriment, to a regular, quiet home, where neatness and regularity were enjoyed and scrupulously practised. I was scrubbed from head to feet, and new and decent garments were made for me. Here I was taught to sew and read, and at length could understand my own dear little Bible. Here I learned the duty of submitting to the will of Providence; and if severity of discipline sometimes made my tears flow, the word of God taught me to bear my lot with patience. Mrs. Leitch was fretful, and often unreasonable; she thought it no harm to keep me confined in her apartment day after day, sewing and knitting without intermission. She could not spare me to go to school; and as she felt it a duty that I should be instructed in reading, as well as in moral and religious duties, she taught me herself in those hours of ease which she sometimes enjoyed. But you can hardly imagine how I longed to run out and play in the sun and air, and to expand my limbs. But I could never go; and it was wearisome to me to sit upright on a cricket* at work, or getting my lessons, the whole day. Sometimes my labor was varied by the necessity of rubbing Mrs. Leitch when she was in pain. I took pleasure in doing anything to procure her ease.

"Such confinement and seclusion from persons of my own age wore upon my spirits, and I began to droop. One day she asked me if I was unhappy, and if I wanted anything. She seemed sorry for me, and I ventured to tell her I wished sometimes to go out as other children did. She was very angry, and called me ungrateful, when she had done so much for me.

"'In one year,' said she, 'you have been transformed from a dirty, ignorant, ragged child, to a neat, well-clothed, and instructed waiting-maid. You have no hard work or drudgery to perform, and have only to sit here with me like a lady!'

"I told her she had been very kind and bountiful to me, and that I would try and be contented. But she became from that time very much dissatisfied with me. I was not allowed to read or write, and was obliged to sew all day. If I rubbed her, she said I took pains to hurt her; if I made the least noise, it was done on purpose to make her head ache; if I looked out of the window, it was because I wanted to be a vagabond about the streets. I had no friends to whom I could apply, and I knew not what to do. I was now twelve years old, and I one day took courage to ask her to let me find another place.

"'No,' said she; 'after I have had so much trouble in teach-

* Term used in New-England for a low bench or stool.

ing you my ways, I shall not let you go.' Finding no hope of getting away, I looked into my Bible for comfort, and saw, 'The Lord preserveth the simple; I was brought low, and He helped me.' I prayed for patience, and it was given to me; I was gentle and docile, and Mrs. Leitch again became kind. At length the physicians ordered her to try a change of climate, and she released me from my service, and found me a place with a friend of her own. She provided me with clothes, and gave me some books and ten dollars. I shed tears at parting with her; for although she was often unreasonable, still I perceived that I had been much improved in her service. I accompanied her friend, Mrs. Grant, to a country residence, and found myself, for the first time, among fields and flowers. There my spirit bounded, and I was happy in those innocent pleasures which spring from the bounties of nature. It was my business here to attend on a sweet little girl of three years old, an only child. I used to drag her in a carriage through the walks in the garden, and pick fruit and flowers and throw in her lap. I arose with the sun, and it was delightful to go out and hear the birds sing, and take my little girl by the hand and walk down to the side of the river, and see the waters glide along! I was not required to perform any other labor than to attend this darling child, and I was allowed to read and employ myself in any way, so that I still kept my attention fixed on her. We were always in the room with her mother, except when little Mary was required to take exercise, which was several hours every day. The mildness of my temper gave Mrs. Grant a confidence in my care, and I was allowed to carry her about without restraint. I now found the value of the discipline to which I had been accustomed; my habits of order and industry made my services quite valuable; and it was a pleasure to me, after my walk in the morning with the little child, to sit down in the room with her, and teach her little lessons and hymns. Never was any young creature so gay and happy as myself. Mrs. Grant gave me leave to attend the Sunday-school, and there I was instructed in those moral and religious truths which teach us our obligation to God and our duty to our fellow-mortals.

"Autumn came and winter, and still found me happy, and thankful to God for this asylum. When I awoke in the morning and looked forth on the fields and distant hills covered with snow, I was overwhelmed with the magnificence of nature. I almost forgot that I was poor and dependant, and that I might at any moment be cast out to seek my bread among strangers. At length the birds began to sing; the flowers sprang up; and the trees put forth their blossoms. I held our dear little Mary by the hand, and had just fixed a nosegay to carry in to her mother, when, as we reached the door, two men came up and asked for Mrs. Grant. I introduced them into the parlor, and one of them handed her a letter; she read it, uttered not a word, but would have fallen to the floor, if I had not sprung to her and supported her. The men looked at her with great compassion. At length she recovered; and when she could speak, said, 'We are ruined, Betsey. Mr. Grant is in jail! I must give up all and go to him!'

"It was even so. He had been unfortunate in some speculations, and all his property was attached. At that moment I did not think of a separation from this dear lady and her sweet child, and thought I should go with her to prison; but she soon convinced me that it would be impossible. She said she must give up all her indulgences, wait on herself, and try to assist her husband. After exhausting myself in unavailing sympathy for her, the forlornness of my situation rushed on my mind, and I felt that I must lose the home where I had been so happy for one whole year; and to part with my dear little Mary was the hardest fate of all.

"After a short struggle, Mrs. Grant summoned up her resolution, delivered the house and furniture into the hands of the officer, and began to make arrangements for her own departure. She collected her domestics, and gave them all she could—good advice, and a good character, with a promise, if it should ever be in her power, to pay them the wages that remained due. They were much attached to her, and begged her not to think of them, but hoped for her sake that her husband would get out of his difficulties. They took a respectful leave, and with many tears departed from a house where they had been treated more like friends than servants. They had friends and acquaintances, knew how to make themselves useful, and could soon get into a new service; but for me, where, alas! could I go? I went to my little chamber, where I had so often kissed Mary to sleep, and there wept bitterly. Presently I heard that sweet voice calling, "Betsey, Betsey, come to my mother!' I wiped away my tears and tried to compose myself.

"My good friend held out her hand to me and said, 'Betsey, this is the hardest task of all; you have been so affectionate and so faithful to my child that I can hardly give you up. Oh, my poor girl, I cannot pay you your year's earnings, or the ten dollars you gave me to keep for you!'

"She had often advised me to take up my wages, and put the money in the savings-bank; but it was some trouble, and it was put off. I begged her not to think of me, but to allow me to assist her in packing up. This was a heart-rending business; and as I folded little Mary's clothes, and laid them one after another in the travelling trunk, my tears flowed afresh. The little child came and put her arms around my neck, and said,

'Don't cry, Betsey; Mary will soon come back and bring you sugar-plums and cake!'

"At length all was ready. Mrs. Grant had selected such articles from her own clothes as she thought would be useful to me, and insisted on my taking them. She also gave me a written certificate of good character and conduct, and recommended me to the care of a poor but respectable woman, who was under obligations to her, and with whom I was to remain until I found a place. The carriage drove off, and I was left the last in the house, to lament alone.

"Those who have the comfort and protection of a father's house, and whose wants are all supplied by parental affection, can little imagine the desolate feeling I endured when I saw the door close which shut me out from a happy home. But it was necessary I should exert myself, and I took up my bundle and walked on.

"I was kindly received by the good woman to whom I had been recommended. After some days, I heard of a lady who wanted a chambermaid. I was now about fourteen, and large of my age. The lady took my certificate and read it, then handed it to her daughters, three young ladies, who sat in the room.

"'Honest, good-tempered, faithful,' were pronounced aloud. 'A very good character, young woman,' said the lady; 'but what kind of work can you do?'

"'I can sew, and knit, and read,' said I; 'and I have been accustomed to attend on a sick lady and little child.'

"At this reply they all burst out a laughing; I thought I must have said something very ridiculous. At length the lady asked me 'if I could wash and iron.' 'No, ma'am.' 'Do up nice muslins and laces?' 'No, ma'am.' 'Clean a room?' 'I have never tried, but could easily learn.' 'Well, young woman, you will not do for me, as we do our own *sewing* and *reading*, and we want a chambermaid who knows how to work.'

"I went away with a heavy heart! On my next application for a place I was careful not to say anything of my qualification for reading and sewing, and merely answered to the inquiries that were made, that I was willing to do any kind of work, and had no doubt that I should give satisfaction. I was so unwilling to be a tax on the poor woman who sheltered me, that I engaged to do more than I honestly thought I could accomplish; and if I was wrong I hope God will forgive me.

"On Sunday evening I entered on my new service. Here was a large family of grown-up people. Mrs. Holt, the mistress of the house, an active, stirring body, kept every one in her employment at work. My companions in the kitchen were a large red-faced woman who cooked, a man who took care of the horses and worked in the garden, and a boy to wait on table and make the fires. They were all vulgar, coarse-looking people. They soon found out that I had been delicately brought up, and conceived a great dislike for me. I was soon known by the nickname of 'Miss Mince.' On Monday morning the clothes were brought forth to be washed, and for the first time I took my place at the washtub. It was not long before I rubbed the skin from my hands, and the pain and smart of the soap was intolerable; still I did not dare to complain. It was fortunate that I was called from the washtub frequently to do other work about the house, or I could not have gotten through the day. At last we got through the long day; the kitchen floor was washed, and the tea things put away, and I took a book of devotion from my pocket and began to read. All my companions laughed at me, and said I should soon be taught better than that. I asked them very mildly if they wished me to do anything for them; they said no, but still kept on laughing. In a few minutes in came the mistress. She lifted up both hands, and exclaimed, 'Heyday, Betsey, can't you find nothing to do but to set down and read?' I shut up my book in some confusion, and said I hoped she would excuse me, as I did not know that she had anything for me to do that evening. Her anger was appeased by my gentleness, and she said, 'Well, child, you should come and ask for work when you do not know what to do, as I cannot afford to pay help unless all their time is spent in my service.' She then produced a large basketful of stockings, and told me to employ my leisure on them, and not sit idling away time with books!

"I had little sympathy from my companions. Still I never retorted when they said harsh or satirical things to me. By this method I gained their forbearance, and I have always found that a kind and gentle temper will conciliate the most unfeeling and ferocious. Thus, although I was not happy, they restrained their taunts; and sometimes, when we were all seated in the kitchen, after our labor was accomplished, they would ask me to read to them. This indulgence almost cost me my place, as Mrs. Holt declared she would have no such doings, and if I continued such a practice I should quit the house. Sometimes I took a little bit of candle to enable me to read a chapter in my little Bible before I went to sleep; but when she found that out, she obliged me to go to bed in the dark.

"By diligence and attention I soon became expert in performing all the work that was required of me, and I should have been contented with my lot if I could have had a little leisure for my own use. When it was found that I performed my work with so much despatch, other labor was added. The young ladies of the family gave me their sewing and mending, and so encroached on my good-nature that they frequently kept me at work until near midnight.

"I continued in this family a year; but their demands on my services increased, and they were so unreasonable, that I resolved to quit them. I told them my intention; they were astonished. I had been so docile and submissive, that it never occurred to them that I should have resolution enough to leave them.

"At this period I accidentally broke a valuable glass dish. I never could tell how it fell from my hand, but it seemed to be without my will and almost without my knowledge. Mrs. Holt was standing by when the accident occurred. I saw her eye kindle with passion, and, before I could apologize, her hand came with a powerful blow on my ear, and the expression, 'Careless huzzy, and trollop!' burst from her angry lips. I felt faint and frightened, and cried as if my heart would break; I wished that the earth would open and take me in. I offered to pay for the loss; the money was declined, but most ungraciously, and the few days I remained I was hourly twitted about the broken dish. And yet it required a great effort for me to get away. I had been in the habit of submitting to circumstances, and it seemed to be my fate to encounter hardships. But I had saved my wages for one year, and felt some degree of independence. I determined to stay a few days with the aged friend with whom I once found shelter; and as I had now the means of paying my board, I felt the less reluctance at claiming the shelter of her hospitable roof. Accordingly, after I had taken a respectful leave of Mrs. Holt and her daughters, and had given a cordial adieu to my companions in the kitchen, I retired to the repose of humble life. I was truly refreshed by the sympathy of my old friend, and the quiet and rest which even poverty can offer to the weary heart. I had time to think of my Creator and my Redeemer; and I shall never forget the feeling of happiness I enjoyed the first Sabbath I found myself at liberty to attend the services of God's holy temple during the whole day. How ardently did I wish to devote myself wholly to Him; and if I ever felt inclined to repine at my lot, it was when I looked round on the well-filled church, and considered what Christian privileges most of the congregation enjoyed, and how little I had hitherto been enabled to mingle my prayers and supplications at the throne of grace, and how ignorant I had remained of my Christian duties.

"This day was an anniversary of the Sabbath-school, and I soon discovered that the privilege of attending it extended to all, and that I had only to make known my spiritual wants to be received as a pupil. From this time my views of life were entirely changed. I felt myself one of God's creatures, and no longer suffered from the humiliation of being an outcast, without relatives or friends. I now realized that I was equally the subject of his providence, and that, by a faithful discharge of the duties of my humble station, I should render a homage equally acceptable to him as if my opportunities were more extensive. 'An humble and a contrite heart, oh God! thou wilt not despise;' and as I breathed in silence a prayer for the influence of his Holy Spirit on my heart, I felt that mine was already accepted!

"It was at this period that I heard of a Southern lady who wished a white servant, and I applied for the situation. She had already a negro attendant of her own travelling with her. For the first few days that we travelled together I was very much struck with the formality of her manner to me, and the intimacy she seemed to feel for Dinah. I had never seen but one negro before, and always had a dread of them; from early prejudice, I could hardly believe my own eyes when I saw the confidence that was placed in Dinah.

"When we arrived in Charleston, I found that I was to go

into the country and *keep the keys* for a Mrs. Randolph, who was an invalid. I cannot describe my home-sickness. A strange fear made me avoid the blacks. When I went to bed it seemed to me as though I should see their faces peering through the doors and windows. Mrs. Randolph's politeness to me was painful in the extreme. I felt as if I was in an ice palace. I had everything I wanted; indeed, I never saw so much elegance in my life, and never had such attendance, but it seemed all above and below me. Mrs. Randolph changing her residence, you were kind enough, ma'am, to take an interest in me, and I will make bold to tell you my feelings. My own voice sometimes frightens me; my dreams are dreadful; and when you and Mr. Marion go to the city, I feel as if I wanted to close my ears, and shut my eyes, and stop the beating of my heart until you come back. Oh, if I could only return," she concluded, timidly, the large tears dropping on her busy needle, "I think I would be willing to work my fingers to the bone."

It will be easily conjectured that, in a solitude like Bellevue, the companionship, even of so humble an individual as Betsey, would be desirable; but, though her heart was in some measure relieved by unfolding its feelings, and by my consequent sympathy, yet I perceived her spirits droop, and determined, on our February visit to the city, to restore her to her native climate. Since that period I have not renewed the experiment of white American servants at the South. Foreigners, from their habit of looking up to fixed classes in society, enter readily into the peculiarities of our institutions, and therefore are better suited to this office; but experience seems to have decided that an attached, faithful negro, is a more suitable servant in our portion of the country, under existing institutions, than any other. It would weary me were I to relate the instances which have fallen under my observation, of devoted kindness from this class of persons to those by whom they have been reared; their jealousy of the rights and reputation of their masters; their kindness in sickness, and the affectionate demonstrations of grief with which they follow them to the grave.

CHAPTER XXXV.

THE PLANTER'S BRIDE.

"She sitteth by his chair,
And holds his feeble hand;
She watcheth ever there,
His wants to understand.
His yet unspoken will
She hasteneth to fulfil."

MISS BROWNE'S "*Woman's Love.*"

"He goes from her chamber straight
Into life's justle;
He meets at the very gate
Business and bustle."

MISS BROWNE'S "*Man's Love.*"

THE planter's bride, who leaves a numerous and cheerful family in her paternal home, little imagines the change which awaits her in her own retired residence. She dreams of an independent sway over her household, devoted love and unbroken intercourse with her husband, and indeed longs to be released from the eyes of others, that she may dwell only beneath the sunbeam of his. And so it was with me. After our bustling wedding and protracted journey, I looked forward to the retirement at Bellevue as a quiet port in which I should rest with Arthur, after drifting so long on general society. The romance of our love was still in its glow, as might be inferred by the infallible sign of his springing to pick up my pocket-handkerchief whenever it fell.

On arriving at Bellevue, which Arthur had recently purchased, with its standing furniture, I perceived the most grotesque arrangement. Whatever was too old or dilapidated for the city, the former proprietor had despatched into the country. The furniture seemed like the fag-end of all housekeeping wares. If a table had lost a leg, it was banished to Bellevue, where the disabled part was supported by a bit of hickory or pine; the mirrors, which comprised all varieties, from heavy carved mahogany frames to gilt ones, with amiable shepherds and shepherdesses pictured at the top, seemed as if the queen of the earthquakes had been angered by her own reflection, and rent them in fissures. In one I had the pleasure of seeing myself multiplied almost indefinitely; in another, an eye or a nose, a forehead or a waist, was severed in two; and in another, unless I stood on tiptoe, a grinning, unnatural thing looked at me above and below the cracks. In one room was an old-fashioned secretary, towering to the ceiling, where a few worm-eaten books leaned against each other, as if for companionship in their solitude; while near it was a finical table, with its defaced gilding hidden by a piece of faded green baize. The sideboard, which was covered with rich silver, was also set off with tumblers and wine-glasses for all sizes and fancies; the andirons, things with long slender stands, and Lilliputian brass heads surmounting their slight bodies, looked as if they were invoking something up the large chimneys; the bellows wheezed as if far gone in the asthma; the tongs lapped over with a sudden spasm, clutching tenaciously the unoffending brands; if I attempted to sweep the hearth, I was left with the handle only in my grasp; the large glass shades, intended to protect the candles from the air, admitted, like treacherous allies, the enemy in at various breaches; small bits of carpet were laid here and there in the apartments, as a kind of hint at warmth; the bed-curtains and spreads were mostly patterns of gorgeous birds and trees, but being imperfectly matched in the sewing, a peacock's plumage was settled on the neck of a humming-bird, a parrot seemed in the act of eating his own tail, and a fine oak came sprouting out of a bird's nest. Arthur was infinitely amused when I called his attention to the china, which varied from the finest Dresden to the common crockery of the dram-shops. The medley, in variety, would have done credit to a modern drawing-room.

The harmonious and joyous frame of our minds rendered these things a source of amusement. For several weeks all kinds of droll associations were conjured up, and we laughed at anything and nothing. What cared we for fashion and pretension? There we were together, asking for nothing but each other's presence and love. At length it was necessary for him to tear himself away to superintend his interests. I remember when his horse was brought to the door for his first absence of two hours; an observer would have thought that he was going a far journey, had he witnessed that parting; and so it continued for some days, and his return at each time was like the sun shooting through a three days' cloud.

But the period of absence was gradually protracted; then a friend sometimes came home with him, and their talk was of crops and politics, draining the fields and draining the revenue, until I (country ladies will believe me) fell off into a state as nearly approaching sleep as a straight-backed chair would allow. Arthur, however, rarely forgot me in conversation with others; he had the art, in which most men are so entirely deficient, of directing a glance to a lady, while conversing with gentlemen on themes apparently uninteresting to her—a glance which seemed not only to acknowledge her presence, but to pay deference to her thoughts. He did not, as is too often the case, forget that a sentient being was without companionship but in him; but seemed to feel what is probably true, that if women are occasionally asked for their opinions, they may be induced to look into the depths of their minds to see if an opinion is there. But Arthur had few aids in this delicate mode of complimenting; after the ordinary questions were answered, I was usually left to ponder on the strip of carpet before the hearth, and wonder why it did not come up to the chairs, while my neighbor gradually hitched himself round with one shoulder towards me and his forefinger on Arthur's thigh.

Arthur was a member of a social club—but he had allowed several citations to pass unnoticed, until it occurred to him that he was slighting his friends; I thought so too, and said so, without permitting the sigh to escape that lay at the bottom of my heart, at the idea of his passing an evening away from me.

"They shall not keep me long from you, my love," he said, as we parted; "I have little joy without you."

But it *was* very long to me. I could bear to be alone in the morning, when I pursued various occupations, and was even happy. When weary with sewing and reading, I strolled to the poultry-yard, and heard Maum Nelly's stories of how twenty fine young turkeys had just tottled backward and died *so;* or how the minks and chicken-snakes had sucked half the fowl-eggs; or see her stuff pepper-corns down the young turkeys' throats, and pick the pip from the old fowls. Luckily for me, I as yet cared little for the pecuniary loss, while I really enjoyed the sight of the healthy flocks, as she exhibited them with a kind of maternal pride, calling the seniors by name. I loved to hear the delicate peeping of the little things, and see how unselfishly the parent bird sacrificed the choicest morsels for them; I loved, too, to stand by the duck-pond, and listen to the plash as the old ones descended to the water, and watch their proud and happy look as their offspring followed with instinctive power. I noted the chaste-robed pea-fowl, with its metallic-sounding cry, and smiled as the strutting and vaporing turkey paraded in "brief authority."

Then I visited the dairy, which was charmingly situated just where a small creek entered among the trees. A clear spring ran directly across the stone floor, and a fine spreading live-oak shaded it above. I enjoyed those days in the week when the little negroes came trooping along with their piggins for milk, the largest bearing the babies on their backs, and obtaining a double portion for them.

There is unquestionably as much a school of *old manners* among the negroes as with the whites, and Dinah, my dairy-woman, belonged to this class, specimens of which are rapidly declining. Her reception of me at the dairy was more that of a dignified hostess than a servile dependant, as, with a low courtesy and wave of the hand, she pointed to a bench for me to be seated. She belonged to the class, also waning, who blend religious expressions and benedictions with their common phraseology. Dinah, too, possessed a native humor and keenness that sometimes amused me. Being short in stature, she asked me to reach a calabash, which was set aside on a high shelf for my especial use when I wished a draught of milk.

"'Scuse me, missis," said she; "when *tall* was give, I no dere."

Observing that she replied in the affirmative to questions of opposite bearing, I asked her meaning.

"'Scuse me, missis," she answered; "I is gitting hard o' hearing, and yes is more politer dan no."

Sometimes I even strayed, for companionship, to the potato-fire, which, though in the open air, was rarely extinguished, and usually found some one roasting or eating. As I lingered there one day, I inquired of an old man, who was hoeing his own ground, about some work neglected by the gardener. He rested on his hoe and shook his head.

"My missis," said he, "you no been hear 'bout Dick?"

"No," I answered; "what of him?"

"He disgrace we all," said the old man, resuming his work. "He tief one sheep—he run away las week, cause de overseer gwine for flog him. He an't desarve a good maussa, like Maussa Arthur!"

My next walk was to the sick-house. Arthur had as yet superintended the duty here, but it gradually became my pleasure to assist him; and, though with some timidity remembering mamma's example, I prescribed and weighed the simplest medicines, and soon became interested in the individuals.

I have said that the morning passed slowly, though happily, even without Arthur; but that club afternoon seemed interminable. The weather was mild, and, tired of the house and of sitting down to *one* plate, that loneliest of all positions, I again walked out to enjoy the declining day and beguile the long hours. I involuntarily paused at the frog-pond, for there seemed a kind of sociality in their voices. Everything depends on the mood of mind. It was but the evening before that Arthur and I had astonished the frogs by our excellent imitation of their melodies. Standing at opposite sides of the little pond, he took the bass and I the treble, until we were hoarse with shouting and laughter; now they had a melancholy sound, and I turned homeward. At this moment a man slowly rose from the bushes near, and looked about carefully. I discerned in him Dick, the runaway. He looked haggard, and, approaching with an humble air, confessed his fault, and begged my intercession with his master to allow him to return once more to his duties. I undertook the office, and the next day he was permitted to go into the field.

The house seemed so deserted, that, though half ashamed of my own want of energy and mental control, I walked to the piazza. I was glad of the salute of the last lingering laborers on their way from the fields; I listened to the swineherd's horn, and saw his uncouth group at a distance, turning towards their pen; the shepherd came next, with his more romantic charge, and I enticed them, by throwing corn from the piazza, to bear me company a little while; but they soon followed the shepherd as he called, individually, their well-known names. Then came the ducks, whose wings were uncut, flying from a neighboring field to seek their night's shelter, sweeping below the deep-tinged sky with flapping wings and happy screams. The sun shot up his last rays on the twilight clouds; the crows wheeled from the field to the forest; the whippoorwill's cry, which the hum of day had stifled, came clearly and solemnly on the air; the young moon rose with her slight crescent, and rapid darkness followed. I returned to the parlor, pushed together the brands on the hearth, threw on lightwood myself, though two servants stood waiting by, and at length heard a footstep. It was Arthur's; I sprang towards him, and we had as much to say as if he had been to India.

This club-engagement, however, brought on others. I was not selfish, and even urged Arthur to go to hunt and to dinner-parties, although hoping that he would resist my urging. He went frequently, and a growing discomfort began to work upon my mind. I had undefined forebodings; I mused about past days; my views of life became slowly disorganized; my physical powers enfeebled; a nervous excitement followed; I nursed a moody discontent, and ceased a while to reason clearly. Woe to me had I yielded to this irritable temperament! I began immediately, on principle, to busy myself about my household. The location of Bellevue was picturesque—the dwelling airy and commodious; I had, therefore, only to exercise taste in external and internal arrangement to make it beautiful throughout. I was careful to consult my husband in those points which interested him, without annoying him with mere trifles. If the reign of romance was really waning, I resolved not to chill his noble confidence, but to make a steadier light rise on his affections. If he was absorbed in reading, I sat quietly waiting the pause when I should be rewarded by the communication of ripe ideas; if I saw that he prized a tree which interfered with my flowers, I sacrificed my preference to a more sacred feeling; if any habit of his annoying me, I spoke of it once or twice calmly, and then bore it quietly if unreformed; I welcomed his friends with cordiality, entered into their family interests, and stopped my yawns, which, to say the truth, was sometimes an almost desperate effort, before they reached eye or ear.

This task of self-government was not easy. To repress a harsh answer, to confess a fault, and to stop (right or wrong) in the midst of self-defence, in gentle submission, sometimes requires a struggle like life and death; but these *three* efforts are the golden threads with which domestic happiness is woven; once begin the fabric with this woof, and trials shall not break or sorrow tarnish it.

Men are not often unreasonable; their difficulties lie in not understanding the moral and physical structure of our sex. They often wound through ignorance, and are surprised at having offended. How clear is it, then, that woman loses by petulance and recrimination! Her first study must be self-control, almost to hypocrisy. A good wife must smile amid a thousand perplexities, and clear her voice to tones of cheerfulness when her frame is drooping with disease, or else languish alone. Man, on the contrary, when trials beset him, expects to find her ear and heart a ready receptacle; and, when sickness assails him, her soft hand must nurse and sustain him.

I have not meant to suggest that, in ceasing to be a mere lover, Arthur was not a tender and devoted husband. I have only described the natural progress of a sensible, independent married man, desirous of fulfilling all the relations of society. Nor in these remarks would I chill the romance of some young dreamer, who is reposing her heart on another. Let her dream on. God has given this youthful, luxurious gift of trusting love, as he has given hues to the flower, and sunbeams to the sky. It is a superadded charm to his lavish blessings; but let her be careful that when her husband

> "Wakes from love's romantic dream,
> His eyes may open on a sweet esteem."

Let him know nothing of the struggle which follows the first chill of the affections; let no scenes of tears and apologies be acted to agitate him, until he becomes accustomed to agitation; thus shall the star of domestic peace arise in fixedness and beauty above them, and shine down in gentle light on their lives, as it has on ours.

CHAPTER XXXVI.

TRIAL OF MY PRINCIPLE.—MY NEW CARRIAGE. —MY GARDEN.

"If we read nature's book with a serious eye,
Not a leaf but some precious thought on it doth lie:
And 'tis good to go forth among scenes like these,
Amid music and sunshine, and flowers and trees,
If 'twere only to waken the deep love that springs
At the sight of all lovely and innocent things."

ANNA MARIA WELLS.

ARTHUR and I, as the period drew near for our town-visit, began to discuss the subject of a new carriage. Long and frequent were the debates with regard to the color, shape, and ornaments; and this, perhaps, is one evil of country life, that it makes us attach a disproportionate interest to trifles. I inclined to a fawn-color, Arthur to deep green. He preferred a coachman's box; I desired an open front, that he might sometimes take the reins. The contest once or twice rose pretty high. I came down to breakfast one morning with a frown, and a determined, if not sullen, taciturnity, and Arthur rode away half an hour earlier than usual. This brought me to a recollection of my *principle* of self-sacrifice in *trifles*, and I was enabled to meet my husband with a smile, and say, on his return—

"On the whole, Arthur, I think your deep green *will* be the best color for the carriage. It will wear well."

"Ah, well, dearest," said he, tenderly smoothing down a curl on my forehead, "I am glad to hear it, and I begin to incline to the open front. I shall often wish to be independent and drive you myself."

Everything now seemed to be going on smoothly, when, in looking over Arthur's letters one day in an old chest, I found the Marion coat of arms. It seemed to me a perfect piece of good fortune. Under what class our arms came, whether of *pretension*, of *concession*, of *succession*, of *assumption*, or of *family*, I could not tell. I only thought that the dots and diagonal lines, and something that looked like two swords crossed would have a very pretty effect on the carriage, and, as soon as Arthur came in, ran and told him. I know not exactly why, but the subject struck him in a most ludicrous light; so far from entering into my views, he took the paper in his hand and proposed comical substitutes that would be in better keeping—cotton-bags *coupé*, sweet potatoes *vert*, alligators *dormant*, shrimps *gulés*, and terrapins *couchant;* and, running every change which his vivid fancy could furnish, he ended with a long, loud laugh, that went tingling through my ears and irritating my system to the very soles of my feet.

Every observer of human nature must have perceived, that lovers not only do not exercise the power of ridicule over each other, but they cannot conceive that the idol of their imaginations should be the subject of it. As intercourse in marriage becomes familiar, and the little graces of etiquette are laid aside, the idol, though not less worshipped, becomes less sacred. She is not the deity of the temple, but of the household; she is no longer the great Diana of Ephesus, approached at a distance with mysterious rites, but one of the Lares, meeting the familiar glance at every turn. This difference is never felt so keenly by a woman, as when she first discovers that it is possible for her to appear ridiculous to her husband. A man who differs from his wife and reasons with her, rather elevates her self-love; but, the moment he laughs at her, she feels that the golden bowl of married sympathy is broken.

How many kinds of laughter there are! The first clear, sweet notes of the infant, like the soft tinkling of a silver bell; the child's laugh, with voice and mind gushing out like a fountain; the maiden's laugh, when sensibility touches her tones like music; the rich, manly laugh, when wit goes to the recesses of intellect, and brings out its echoes; the girl's giggle behind her fan; the old man's laugh of habit, that sounds like the wind through an empty house; the maniac's laugh, sad and dreary as the last leaf on a withered tree; the parrot's laugh, calling out and yet repelling sympathy with its natural unnaturalness. Arthur's was like none of these at the moment of which I speak; it was one brought out by a sense of the ridiculous; and if a sister, or wife, or child can stand quietly by and hear such a one, she ought to be immortalized. I did not. I sat down deliberately and had a hearty cry, notwithstanding my *principle*. Poor Arthur, who had never thought about all this, and fancied I was enjoying his jests, was dismayed. He clasped me in his arms, apologized with all the tenderness and sincerity of his nature, and I never heard that laugh again.

I was, in the sequel, perfectly satisfied with my airy and elegant carriage, entered into the city amusements with animation, went through a February campaign with *eclat*, and had no wishes ungratified that wealth could procure. Letters of introduction were poured in upon us from all quarters, and we were glad and proud to be hospitable.

I was prepared one morning to call on a stranger, when visitors were announced; and, glancing round the drawing-room, I perceived on the sofa a ratan, which had been brought in by one of my young brothers. I caught it up, and twisting it into a coil, thrust it into my velvet reticule, and received my guests. As soon as they departed I sprang into the carriage, which was in waiting, and drove away. The ladies were at home. In the course of conversation I unthinkingly drew my scented pocket-handkerchief from my bag, when out flew the ratan with a bound, and rolled to the feet of the stranger. My deep and inextinguishable blush probably helped on any uncharitable surmises that she might have made, and who can blame her, after such evidence, for reporting that Charleston ladies carried cowskins in their pockets!

I was the personation of benevolence in my new carriage, and unaffectedly enjoyed the pleasure I conferred, yet every happiness has its alloy. If an acquaintance expected a friend at the wharves, Mrs. Marion's carriage was sent for and detained half the day; I was kept the very latest of the company at parties and balls, because my carriage had so many turns to make; when invalids arrived in the city my carriage was borrowed, and the credit went to the borrower, not to me. A child of one lady was allowed to rub its sugar candy over the fine cloth linings, and another preferred standing on the cushions to sitting down. Some fair rioters broke a glass returning crowded from a ball; one of my horses took cold by being overheated in a long drive out of town; another was injured by being delayed until twelve at a party, which the borrower said would break up at nine; my best coachman became chilled, irritable, and at length intemperate; and what capped the climax was a remark from my most frequent borrower, that she was surprised that Mrs. Marion could sport such a shabby carriage with a drunken coachman!

* * * * * * *

I found a small but favorable gardening-spot attached to our city residence, and a taste for the beautiful, which can always touch the humblest spot with grace, did not allow me to let it go to waste. The mere aspect of a bud or flower, without a higher association, is so pure and soothing to the lover of nature, that it repays the glance which bends over its daily growth; and I envy not him who can look coldly on a blade shooting from its unsightly seed into verdure, the sacred and startling emblem of that mortal which is to put on immortality.

And how much of the poetry of life springs from flowers! How delicate a pleasure is it to twine the orange-blossom or japonica for the bride—to arrange a bouquet for the invalid—to throw simple flowers into the lap of childhood—and to pull rosebuds for the girl of whom they are the emblem!

But gardens are not all poetry: witness the long-drawn countenance of the lady whose delicious geraniums are crumbled to yellow weeds by the frost; witness the housewife, whose imagination has sprung forward to the moment when her savory cabbages shall enter on her dinner-table, as fit companions to boiled pork or beef, when she visits her garden, and finds that a hard-hearted fowl has deliberately picked the plants up by the roots, rifled their green leaves, and left only withered relics; witness the gentleman who has watched his figs and grapes with such interest that even the daily paper has been laid aside to note their development, when he finds that the insects, with keener instinct than himself, have seized upon the ripe subjects and rifled their very cores!

There are other mortifications, that seem petty in detail, but which inflict a real pang on the florist. How often have I spent hours of culture on a rare blossom, and presented it as a valuable gift, seen it received with smiles and thanks, and then observed the thoughtless recipient crumble up the leaves in her fingers, or pull and throw them on the floor, or deliberately *chew* them!

Sometimes individuals have visited my garden and gathered flowers which have cost me not only time and labor, but heavy pecuniary sums, as unconcernedly as they would a blade of grass; sometimes, when I have cherished a little slip until it has shown signs of independent existence, a considerate lady has begged me for a *cutting!*

Other vexations, too, occur, on which the florist does not calculate when she yields up her heart to flowers. An Englishman presented me with four seeds, on the envelope of which was written an almost unpronounceable name, long and imposing. I was never selfish, and, in the warmth of my heart, gave two to botanists. I planted mine, and watched them day by day. At last they came up, and, with the pride of a florist, I carried my friends to see the first leaves. At length they grew, they budded, they blossomed—and behold, they were common four-o'clocks!

A botanist from Georgia favored me with two fine bulbs of the delicate Iris Persica. I valued them highly for their giver's sake as well as their own, and planted them with care and hope. A few mornings after, a little negro waiting-boy ran into the house exclaiming—

"Oh, missis, de cat pull you *inion* out of de jar!"

A friend of mine, however, was still more unfortunate in having a dish of Prince's best bulbs boiled for dinner!

Yet all these things will not rebuff the true lover of nature. She will enjoy the sparkling bud in the morning's ray, and love the perfume as daylight dies; and a moral freshness will settle over her thoughts like heaven's dew, as she traces the hand of Providence in her flowers.

CHAPTER XXXVII.

A MOTHER.—THE CONCLUSION.

"To teach rooted sorrow the lesson of submission; to succor virtue amid mighty temptations; to dispel the awful sadness of the inevitable hour; these are the victories of the Christian faith; the grand, and peculiar, and imperishable evidences of its power."—PROFESSOR GODDARD.

OUR country solitude was made glad by the birth of a son, and my parents were with me to heighten my joy and gratitude. On no other occasion does a woman's heart open so sweetly to sympathy as when, clasping her first infant to her breast, she feels that she has added, with tremor and suffering, another link to that human chain which, descending from heaven, will reach to heaven again. There is something still inexpressibly affecting to me in infancy, in its earliest stage, before *will* has put forth its impertinent little feelers. I love to take the tiny hand, which almost melts in its fragility, in mine, and press the unconscious cheek, and see the pulses of the protecting lid that covers the still unopened eyes. Papa was in raptures. His natural hilarity burst forth into almost boyish frolic. He thrust a ramrod between the fingers of the frail little thing, threw a powder-horn round his neck, and sang hunting choruses until I was obliged to stop my ears.

No other state of society can show a scene like that which was presented at Bellevue on the third Sabbath after the birth of our son. All the negroes, dressed in their best, came to welcome their *young maussa*, bringing offerings of eggs and chickens, and pronouncing prayers and blessings as the unconscious sleeper, decorated, too, in his little finery, lay in his nurse's arms.

The child grew, and called up in Arthur and myself a new fount of affection for him and for each other. Why should I detail what millions have felt and described? and yet I may, for infancy, like flowers, is always fresh. I may tell how, as he rested in my arms, before expression began to mould his features, imagination traced the mind that would come and light it as a torch the vase, which owes its chief beauty to the flame within. I may tell how Arthur left me late and returned early, while the romance of first love seemed renewed; how we hung together over the boy's little crib, and laid our ears near the sleeper's mouth, fearing in his soft stillness that he breathed not; I may tell, at least to mothers, how I gazed at his first smile, listened to his first laugh, supported his first footstep, and made him repeat again and again his first word, and how his being shone like a new planet on Arthur's life and mine.

Our little Arthur was a miniature likeness of his father; on that full brow, in those dark eyes, I loved to trace my husband's image. For the first two years of his life, until the birth of a little girl, I thought, as is the case with most American mothers, of little else but him; and even after that event, the child's companionship was everything to me. He was precociously musical, and I taught him many nursery songs. At the age of three years, secluded as we were in the country in winter, I felt it a privilege to let him fall asleep in my arms. When he became drowsy, he ran instinctively towards me, sprang into my lap, and began to sing. The notes gradually grew fainter, like the voices of birds in a twilight forest—then, starting up afresh, he smiled and sang until his lids closed over his dark eyes like a moon-tinged cloud on the night sky; and thus it was, with song and smile, that sometimes, in the midst of a word, consciousness forsook him, and the mantle of sleep folded his little spirit. One night he was reposing thus in my arms when Arthur came home. He knelt down before us, clasped his arms around us, laid his lips against the rosy cheek of the boy, and sighed in the very fulness of his love.

That night we were awoke with the struggling sound of the croup, which has so often sent a death-chill to a mother's heart. That night passed in wild and fearful struggles on his part, and desperate yet unceasing efforts on ours; medical aid arrived early the following day, but the boy was dying. He knew me not; his glazed eye was upward and away from mine; his hand, now tossing and restless, and then, as life quivered, feeble and helpless, returned not my pressure, that sought for life and feeling with maddened eagerness.

He died; I caught the last flutter of his breath, felt the coldness of death gather on his hand, still full and beautiful as the artist's dream of a cherub.

I was borne to my room, and Arthur followed to comfort me, himself despairing. Night drew on rapidly. Oh, that first night of bereavement! how coldly and darkly settle its shades over breaking hearts!

Arthur slept, and at midnight I arose to visit my boy.

He was laid on his little couch, and the negro watchers were singing hymns over him.

I tried to touch his deathly brow and hand; I could not; he seemed no longer mine.

The moon shone with strange brightness into the window, almost obscuring the single lamp that flickered in the aired and chill apartment; and lighting up with supernatural vividness the face of the dead, brought out in wild relief the dark forms around him.

How differently that soft planet rises on different eyes! The child looks on its beauty like a plaything, and clasps his hands in joy; the young girl cherishes its sweet, mysterious rays, and images, dearer and more tender, pour their light on her romantic spirit; the traveller blesses it on his way, and thinks of eyes softer and brighter than its beams at home; the husbandman prophesies in its silver radiance sunshine for the morrow; the lover, like the Pythagorean, fixes his earnest eye on the glittering orb, longing to trace there the thought of a dear one and inscribe his own; and the astronomer gazes on the beautiful glory in scientific pride; but alas, for me, on that night it rose like a separate ball of fire, without blending or harmony. There was no light on earth; nature was chaotic. I saw but one object, the dead form of my boy, stiff and cold, unsmiling, unanswering.

My kind women looked at me pityingly, and were eloquent with their simple religious consolation. They were idle words to me. God had struck the rock of my soul, but the blow had hardened it. The waters gushed not forth. Arthur still slept; men *can* sleep. I went hurriedly and sought the materials for a shroud, and sat down by my boy, and some wild association made me bind the white ribands from my bridal dress on his last garment.

I could not look at him, and yet his image was indefinitely multiplied; wherever I turned then, and for weeks after, amid sunshine or darkness, by the social hearth or in the solitude of my chamber, all was darkness, except where luminous points shone on a dead child.

We carried our boy to Roseland, and deposited his precious remains at Cedar Mound. It stormed that night after he was laid in his cold bed. I shuddered; the change was too horrible between my loving arms and that pelting rain. I asked why God could not have translated his cherub form to heaven? I could have borne his happy, upward flight, and waved my hand to him as in an earthly parting, when the white clouds opened to take him in; and I would have fancied that young mellifluous voice chanting its new-born tones, and the sweet surprise of his unclosing gaze; but to leave him there! Father in Heaven; thou hast pardoned the rebellion of a heart in its first gush of grief!

The sympathy of my parents was consoling; but I missed my boy on his grandfather's knee, and his prattle by his grandfather's side. In the restlessness of my soul I returned to Bellevue. Everything had been removed that could remind me of him. His little hat and cloak hung no more in the passage; his barrow and whip were gone from the garden-path; his carved alphabet no longer strewed the floor, nor did his disfigured toy-books meet my eye; all was dreary order and decorum; but, with all their care, could they prevent his graceful image from haunting those familiar scenes? How often did I hear his footsteps on the stairs, his shout in the court-yard! How often fancy his arms about my neck, and feel his eager kisses on my cheek! How often did I press my struggling heart and cry, "My son! my son! would to God that I had died for thee!"

Arthur watched my feelings tenderly. He sat by me hour by hour, silently, but with looks that said, "My poor stricken one! The storm has dealt hardly with thee, but flowers will not grow unless water and winds descend as well as sunshine. I will be very patient, and hold my heart all ready for thee, when thy love and hope shall ask for their accustomed nest."

What an education poor humanity requires to train it for Heaven! I had thought myself religious, and yet, when God took back the gift he had bestowed, a gift that had brightened my being for three happy years, I could not bless him for the past joy. My rebellious spirit charged even Heaven with injustice.

Arthur's unwearied love, my little Anna's caresses, and the softening hand of time, slowly wrought their sweet and natural influence. I began not to look exclusively on the grave; I listened as the buds of spring told their beautiful story of a new-clothed soul; I loved to think that the chill feel of earth was giving place to the flowers that began to gem my darling's distant bed; and, as time passed on, I forgot the flowers of earth, and thought only of heaven's garden, where my boy was waiting for me to come. Death, since my first bereavement, has never borne the same aspect. I have lost a gentle girl, and let her pass quietly, with scarce a tear on her grave; my thoughts went upward to my growing family above. I could bear to look on the soft curl that had lain on her brow, and fold the garments that had clothed her living form.

My mother followed; I fancied the meeting between her and my cherub children, and did not ask her back to a world where she could die again. I closed Richard's eyes of love, and my heart said, "God's will be done."

Long and refreshing, when my mind became calm, were my conversations with Arthur on the death of our boy.

"We had commenced a bright career, dearest," he said; "who knows but the world might have engrossed us, and made us sell our heavenly birthright? Our social pleasures will hereafter be modified by higher hopes. We have never given our public testimony to Christianity; let us go, beloved; let us plant this seed of immortality. Our precious boy rushed like a fresh fountain, and emptied himself in his first purity into the ocean of eternity; but we are checked and clogged by earthly obstacles, and must ask for aid to clear the onward stream, that it may reflect heaven from its bosom. Christian ordinances are noble aids; they degrade no lofty association, they wither no social affections, but, like the supports to the failing arms of the prophets of old, they lift up our souls until our earthly fight is won."

We went together to fulfil the command of Jesus. I do not say that any mysterious power was communicated to elevate us *above* human nature; but still I feel that, from time to time, after the self-examination of those holy hours, a truer zest is given to social happiness, a juster feeling of duty, and a clearer sense of our relations as immortals.

RECOLLECTIONS

OF

A NEW ENGLAND BRIDE

AND

HOUSEKEEPER

Quickly. Look you, I keep his house, and wash, wring, brew, bake, scour, dress meat and drink, make the beds, and do all myself.
Simple. 'Tis a great charge to come under one body's hand.

NEW YORK:
G. P. PUTNAM & CO., 10 PARK PLACE.

1852.

TO MRS. FAY,

OF CAMBRIDGE, MASS.,

THE FOLLOWING AUTHENTIC SKETCHES,

THE MINGLED RESULT

OF OBSERVATION AND EXPERIENCE,

ARE AFFECTIONATELY DEDICATED BY

THE AUTHOR.

CHARLESTON, S. C., 1834.

RECOLLECTIONS OF A HOUSEKEEPER.

CHAPTER I.

Ici tout est vivant, tout parle à ma memoire.
TRENEUIL.

Far up the tide of time I turn my sail.
ROGERS.

MY maiden name was Clarissa Gray. I was born in the neighborhood of Boston (Mass.), in 17—, and educated with the few facilities at that time afforded for the young; that is, I read "No man may" in Webster's spelling-book, then advanced to the more elaborate "Art of Speaking," and committed to memory, page by page, Morse's Geography, without maps, of course in glorious uncertainty with regard to the position even of my own country. My ciphering-book, however, was my pride, and my mother's too. With what delight did she display those sums, that rose like Banquo's ghosts,

"And drew at each remove a lengthening chain."

At the age of eight years I recollect seeing my mother reading a thin black book, which attracted my attention. It was "Blair's Grave," and she read me the passage,

——"But see, the well-plumed hearse comes nodding on."

How distinctly my imagination pictured that hearse and those nodding plumes! I recollect no other books, until I saw and *devoured* Shakspeare, at the age of nine, except an odd volume of Pope, containing "The Messiah," and "The Rape of the Lock." I sometimes look around on the mass of books collected by my children, and am half skeptical with regard to the value of juvenile literature, when I remember how my mind opened under the mysteries of those writings.

In justice, however, to the good tendency of engravings, I must mention, that the effect produced on me by the only two picture-books I possessed was an important one. One of them was "Watts's Hymns for Infant Minds," where fighting animals are portrayed. When friends have wounded or foes oppressed me, the strong but simple lines which elucidate the picture,

"Let *dogs* delight to bark and bite,"

have arisen to my memory, and calmed my chafed spirit, when mere flimsy sentiment would have afforded me no shelter against wrong.

The other book, and it is as distinct to my imagination now as the rich landscape by Fisher which hangs before me, contained a representation of Miss Kitty Greedy leaning both elbows on a table, with her mouth crammed to repletion, trying in vain to address her mamma. The *morale* has clung to me to this day, and I never see a young or old *gourmand*, or detect myself in a superfluous mouthful, without thinking of Kitty Greedy.

The utmost term of my *solid education* was one year of attendance at the town school—a square building, with one room for both sexes, near an open common, without a shrub or tree to grace or shade it. Thither, bearing my own satchel, I walked a mile, being a journey of four miles daily, to make my "young idea shoot." I will not say much for my ideas, but my limbs were not backward in the process. I *shot* up into a tall girl, and was allowed to go occasionally with my mother to take tea sociably with her friends at four o'clock, carrying my knitting-work for occupation.

My accomplishments are soon told. I opened an exhibition ball with one of the slow minuets of the last century, and I cannot but stop to render a tribute of admiration to that charming movement, in spite of the admirers of the lazy quadrille, or the seductive waltz.

A single courtesy or bow, when well ordered, is graceful; think then how delightful must be the spectacle of a series of these beautiful curves, performed to slow and appropriate music, by so attractive a couple as I certainly believed Clarissa Gray and my partner Benjamin Homes to be. He was a red-cheeked boy of thirteen, and had a pair of new white gloves for the occasion, unharmed by contact with mine, for the minuet allows but the meeting of the extremities of the fingers, and that lightly. I know not thy destiny, Benjamin, but I have sometimes wished thou mightst tread through life on such polished footing, with sweet music to lead thee, and a partner as kind.

My teacher honored, or rewarded me with a choice of fancy dances, and I decided on the slow minuet. How brilliant was the scene! Our old clergyman and his lady were stationed in conspicuous seats, and looked on with benevolent smiles. We scarcely felt the floor while moving with a step closely resembling the waltz, our hands raised the top of each forefinger making a circle with the thumb, then slowly descending, while with sidelong glances, and sidelong steps, with measured obeisances, we evolved the "poetry of motion."

I commenced learning music upon an old spinet of my mother's; but her indulgence soon imported me for a harpsichord of the latest fashion, and though my more fastidious ear may be critically pleased with the improvements in the modern pianoforte, I have never felt so rapt and raised as when I sang to a silent circle, "Henry's Cottage Maid," or "Her mouth which a smile," to my own harpsichord.

My sampler was one of unrivalled beauty. It possessed every shade and glory of tent-stitch. At the upper corners were cherubs' heads and wings. Under the alphabets stood Adam and Eve, draperied with fig-leaves, and between them these appropriate lines—

"Clarissa Gray is my name,
My age is ten.
This work in hand my friends may have,
When I am dead and laid in grave."

This sampler was a matter of curiosity, and sometimes of ridicule, to my children; but now that they perceive my gray hairs and increasing infirmities, I find the sampler neatly folded and laid aside, and sometimes a conscious look reveals to me that they think I may soon be folded to rest in the grave.

Our pecuniary circumstances enabled us to indulge in the luxuries of life; but none of these interfered with my education for usefulness. My mother was proud to say that I could manufacture a frilled shirt in two days, with stitches that required a microscope to detect them. I made my own bed, swept and dusted the apartments, mended my own clothes, and when pudding or cake was to be made, rolled up my sleeves, and went to beating eggs, with strokes that I should half like to see given to lazy modern girls, lolling over new-fangled cookery-books. But this was not all.

"Clarissa," said my judicious mother, "by not knowing how to make puddings and pies, you may be occasionally mortified;

but if you are ignorant of roasting and boiling, you may be annoyed every day."

On washing and ironing days, therefore, I spent a large portion of my time in the kitchen; well known, on such occasions, as the New-England Pandemonium. Quite contented did I feel, if able to retire to my bed-room, "my loop-hole of retreat," by four o'clock in the afternoon. The only domestic I distinctly remember in my mother's establishment was a washerwoman, called Ma'am Bridge, whose mouth and chin resembled the modern pictures of old Mother Hubbard, and who was an extra assistant on washing days. She wore a mob cap, with a broad unstarched frill, which, in hanging out clothes against the wind, fell back, displaying her sharp physiognomy. One day I was laying some ham on the gridiron, my mother preferring it broiled to fried, while Ma'am Bridge was *sudsing* the clothes in a tub before her, and dexterously throwing them into a *rinsing* tub behind. A sudden thunder-gust had arisen, and a brilliant flash of lightning blazed through the kitchen. I heard a great splash, and turning round saw Ma'am Bridge seated in the wash-tub, with the water gushing out on all sides; her head was thrown back, and her broad frill with it, developing a mingled expression of consternation at the danger, and joy at her escape. It was one of those odd combinations in which the ludicrous triumphs over the fearful. As she rose from the tub, like Venus from her shell, or Cowper's Rose, "all dripping and drown'd," I laughed until I brought upon myself her just indignation.

I do not feel myself called upon to say how many loaves of bread, under my apprenticeship, came out of the oven as heavy as a bad joke, or as sour as an unkind one; how my pickles turned soft and yellow; how I filled a bed without curing the feathers; how I put pepper instead of alspice into a batch of mince-pies; how many chemical separations instead of affinities took place in my baked beans and Indian puddings; and how my pan-dowdy disconcerted all the family, except my cousin Sam, a black-eyed boy, with a raging appetite, who dined with us every Sunday, and who affirmed that the paste was *not* tough, and that he did not mind if the apple cores did choke him a little. These mischances will happen in every department, and I may claim the sympathy of the lawyer who blunders in his maiden speech, of the doctor who kills his first patient, and of the preacher who soothes his first hearers to sleep. This acknowledgment, however, I will make *en passant*, that my mother's persevering tuition in cookery has saved me a thousand mortifications, to which I have seen ignorant housewives exposed.

CHAPTER II.

THE FIRST TRIAL.

PARSON EVANS.—It were a good motion if we give over pribbles and prabbles, and desire a marriage between Master Abraham and Mistress Page.

IT was beginning to be a subject of deep calculation with me, whether a brunette should wear pink or yellow riband on her bonnet; and I had decided on the former, when one Sabbath, on entering the meeting-house, I observed a stranger outside the porch, and on glancing at the gallery after I was seated, I again perceived him there. I thought he looked at our pew more than was correct, but, somehow or other, I kept looking at him to see whether he would become more attentive to the exercises, and thus our eyes repeatedly met.

After service he came to the porch, for in New England people retire from their pews with a silent bow to their acquaintance, and introduced himself to my mother as Mr. Packard from Boston, the son of a friend. He remained a few days at the village on law business, for he was an attorney, and though my mother was one of the most unostentatious women in the world, yet before he left us she made him understand that I could skewer a goose, roll puff paste, complete a shirt, and make a list carpet, as well as I played on the spinet and worked tent-stitch. She was on the point of telling him that I could spin a little, but I protested against anything so old-fashioned.

According to my motto, I "gave over pribbles and prabbles," and married, at the age of seventeen, Edward Packard. I remember the moment, when, after a short drive, I first entered my adopted home in the North Square, one of the most genteel quarters in the then town of Boston. The new carpet, new chairs, and new mahogany, with its virgin hue, undarkened by wax or turpentine, are all before me. My mother was with me, and though she held one of my hands, and my husband the other, I could not restrain my tears from falling, happy though they were.

I felt half ashamed to praise the parlor-furniture, though I secretly said, "It is mine." On recovering from my shyness, I visited the various apartments, and I think I was most attracted by the nicely sanded kitchen, not even excepting a closet, which I might now call a *boudoir*, fitted up expressly for me by my husband.

How bright were those new tins and brasses, arranged with ostentatious glitter on the walls and dresser! How comfortable that suspended warming-pan! How red and clean those bricks, extending to the right and left, leaving space for a family in the corners. A *settle*, too, that glory of New-England kitchens, was there, now banished for the inhospitable chair, which accommodates one instead of three! I had often presided in a parlor, but never before was mistress of a kitchen!

A council had been called previous to my marriage of the number of "help" which we should require, and it was decided that a female cook, and a little girl to "wait and tend," would answer our purpose, and be sufficiently genteel.

I was introduced, on that memorable evening, to Nancy, the cook. She was the picture of cleanliness. She had on, what is called in New England, a "calico short loose gown," and at the south "a chintz wrapper," with a check apron, a little starched, tied round her waist. Both cook and kitchen were in perfect keeping.

"Well, Nancy," said I, with a half modest, half patronizing tone, "I am a young housekeeper, but I dare say we shall get along very well."

"Oh, ma'am," replied Nancy, "*I* am not at all petikelar. I never has no differences with nobody."

How amiable! thought I; and I gave her a calico bag, containing iron-holders, kettle-holders, wipers, and dishcloths, presented me by an old aunt, who had quilted them for the occasion, and who said, with a commiserating voice, as she presented them, "Young housekeepers have no rags, poor things!"

The same kind friend gave me a rag-bag, and repeated to me an anecdote she was fond of relating, of a lady in Cambridge, who sold rags enough at four cents a pound to buy herself a silver porringer. "And mind, Clarissa," continued she, "that you do not throw away the ends of your thread—they all help to fill up." I heeded her directions; and who knows but some act of diplomacy, or some effusion of genius, may have been perpetuated on the paper made from my "shreds and patches?"

My husband was at home nearly all the first week, and my mother, nominally my guest, relieved me from every care; but on the Monday following, she returned to her own residence, Edward went to his office, and I was left alone. I soon felt weary of idleness. How willingly would I have darned a stocking, or clear-starched a muslin; but, alas, everything was *whole*, and in order. I tried to find a withered leaf on my geraniums, but they all looked as fresh as if they too were just married. Centre-tables were not then in fashion, or I could have beguiled a little time in disarranging them for effect; but no! every article of furniture was in its proper parallel, and every chair at right angles with its neighbor, while books and knick-knacks, as drawing-room luxuries, were unknown.

To amuse the tedious hours of my husband's absence, I went into the kitchen, and offered to assist Nancy in making a pudding. My overtures were coldly received, but I thought that that might be "her way," and I proceeded to break the eggs, and measure the milk, giving little Polly the raisins to pick.

"*We* don't put so much milk as that ere in puddins," said Nancy, eying me keenly.

My mother had taught me culinary arts with great care, and I felt on strong ground while I defended *my* quantity of milk. Nancy answered me again with some heat, and when she found me following my own recipe in silence, dashed the sieve full of flour on the table, and putting her arms akimbo, said,

"Well, *Miss* Packard, if you will spile the puddin, you must bake it yourself."

I was thunderstruck! A bride, to whom for a week all had submitted as to a queen; from whom commands were favors, and requests privileges! I felt the blood rush to my face, my hands trembled, and fearing to expose my agitation, I quietly laid down the materials I was preparing, and said, with a great effort at calmness,—

"Finish this pudding, and bake it for dinner."

I just made out to reach the parlor, when I burst into tears, and sobbed like a child, comforting myself, however, with the idea that I should compose myself and bathe my eyes before Edward came home. But that was not to be. With a young husband's impatience, he had hurried through his business, and thinking to give me a pleasant surprise, stood by my side.

I cannot describe his concern at my situation, while I, mortified to the heart at having exposed myself in tears for such a trifle, could scarcely explain the cause of my distress. When I did make him understand the nature of the provocation I had received, he grew angry (I had never seen him angry before), and walking with long strides into the kitchen, he dismissed Nancy on the spot.

With a woman's glance, I saw the consequences. Nancy laid aside a raw steak, that she was making tender by her passionate treatment, and walked up stairs in high dudgeon, not forgetting to take up the wages which Edward had thrown on the table. Five minutes after, we heard her departing tramp on the stairs.

It was no time for crying now. Little Polly and I had to go to cooking in good earnest. My husband turned off the affair, when his temper was cooled, with a very pleasant grace, and as I placed the before-mentioned steak on the gridiron, exclaimed,

"Haste hither, Eve, with speed;
And what thy stores contain bring forth, and pour abundance."

When our dinner was cooked, we formed a procession from the kitchen to the parlor. Edward bore the steak, whistling a march; I followed, laughing, with the pudding, for we had to economize time, and little Polly, enjoying the joke, trudged after with the potatoes.

Still we felt that there was an effort in all this, and when my husband looked at me for the first time alone, at his table, he perceived that the kitchen fire, added to the effects of weeping, had deepened the hue of my complexion beyond the delicacy of beauty, and as I was assisting him to a potato, detected a spot of "smut" (pot-black) on the finger on which he had placed a pearl ring. I blushed deeper crimson; and tears, those trials to young wives, started to my eyes. Edward seemed not to notice it, and I transferred the sable stain to one of my bridal handkerchiefs.

CHAPTER III.

SALLY CURRY.

> She is not the fairest, although she is fair,
> O' nice education but sma' is her share,
> Her parentage humble as humble can be.—BURNS.

NOTHING could be more calm than our evening meal after the excitement of our cook's departure. We felt the happiness of that intercourse where "love is." It was autumn. The beauty and freshness of summer were in the heavens, and the warmth of winter on our hearth.

I felt no embarrassment in carrying my shining brass tea-kettle into the parlor, and making tea there, which, with blushing importance, I poured out for my husband. He was full of the gentle pleasantry of satisfied affection.

Little Polly superintended the toasting iron, that luxury so little known in some places, where forks are destroyed daily in *burning* one piece of bread, while the iron *toasts* three in less time.

My mother was soon apprized of the loss of my cook, and the very next evening "help" came in the form of a gentle, but ignorant-looking girl of eighteen. She was one to whom I would willingly have extended my hand, and given my heart. I dreaded to think that so soft a creature should be visited by the elements "too roughly." She was however active, and her duties were soon well performed. Sally had been an inmate of my family but six weeks, when one day she came into the parlor, and, coloring very deeply, handed me a letter, which was written as follows.

"SALEM, ———.

"Dear Sally,—I've got home safe from Calcutta, and reckon that you will be glad to see me, tho' sometimes I aint so sure. I calculate to be in Boston by to-morrow, and shall find you out. If you haven't got another sweetheart I shall want to marry you Sunday night; if you have, I shall take ship Monday morning and be off again.

"Yours till death,

"SAM'L CURRY.

"P.S.—I have had two lucky 'ventures, and we shan't want for nothing. I hope you aint lost the ring."

"Well, Sally," said I, smiling, "am I to lose you on Sunday night?"

"I am afeard so, ma'am," replied she, sliding behind the door.

"Don't be ashamed, Sally," said I. "I have shown you such an example of marrying one whom *I* preferred, that I am sure I cannot blame *you*."

Upon this Sally looked up, and I asked her how long she had known Mr. Curry.

Sally began twisting a gold ring that was on the fore-finger of her left hand, and said,

"My mother, ma'am, was a poor woman in Salem, the widow of a sea-captain. He was lost on a voyage, and she fell sick, declining, like. I was her only child. It was a very stormy night, a year ago, and my mother was very ill. I sent to a neighbor to say that I was afeard she wouldn't stand it. Our neighbor sent back she daresn't leave her baby, who was sick, but a young man what was boarding there, a sailor named Curry, a very decent person, would come and watch with me.

I was thankful to see a living countenance, and said he might come and welcome.

"That was a forlorn night; but Mr. Curry helped me a sight. My mother was in a kind of faint like all night, and he was as tender as a child to her. Once he began to tell a sea-story, to try and cheer me up, but he found he made me cry more, because it didn't seem somehow respectful to talk of the things of life by a death-bed, and he stopped talking, and only now and then, when he found he couldn't comfort me, nor raise her neither, he would fetch up such a pitying look, as if he wished he could.

"The day was just dawning when my mother seemed to come to a little, and spoke right out, 'Sally, dear.'

"'What, mother?' says I, and my heart beat as if it would come through.

"'Is there anybody with you?' says she.

"'Yes, dear mother, a friend,' says I, whispering.

"'Will he take care of you?' says she, and she looked with her sunk eye full on Curry.

"Curry got right up, and came by the bedside, and knelt down, and took her thin hand, and said, in a voice quite loud and solemn, 'I *will* take care of her, so help me God.'

"She didn't say another word, but just gave a kind of sigh, as it were not sorrowful, but as if she was satisfied, and squeezed his hand, and so she died.

"The sun rose then quite glorious. The light didn't look right to me; it shot to my heart like ice, and I would rather have had it dark again.

"Curry was very kind and serviceable to me, but just as he was going to call in the neighbors, one of the crew came, and said, the vessel was gettin under way, and he must go.

"There wasn't much to be said, because he had to go so

quick, but he kissed me once (you know I was in trouble, and that somehow brings us all equal), and took a gold ring out of his waistcoat pocket, and putting it on my finger, said, 'I bought that ring for my sister ; but, Miss Sally, I love you more than I do her now, and if I live to come back, you shall see that I do, that you shall.'

"I felt as if my mother had died over again when he went out, but the neighbors soon came in, and she was decently laid out. Curry left twenty dollars to pay expenses. I was the only mourner at her funeral, and I cried enough for a hundred ; and it seemed to me, the night after the funeral, that I should like to go and throw myself into the ocean that poor Curry sailed on.

"Time passed on, and the ring was a kind of comfort to me. Sometimes I was so foolish as to talk to it, as if it could understand, and I would ask it questions I wouldn't like to ask anybody else.

"The folks told me I should get higher wages in Boston than in Salem, and I have made out tolerable. I don't know how it was, it seemed to me that I would give myself a year to hear good news in, and I thought I might as well be laying up things with my earnings when they turned up cheap, so that I have got pretty considerable beforehand.

"I hope, ma'am," said Sally after a pause, for I was silent from the emotion her simple story caused me—"I hope you don't think I've been over-quick in my liking. I heard a very good character of Curry from the folks he lodged with, and the image of him that night seemed to take the place of my mother's, and filled up a very heavy want in my heart."

"Oh no, Sally," said I, quite charmed with her simplicity, "I do not blame you, but I hear the sound of a chaise on the pavement at the side door."

Sally's color went and came, but she answered a sailor-like knock from the outside, and I believe Curry was very well satisfied with his reception.

This was Friday. On the following day the kitchen had an extra cleaning. I beat up a wedding-cake, and we made busy preparations for Sunday evening.

The bride looked very sweetly in a plain white cambric frock, and as she stood beside Curry, reminded me of those figures we sometimes see delicately chiselled on the sterns of vessels; while he appeared like the good stout ship, which, though destined to bear her through winds and waves, was powerful enough to do it safely. When our good pastor, the Rev. Mr. Lathrop, asked him the customary question, "Will you love, protect, and cherish this woman?" &c., Curry was not content with the simple bowing affirmative. Something seemed struggling in his mind. He grasped Sally's hand, and with such an utterance as she told me he had used on the night her mother died, said, "I will, so help me God.'

On Monday morning my husband presented Sally with a large brass kettle, a common New-England present on such occasions, and the happy couple bade us farewell. As they rode away, Curry waved his red handkerchief, and Sally put her new cambric one to her eyes, between tears and smiles. I never saw my pretty cook again.

CHAPTER IV.

CINDA TYLER.

How now, my headstrong?
Where have you been gadding?
Romeo and Juliet.

I HAD become so much attached to my gentle Sally, that I was really quite dispirited at her departure; but, not being provided with immediate assistance, was soon engrossed with household cares. And let no one underrate the value of those cares to an unoccupied or even a harassed mind, whose mental resources are limited. Who has not seen the tear of sorrow dry away amid their gentle but imperious demands? Who has not seen oppressed and tender women forget, in the routine which constitutes the comfort of a husband, that husband's unkindness? And then, what an admirable outlet are household cares for a scold! View that face screwed up to moderation and even courtesy at the breakfast table. How gracefully is that cup forwarded! What gentle accents accompany it! But the lord and master of the household departs! Hear his last footstep, and then notice how the clouds gather round that delicate creature, until the brow is contracted, the voice is sharpened, the eye darts withering beams, and those lips open (shall I say it?) for the unequivocal terms *slut and hussy!* While sometimes, rarely I hope, the tender palm comes vibrating in unthoughtof vigor on some uncovered ear, or (alas for delicacy !) that little implement which once won the heart of an Eastern Prince,* is flourished over an extended and trembling hand.

My mother, with a mother's care, supplied me with new "help." She was from Vermont, and as green as her native hills. Cinda Tyler was her name, though she took some pains to tell me she was christened Lucinda.

What a contrast to my Sally! No one could look at her without thinking of *strapper*, *bouncer*, or some such inelegant association. She had carrot-colored hair of unmanageable thickness, even when the experiment of a comb was tried, which was rarely done except on the Sabbath, when even the poorest in New-England feel as if the purity of the body should honor the day, whatever may be the undress of the soul.

Cinda's arms were bare and red, large and short. She had a perpetual look of eager curiosity. There were a few things I never could break her of. She invariably nodded her head to my visitors, even if she had a dish full of meat in her hand, and said, "How fares ye?" And say it she would, until an answer was extorted, whatever might be the repulsive dignity of the person addressed. I endeavored, at first by nods and signs, to make her understand that this ceremony could be dispensed with, but all in vain; with her eyes wide open, she stood at my parlor door, "making her manners" (little bobbing courtesies), until she obtained the sought-for notice. Finding her incorrigible to hints, I told her, as she was using one evening the whole artillery of her politeness on Judge ——, a friend of my husband's, that she might go out. She opened her great gray eyes wider than ever, and said, somewhat gruffly, "I ain't a goin to let his honor s'pose I was brought up mungst wild criters." His honor, who had been stating a case of great interest, roused

* See Cinderella, or the Little Glass Slipper.

by her voice, perceived her for the first time, and said, with perfect good-nature, "Ah, how d'ye do?" and Cinda set him down from that moment as a gentleman; and so he was. It is that immediate conformity to the *feelings* of individuals that marks a gentleman or lady, whether they address their equals or inferiors.

One morning, in my absence from home, a lady called to see me, and Cinda, from sheer curiosity, anticipated little Polly in going to the door.

"Is Mrs. Packard within?" said the lady.

"No ma'am," said Cinda, with great promptness, "but you'd better come in and set with me a spell."

I met my intended guest at the gate, and could not account for her look of ill-suppressed mirth, until Cinda gave me a hint of what she called manners in her reception.

Another peculiarity of Cinda's was to examine every new purchase of mine, and ask the price, and sometimes the ornaments of my visitors did not escape this ordeal. I was getting somewhat wearied with these oddities, notwithstanding her skill in washing, hanging on pots and kettles, and all the drudgery of her calling, when one evening a few ladies visited me, and Cinda, after sufficient drilling, undertook to hand tea, solemnly promising me not to address them. As she passed from one to another, I felt a little anxiety at the look of scrutiny she cast, from the head downward, on every individual. Her appearance began to attract the attention of my friends, but she preserved silence, until, at the close of the service, a very sweet-looking girl bent her blue eye upon Cinda with a smile. The temptation was irresistible. She had an empty tray in her hand, and lowering it suddenly, said, "I guess, miss, them 'ere beads of your'n cost considerable." The younger ladies thrust their pocket-handkerchiefs into their mouths, and the elder ones stared, while Cinda, catching my eye, and perceiving a frown, cried out, "Lud, Miss Packard, if I ain't spoke in the party;" and then, with a look of greater horror, "Lud, lud, I've spoke agin!" then catching up the tray, she retreated in confusion.

It was impossible for the most rigid muscles to refrain from laughter. The shouts reached poor Cinda's ears in her culinary domain, and it required all the inducements I could urge to prevail on her to carry the tray again.

Curiosity, which seemed to be her master-passion, prompted her to try on the garments of others. A French lady from St. Domingo, for whom Edward was employed in a law-suit, came to pass a few days with me. Her dress was fashionable in the extreme. It was Cinda's province to arrange the bed-rooms while we breakfasted. Mam'selle Ligne had occasion to leave the table one morning in quest of her handkerchief, and her light step was unperceived by Cinda, who stood before the glass. She had placed on her carroty locks Mam'selle Ligne's beautiful evening cap, and thrown a slight scarf over her shoulders; and there she stood with an air of the most complacent satisfaction, gazing at her own charms. The joke was too good to be lost. Mam'selle tripped down, and asking Edward and myself to follow, we all went up softly, ignorant of what we were to behold.

Human gravity could not hold out at such a spectacle. Edward gave one of those laughs through his nose that always sound louder than a natural one, and poor Cinda started in dismay at beholding us. She took off the scarf in her hurry, but forgot the cap, which was of very light material, and began making up the bed with great zeal.

Just at this crisis the butcher knocked at the outer door, and Cinda, glad to escape, raced down, cap and all, to receive him.

"Holla, Cinda," said he, "are you setting that 'ere cap at me?" This was too much for Cinda's nerves. She caught up the leg of lamb he had extended to her, and running into the kitchen, hid her blushes in her check apron.

CHAPTER V.

LUCY COOLEDGE.

> Servitude is honor, not
> Disgrace, when falling fortunes make it needful.
> GOETHE. *Herman and Dorothea.*

CINDA blundered through ten months in my service, sometimes fretting and sometimes amusing me with her oddities, before her curiosity and love of change induced her to leave me. At length, with some little emotion, she announced her intention of removing.

"I know, *Miss* Packard," said she, "that you'll miss me more than enough; such a bird is not to be caught on every bough. 'Tisn't everybody that has my knack at thrashing about among the pots and kettles. I'm not the person that holds a frying-pan with white gloves on. But I've a notion to see a little more of the world. *Miss* Bachelor is going out to Roxbury to live, and I'm to try how she suits me a spell. Howsomever, as I don't want to leave you without nobody, Mr. Tucker, the butcher, says one Lucy Cooledge is in petikelar want of a sitivation, being as how old Miss Amory died two weeks ago, and ain't left her no provision."

On the following morning I had a conversation with Mr. Tucker about Lucy Cooledge. The narration interested me, though I drew the inference that she would not be as dexterous in "thrashing about among the pots and kettles" as her predecessor. She had been adopted in orphan-infancy by Mrs. Amory, and educated as well as her slender means would permit. The tendency of her teaching, it appeared, was to form a religious character, and cultivate great original sensibility in her young charge. For two years, Mrs. Amory had been lingering with a chronic affection, and left Lucy, at the age of seventeen, without a shelter, except from the charity of neighbors.

"It was a crying sight," said Mr. Tucker, "to see the poor thing the day Mrs. Amory died, looking around so piteous, as much as to say, 'I have nothing left now!' She sat as still as could be, for you know there are folks enough always busy at layings-out, and just watched what they did in a wistful kind of a way. I made a shift to get a neighbor to ride around with the meats for me, first picking out a real tender bit of mutton for some broth for Miss Lucy; and made as good a bargain as I could about the coffin. I happened in again on the afternoon of the burying, and I was scared to see her so quiet. When her name was called out to walk with Deacon Hodges as chief mourner, she just went straight forward, without putting her handkerchief to her eyes, and didn't seem to care to lean on his arm, even. She walked right on to the grave, and gave a look as if she could not look far enough, nor long enough, and then came back—but no crying, not a drop. She went into the sitting-room, where the chairs still stood thick and close, and sat down, and there wasn't one of us that know'd what to say. You know, ma'am, if she had only took on, we could have comforted her. At last Deacon Hodges' wife went to take off her bonnet, seeing she didn't move, and took hold of her hand. 'My gracious, Lucy,' says she, 'your hand is like ice;' and so it was, though it was a warm day, and her cheeks were like ice too; and says she, with a kind of shiver, 'My heart is ice.'

They fell to rubbing her hands, and gave her some wine to drink, and in a half an hour or thereabouts, she fetched a sigh, and large tears rolled down her cheeks; and them as stood by wiped them off, for she seemed not to know that she was a crying. She has come to now pretty much, but has an ugly cough, and I don't like the look of her eyes. Mrs. Amory taught her all kinds of housework, and I've a notion, if she was in a reg'lar family, she would be quite pert again. A man, you see, *Miss* Packard," continued Mr. Tucker, clearing his throat, "can worry through these things, and make a shift for a living; but it's hard for young women to push on through thick and thin."

I should have been glad to assist Lucy in a pecuniary way, but to a character like hers independence was the better charity; and as Cinda had fixed on the day for quitting me, Mr. Tucker promised to engage a seat in the Newton stage for her to Boston.

The stage arrived about ten o'clock on the day appointed, and Lucy was the only passenger. It was a great unwieldy vehicle, without glasses, the leathern curtains flapping all around, the worn cushions as slippery as glass, and so little spring in its construction, that Lucy's slight figure was thrown from side to side as the horses, for city display, whisked up to the door.

She was dressed in simple mourning. There was no affectation of better days about her; she entered the kitchen as the scene of her duties with quiet gravity, and went through her work with precision and fidelity, and only on Sunday evenings allowed herself the luxury of reading.

Servants' apartments, in New-England are always in the house with the family; Lucy's bed-room was near mine, and every night before she retired, for three months, we heard her sweet voice in an evening hymn. Gradually, however, from five or six verses she diminished to one, until at last no music was heard; but a hoarse, deep cough broke in even on my midnight slumbers.

Still she moved on in her daily duties, though I could not but regard with anxiety the color that lit her cheek at evening, and made her intellectual face even beautiful. I gradually lightened her heavier employments, and gave her sewing in the parlor, for Polly had by this time become familiar with my arrangements, and with occasional assistance was strong enough to engage in carrying them out.

But Lucy drooped daily, struggling on; I was often obliged to take her work from her forcibly, so conscientious was she. I sent for a physician. She met him with a gentle smile. After parting with her, he said to me, "There has been some heart-sickness in this case, I suspect.—There is a fine organization in some systems, tending to early decay, and yielding alike to mental and bodily pressure; and hers is of that stamp. The case is a call on your charity, and I will cheerfully co-operate with you."

When I returned to the parlor Lucy had laid her sewing on her lap, and sat with her hands folded, as in reverie.

"I see, by your countenance, Mrs. Packard," said she, "what Dr. Webster thinks of my case, and I am not *very* sorry. I am *only* sorry because I shall be a source of care and anxiety, in such a scene of quiet happiness as your house always presents.

"To me, dear madam," continued she, after a pause, turning her large dark eyes upwards, "to me, *to die is gain.*"

I had been educated religiously, attended church regularly, learned appropriate catechisms and hymns, and found in the example of my dear mother the best of all instruction; but I had never suffered, never seen death in any form, and my religion was the overflowing of gratitude, not the want of poor humanity. I could not realize the force of Lucy's expression. To be willing to leave this bright world, so full of the blossoms of hope and love, to quit the pure air, and the bright skies, and be the mouldering tenant of the solitary tomb—how could it be *gain?* I looked at her thin pale cheek inquiringly, and could not restrain my tears.

Lucy smiled sadly—"Life appears," said she, "very differently to one who, like you, enjoys the sympathy of friends, of such friends too! I am now only a weed on the stream of time. When I pass into the ocean of eternity, who knows but that I may be attached to something bright and beautiful too?"

From that moment, that little moment of heart and sensibility, my relations with Lucy assumed a different aspect. I drew a chair near her—"Lucy," I said, cheerfully, "*I* will be the beautiful thing to which you shall be attached in *this* world; so do not talk of another, dear." I was checked by the pressure of her thin hand, where even labor had not been able to shade the blue veins, so light was their covering.

From the moment that this delicate chain of sympathy was thrown over our minds, there was a quiet but distinct course of action between us. My part was to strengthen and animate her sinking frame. I brought her fresh flowers, new books, kind friends, and little luxuries that cool the feverish lip; but Lucy had a higher task to perform. It was, to direct my thoughts to a feeling of the value and necessity of Christianity; to teach me to subdue the idolatry of my affections, and give them a *spiritual* bias.

She spoke of Edward as a "being of *soul*, a candidate for immortality."—"He is too beautiful for the grave, Lucy," said I; "I can never, never let him die.—I can go myself, if God calls me, but I cannot spare him; that manly form, those high and generous feelings, that warm, warm heart,—oh, they are my *life*. Talk to me of anything but the death of Edward!"

Still she gently recurred to high and spiritual topics, and led my thoughts at times beyond earthly affections. She marked passages in the Bible of the most attractive character for me to read to her, and, when her cough would allow, breathed out a hymn in sweet and happy strains, in which I soon loved to join. Time wore away, and she revived a little with reviving spring. She still had strength to carry her plants from window to window to catch the sunbeams, and could sit to watch the twilight in its dying glory.

But soon she failed again, and one night Edward and I were awaked to go to her. She could but whisper to us as we bent over her, "Do not love each other too well. Pray with and for each other. Forget not that Christ lived and died for you. I shall expect you *both*, *both*—in Heaven." And thus she died.

One favor only had she asked of us. It was that she might be buried in the country church-yard of her native town.

"I would have overcome that little preference," she once said, "did I not know there is something soothing in complying with the wishes of the dying. How idle a fancy," she continued, smiling, "to wish that trees should wave and birds sing over this wasted form; but nature has been so lovely to me that I have a kind of gratitude to her, and it is sweet to think that I shall repose among those objects which God has given me sensibility to enjoy."

She was carried to her favorite resting-place. From that period a religious repose chastened the intense tenderness of our hearts, as we remembered Lucy's character and death; and when we occasionally left the city to breathe the country air, our souls were refreshed by a visit to her grave.

CHAPTER VI.

JEALOUSY.

Ever at early dawn, and close of day,
Oh! be Amanda's toil to thine allied—
Labor shall lead me smiling by thy side,
So but a smile of thine my toil repay.—WIELAND.

MY next domestic trial was unconnected with household cares. My "help" was "the perfectest pattern of excelling" housekeepers, and my affairs went on like clockwork. Our meals "came like spirits." No half-cooked potatoes betrayed a cold and hard heart beneath a soft surface—no half-picked poultry came to the table as if reluctant to resign the feathery insignia. The amalgamation of sauces and gravies was like the intercourse of society, where the piquant is softened by the modest, and the feeble animated by the strong. My windows were clear as a good conscience, my brasses bright as ready wit, and like Narcissus in the stream, I half fell in love with myself in the polished mahogany.

From whence then came the cloud to shade this happy picture? I was jealous. Not of women, for my husband not only professed to love me, but treated me with marked attention in the society of others; and often when I saw married men display their gallantry to any *but* their wives, I felt proud of those *preferring* attentions, which Edward directly, but without display, tendered me. My jealousy, and I write it with half a blush, was of books.

Edward was becoming an ambitious lawyer. His singleness of character and clearness of intellect gained him unexpected friends, and the strongest efforts of his mind were directed to eminence in his profession. Gradually, book by book was brought from the office. Blackstone was on one window-seat, Coke upon Littleton on another, and Chitty's Pleadings lumbered the well-dusted mantelpiece. An instinctive regard and respect for my feelings prevented his passing his evenings abroad; but he read and read, while I silently pursued my sewing, until at last the heavy *whitish* looking volumes were laid on the breakfast or tea-table, beside the cup of coffee, which was often allowed to cool before it was tasted. He no longer asked me for a song at evening; and when I found my voice unheard by him, I shut the harpsichord in disgust. Our sunset walk was often forgotten; and when I sometimes said, "Come, Edward, I am ready;" he answered, "Yes, dear, directly—just let me finish this paragraph." The paragraph might be finished, but I, sitting in silence, felt a languor steal over me; and when in a half-hour he closed his book, and said briefly, "What—are you waiting? Let us go," the walk seemed heavy, and the twilight sad. Perhaps, had I rallied him, he might have perceived that he was trying a dangerous, though unintentional experiment with a devoted heart; or had I seriously opened my feelings, he would probably have understood them; but I was ashamed, and tried to think that *I* was unreasonable, and he in the performance of his duty. I remembered that it was for my subsistence he toiled, and lingered through even the midnight hour.

But with a feeling of unconquerable diffidence in the expression of my thoughts, I grew reserved. My step was slow and careful, or quick and agitated, and I sometimes said cutting things in the impatience of my spirit. He was all truth and openness, and occasionally looked perplexed at my manner.

"I should think you were unhappy," said he one day to me, after he had been studying a horrid-looking, parchment-covered book, at the breakfast-table, "if I did not see everything around you appearing so cheerful and comfortable. There never was such a sweet home as ours."

My eyes filled with tears, but I hid them, and was silent.

"Clarissa," said he, "you look thin, and now I think of it I am afraid your appetite is not good. Those nice cakes, did you eat some this morning?"

"We had *toast* for breakfast," I replied; before I could say more, he was absorbed in his book.

I took my sewing, that I might be with him the half-hour before he went out. Just at this period a little boy who lived opposite, and who was in the habit of visiting us frequently, came in, and began his customary prattle.

"Oh, Mr. Packard," said little John, running to him, "let me see that book."

"What for?" said my husband, keeping his finger on a paragraph.

"Why, because," said the rogue, "aunt Clara (the name he always gave me), aunt Clara got angry with it yesterday."

"Angry, my boy; how so?" said he.

"Why, sir, after you had done sipping your coffee, with the big book by your plate, and took your hat and walked out like a judge, she went to gather the cups to wash, and when she came to the big white book by your cup she dashed it down on a chair, and said, 'I hate you!' and looked as if she was going to cry."

Edward leaned his head a moment over the chair on which he sat, and mused. I sewed as if life hung on my needle.

"Clarissa," he said, at length, with a sweet, earnest voice and look, taking my hands in his, "I know now what is the matter with you. I have been to blame, dearest, in not consulting more affectionately the feelings of my own wife. It was not enough, it *ought* not to be enough for me, to have given you comforts and luxuries; you require sympathy. You have been struggling with the wants of your heart. I wish I had understood them before. As for this book," said he, playfully, "I cannot 'hate it,' since it has given me such a revelation of my duty."

From that period his deportment at home had a perpetual view to my happiness and improvement. He brought books to read to me, calculated to interest while they elevated my literary taste. He referred to me for opinions, and by sounding the depth and power of my intellect, found, that under his guidance there were occasions when even my advice might avail him. When a case occurred which obliged him to study at home, he detailed it in simple terms to me, told me the course he should pursue, and its probable results; while, satisfied and happy, I would sit by his side like Klopstock's Meta, "looking so still in his sweet face." Understanding his conduct and feelings, I began to be ambitious for him. Step by step he mounted the ladder of fame. I saw all eyes gazing on him with delight, heard every lip echoing applause; and those sights and sounds were doubly dear to me, for I knew every spring that moved his noble heart, and that his thoughts were mine before they were the world's.

CHAPTER VII.

GREASE.

> Chattels which, yesterday, good housewifery
> Had rang'd, in cleanly and delightful order,
> Lay now disjointed, broken, rent.—GOETHE.

IN the subject I am about to introduce, I am confident of the sympathy of housekeepers.—The theme is *grease*, which, if I may be allowed a poor pun, has produced as many domestic disturbances in modern, as it did political in ancient times. Who can tell the amount of temper that has been roused by this evil, from the single drop of lamp-oil on the finger, to which the olfactory sense, though driven back, returns with painful tenacity, to the mass which, sinking in your white floor, looks fresher, like the stain on Blue Beard's key, for many a scouring?

I hope I may be excused here for a homely piece of advice, which is, that wives should not only keep the lamps of their souls trimmed and burning, but attend to that department in their household economy. If they do not, their husbands may as well sit down to sup with the ladies of Queen Charlotte's Sound, whom Captain Cook describes as not only "drinking the oil from his lamps, but eating the cotton wick."

In return for the various attentions we had received, Edward and myself sent out invitations for an evening party. We had not the facilities for lighting our rooms which make it so little trouble now, by sending for a *professor* in the art, to produce a blaze that shall *cast no shadow;* but we treated ourselves to an astral lamp, they having been newly brought to this country. Being somewhat ambitious of intellectual display, and the time beginning to pass away when ladies did not feel themselves pinned to the same seat for three hours, we managed, by buying and borrowing, to collect some amusing novelties; among them was a magnifying glass, with splendid Italian views. These were arranged on the sofa table, illuminated by our new lamp, which attracted universal admiration. The Italian views became the chief subject of attention, but alas! as our guests crowded around the table it was suddenly overthrown, and the lamp shattered to pieces. Satin slippers and gentlemen's pumps received the indiscriminate shower of oil, and the beautiful engravings coming in for a share, a young beau, who never lost a pun, even in calamity, whispered to me that they were "oil paintings."

A general shock was given to our before complacent group; first were circulated whispered complaints and commiseration, then in a louder tone followed details of similar misfortunes, and recipes for extracting them.

I contrived to affect great indifference, and Edward got up his best jokes, but after a struggle at general sociability the company retired, and left us, at an earlier period than we expected, gazing on the wreck.

It is easy to preserve a sweet smile in the presence of fifty people, but the test of good nature follows in a *tête-à-tête.*

"What an awkward wretch that Mason is," said Edward. "I wish people would not go into society until they are civilized!"

"I am surprised at your blaming Mr. Mason," said I. "It

was Miss Otis who knocked over the table—that girl thinks she must be first in everything."

"Mrs. Packard, I am confident that it was Mr. Mason," returned Edward.

"Mr. Packard," replied I, "I saw Miss Otis do it with my own eyes."

"Women are always obstinate," said he, turning away.

"And men are always domineering," I answered, in the same tone.

There ended our first party, and began our first quarrel; but it seemed so odd, that turning round, our eyes met, and we burst out into unaffected laughter.

I will not enter into a detail of similar misfortunes. Who has not, after long deliberation, purchased a set of expensive lamps, only to suffocate himself or his friends with smoke? Who has not heard his glass shades pop one after another, with a report as harassing as the small arms of an enemy? Who has not welcomed "the tall mould candle straight and round," while the costly lamp, that gave for five minutes a gleam of light, is

"Wisely kept for show."

But I have other themes of varied trouble to relate. One commencement day a large party assembled to dine with us, after the college exercises. Edward had presented me with a new silk dress. It was a rare and important addition to my wardrobe, and I made my toilet with many resolutions to be careful of it. As I sat at the table, with the consciousness of a well-ordered dinner and an appropriate dress, whose value to me was doubly enhanced by its being Edward's choice, one of the waiters, with a zeal worthy of a better cause, jostled by another, who was reaching above my shoulder to deposit a gravy-boat, and knocked it over. I felt the warm stream trickle through my lace tippet, and saw it pour into my lap. *Selon la règle*, I was obliged either not to notice or make a jest of it. I had the resolution not to *look* at the servant (how often have I seen looks speak more than words!) and turning quietly to my left-hand neighbor, I said, "Pray, sir, excuse my being helped first."

A short period only elapsed before Edward was called upon to sympathize with me in a similar experience. Being invited to a ceremonious party, he mounted a new coat. I could perceive considerable complacency in his manner of pulling down the waist and turning out the collar. He was in excellent spirits through the evening, and on his return said, laughing,

"Either I or my new coat was a great favorite this evening, for my friends certainly regarded me with uncommon interest."

"And well they might!" I exclaimed, in alarm, on looking at him, "for you have half of one of Mrs. Winthrop's candles streaming down from your collar to your elbow."

Poor Edward was thrown all aback. "Hang it," said he, quite off his guard, "I can interpret their looks now. They could not quite resolve to tell me what a figure I cut, and I thought they were admiring my genteel person, while I was strutting about with the sign of a tallow-chandler on my shoulder."

Speaking of a new coat reminds me of an anecdote of Mr. Shaw, a literary friend of ours. In the pride of his heart *he* too put on a coat fresh from the tailor's, to attend a party, and while bowing to the ladies, an acquaintance tapping him on the shoulder said, "Shaw, your coat was very reasonable," pointing at the same time to the tailor's mark, which was pinned conspicuously on the skirt.

When albums were first in vogue, a choice one was sent us for our contributions. I have always loved albums, much as they have been ridiculed. They seem to me the leading-strings of literature, and it interests me to see the ardor of a young lady, when, opening the gilt leaves, she finds there sentiments dedicated to her alone. Woe to him who shall dare to trace impure characters on those unsullied leaves! Indeed, so sacred are they, that though folly often intrudes upon them, vice rarely profanes them.

The album sent us was elegantly bound, and enriched by contributions from native poets. Edward and I communicated our mite immediately. It is a good rule. The next day I looked at the book to review what I had written, but what was my dismay at finding its beautiful pages discolored with lamp oil. Down it had streamed over a sentimental effusion of Wilde; Percival's wing was clogged, and even Bryant's purity was marred by the contact.

"I did not think to shed a tear"

over my silk frock or Edward's coat, but this was really alarming. An album I could purchase, but how restore the handwriting of those poets on which I knew the enthusiastic owner loved to dwell with natural pride? I summoned Becky Rand, "*my woman in the kitchen*," (the New-England circumlocution for cook).

She confessed that after I had retired she thought it would do no harm to read a little, and being "dozy," she let the kitchen lamp fall on the book and "il'd" it.

I suspected as much from Becky's literary taste. I had often observed a volume of "Zimmerman on Solitude," covered with blue homespun, lying on the dresser, and once, being in want of a skewer, detected one put for a mark at the following anecdote.

"The celebrated Armelle, who died in the convent of Vannes,

was placed by her parents who were villagers, as a menial servant in the house of a neighboring gentleman, with whom she lived five-and-thirty years (just Becky's age). During this time his groom, finding the kitchen-door fastened, had the curiosity to peep through the keyhole, where he discovered the pious maid in a paroxysm of divine ecstacy spitting a fowl. The youth was so much affected by this religious fervor, that he devoted himself to a convent."

Becky was very sentimental, and usually had an interjectional remark whenever I entered the kitchen.

"Oh, ma'am," said she to me one day, pointing to a bean she had trained over her kitchen window, "how can the human natur's heart help for to see how miraculous beans is!"

I did not ridicule Becky's sentimentalities, but found pleasure in moralizing over the progress of her bean vine, and even kept my countenance when, the morning after a frost, she assumed a pensive attitude, and said, "Ah, *Miss* Packard, so frail is the human natur's life of a bean!"

I heard, however, a conversation between herself and Polly, as we were preparing for a guest at dinner, that completely excited my risibility.

"Who is coming here to day?" said Polly.

"A tutor from Cambridge," answered Becky.

"What *is* a tutor?" asked Polly.

"Mercy! child, don't you know?" said Becky, "why, a person that tutes!"

Becky's sentimentalism was not confined to her bean vine. She rarely took up the gridiron without a sigh over the remains of the beef and poultry, and one would think from her looks she was about to bear the martyrdom of St. Lawrence on its well-scraped parallels.

But the place where her mind was most under my inspection

was the ironing-table, where, as Mr. Packard's shirts and cravats were my first care, I felt a feminine pride in smoothing their snowy texture.

Many were the experiences detailed by Becky as we gave the sheets a finishing *snap* in folding, or wielded our irons with the skill of artists.

And when on Tuesday evening every article was translated to its appropriate drawer, and Becky sat by the kitchen fire, at her pine table, with her *mending*, I have often heard her say,

"Polly, child, always regulate your concerns in the day, and then when you come to set by your taper (looking at the small tallow candle), you can have time to meditate on the human natur's heart."

Alas, for romance! Becky married my butcher, and became Mrs. Ichabod Whittemore!

CHAPTER VIII.

THE FIRST-BORN.

As mine own shadow was this child to me,
A second self, far dearer, and more fair.
SHELLEY.

THERE can be but few domestic trials, comparatively speaking, without children. In their absence, that combination of articles expressively designated *clutter*, seldom alarms the eagle-eyed housewife. From day to day, from week to week, from year to year, may she descend to the breakfast table with her smooth morning dress, her well-combed hair, and her face unwrinkled by nursing vigils.

Such was my happy predicament until Master Frederick Packard entered on the before tranquil scene, when forthwith appeared an accompanying train of vials, fennel-seed, and pap. He was blessed from the moment of his birth with a pair of lungs that needed no Demosthenean pebbles to bring them into play. Two thirds of the time his face was in lines as thick as the rivers on a well-drawn map, and his roaring brought kind inquiries from the neighbors " if anything was the matter with the baby ?" His father flattered himself that he was destined to make a noise in the world, and descanted long and loud (for we were obliged to speak at " the top of our voices") on the kindness of Providence in permitting infants to scream, since it was necessary to the healthy action of the lungs; he added, moreover, that all *sensible* children were cross, and that his mother had often said *he* was the most fretful child in the world.

Polly, now thirteen years of age, succeeded the regular nurse in assisting me to attend my little boy, and if ever any one, with the kindest attentions, had a knack at making a child scream, it was she, notwithstanding *my woman in the kitchen* would occasionally put her head into the parlor door and call out, "Polly, Polly, why don't you *shue** the child?" but alas! Polly's sole ability lay in trotting and walking, walking and trotting, with all the energy of human muscles; her last resource, and it was often effectual, was to sit on a particularly hard chair, and rock backward and forward on an uncarpeted floor. At each jolt Master Frederick's voice grew fainter and fainter, until at length, overpowered by superior physical strength, he dropped asleep, and looked as if no storm had ever hung over his placid brow.

How beautiful is the sleep of infancy, with its breathing like the uplifting of lily leaves on a summer wave! It would be sculpture-like, did not the motion of the lips betray a sweet remembrance of its natural wants,

"As the shifting visions sweep,
Amid its innocent rest."

Edward often stole from his office at the hour of our infant's slumber, and we knelt together by his cradle, our thoughts leaping from baby-hood to manhood, living long, long years in that lingering gaze. He always blessed us by awaking with a smile. An unutterable sweetness played over his lips, and his hands were outstretched in gentle joy.

* Probably meaning *hush*.

"His hair is growing darker. He *will* look like you, Clarissa."

"No, Edward, his cradle shades it. See now, as I turn it to the light, your own sunny brown, and Polly thinks his eyes are blue."

To this day the point is not settled. Frederick, who is now a successor in his father's office, has dark eyes when shaded by fatigue or sorrow, but in health and joy they light up with his father's hue.

Notwithstanding Mr. Packard's arguments about expanding the chest, and though he was as brave as a lion, and, in the old uniform of "The Ancient and Honorable Artillery," white broadcloth, faced with red, with a gold-laced *chapeau bras*, he looked as though

> "his eye
> Could create soldiers, and make women fight,"

yet was he a mere coward when Frederick opened his infantile battery of screams; and from this weakness arose the uncomfortable habit of walking with him at night. Even after my husband became Judge Packard, you might have seen his honor at the dead of night, with a half naked baby in his arms, whose whims increased in proportion to their indulgence. For myself, I scarcely knew whether to laugh or weep one night, when, as peeping from my comfortable pillow, I saw the judge dividing the remains of a cold turkey between little Martha, my eldest daughter, and her brother. Fred was then four years old.

When Frederick ceased to be fretful, he became mischievous. By a well-timed slap, I cured him of some daydawn experiments on me; but his favorite plaything at that hour so delightful for repose after a disturbed night, was his father's nose; and when with a groan or remonstrance he turned away, the boy's scream became so tremendous that the nasal toy was restored.

Nothing is more helpless than a kind-hearted man with a passionate child. Its very weakness is its strength, and though one finger of his masculine hand could terminate its existence, yet the infant's feeblest touch can conquer both body and mind.

It is not my intention to theorize on the subject of managing children; I am simply practical. When Frederick was a week old, his father brought home the treatises of Hamilton, West, Edgeworth, &c. on education. I had previously seen him poring over Rousseau and Xenophon. He read them faithfully, and discussed them eloquently, yet not one of these writers could induce him to deny Fred his nose; therefore, finding them insufficient to establish his authority, and not having much taste for reading, I did not look into these celebrated works, and yet my boy obeyed my words, and even my looks. I found great virtue in a rational, well-managed rod. Scolding is every way injurious. It is pouring water into a sieve; your child becomes accustomed to threats, and the passions of both rise with the voice.

"How did you contrive to be so cool," said a gentleman to a Quaker, "when that rascally porter cheated you?" His reply is a lesson to parents and housewives. "Friend, I long ago obliged myself not to *speak loud*, and therefore I never lose my temper."

I have seen so many well-regulated families brought up under Solomon's discipline, and sometimes controlled by the mere sight of a switch hung over the mantelpiece, that I am tempted to think he is getting too much out of fashion, and modern theories, with their feather rods, seem to me like "the crackling of thorns under the pot."

My first sally from my bedroom was to ride; a common custom in New-England. My babe protested with all his lungs, and well he might, against the preparations of his cumbrous toilet. He instinctively raised his trembling hands to his frilled cap, and when a smart blue satin hat was perched on the top of that, making him by contrast look the color of a mummy, his indignation was beyond all bounds; and the flannel blanket, enveloping the whole, scarcely smothered his screams. The motion of the chaise fortunately soon lulled him to sleep, and I was enabled to enjoy the repose of nature.

Every object was as fresh as though it had just sprung into being before my eyes. The beautiful sloping hills of Brookline, the sparkling fulness of Charles river, emptying into the bay, the apple orchards filling the senses with gentle colors and odors, the sweet-brier throwing out its perfume at the very feet of passengers, the barberry bushes, with their delicate yellow blossoms, preludes to the scarlet fruit of autumn, and even the palace-like buildings, placed at almost regular distances along the road from Cambridge to Sweet Auburn, seemed all made for me. I pressed my boy close to my heart, with a gush of gratitude to Him who had thus blessed me. The cares of life had not taken rough hold of Edward or myself, nor were we satiated with its pleasures. There was ever a fount of gayety in our hearts, that threw its sprinklings over the deeper shades of parental consciousness, and gave that relish to the ludicrous which is almost always discernible in delicate minds.

But rides, like all things else, must end. Fred awoke, and began to grow restive beneath the "bonnet of blue." I "*shued*" him as well as my strength would allow, but his clamor increased. Every father and mother, who have ridden through a populous city with a screaming child, will know how the perspiration stood on our faces at this awful publicity, and how we imagined that every eye was fixed on us, and every individual condemning the breeding of Master Packard.

I gave my hopeful baby into Polly's arms on our return, and reconnoitred my establishment below. A good-tempered woman was governing all its various departments. Mrs. Philipson was one of those who seemed to think the old allowance of a "peck of dirt" to a man was too small, for her practical allowance was a bushel.

In vain did I seek for my own reflection in the dim looking-glass; a kitchen towel was thrown on the sofa; Edward, forgetful of all my hints and hopes, "that everything was in order down stairs," had suffered his slippers, coat, books, &c. to accumulate with utter unconsciousness of the effect; no dusting-cloth had passed, like the wing of a good angel, over the furniture, and a waggish friend had written in plain characters on one of the tables, with his finger, "Mr. B——'s compliments."

CHAPTER IX.

INTELLIGENCE OFFICE.

Voyons donc, je vous prie;
Mettons l'original auprès de la copie.
Par ma foi, c'est vous-même;—
Jamais peintre ne fit portrait si ressemblant.—Regnaud.

What charm can soothe her melancholy,
What art can wash her guilt away?—*Vicar of Wakefield.*

Mrs. Philipson, the votary of the Penates mentioned in the preceding chapter, had been obtained for me by my mother at the intelligence-office. It often startles me when I reflect what unprincipled wretches may be brought into the very heart of our domestic circles, and how the pure minds of our children may be blighted in their very unfolding, by these necessary but vicious instruments.

Mrs. Philipson was a chubby woman of forty, with a scarlet face and scarlet throat laid in fat folds. Her eyes were prominent and whitish. Her round elbows rested upon her hips, from whence her short arms projected, and her hands hung from her wrists with an imbecile air. She spoke softly, and was liberal in promises. Polly, whom my readers may recollect as the *little girl* of our establishment, was necessarily greatly under the influence of the cook, particularly as she occupied the same room. She was an orphan from the Female Asylum, bound to me until the age of eighteen. She was so docile and innocent, that could I always have sheltered her under my own wing, she would have been pure as a bird, and might have plumed her flight from me to Heaven; but after the birth of Frederick, new affections came to me, and new cares to her. I could no longer confine her to the parlor, in her half-sized chair, with her calico frock and apron, and her hair simply parted. One morning I discerned a row of ambitious paper-curls on her head; soon, a soiled muslin frill was pinned round her neck; and on the following Sabbath, when I was conjecturing what stranger was passing the window stealthily, a second revealed to me Polly, with a bunch of faded flowers surmounting the simple green riband on her hat, and an old silk dress, which, hanging like a bag about her trim figure, betrayed at once the ungainly circumference of Mrs. Philipson. I called to her to come back. She blushed, and said, "the last bell was tolling."

"Come in immediately," said I.

She walked slowly and sulkily back, and I asked her why she wore borrowed clothes?

For the first time in her life she looked pertly as she answered, "I don't see why I can't dress as well as other folks."

I reasoned with her, and used affectionate persuasions, but finding her obstinate, ordered her to take off finery so unsuited to her age and situation. My anger was new to her, and she obeyed. For several days she was sulky and silent; every action seemed forced, and she looked at me as if I were a tyrant. This expression wore off, and I hoped for better things. I would willingly have discharged Mrs. Philipson, but how could I, with an infant in my arms, my husband's comfort to study, and the fang-like chains of custom clinging to me?

Two weeks elapsed in apparent acquiescence to my wishes. My whole soul was absorbed in Frederick, or perhaps I should have noticed the under-current that was hurrying Polly to destruction. To see his intelligent smile awakening like young creation, to kiss his rounded limbs as they came flushed like the heart of a white rose from the morning-bath, to feel his dimpled hand on my cheek, or press the little velvet luxury in my own, to dress him with maternal pride in robes wrought by the hand of friendship, to sing him lullabies conjured up from the breathings of love, and to whisper to my own heart a thousand and thousand times, "he is an angel"—was not this occupation enough for a young mother?

I was surprised one morning not to hear the usual movements in the house below, and on descending, found the shutters unopened, no fire in the kitchen, and the outer door unlocked. I repaired in some trepidation to the kitchen-chamber. It was untenanted. Astonished and agitated, I ran to acquaint Edward, and we proceeded to examine the premises. Polly's reasons for departing were told in language as strong as words, by a bundle of her plain clothes directed to me.

With what a crash comes the first breach of confidence on the affections, as the circle of agitation is more violent when a stone is thrown on a smooth lake, than on the wilder ocean! I had loved Polly like a younger sister. She came to me when my cup of happiness was full, and I was glad to see her taste her daily draught with me. She had looked at me with a trustingness that seemed to say, "you are my oracle!" She had confided to me her childish sorrows, and was a willing hearer when I talked of Edward. I had administered to *her* in sickness, and when *my* head ached, if every other step was heavy, hers was light and careful.

I looked round her chamber. There was the little glass hung against the wall, before which she had so often combed her parted hair, and which had recently reflected the first awakened glance of vanity. She had forgotten her Bible, Edward's gift. It was lying on the pine dressing-table, with her pocket-handkerchief folded over it, as if it had been her intention to take it, *but it was forgotten!* I glanced at Edward, and sinking on her bed, burst into violent and bitter tears. Edward comforted me with a husband's better love, but though a neighbor sent us breakfast and assistance, and we were at length seated at table, I could not speak; my voice was choked, and large drops fell from my eyes on Fred's silky hair, as he lay sleeping on my lap.

My dear mother hastened to me as soon as Edward sent her intelligence of my misfortune. She insisted on my returning with her, and passing the remainder of the season; and as Edward was deeply engaged in business, he urged it too. In making the necessary arrangements for my removal, I perceived that several articles of my dress were missing, together with some silver, and my miniature. The sorrowful conviction burst upon me, that Polly, instigated by that human fiend, had robbed me.

Several months elapsed, and all inquiries for the poor child were unavailing. How gladly would I have taken her back to my protection, and showed her the "better part," for she was young in sin.

On entering the court-house one day, Edward understood that the suit in which he was engaged would not be brought up immediately, and having some pressing business, he commenced writing. Quite absorbed, he knew not what was occupying the bar, until he heard a lawyer before him exclaim,

"By heavens! it looks like Packard's wife."

Edward started, and saw a miniature passing from hand to hand among the gentlemen. He rose to join them, and it came to him in turn. It was my likeness. I may write, for the sake of my narrative, what Edward said in his enthusiasm, for my age of vanity, if I ever possessed any, has departed. A brilliant eye, a rose-tinged cheek, and an airy form, speak only to me now of the Great Architect who made them, and who has beauty for us in reversion that will be as the fine gold to dross.

"Clarissa," said my husband, "think what must have been my sensations at that moment, when the low jests of some of my brethren, and the unsubdued admiration of others, ignorant of my connection with the picture, fell on my ear. I gave one long glance at their lineaments to assure me of their identity. There were your dark flashing eyes looking a sweet defiance on that heartless crowd; there were your ruby lips softening those eyes with smiles; there were these very curls, nature's handiwork, falling over the polished brow; there was this white hand, pledged to me in truth and innocence, and those slight fingers, with their one golden circlet, holding back the clustering locks, and glancing among their darkness like breaks of the galaxy between parting clouds. I thrust the miniature next my heart, and held my hands crushed over it as a miser holds a rescued treasure. I was recalled to my recollection by an astonished smile from those around me. A few words to the counsel convinced them of my claim on the picture, and my interest in the disclosures to be made."

But Edward soon forgot even me, for stationed at the bar were two female figures familiar to his memory. It was impossible to mistake the vulgar air and face of Mrs. Philipson. As the various testimony was given in, her eyes rolled in uneasy impudence from side to side, her red hands were clenched in anger, or she gave an hysterical sob, half affectation, half alarm, and raised the corner of her shawl to wipe pretended tears. But a deeper feeling absorbed him when he scrutinized the timid-looking figure by her side. Her bonnet, a mixture of sorry finery, scarcely hid her face, but it was closely covered with both her hands. She looked like one who would gladly have called on the rocks to cover her, and a feeling of shame could be seen in the very bend of her figure as it crouched by the side of the bolder criminal.

Mrs. Philipson had committed a series of thefts on the individual at whose charge she was summoned, and it was proved but too clearly that her young companion was her accomplice. When Polly was requested to uncover her face, she only pressed her hands upon it more closely. The necessity was explained to her, and she complied. It was pale as death, and care-worn as though age had trampled over it. She gave one frightened glance around, but that glance took in the face of Edward, who was leaning forward with harrowing interest. It was too much for poor Polly. A scream of joy and horror burst from her, and extending her arms towards him, she fell senseless. He came forward, and stating his relation to her, begged to be allowed a few moments' conversation with her in presence of counsel. The poor child soon recovered, and shrinking from the baleful touch of her seducer, met Edward's compassionate eye, who spake soothingly to her, and she gathered courage.

"It was first flattery, then fear, that ruined me," she said, in a low voice; "but I have never loved wickedness. I would have come back to you if I could, but that wicked woman frightened me, and gave me vile drinks, and then I did her bidding. I never stole for myself. She *gave* me these clothes," continued she, earnestly, "they are all I own in the wide world. If it hadn't been for the picture, sir," and she shuddered as she spoke, "I might have been worse. I hid it where she could not find it, and I knelt down and looked at it when I was afraid to pray to God, and it seemed to strengthen me, and make me bolder in the right. They took it from me, or I would give it to you, sir." Here her voice was very mournful, but looking again terrified, she said, "Do you think they can hang me for this? I am sure I shall grow good again."

The trial closed, and Mrs. Philipson was sentenced to the heaviest penalty of the law. Polly's youth and inexperience were mitigating circumstances, and her punishment was almost nominal.

About twilight on the evening of that day, Edward came home, as I thought, with a stranger. In a moment, Polly was at my feet, asking pardon through gushing tears. Her story was soon told, and I comforted the young penitent with Christian promises.

The next morning she came down with her calico frock and apron, her hair parted again with girlish simplicity, and hid her bashfulness in caresses of my Frederick.

She has been my tried and faithful friend, through joy and sorrow, for many years; and is now sitting in her low chair, with a plain, respectable looking cap over her hair, which is just revealing the first tread of time, while my grand-daughter Clarissa is roguishly trying on her new spectacles.

CHAPTER X.

KITCHEN COURTSHIP.

—— his aspect breathed repose,
And in sweet torpor he was plunged deep,
Ne could himself from ceaseless yawning keep.
CASTLE OF INDOLENCE.

IT was winter when I returned to housekeeping, and installed Lydia, commonly pronounced Lyddy Pierce, as president of the dishcloth. She was of the demure sort, as silent and regular as the stars, past the heyday of youth, and had reached an age which the eagle-eyed housekeeper loves. I had restored Polly to full confidence. The sooner you trust in a generous mind after error, the more hold you possess over its returning rectitude, and the more it feels the practicability of virtue.

One of our visitors was Mr. Stockton, a gentleman of broken mercantile fortunes, about thirty-five years of age. He had reserved from his creditors just sufficient for his own support; but not having much energy of character, stood still at that point, and kept himself alive by calling about once a week to pass an evening with his friends. His ideas were all in a circle, and to us it was a mental tread-mill. We soon learned to distinguish his knock at the door, and what a death-peal was it to our imaginations when, after having put Frederick to bed, I sat sewing and Edward reading, in the luxury of winter evening repose. We could have tolerated his visits with cheerful politeness had they been of moderate length; or had he possessed any conversational powers, we would have listened patiently; but Mr. Stockton seemed to have nothing on earth to say. Why he came to see us, and why he tarried so long, I have never learned to this day. I once heard a father say to a son who was going to college, "Samuel, however intimate you may be, never make *long* visits." This good advice Mr. Stockton either never heard, or disregarded.

He had been sitting with us one evening five hours, having come to a sociable tea. A pause in the conversation being unusually long, I looked up from my sewing, and saw Edward asleep. I felt a little fidgety, and took the tongs to mend the fire. Edward stretched forward his legs and called out, "May it please your honor, the plaintiff—" I contrived to pass near him, and trod upon his foot. He started and recovered, somewhat refreshed, while Mr. Stockton, brightening up with the incident, thought proper to sit an hour longer.

Another evening (it was the Sabbath), when Edward had taken two or three nods I went into the kitchen, and with a preliminary yawn told Polly that I could keep awake no longer, and bade her come in and collect the silver to carry to my bedroom, and close the parlor shutters. "There is some hope," said I, "that Mr. Stockton may observe what you are doing and depart." It was then ten o'clock. Polly bustled about and closed the shutters, and as she passed me I whispered, "Make as much noise as possible."

"An excellent plan that," said Mr. Stockton, "to close the shutters; it keeps in the warm air;" and he buttoned up his coat, drew his chair nearer the fire, and put his feet on the fender.

Edward almost groaned, and we sat cogitating until eleven o'clock before Mr. Stockton said, with a hem and a little hitch of his chair, that he "believed it was getting late." Edward and I were silent.

"The evenings are growing long," said he.

"Very," rejoined Edward and I, in a breath.

"These are fine nights for sleep, Mr. Packard," said our imperturbable visitor.

"Very," answered Edward, and I echoed "Very."

"The fire treads snow,"* said Mr. Stockton, "I think we shall have falling weather."

Edward rose, unbolted a window, and looking out, said, "Yes, falling weather;" and bolting the window-shutter again, sat down.

"I believe I must *think* of going," said Mr. Stockton. A dead pause.—At length, for all late sittings, whether in Congress or parlors, will have an end, our guest departed.

I usually visited the kitchen before retiring, to observe whether all were safe. For several evenings I found the ashes raked up in a symmetrical mound, the hearth swept clean, the boiler filled and placed upon the trammels, and the dough in its white trough, with its whiter towel, set at a safe distance to rise.

After Mr. Stockton's departure I went as usual to inspect the premises, leaving the parlor door open to light the passage. Everything was quiet, but I fancied that the settle, the back of which was towards me, was too near the fire. In the act of removing it I caught hold of a head of well-greased hair, and heard, though too late, a warning hem!

I screamed, and Edward ran with a light. Lyddy and a young man who sat beside her rose in some confusion, but the maiden soon recovered, and said with great composure,

"I forgot to tell you, ma'am, that I had a *spark.*—This is

* A phrase for a crackling sound in ignited wood.

Nathan Osgood, Mr. Hill the tailor's 'prentice, a very reputable person."

I apologized in my turn, and left Mr. Osgood to "smooth his raven darkness."

There is a tacit agreement in New-England, allowing this midnight intercourse in the best regulated families; families who would raise their hands and eyes at every breach of decorum; I therefore retired, and left Nathan and Lyddy in undisturbed possession of the settle.

It so chanced, that Lyddy having as little to say in the kitchen as Mr. Stockton in the parlor, the happy couple fell asleep. In the meantime the elements, which pay regard neither to Leanders nor Nathans, were brewing a quiet but potent snow-storm. They formed a regular and sure barricade of snow-flakes through the silent hours of night; a drifting wind bore them against our doors and windows, and settling into a biting northeaster cemented them there; and when Nathan, stiff from his sitting posture and chilled with cold, awoke at the mechanic's early hour, he found himself imprisoned by these Alpine banks.

He awoke Lyddy, and called a council of love. The snow-banks reached to the second story over the kitchen. He might have gone out at the front door, but was he a man to leave his Lyddy struggling with the powers of frost? Not he. With shovel in hand he commenced operations, and in an hour she was able to follow him with a broom, sweeping away the lighter particles, under an arch of snow, to the wood-house; and in half an hour more he cleared his way to the street, claimed a lover's reward, went home, mounted his week-day clothes, and for six days was as faithful a tailor as he had been lover on the seventh.

I arose at eight, and found snow-patches in every crevice of my windows, a tracery of frost-work on the panes of glass, and the water in the ewer a mass of ice. With chattering teeth and purple fingers I descended to the parlor. It was in perfect order; a cheerful fire blazed on the hearth, and Edward's boots, polished to the highest, were warming by the fender. The scene in the kitchen was equally auspicious. Lyddy, with as grave a look as though she had never felt *la belle passion*, stood at the wash-tub (in which she had made far advances), watching the baking cakes. Polly had Fred between her knees, wrapped up in a flannel gown, his scorched face looking like a full moon. She was dexterously keeping her sewing from his mischievous grasp, and persevering in spite of him in her industry. What could rival the comfort of such a home, when, to complete the luxury, Polly with her smiling face brought to the breakfast-table the hot coffee, which, as the poet sings of something else, was

——"deep, yet clear,
Strong without rage, without overflowing, full."

And all this with the thermometer below zero!

I have not yet mentioned that Lyddy was excessively deaf. Polly used to say "she was as deaf as a haddock." I have sometimes speculated about this New-England phrase, but have not been able to trace its origin, and I do not find that naturalists refer to any peculiar organization of the species which authorizes it.

It was not the fault of my lungs if our neighbors did not know the items of our daily food. I often forgot that others were not deaf, and caught Edward smiling at my trumpet-tongued style. One day in particular, when a stranger was dining with us, I had been unusually occupied in preparing for dinner in the kitchen, and had pitched my voice very high. Quite unconsciously I turned to our guest, and his politeness could scarcely prevent his starting when I screamed, "Allow me to give you a piece of ham, sir."

"Clarissa," said Mr. Packard, greatly amused, "Mr. Stevens is not deaf."

I was sadly disconcerted, and it was some time before our courteous visitor could bow and smile me into self-possession.

One of the accidents which Lyddy's infirmity caused was particularly provoking, and occurred in the following manner at a fruit-party, given by us to some New-Yorkers, who brought us letters. I made unusual efforts to procure fresh cream, and had succeeded so well, that dishes with ladles stood at the head, foot, and centre of the table; enough indeed for a housekeeper's measure, which is, to make every one help freely, without looking round to see how far a thing will go. My sensitiveness was perfectly satisfied with the display, as I saw the thick white volumes poured over the rich red raspberries and strawberries, but as quickly I detected a change in my guests; here a half look of disgust, there a glance of concern, in one quarter unusual eloquence, in another unusual taciturnity. Every one knows that the lady of the house is the last person to taste at table of her own delicacies, and so confident was I in the perfection of the cream, that I would have volunteered to stand in Hebe's place with it, as cup-bearer to the gods. Edward's turn came before mine. "Bless my soul, my dear," said he, with a wry face, "what is the matter with the cream?"

I dipped my spoon in the compound which has furnished the poet with so exquisite an illustration of beauty,

> "Her lips looked like strawberries smothered in cream."

and

> "When fondly thinking to allay
> My appetite with gust, instead of fruit
> Chewed bitter ashes which th' offended taste
> With spattering noise rejected."—

Or, to be less Miltonian, I tasted, and would willingly have thrown from my mouth a nauseous mixture of salted cream.

Lyddy, who, as is not unfrequently the case, had doffed her cook's habit and acted as waiting-woman, perceived in helpless ignorance of wrong, the consternation that prevailed. I had tact enough to know tnat to question her would be worse than useless; but Edward, forgetting her deafness, asked her, as she stood near him, "what was the matter with the cream?"

"Very sweet and fresh, sir," said she, in the guttural tone peculiar to very deaf people; "kept down the cellar all the forenoon."

This *malapropos* answer came in very well, and turned mortification to mirth, which was increased when Edward said, in a louder tone,

"But, Lyddy, what have you done to the cream?" and she answered,

"Yes, sir, very fresh; Miss Hatch was spoke to aforehand for the best, and I thought I would salt it to *presarve* it, as *Miss* Packard tell'd me."

This grave answer let loose the flood-gates of wit and laughter, and we finished our dessert with attic salt, as a substitute for poor Lyddy's mistaken mixture.

But while I thus detail circumstances which, if taken by the housekeeper in a right spirit, produce at worst but a passing shade over the brightness of her régime, let me stop a moment to pay a tribute to Lydia's unpretending virtues. Happy shall we be if, like her, we only *mistake* our duty. Through her long days of toil, her onward course was calm and steady, unruffled by passion, studious to please, contemplative and prayerful. Her study was to serve God and her fellow-creatures. Peace to thy memory, my humble friend! When the lords of this world are summoned to the test of a high tribunal, will they not envy thee?

CHAPTER XI.

THE HELPLESS BRIDE.

For the maist thrifty man could never get
A well-stored room, unless his wife wad let.
Gentle Shepherd.

In short, 'twas his fate, sir,
To eat mutton cold.
GOLDSMITH'S *Retaliation.*

A LETTER which I have recently received seems so appropriate to my recollections, that I hope I shall be excused for presenting it in these details. Its writer, Emily Lawrence, seemed never made for a coarser implement than a No. 12 needle. Before her marriage she breathed the very atmosphere of indulgence, the acquisition of various accomplishments being the only discipline she was called to endure. Her hands were white and soft as infancy, her step untroubled and elastic, her spirits joyous and gentle, her smile delicate as moonlight; she was a sweet creature, and her friends loved to lift her along the road of life without her touching the earth. Her experiences after her marriage will be best illustrated by her letter.

"QUINCY, Mass., Aug. 9th, 18—.

"MY DEAR FRIEND,

"I have been for some time intending to write to you, as I promised at parting, to give you a description of our establishment, and the beautiful scenery about this delightful region. I have but little excuse for my delay, and will make amends by a long letter.

"You recollect that when I left my dear maternal home, my mother provided me with excellent domestics, and everything useful and elegant suited to our large fortune. Indeed there seemed no deficiency throughout the whole establishment, and she departed for England, happy in the belief that the care and expense bestowed on my education had been attended with complete success; that I was fitted to adorn the fortune I inherited, and to preside over a family with grace and dignity. Alas! she had only seen me in my drawing-room, surrounded with taste and elegance, beautifully dressed, with an admiring husband who studied every wish. But, my dear friend, I soon found myself involved in perplexities. Oh how I wished you were here to enlighten me by your experience!

"The domestics I brought with me from Boston soon began to grow dissatisfied with the monotony of a country life, and to feel the want of those social pleasures to which all human beings aspire. My cook, an excellent woman, pined for her own *minister*. She had been a very respectable member of the Congregational church in her native town, and feeling the want of those respectful attentions to which she had been accustomed on the Sabbath, it was always a melancholy day to her. In vain I took her in our comfortable coach to the Episcopal church, which was under the especial patronage of my husband, and seated her in a respectable pew; she said 'she did not like to hear prayers *read*, she wished to hear the minister pray from his heart, as she had been accustomed to hear.'

"My chamber-maid Amanda, who was something of a coquette, and very fond of dress, complained that she 'might as well be shut up in a prison; to be sure the house was well enough, and her wages were high, and she hadn't much to do, and got presents from the visitors, but what did all that signify if she was to be *moped* up in a great castle of a place, with nobody to speak to? Besides, she didn't like the *prospect* from the kitchen *winders*, and Mr. Lawrence had not given her a rocking-chair—she had always been used to a rocking-chair in kitchens.'

"My own little waiting-maid, who knew nothing but how to dress me, and whose whole happiness consisted in making me look beautiful, was, except the coachman, the only contented one in the establishment; her happiness was complete when my dear Henry came into my dressing-room, admired my charms, and the taste with which Jane had adorned them.

"Complaints daily increased, although Mr. Lawrence cut down a fine tree to open the view from the kitchen, and provided a rocking-chair for Amanda; and she soon left me, because, when a smart young gardener in our employ wished to *stay* with her, I would not allow them a separate room from the kitchen to *court* in.

"My footman was equally discontented; he was tired of a subordinate situation, and having accumulated a considerable amount in the Savings Bank, decided to go back to the city and set up in trade; and this decision seemed accelerated by Mr. Lawrence offering him a second-hand hat, upon which he took up his own and departed.

"Our cook, who was a woman of principle, gave us formal notice of her intention to go away, and really seemed to feel for my situation; but she said her *conscience* wouldn't let her stay. She remained, however, until we were accommodated with such domestics as the country afforded.

"The mistakes which occurred the first few days after her departure we ascribed to accident, and, as we were without company, they rather amused us. The waiting-man, John, on his first *début*, placed the dinner-service on the table, putting a small dish of vegetables at the head, a piece of roast-beef at one corner, and deliberately moving the pickles in front of my carver. I followed him, and gave him directions, to which he paid very respectful attention. As we seated ourselves, he took up a newspaper and sat down by the window to read. Mr. Lawrence was exceedingly annoyed, because he could not instantly decide whether he was impudent as well as ignorant. After some embarrassment he said,

"'Young man, it is not customary for a person employed to wait at table to sit down.'

"John started up with great alacrity, and said, 'Oh, isn't it? Well, I'd as lief stand, I ain't the least grain tired. You havn't a power of work for a hired man to do.'

"We felt some comfort in the idea that we had only ignorance to contend with, though that was bad enough, considering our inexperience. Henry very good-naturedly instructed him in his business, and although it seemed very strange to him that two persons should require a third to stand and watch them while they were eating, yet finding the work easy and profitable, he soon acquitted himself to our satisfaction.

"As we lived at some distance from town, I was frequently without the common necessaries for cooking, from my total ignorance of what ought to be furnished beforehand. My new cook, though perfectly obliging, knew nothing of her business, and it was deplorable to see her serve up a dinner. It happened, perhaps unfortunately, that we had no company for several weeks, and Henry and myself were too much engrossed with each other to observe the gradual decline of good order which had taken place since the departure of our city help; but we were at length aroused by a letter from Henry's uncle and former guardian, announcing that as we had been at housekeeping long enough to have everything in fine order, he would pay us a visit. We were delighted at the prospect of seeing him, and it did not occur to us immediately that he was very particular, and our domestics very ignorant.

"When he arrived I felt some anxiety that he should have a comfortable dinner, and went into the kitchen for the first time to consult with the cook. I confess, with all my inexperience, I felt shocked and alarmed at the dirt with which I was surrounded, and at the singular appropriations of the various articles of kitchen furniture. One of the best tin-pans was on the hearth, full of ashes; a fine damask towel had been used to wipe the dishes; the oil-can and rags stood in a chair; and a pair of Henry's good boots were thrust under the sink with some iron pots, in which were the accumulated *skimmings* of weeks.

"I found that the butcher had left a leg of veal, and nothing else; but recollecting that my uncle was very fond of stuffed veal, I told the cook to stuff and roast it. She asked if I had any sweet herbs. I told her that I believed the herbs in the kitchen were used, but that my mother had put me up several paper bags of sage, catnip, &c., which I supposed would do as well, and ordered her to put in a plenty, as my uncle liked his food high-seasoned.

"My husband invited two neighboring gentlemen to take a family dinner. When the veal was carved and tasted, I leave it to your imagination to conceive of my distress and Henry's mortification, on finding that our only dish was ruined. A half-picked ham-bone was summoned from the store-room, on which our guests satisfied the cravings of appetite.

"The following day we made more elaborate preparations, and Mr. Lawrence asked me, in the most gentle manner, just to look into the kitchen and see that everything was going on right. Being sincerely desirous to please my dear husband and discharge my duty, I determined to spend the morning in the kitchen. But there I was in everybody's way and only worried by trying to hurry my unskilful domestics; indeed, I was wholly incompetent even to advise them.

"I began to feel some trepidation as the dinner-hour approached; and when I saw the heterogeneous mass on the table, in a style so different from our former elegant dinners, I had scarcely courage to take my seat. My uncle sat next to me, and offered to carve a pair of roasted chickens. When he cut off the wing, out dropped from the crop (as I have since heard it is called) corn, and beans, and grass, just as they had been eaten by the fowl. I perceived by his countenance that something was wrong, but he adroitly concealed the unsightly objects from our visitors, and refrained from making any remark.

"When our guests departed, he took me aside, and said,

"'My dear child, you had materials enough on your table for twenty persons, but your cookery is deplorably deficient. Your mother neglected a very important part of your education. You will spend your fortune to very little purpose if, amid the abundance with which you are surrounded, you cannot procure a well-cooked dinner.'

"I felt at that moment as if I would have given up all my French, German, and every accomplishment, in exchange for the knowledge which would make me a good housekeeper. Every young married woman who is ignorant of her duties will meet mortifications at every step; an elegant establishment, an ample fortune, and even a devoted husband, will not secure her happiness.

"You may suppose that my nerves became considerably excited; indeed, I could not always control my feelings during my uncle's visit. The day before his departure Henry again had company, and had been at some pains to procure a brace of partridges for dinner. They looked very well, for I studied a cook-book that morning, but when my husband cut them, they were nearly raw; he gave a glance at me, I burst into tears, and was so much agitated that I was obliged to quit the table. He followed, and said everything he could to console me, but utterly unable to command myself, I begged him to carry my apology to his guests, and I sobbed away the afternoon.

"My uncle has promised to look out for an experienced housekeeper for me, and I have engaged to take lessons of her, so that when he comes again I can show him my own cookery. I told him I should be more proud of serving up a well-dressed turkey for him, with all the accompaniments in good order, than in performing the most difficult piece of music. Both he and Henry smiled encouragingly on me, and said that with such a disposition to do right I could not fail of succeeding. But how much better would it have been to have been taught these things under the eye of a mother! My husband is very social in his disposition, and frequently brings home guests unexpectedly, and I often see his brow clouded and his temper disturbed by the total ignorance of his wife. Not that he complains, for he knows how desirous I am to please him ever to say a word to wound my feelings, but I can perceive that he is anxious, and instead of feeling light-hearted with his guests, is dreading blunders which will make me ridiculous.

"And now, my dear and respected friend, let me ask you to come, and counsel and teach me. I find that wealth cannot produce order and comfort, and I long for your example and advice in the absence of my mother.

"Affectionately yours,

"EMILY LAWRENCE."

CHAPTER XII.

A STRUGGLE FOR POWER.

He reprimands, by glancing with his eye—
And *she* inflicts her soft reproach—a sigh.
That's all—and that's enough for man and wife;
Did you expect an Iliad of strife?
Why need invective to make error smart,
When looks and signs as deeply touch the heart?
S. GILMAN.

THREE years passed quietly away before Lyddy gave her hand in marriage to Nathan Osgood. Notwithstanding her attention to the duties of my family, Lyddy made two quilts of marvellous beauty. One was in hexagon pieces, each the size of a dollar. The other displayed in the centre a tree, on which were birds larger than the limbs thereof, while each corner contained what I was glad to be informed was a shepherd with his flock. To accomplish these *chefs d'œuvre* I had seen several yards of good chintz destroyed; but, as the gentlemen say, *de gustibus non est disputandum.*

Lyddy's successor, Hannah Sanders' first request on becoming my *help* was, that she might attend night-meetings. I readily agreed to this, thinking that she was attached to some church, and would be more conscientious from her religious profession; but she proved to be the mere child of excitement. She attended every denomination,—was out every evening. The tolling of a bell unhingèd all her faculties. When I said to her, "Hannah, I should like to have you reflect one evening on what you have heard the evening before," she answered, " Oh, *Miss* Packard, you don't know anything about it. When I am at meeting I feel like a gill cup running over."

But I must not omit to introduce at this period a department of my establishment which, though humble in itself, wrought important effects on my after-happiness.

I carried with me from my mother's house a cat, which was so beautiful that I named her Fairy, in honor of the damsel who was changed to Grimalkin in the old romance. If I had a prejudice it was in favor of cats and against dogs; this was unfortunate, for soon after my marriage I was introduced to a mastiff of Edward's nearly as large as myself. I had often heard him speak of this dog, and praise the faithfulness with which he guarded the office. I was too busy in other interests to think much of Growler for some time. I only observed, that on his occasional visits (for the office was his head-quarters), Fairy's back rose indignantly, and I felt mine disposed to mount too.

At length, Growler finding the house so comfortable, came home at night with his master, and daringly laid his unwieldy form on the centre of the hearth-rug, while Fairy, routed from her luxurious station, stood upon her dignity, hissing and sputtering in one corner.

For a long period a single look from me would make Edward banish Growler from the room; but a present of a new office-dog from a friend completely established him at home, and my husband became accustomed to my *look* and Growler's presence. When he grew indifferent my ire was roused. I affirmed, that of all created things dogs were the dirtiest,—that the house was filled with fleas,—that my visitors never could approach the fire,—that Growler ate us out of house and home,—and if he were to be indulged in tracking the Wilton carpet and painted floors, we had better live in a wigwam.

Edward sometimes gently excused his dog, sometimes defended him, and always turned him out of doors. The animal, knowing he had an enemy in the cabinet, would sneak in with a coward look, his tail between his legs, but invariably succeeded in ensconcing himself on Fairy's rightful domain.

At length I became quite nervous about him. It seemed to me that he haunted me like a ghost. I was even jealous of Edward's caresses to him, and looked and spoke as no good wife should look or speak to her husband.

It is from permitting such trifles to gain the ascendency over the mind that most connubial discord proceeds. We dwell on some little peculiarity in manner or taste opposed to our own, and jar the rich harp of domestic happiness until, one by one, every string is broken. I might have gone on in this foolish ingenuity in unhappiness, and perhaps have been among those whose matrimonial bands are chains, not garlands, had I not, when reading one Sabbath morning the fifth chapter of Ephesians, been struck with a sudden sense of my duty, as I met the words, "and the wife see that she *reverence* her husband."

Oh, young and lovely bride, watch well the first moments when your will conflicts with his to whom God and society have given the control. Reverence his *wishes* even when you do not his *opinions*. Opportunities enough will arise for the expression of your independence, to which he will gladly accede, without a contest for trifles. The beautiful independence that soars over and conquers an irritable temper is higher than any other. So surely as you believe faults of temper are beneath prayer and self-examination, you are on dangerous ground; a fountain will spring up on your household hearth, of bitter and troubled waters.

When this conviction came over me I threw myself on my knees, and prayed to God for a gentle, submissive temper.

After long and earnest inquiry into my own heart, I left my chamber calm and happy. Edward was reading, and Growler stood beside him. I approached them softly, and patting the dog's head, said, "So, Growler, helping your master to read?" Edward looked at me inquiringly. I am sure my whole expression of face was changed; he drew me to him in silence, and gave me a token of regard he never bestowed on Growler. From that moment, though I might wince a little at his inroads on my neat housekeeping, I never gave the dog an angry word, and I taught Fairy to regard him as one of the lords of the creation.

Growler's intelligence was remarkable, although it did not equal that of Sir Walter Scott's bull-dog terrier, Camp, who could perceive the meaning of words, and who understood an allusion to an offence he had committed against the baker, for which he had been punished. In whatever voice and tone it was mentioned, he would get up and retire into the darkest part of the room with an air of distress. But if you said, "The baker was not hurt after all," Camp came forth from his hiding-place, capered, barked, and rejoiced. Growler, however, had many of those properties of observation which raise the canine race so high in the affections of man.

When Edward made his forenoon *sortie* from the office to look at his sleeping boy, Growler always accompanied him, and rested his fore-paws on the head of the cradle. As the babe grew older, he loved to try experiments upon the dog's sagacity and the child's courage.

Sometimes Fred was put into a basket, and Growler drew him carefully about the room with a string between his teeth; as the boy advanced in strength, he was seated on the dog's back with a whip in his hand. When my attachment to Growler increased, new experiments were made, particularly after the birth of Martha. She was an exquisite little infant, and it seemed to us that the dog was more gentle and tender in his movements with her than with Frederick. When two months old, Edward sometimes arranged a shawl carefully about her, tied it strongly, and putting the knot between the dog's teeth, sent her across the room to me. No mother ever carried a child more skilfully. Of course all these associations attached him to the infant, and after a while he deserted the rug, where Fairy again established herself, and laid himself down to sleep by the infant's cradle.

There is nothing more picturesque than the image of an infant and a large dog. Every one has felt it. The little plump hand looks smaller and whiter in his rough hair, and the round dimpled cheek rests on his shaggy coat—like a flower on a rock.

Edward and I and Frederick rode one afternoon to Roxbury to take tea with a friend. Our *woman in the kitchen* wished to pass the night with a sick person after the evening's lecture, and I felt no hesitation in leaving Martha to Polly's care. We were prevented, by an accidental delay, from returning until ten o'clock. The ride over the *neck*, although it was fine sleighing, appeared uncommonly long, for I had never been so far and so long from my infant. The wind was sharp and frosty, but my attention was beguiled by sheltering Frederick with my furs, who soon fell asleep, singing his own little lullaby. As we entered the *Square* we perceived that the neighboring houses were closed for the night, and no light visible, but a universal brilliancy through the crevices of our parlor-shutters. Our hearts misgave us. I uttered an involuntary cry, and Edward said, that "a common fire-light could not produce such an effect." He urged his horse,—we reached the house,—I sprang from the sleigh to the door. It was fastened. We knocked with violence. There was no answer. We looked through a small aperture, and both screamed in agony "fire!" In vain Edward attempted to wrench the bolt or burst the door, that horrible light still gleaming on us. We flew to the side-door, and I then recollected that a window was usually left open in that quarter, in a room which communicated with the parlor, for the smoke to escape when the wind prevailed in the quarter it had done this day. The window was open, and as Edward threw down logs that we might reach it, we heard a stifled howl. We mounted the logs, and could just raise our heads to the window. Oh, heavens! what were our emotions, as we saw Growler with his fore-paws stationed on the window, holding Martha safely with her night-dress between his teeth, ready to spring at the last extremity, and suspending the little cherub so carefully that she thought it but one of his customary gambols! With a little effort Edward reached the child, and Growler, springing to the ground, fawned and grovelled at our feet.

Edward alarmed the neighborhood and entered the window. Poor Polly had fainted in the entry from the close atmosphere and excess of terror. She could give no account of the origin of the fire, unless she had dropped a spark on the window-curtain. The moment a blaze appeared she endeavored to extinguish it; "but," said she, "the flames ran like wild-fire; and when I found I could do nothing, I snatched Martha from the cradle, and ran into the entry to go out by the back-door; after that I recollect nothing."

With prodigious efforts the house was saved, though with a great loss of furniture. But what were pecuniary losses that night to us? We were sheltered by a hospitable neighbor; our little cherub was clasped in our arms, amid smiles and tears; and Growler, our good Growler, with a whimpering dream, lay sleeping at our feet.

CHAPTER XIII.

FACTS AND REFLECTIONS.

Mistress of herself, though china fall.
POPE.

But see, the well-plumed hearse comes nodding on.
BLAIR'S GRAVE.

EVERY housekeeper has experienced what is called a "breaking season," when the centre of gravitation seems shaken, as far as crockery is concerned. Such an era followed the departure of Hannah Sanders, who left me to reside with a minister's lady.

I will offer no excuse for this subject, since it forms the point of discussion for half my sex in their select circles, and constitutes, in some measure, the conversational boundary line between men and women. True to my character of housekeeper, let me proceed.

Compassion and interest induced me to offer the situation of cook to a Mrs. Sliter, whose husband had recently died in the neighborhood. She was one of those persons who may look decently in new crape, but who generally, with a great display of pins on their waist and sleeves, put them nowhere else; or who apply them as if totally ignorant of the "fitness" of dress, as well as of things. I took her as a forlorn hope—one of those experiments that New-England ladies are so constantly obliged to make of the morals and dispositions of strangers.

Edward was detained late at court the day on which she came, and I ordered some hashed lamb and roasted potatoes for his supper. Mrs. Sliter, with the hash in one hand and the hot potatoes in the other, issued from the kitchen, but unfortunately turned towards the cellar instead of the parlor passage. We were startled by a sudden noise, and hastened tc the kitchen; but neither cook nor viands were there, and we heard a stifled voice from the cellar, crying, "Marcy me, marcy me!" Following the sound, and descending the stairs, we found Mrs. Sliter lying at the foot, who with her meat and potatoes had rolled down into the ash-heap, and, in attempting to rise, pulled over a barrel of soft soap.

It is difficult to describe her appearance as she arose from this alkaline immersion. The soap trickled from the deep frill of her widow's cap in streams over her cheeks, and commingling with the ashes, left scarcely a trace of the "human face divine;" and what added to the grotesqueness of the scene was her holding up the mutton dish unharmed. How this was accomplished in her necessary gyrations down a deep flight of stairs, we never could comprehend. Her complaints were eloquent enough, mingled with some irritability at our ill-restrained laughter.

In arranging the bed-rooms the following morning she broke a toilet glass, and was in still deeper consternation.

"Oh, *Miss* Packard," she cried, "there will *sartainly* be a death in the family. It was only two months ago, poor Mr. Sliter that's dead and gone broke his shaving glass, and you see what's come on't. I'm left, as it were, a poor lone *vider*, without a partner; and it was but a year ago that my neighbor, Miss Stone, that keeps the *wittle* (victual) house, broke her parlor-glass, and that same day, as she was *chawing* some fish, a bone choked her, and she was as good as dead for an hour."

To verify Mrs. Sliter's prediction, Polly, a month from the date of the broken toilet-glass, heard of the death of a great-uncle whom she had never seen, and Mrs. Sliter went about the house with a self-congratulatory cackle at the birth of the disaster. To me, however, the prediction of trouble, if not of death, seemed realized. Piece after piece of my dinner set (a rare and beautiful style at the time, white ground with a rose-colored vine on the edge), came tinkling on my ears with a sound that a housewife can detect from afar.

I early obliged myself not to stir on such occasions. If one can sit still a few moments, quietly lay down a book, or fold up one's work, or knit to the middle of one's needle, there is a favorable prospect of keeping the temper smooth; but as surely as you start up with "there, now," your feminine dignity is gone. I had a friend who once conquered an irritable temper by obliging herself to count twenty when under sudden excitement.

Mrs. Sliter's next feat was to lose the balance of the breakfast-tray, and deposit the whole apparatus on the floor. Every housekeeper will give me their sympathy when I describe to them my sugar-bowl without a cover, my cream-pot without a handle, my coffee-pot indented at the side, and an unmatching slop-bowl called in from the kitchen to complete the muster-roll.

An honest, open breakage, one can bear with a tolerable grace, but it is hard to be the subject of duplicity as well as carelessness. Mrs. Sliter's favorite practice was to conceal the results of her organ of destructiveness, until they were discovered in some nook or corner, in the form of irregular triangles of glass or china. Frederick, who was as great a collector of old china, in his way, as Monkbarns, discovered, in Mrs. Sliter's short but emphatic reign, treasure upon treasure; and his broken dishes, as he called the pieces of crockery, were gathered up from the cellar, the ash-heap, the wood-house, and every other spot where his busy little feet resorted for what is miscalled mischief. At length, one day, he brought in a sample to his grandmother, who was visiting us. The moment she saw it she detected the cup, the very teacup from which Dr. Franklin had once drunk. It had been a family boast, and she had given it to me at my earnest solicitation. My mother was really affected; she took Frederick in her arms, and told him the story of the cup; how Benjamin Franklin sat and talked with her parents as he sipped his tea; how her mother whispered to her that he was a *great man;* how she took the cup from his hand, and said, "No one shall use *this* again."

We were all silent as she sat polishing the fragment with her pocket-handkerchief, and even the boy laid it aside carefully.

To heighten my troubles at this period, I found the contents of my decanters sensibly lowered, and perceived that Mrs. Sliter was frequently intoxicated. When accused of purloining the liquor she denied it until the proof became too glaring, and when no longer able to evade, said to me, "*Miss* Packard, you're the *unfeelingest* person I ever *see*, to speak so *onkind* to a lone *vider* that ain't got no consolation, and *vishes* to raise her *sperits.* I ain't a going to stay with a person that begrudges every mouthful that's ate and drank, and you needn't expect me to give you a character, for I shan't recommend your house to nobody."

She decamped in violent wrath, and we were thrown for several weeks on our own resources.

There could scarcely be a more striking illustration of the lamentable dependence of housekeepers on servants, than in the obligation I felt myself under when deserted by Hannah, to take under my roof this woman, with whose character and disposition I was so little acquainted. Mrs. Sliter was the wife of a wood-sawyer, and sent for me in haste, as a neighbor, to see her after her husband's decease. I went with as much promptitude as possible. Mr. Sliter had died in a fit of drunkenness, and his bloated body was laid out in all the state that extreme poverty could assume, in the small apartment, the common bedroom and parlor of the miserable pair. In an old chair, from which hung the broken rushes, sat his wife, rocking in the restlessness of unoccupied grief.

I took her hand, and was about offering her consolation; but her sorrow was not of that sort that breaks the heart in silence, and I was interrupted by her dolorous voice, preceded by a long-drawn sigh.

"Death is a dreadful thing, ma'am. Mr. Sliter, poor man, that's dead and gone, and I have lived nigh twenty year together. It's hard to be left a lone *voman*, as it *vere*. He was nobody's enemy but his own. I shall be a lone body indeed,"—and she put her handkerchief to the corners of both eyes.

I commenced once more the usual common-place attempts at consolation, when looking up, she said briskly, "*Miss* Packard, do *viders vear weils* now?"

This miserable attempt at the semblance of mourning first led me to speculate on the propriety of black apparel for the bereaved. If our friends are virtuous, and our belief in Christianity sincere, why assume a mourning robe, when they are clothed in the white garments of immortality? Why shroud our heads, when theirs are crowned with amaranthine wreaths? Why utter sighs of woe, when they are hymning to celestial harps, amid celestial choirs? And when a case occurs where those who should have loved us have rent our hearts by sin, or broken them by harshness, and the weary spirit shrinking from observation, turns on itself to commune in silence, why assume the ostentation of regret before an unsympathizing world?

Yet let me not treat lightly or harshly a prejudice founded on the delicate impulses of nature. Perhaps the hand that writes these strictures might be the first to mould those sombre monuments which affection raises to departed friends, and would be the last to lay aside the time-honored associations that cluster in the day of earthly separation.

However this may be, Mrs. Sliter, with a veil of proper dimensions, followed *him* to the grave who had thrice kicked her out of doors; actually, if not nominally, caused the death of her only infant by brutality; left her whom God and society demanded him to support, a miserable pauper, and gone down to the tomb, a bloated carcass, to meet the changes, for weal or woe of an endless immortality.

CHAPTER XIV.

A TEMPERANCE LECTURE TO MY COUSIN WILLIAM.

She could go near the precipice, nor dread
A failing caution, or a giddy head;
She'd fix her eyes upon the roaring flood,
And dance upon the brink where danger stood.

The Borough.

IT seems to me a dream, that I once cleansed and replenished a gin and brandy decanter every Saturday morning. My "swords are turned into ploughshares, and my spears into pruning hooks;" for there they stand, the pictures of innocence, converted into water-crafts and molasses bottles.

Let every housekeeper seriously look back through her past experience, and ask herself how many individuals (unintentionally of course) she has led into temptation with these polished seducers: and if she has herself escaped a pit where so many of the bright and good have fallen, offer up a prayer of thankfulness.

I know not how others may have felt, but my soul has often been wrung with anguish at the utter hopelessness of preventing any individual, who has betrayed a tendency to intemperance, from plunging daily further and further into sin, when the means were spread out before him, leaving unchecked his vitiated taste.

Edward, like others, provided liquors for his sideboard, but only drank them as the compliment which society demanded with his guests. William Ingols, my cousin, an interesting young man, entered his office as a student, and resided with us. He was confiding and communicative, and I soon began to love him as a member of our household. At his first dinner Edward joined him in a glass of brandy and water; on succeeding days he took it unsolicited; in a short time he drank at the sideboard before dinner; and, in a few weeks, repeated the draught at bedtime.

I asked Edward's advice on what was to be done. He answered with a smile, "You are a woman, and can manage these things better than I. Talk with Ingols on the subject. You know my detestation of this genteel tippling, but I have no authority over him."

A fair opportunity offered, in Edward's necessary absence at a circuit court for a week, to speak on the subject without implicating my husband.

As Ingols was visiting the sideboard as usual, and (what seems to me an alarming symptom) covering the lower part of the tumbler with his hand, I asked him, with a little hesitation, if he drank brandy for his health.

"I cannot say that I do," said he, smiling. "Will you take a little for yours, cousin?"

"No, I thank you," said I; "I am afraid of it."

"Afraid of it, cousin? It will not hurt you. You would be all the better for a little tonic."

"A little tonic might not hurt me, cousin William, but I fear being tempted. I distrust my own strength of character."

"Pshaw! you are not serious! I have been drinking a *little* several years."

"Why do you drink it?" I asked. "Your mind is naturally active, your conversation agreeable, you have no mental or bodily suffering, and you have a thousand rational modes of enjoyment. If you will only look into your own feelings, you will find a cormorant settling over them, whose guilty cry is 'give, give!'"

"You are a sweet monitor, cousin Clara; I believe I must take a little brandy, if it is only to hear you scold so prettily."

"Oh, Ingols," I answered, "do not, in mercy to yourself, treat this subject so lightly. Why society tolerates its abuse, I know not. I see already a look directed to that bottle when you are about to pour out its libations to your incipient sensual desires, which speaks an awkward consciousness. You are already screening the quantity you take. If you love my schooling, hear it plainly. Your manly and graceful form will soon begin to lose its firmness, your brilliant eyes shine with a drunkard's glassy inexpressiveness, and your mind

——" where God has set his seal
To give the world assurance of a man,"

reduced to childishness, worse than childishness, since its weakness will have no redeeming innocence."

"But, Mrs. Packard," said Ingols, "you forget how many indulge in ardent spirits without injury."

"I do not forget that, William, but I remember more vividly how many have been destroyed, soul and body, while these moderate drinkers, favored perhaps by constitutional resistance, have been unscathed by the burning trial. But they will not escape, cousin William; they cannot escape His eyes who watches motives rather than deeds. They may be strong enough to carry until death the unrighteous banner of the drunkard without reeling, while others are falling on the right hand and on the left, but they lead the way to the destruction of others, and they must answer for it."

"My dear cousin," said Ingols, "you take this matter too seriously. You make a bugbear of a trifle."

"A trifle!" I exclaimed; "call not that a trifle which rifles the mind and body of their best gifts. If I were permitted, I would go (not in the wildness of quixotism, but in the spirit of him who drove the profaners from God's temple) and destroy every implement like *that* before you, which attracts you and others from the simplicity of nature. They disgrace our homes, they deform the purity of domestic scenes, and often convert them into bacchanalian orgies. I had a friend once, William, young and lovely; such a one as your warm heart would have loved, and your discriminating mind would have appreciated. She received a shock from the early disappointment of her affections, pined, sickened, and drooped like a withering flower. Would to God she had died in the unstained paleness of her beauty! Tonics were recommended, and as medicine they were right. Her health was restored, and all would have been well, had they not been spread out among the wants and luxuries of life. Her sensual appetite increased. I sicken as I remember the miserable subterfuges that marred her fair character, first chilling the confidence of friends, and then by open exposures disgracing them. The enemy wrought surely, baffled but not subdued by reproaches, by sarcasms, by entreaties, by the shunning eye of retreating friendship, by the agonizing appeals of a dying conscience. She died a drunkard. Her mother wept bitterer tears than should ever fall over a daughter's grave; her sister's cheek paled with a sorrow sadder than grief; and her father, I tremble while I say it, cursed his first-born child."

Ingols had not tasted his draught while I was speaking, but held it in his hand, and when I ceased, quietly placed it on the table and said, "Cousin, I have not the heart to drink this now, and will give it up if only to please you."

"You are not angry, then," I said, eagerly.

"Angry? no," he replied. "How can I be angry with a true friend, and a lady too?" with a low bow.

"Thank you," said I, "and now that I have gone thus far, may I proceed?"

"Yes, cousin, I give you *carte blanche.*"

"I shall do it by actions, not words," I said, with solemnity; "and I warn you to be prepared, for I have solemnly pledged myself in prayer to God that I will never again aid the cause of the destroying angel. But promise me (not that I claim any right over you but that of interest in your welfare) that you will abstain from ardent spirits, now in the sunshine of your youth, 'before the evil days come.'"

Ingols hesitated, reflected, and promised half earnestly, half jestingly.

On the following day, no decanter was to be seen on my sideboard or table, and I carried the keys up stairs. Ingols was very amiable, and our week passed happily away. Edward returned, and took no notice of the withdrawal of the decanters.

I had retired to my bedroom early one evening, when I heard Ingols enter, and ask Polly for the keys. She came up stairs, and I gave them to her in silence. I heard her transfer them to him, and held my breath. He opened the door. I trembled so much that I could not stand. *I had emptied every decanter.* I heard the rattling of the keys as the door closed, and a faintness came over me at my own daring. A half-hour passed away, and Polly came back with a slip of paper, on which was written, "You have conquered, cousin. I thank you, and thank God."

I burst into tears, and sobbed as if my heart would break; nor was I relieved until Edward returned and said he loved me better for my moral courage.

CHAPTER XV.

CONCLUSION.

Frae morn to e'en it's naught but toiling,
At baking, roasting, frying, boiling.
The Twa Dogs.

THE successor of Mrs. Sliter was Sukey Hopkins, an untamed damsel from Nantucket; and as Edward required some attendance at the office, he engaged a friend of hers, Aaron Wheeler, who had *driv her down*, to remain with us. I passed every forenoon for a month in the kitchen, to initiate her in cookery; and even after that period was obliged to be with her whenever I had guests, of course at the period when I ought to have been most unincumbered with care. I was obliged to watch the last turn of the spit, and the last bubble of the boiling gravy, and even lay the meats in their right position; for know, inexperienced reader, that a lady may as excusably stand on her own head at her table, as have her turkey or goose in an unauthorized posture. One bleak autumnal day we had company to dine; but I became so much heated with my business and anxiety as not to dream of the necessity of a fire. Just five minutes before dinner was carried in, I ran up stairs, changed my dress, and seizing a fan, descended to the drawing-room. My zeal in fanning was proportioned to the kitchen thermometer; and it was not until I detected a shiver in a lady who sat within the influence of my Æolus, as Edward prettily called a fan, that I perceived my *faux pas.*

The day after Aaron's induction into his duties, I went to Cornhill, shopping; and Edward left word with him that if a certain gentleman called, he must ask him in to sit until he came. When Edward opened the door, what should he behold but Aaron, sitting with his feet on the fender, entertaining Mr. —— with the last Nantucket news!

A few evenings succeeding I invited company to tea. I was the whole morning drilling Sukey and Aaron, and as I went to make my toilet, I said, "Be very careful, Aaron, that the ladies and gentlemen are all supplied with sugar and cream in their coffee." When the company had assembled, and the very last visitor, according to the old and formidable rule, had arrived and was seated, Aaron entered with his tea tray, followed by Sukey with the cream and sugar. He walked round as carefully as if he were treading on eggs. When the circuit was over, and he had reached the door, his mind seemed to misgive him; and with an anxious look, standing on tiptoe, he said, "I say, how are ye on't for sugar and cream in that corner?"

On that memorable evening, a lady spilled some quince syrup on the carpet, when, to my utter dismay, Sukey set the waiter on the floor, rushed out, and brought in the mop to wipe it up.

I have inserted these lingering reminiscences in this chapter, to show that the most skilful housewifery cannot counteract the mortification and embarrassment of our present system. I took infinite pains to make my daughter useful. She was a sweet, docile girl, and at the age of eleven often made our tea, arranged the table, and assisted in handing it when we had company; but notwithstanding this early discipline, the awkward blending of lady and housewife led to countless anxieties; indeed, it requires an omnipresent eye to meet one's guests with the personal welcome they demand, while providing for their grosser wants. How many girls like Sukey have I passed months in drilling, when, just as I began to realize the effects of my care, they have taken a sudden whim and departed! How many were there whom I never *could* teach, whose inattention or wilfulness rendered me miserable! How much hard labor have I performed while paying high prices for that of others! What then can be done to remedy this evil? It is the opinion of Adam Smith, and an humble housekeeper agrees with him, that the perfection of society consists in the division of labor.

Is it not monstrous that educated, intelligent women, should be obliged to give over their children to the care of servants, and pass their days in the most menial occupation? And must our lovely daughters be called from intellectual or graceful accomplishments, to associate with the vulgar inmates of the kitchen?

We have a partial system, which it appears to me might easily be carried through the whole order of social life. We have our chimney-sweeps, our wood-sawyers, our bakeries; why not have our grand cooking-establishments, our scourers, our window-cleaners, &c? I will give one example, a direct one however, of the helplessness of a housekeeper on the present plan of life. She perceives, and none but those who have witnessed it can tell how irritating is the feeling, that about five hundred panes of glass in her house require washing. How can they be cleansed? It is properly a man's business, but she must put an inexperienced female to the work who is required for a hundred other things; one, too, who perhaps never wiped a glass before. A particular set of cloths is required, step-ladder, hammer, and a *knack* at *cleaning* glass. By the time she has accomplished her task,. which is probably imperfectly done broken a few panes, and left the sashes loose and clattering, dust and flies have been equally active, and the *gude man* begins to say, "My dear, our windows require a little cleaning." What a cheering sound would it be to a lady so circumstanced, if she could hear in the street "any windows to clean to-day?" or, what is better, know where to send to an establishment for a person devoted to that object.

What a desideratum is a cooking-establishment, where families can be provided with prepared food, and a still greater to have our meals brought to us, now that the improvements in steam can give them hotter than from our own hearths. They could probably be furnished cheaper than on the present plan. Our husbands would no longer be seen haggling with butchers at their stalls, or balancing raw meat in the open streets; nor should we see decent women, in utter uncertainty of their dinners, throwing up their window-sashes to the passing countrymen, with "Mister, what's you got to-day?" A friend could *drop in* without disconcerting a family, and the lady of the house sit without a thorn. How many more smiles would kindle up around the domestic board, could the wife be assured of her husband's comfort. She has enough to do in the agitating responsibility of her maternal cares; her little ones may be sickly, her own health feeble. Many a woman breaks and sinks beneath the wear and tear of the frame and the affections. She rallies before the world, and "her children rise up and call her blessed," and she is blessed in the conscious attempt to discharge her duty; but cares eat away at her heart; the day presses on her with new toils, the night comes, and they are unfulfilled; she lies down in weariness, and rises with uncertainty; her smiles become languid and few, and her husband wonders at the gloominess of his home.

How great a duty is it, then, to study modes of comfort, and preserve the song of cheerfulness in the routine of domestic industry. It is not below the task of legislation, if legislation is a study of the order and happiness of a community, or if legislators would have neat houses, good dinners, and smiling wives.

THE END.

www.ingramcontent.com/pod-product-compliance
Lightning Source LLC
LaVergne TN
LVHW020105110826
845151LV00001B/71

* 9 7 8 1 4 2 5 5 4 4 3 5 5 *